THE ALPINE PURSUIT

THE
ALPINE
PURSUIT

MARY DAHEIM

BALLANTINE BOOKS • NEW YORK

A Ballantine Book
Published by The Random House Publishing Group
Copyright © 2004 by Mary Daheim

The Alpine Pursuit is a work of fiction. Names, places, and incidents are
either a product of the author's imagination or are used fictitiously.

www.ballantinebooks.com

Library of Congress Cataloging-in-Publication Data is available from the
publisher upon request.

ISBN 0-345-46715-9

Book design by Susan Turner

Manufactured in the United States of America

First Edition: April 2004

10   9   8   7   6   5   4   3   2   1

To Joe Blades
Not only a terrific editor, but even a better friend.

ONE

My brother, Ben, and I had flown into Rome on a dark October day. A heavy rain fell all the way into the city from Da Vinci Airport, making it almost impossible to see through the train windows. It was eight-thirty in the morning when we got a taxi at the stazione *to head for the Hotel Bramante near the Vatican. The buildings in the oldest part of the Eternal City showed their age, with bright colors dulled, wavery glass, worn wrought iron, and cracked stucco exteriors. Rome seemed as gloomy as Alpine, where it had rained for a week before I left. If this trip was my brother's effort to raise my spirits after Tom's death, I was afraid Ben had made a big mistake.*

※　※　※

AN ALPINE WINTER IS EVEN GLOOMIER THAN MOST AUTUMNS, BUT I'm used to it. Changes in the weather pattern during the past century have raised temperatures, however. No longer is the mountain town snowed in from October to April. The current fall had accumulated to over four feet, but it was the third week of

February and that was ordinary at the three-thousand-foot level of the Cascades. Seventy years ago Alpine was completely isolated except by train—when the locomotives could push through. We still had the trains, but we also had roads and streets, and we usually had access to the highway. Stories were still handed down about snow up to the housetops and how close the community of two hundred hardy souls became when there was virtually no contact with the outside world. Listening to the legends, it almost sounded like fun.

But the good old days weren't always so good. I was reminded of that fact when a group of Alpine residents decided to revive a theatrical tradition that had begun before World War One. Forced to rely on their own resources for entertainment, the diversions included lectures, musicales, sports competitions, and plays starring local amateurs. Judging from cast photos, the actors had a wonderful time. I'm sure the audience did, too. Maybe everybody was juiced on moonshine.

"Very professional productions," declared my House & Home editor, Vida Runkel. "That is, given the limited amount of talent."

Vida hadn't been born until after the troupe shut down along with the original mill in 1929. But as a native Alpiner, she was loyal to the core. As a non-native, I was skeptical. Looking at the pictures of people in outlandish wigs and grotesque makeup, I sensed that the productions had been god-awful.

But the locals couldn't leave good—or bad—enough alone. They had revived the tradition after World War Two, only to abandon it for a second time when the logging industry was hit hard in the early 1980s by environmental concerns. Then, two years ago, a group of misguided souls again reverted to tradition. Aided and abetted by the drama professor at Skykomish Community College, The Alpine Council Dramatic Club was resurrected, original name and all.

I'd seen only one of the first four plays—they did two a year—an uncut version of *Long Day's Journey Into Night*. It certainly was. I felt as if I were nailed to my seat for twenty-four hours.

At least Eugene O'Neill could write. The current rehearsals were for a play called *The Outcast*, written by Destiny Parsons, the aforementioned college prof. It was described as a ". . . black comedy, revealing the inner struggle of a young woman to find herself in a small town."

I could identify with the concept. Thirteen years ago, I'd come to Alpine as a thirtysomething woman. Despite my best efforts, it had been difficult to fit in. It wasn't just my controversial status as editor and publisher of the local weekly, but that I'd committed the unforgivable sin of being born elsewhere, and in the big city of Seattle at that.

"Wait a minute," I said, rereading the play's premise. "Does this mean the protagonist is searching for her identity or trying to get out of town?"

Vida, who was sitting at her desk in the corner of the newsroom, whipped off her big glasses. "Of course not! Why would she want to leave?"

I'd been standing next to Leo Walsh's desk. Leo, my ad manager, looked up from his computer screen. "Does the town have a name?" he asked with an innocent expression on his leathery face.

"Certainly," Vida snapped. "It's called Evergreen. But it's obvious that it stands for Alpine."

Leo retained his air of naïveté. "How miserable is she in . . . *Evergreen,* Duchess?"

Vida leaned forward, her imposing figure exuding hostility. "For the last time, don't call me Duchess. You know I despise that nickname. As for the heroine, Dorothy Oz, she isn't miserable— merely confused."

I had to admit I hadn't yet read the script. Nor did I intend to. Destiny Parsons was in her second year at Skykomish Community College, teaching drama, literature, English, and women's studies. She seemed intelligent, if a bit stiff. In the normal course of events, I would rarely have seen her, but she'd recently bought a house across the street from me. We saw each other in passing, though neither of us had gone out of the way to become further acquainted. One of these days I'd have to make an overture, and it probably wouldn't be a pleasant encounter. Destiny not only allowed her fox terrier to use my front yard as a rest room, but some mornings I'd seen Destiny urge the animal to cross the street and head for my property. I was growing tired of cleaning up Azbug's messes.

"Maybe," Leo remarked, lighting a cigarette while Vida shot more daggers his way, "I ought to take in a performance. What's the schedule?"

I grabbed a copy of the *Advocate* and waved it at Leo. "Read all about it! Jeez, Leo, don't you read anything except the ads?"

Leo didn't bat an eye. "Hell, I don't read those, either. Not after I put them together. If I want news, I go home and watch CNN or one of the Seattle stations."

"Watch your language, Leo," Vida murmured before our ad manager finished speaking. When he did, she really exploded. "That's blasphemy! You must be joking! Though in very poor taste, if you ask me!"

Leo must have caught the look of dismay on my face. He knows better than anyone how a publisher reacts to TV-only news viewers. "You know I'm kidding," he said in a reasonable tone. "It's Wednesday, pub day. The paper just came off the press ten minutes ago. When would I have time to read it?"

"Start now," Vida commanded. "Scott and I both have stories on the play. And in case you forget, the performances are Friday, Saturday, and Sunday. Indeed, the play will be presented twice Sunday, at a matinee and in the evening."

"I'll have to check my social calendar," Leo responded. "I may have opera tickets or the symphony or an NBA game."

I left Leo to fabricate and Vida to froth. In my small office, I sat down to look at the latest edition of *The Alpine Advocate*. My sole reporter, Scott Chamoud, had managed to fill up the front page all by himself. The recent snow—with more in the forecast—had partially made up for the lack of winter moisture in western Washington. There was hope for the ski industry after all. The weather had also given Scott an opportunity to take photos of children playing in the snow, trees in Old Mill Park covered with snow, and a traffic accident at First and Front caused by snow. We'd save the icicle pictures for next week.

Below the fold, there was Scott's story about the play. It ran for six inches and jumped to page three. Vida had two rehearsal photos on her House & Home page, along with a head shot of Destiny Parsons and a feature on various cast members. Since Mayor Fuzzy Baugh was one of them and we hadn't run his stock studio portrait, I expected the phone to start ringing any minute.

I looked up as Sheriff Milo Dodge loped into my office. At six-foot-five and wearing his regulation Smokey the Bear hat, he filled the door.

"I suppose it's too late for a dead guy," he said.

"You know it is," I retorted, mentally cursing the prospect of losing a big story. "Who is it?"

"No idea yet," Milo replied, lounging against the door frame. "Somebody in a pickup just got creamed on Highway 2 by Deception Falls. Sam and Dwight haven't called in with the ID."

"Milo," I said sternly, "you know damned well that our deadline is five o'clock Tuesday. Are you pretending to forget or pretending to be stupid? And why don't you sit down? You're looming."

Milo rubbed his long chin. "I guess I've never figured out how you can have a Tuesday deadline, but the paper doesn't come out until Wednesday afternoon. What about all this new technology? Why can't the deadline be Wednesday noon or else have the paper come out in the morning? You've got a whole week to put the thing together."

I tried not to gnash my teeth. "I've explained this to you a dozen times. We hold the front page open for late-breaking news. If there is any. We put features inside, I write editorials, we watch the wire services for anything connected to Alpine and Skykomish County. We have ads and classifieds and legal notices and vital statistics. Not to mention photographs and occasional artwork. The paper has to be laid out, and even with PageMaker technology, it takes time. There are headlines to—"

"What artwork?" Milo interrupted.

He caught me off-guard; I was stumped. "Maps," I finally said. "Graphs. Are you going to sit down or not?"

"Nope." Milo stopped leaning. "I'll let you know when we get an ID on the crash victim. See you."

I watched him walk away. Recently the sheriff had become very aggravating. Over the years we'd had our ups and downs. Being friends was tricky. As lovers, we'd failed. Milo had wanted to take the relationship further. I hadn't. Not then, when Tom Cavanaugh was still alive. Six months ago, I thought we'd reached a new, comfortable level of companionship. But lately Milo had been acting oddly, or at least showing me his prickly side. I'd seen it before. I supposed I could endure it again. I only wished I knew what had triggered the change.

Milo had been gone less than a minute when the phone started ringing. Obviously, the latest edition of the *Advocate* had hit the streets, no easy feat considering that only the main thoroughfares—both of them—had been plowed in the last two days.

The first call was in fact weather-related. It was from the ranger station, a couple of miles west of Alpine, informing me that it was snowing up at the Stevens Pass summit. They expected the state to close Highway 2 before dark. For now, vehicles with chains and traction tires could still get through.

"Tell that to Spencer Fleetwood," I said, but thanked the ranger who'd called. His name was Bunky or Punky Smythe, a newcomer to the Skykomish area. Or maybe it was Hunky. I could but hope.

Speaking of which, Scott Chamoud entered my office. Even bundled up in a Gore-Tex parka, he looked good.

"Are you going to the dress rehearsal tomorrow?" he inquired.

"I hadn't thought about it," I replied. "Are you?"

"I can't," he said, unzipping the parka and sitting down in one of my two visitor chairs. "I've got that special county commissioners' meeting. You know—the one where they're going to decide if they should build up the banks on the Sky."

The riverbanks through town had been heightened once, some forty years earlier. But natural erosion and new construction had taken their toll. The Skykomish had flooded twice in the last four years, though damage had been minimal. Since the troika of county commissioners was getting so old that I was surprised they could tell wet from dry, I'd been gratified to learn that they still had some rational concerns about the town's welfare.

Had I possessed a kindly heart, I would have volunteered to cover the county commissioners myself. But I'd been stuck with most of their regular meetings ever since I came to Alpine. Somehow, an emergency meeting didn't equate with an added attraction. Even in the days when all three were relatively lucid, most of the sessions were taken up with how much barbed wire was needed to fence in the Fabergasts' prize bull, where a new trash can should be placed at Old Mill Park, and should the name of a Korean War veteran be stricken from the courthouse's military service plaque because almost fifty years after the cease-fire he'd gotten drunk and run over one of Grace Grundle's cats.

On the other hand, a dress rehearsal of *The Outcast* didn't create much enthusiasm in my breast. Sitting through opening night was obligatory. But watching the troupe stumble and mumble for an extra three hours seemed above and beyond the call of duty. In fact, it sounded a lot like the county commissioners' meeting.

"I'll drop by for the rehearsal," I promised as the phone rang.

Expecting the mayor, I was surprised—but not pleased—to hear the voice of my former ad manager, Ed Bronsky.

"What's the deal with my name being last in the cast list?" Ed demanded in his whining voice. "Shouldn't the actors be in alphabetical order? I don't mind Hans Berenger being ahead of me, because *B-e-r* comes before *B-r-o*. But how do I end up dead last? Has everybody forgotten who the fairy is for this production?"

"I think," I replied, trying not to laugh out loud, "you mean *angel*." Some angel! As our local millionaire through inheritance, Ed had volunteered money to back the production. He'd bragged about five figures, but I learned later that included a decimal point.

"Whatever," Ed huffed. "I know it's too late to change it— after all, I'm an old newspaper hand myself—but I want better treatment when the review appears next week."

"Actually," I remarked, scanning Scott's story, "your name appears before Dodo's."

"I should hope so," Ed retorted. "Dodo is a dog."

"A clever dog," I noted. Dodo belonged to Jim Medved, the town's veterinarian, who also had a part in the play. I didn't mention that Dodo probably could act circles around most of the cast, especially Ed. "Here's how it works," I explained. "The cast list is made out according to the order of speaking roles. You play a customer at the Emerald Café. I assume you don't have a great many lines."

"Well." Ed paused. "Maybe not. But I'm onstage for most of the play. I sit at the counter and eat."

Typecasting, I thought, picturing the rotund Mr. Bronsky's backside overlapping the stool. "If you look at the program—which we'll have printed by tomorrow for whoever is picking them up—you'll see your name appears in the same place there as it does in the paper. If you've got a beef, talk to Destiny Parsons."

"Destiny obviously doesn't know what side her bread is buttered on," Ed declared. "She'll hear about this. She seems to have forgotten that I'm going to run for mayor in the off-year election this fall." He slammed down the phone.

I seemed to have forgotten it, too. Recently Ed had made a couple of passing remarks about seeking office, but I had dismissed them as mere bluster. Fuzzy Baugh had been mayor since before I moved to Alpine. No serious candidate had ever challenged him. It wasn't that Fuzzy was so effective in office, but that no one else seemed to want the job. The real power lay in the arthritic hands of the county commissioners.

Ginny Erlandson, her dazzling red hair in disarray, rushed into my cubbyhole. "Nat Cardenas has been on hold for five minutes. Didn't you see the red light on your phone?"

I heaved a sigh. "No," I admitted to our office manager. "I was too busy soothing Ed Bronsky's ruffled feathers."

I punched in the call and immediately apologized to the college president.

Nat, who rarely shows his human side, sounded almost meek. "I'd like to get together with you tomorrow or Friday," he began. "I didn't want to bother you on press day. Would lunch at the ski lodge work for you?"

If Nat wanted to see me, there must be a problem. I assumed it had nothing to do with his part in *The Outcast.* He was playing Sheriff John Brown, an apparently heroic figure, though it had surprised me when he took on the role. Nat Cardenas guarded his dignity closely.

"Tomorrow's fine," I said, "assuming we don't get more snow and the road to the lodge is open."

"Let's hope for the best, despite the forecast," Nat replied. "Would twelve-thirty be convenient?"

I said that it would. "Is there a crisis at the college?" I asked.

Nat didn't answer right away, and when he did, his voice was very formal. "There are some challenges emerging. I'll tell you about them tomorrow. Thanks for agreeing to meet me."

The calls that followed included the usual irate readers, three of whom didn't agree with my editorial advocating the flood control project. One of them was Rita Patricelli, the Chamber of Commerce secretary and a member of a large Italian family that had been in the area for years. I had first known her as Rita Haines, but she'd dumped both Mr. Haines and his last name some time ago.

"I've lived here all my life, more or less," Rita declared in her brisk voice. "I'd write a letter to the editor, but I don't want the merchants to think I'm speaking for all of them. You've been here for at least ten years, Emma. How many times has the Sky flooded?"

I thought back over the decade. "Twice."

"How much damage?"

"Some of the businesses and homes along River Road got almost a foot of water the last time," I said.

"Which they could bail out with a couple of buckets and a dishpan," Rita retorted. "The Sky's not big enough this close to the source. It's a waste of money. The project wouldn't even bring more jobs to Alpine. You know damned well the county would hire some outsider."

"I appreciate your opinion," I said, trying to be gracious even though I'd never been particularly fond of the abrasive Rita Patricelli. "You may be right. But I'm not backing down. In any event, it's up to the county commissioners."

"Those old slugs," Rita sneered. "Maybe that's a good thing. They'll dither around until the river dries up. The three of them already have. Now if they'd only blow away."

I wouldn't admit to Rita that I agreed with her.

"And by the way," she went on, "that picture of me in this week's *Advocate* is god-awful. I look like I weigh four hundred pounds."

Rita referred to the group photo of *The Outcast* troupe. She was playing a waitress at the Emerald Café. I wouldn't exactly call Rita fat, but she had put on some weight in recent months.

"You look fine to me," I said blithely.

"Speak for yourself," Rita grumbled. "I still wish you'd visited Avezzano when you were in Italy. It's not that far from Rome. I'd have liked a souvenir from my ancestral home."

"You ought to go there yourself," I said, aware that I had another call on hold. "Got to run, Rita. I think Fuzzy's on the other line."

"Good-bye." Rita hung up.

❈   ❈   ❈

There hadn't been time to visit the countryside that surrounded Rome. I'd never been there before, but my brother had made three previous visits, including a six-month stint several years earlier when he'd studied how to be a missionary priest. If he'd learned nothing else, he'd discovered that his vocation was not in the jungles of Papua New Guinea or the deserts of North Africa. Ben had opted for the home missions and had been sent to the Mississippi Delta, where I had gone when my son, Adam, was born.

Thus, Ben knew Rome fairly well, though he was surprised at the city's expansion since his last visit seven years ago. While he attended meetings in the Vatican, I followed his instructions on where to go and what to see. I started at Piazza di Porta San Giovanni, where I visited the basilica dedicated to St. John the Evangelist and St. John the Baptist. The church, which frankly isn't all that imposing on the outside, is also Rome's cathedral. I stumbled over an uneven place in the floor and fell to one knee. If any on-lookers saw me, they probably thought I was genuflecting and praying. Instead, I was wobbling and cussing.

If this was a pilgrimage, it had gotten off on the wrong foot.

❄   ❄   ❄

As Rita rang off abruptly, I knew it was because she wouldn't want to keep the mayor waiting. But the call wasn't from Fuzzy Baugh. Instead, it was from Sunny Rhodes, the mother of one of our carriers. Her son, Davin, had fallen off his bike and possibly broken his ankle. If he was laid up, could the family collect disability from the *Advocate*? I told her I'd have to check into it with our attorney, Marisa Foxx. I felt like telling Mom that her son should have been using snowshoes, not a bicycle.

Deputy Sam Heppner phoned in the name of the highway accident victim, a resident of Wenatchee, on the other side of the Cascades. Crass as it sounds, his lack of association with Alpine didn't mean we'd missed a major story. Next week, the fatality would take up no more than two inches on the inside pages.

As it turned out, the mayor never called that afternoon. Apparently, he wasn't upset over the omission of his formal portrait. Maybe he didn't want to annoy me. Maybe he was taking Ed Bronsky's electoral challenge seriously.

Despite the gloomy gray clouds, it was still light at five o'clock when I left the office. Spring was exactly a month away, but it was hard to believe with the snow piled high at the sidewalk's edge. Not that it was unusual for Alpine to get snow even as late as April. We'd been spoiled the past few years by warmer weather that might have been easier to live with but hurt the winter sports industry. The lack of a sizable snowpack also kept the rivers low and caused a shortage of hydroelectric power.

Tire chains weren't practical in town, since Front Street and Alpine Way were kept clear. But the moment I turned onto Fir Street and headed to my little log house, I had to rely on studded tires. After returning from my two-week vacation in Italy, I'd sold the Lexus that Tom Cavanaugh had virtually given me and replaced it with an almost-new Honda Accord. I couldn't ever replace Tom and I had only sad memories of the Lexus. He'd been dead for going on two years. Yet I still awoke some mornings thinking he was alive.

"Time," people kept telling me. "Time heals. You'll get over the worst parts."

I was feeling more stable. But I'd never heal completely. Tom was the father of my child, the only love of my life, the man I had been about to marry after waiting for almost thirty years. I was reminded of a song, something about the sea being wide and ". . . I cannot get over it."

I would never get over Tom Cavanaugh.

TWO

THERE WAS NO NEW SNOW ON THE GROUND THURSDAY MORNING.
I'd almost hoped for a blizzard that would shut down the town
and make it impossible for the show to go on.

"Well!" Vida exclaimed as she entered the newsroom almost
fifteen minutes late. "Guess what?"

Leo, Scott, and I all looked up from the Grocery Basket layout we'd been studying.

"You skied to work," Leo said. "That's why you're late. We
were about to send Dodge out to look for you."

Vida dismissed the remark with a wave of her hand and an
amiable laugh. "Nothing of the sort. Amy called just as I was
leaving. You'll never guess what she had to say."

Scott stared at Vida. "Your daughter won the lottery?"

"No, no, no." Vida made another gesture of dismissal, as if
a few million dollars wouldn't cause such excitement. "Roger is
in *The Outcast*!"

I wanted to say that Roger *was* the outcast. Vida's spoiled
grandson had been a thorn in my side ever since I arrived in
Alpine. Now he was a teenager, a high school junior, and—in
my mind—licensed to kill since he'd passed his driver's test.

"Wait a minute," I said, unable to hide my shock. "Roger's not listed among the cast members. Did they add a part?" *Like Spawn of Satan?*

"Of course not," Vida replied. "Davin Rhodes was supposed to play the role of the runaway youth. Davin hurt himself yesterday. According to my niece, Marje Blatt at the clinic, he sprained an ankle, tripping over his own feet. Roger is taking his place."

Sunny Rhodes hadn't been entirely truthful in her report to me. Maybe she and her husband, Oren, were hoping they could sue the *Advocate*.

"How can Roger learn the part so fast?" I inquired, putting aside the evil thought that I didn't think the kid had learned to read yet.

Vida was removing her hat, a gift I'd brought back from Rome. It was a replica of the headgear previously worn by the Italian *carabinieri*. The shape was reminiscent of an eighteenth-century tricorn, complete with the police force's official red-and-white flame-shaped badge. I couldn't decide if Vida looked like a Revolutionary War general or a Stealth bomber. But she adored the hat and patted it fondly before placing it on the windowsill above her desk. "The part of Jamie Jejune," she explained, "doesn't have a great many lines, though he's onstage quite a bit. Roger will have no trouble. He's been thinking about becoming an actor, you know."

Leo cocked his head to one side. "Really."

"Is that sarcasm I hear?" Vida demanded.

Leo had assumed his innocent expression. "No. I think it'd be great for him to become a good actor."

As opposed to a bad actor, I thought, and was certain that Leo had implied the same.

Vida, however, couldn't lose her euphoria. "Roger has always enjoyed playing parts. His imitations of movie and TV actors absolutely astonish me. Of course I don't know all the characters he mimics, but there's one named AJ from a show called *The Sopranos* that's just hilarious. I can't wait for him to start singing some of the music. He has quite a good voice, you know."

Scott shot me a look that indicated he felt it was a good thing that Vida had never watched *The Sopranos*. "It's cool when teenagers have some idea of what they'd like to do with their lives," he said, keeping his back to Vida as he went over to the coffeemaker for a refill. "Most kids don't. I knew in high school that I wanted to be a journalist. One of these days I'm going to try to freelance as a photojournalist."

"Don't rush," I urged. Scott was, in fact, a better photographer than he was a writer. At least his copy wasn't prone to the typos that his predecessor had come up with on an almost weekly basis. Carla Steinmetz Talliaferro had written some pips, including her final issue, in which she referred to Grace Grundle as Grace Griddle, mentioned Justine Cardenas's energy-efficient fishwasher, and reported that there was ". . . a new crook at the Venison Inn." Fortunately, I had caught the mistakes when I proofread her copy.

The morning passed quickly, though the creaking of the tin roof over my office seemed to have gone up a decibel or two. Our production wizard, Kip MacDuff, had promised to remove the accumulation of snow from the building before it collapsed. But Kip, who is usually extremely competent, was recently married and seemed to have other things on his mind.

So did I. Scott's hint of future departure wasn't the first time I'd heard such an idea from one of my staffers. Every so often, Kip remarked that he'd like to find some greener pastures for his computer skills. I couldn't blame either of them. They were both young, and their jobs on the *Advocate* were dead ends. As was my own. I wasn't so young, but increasingly I felt the need for change. Maybe it was middle age. Maybe there were too many sad memories in Alpine. Maybe you can't keep a girl down in a small town after she's seen Rome.

At twelve-fifteen I headed off for the ski lodge. To my relief, the road had been plowed that morning, perhaps in preparation for weekend skiers. The restaurant, with its Norse mythology theme and a waterfall tumbling among artificial trees, was fairly full. There aren't many choices when it comes to better dining in Alpine.

The fair-haired hostess, who looked vaguely familiar, informed me that Dr. Cardenas—as he preferred to be known to the public—hadn't yet arrived. He'd made a reservation, however. Would I like to be seated?

I said I would. Unfortunately, she began leading me to a table next to Spencer Fleetwood and Rita Patricelli. Apparently Mr. Radio was buttering up the Chamber of Commerce—or vice versa. If Nat Cardenas wanted to speak to me privately, it wouldn't be wise to sit so close to my news rival. I asked if we could be seated elsewhere. The hostess seemed surprised but cooperated and took me to a corner table next to two older women I also vaguely recognized. After over a decade in Alpine, I recognize almost everybody.

❄   ❄   ❄

I'd liked the anonymity of Rome. I didn't have to worry about being accosted on the street by irate readers or getting stuck in the produce aisle at the Grocery Basket listening to somebody tell me what to write in my next editorial. I was free from the constant telephone calls, indignant letters to the editor, insulting E-mails, and boring meetings.

I moved about with caution, aware that tourists are prey to thieves, con artists, and, in the case of women, the occasional hands-on lecher. Yet, as the days passed by, I felt a nascent sense of freedom.

But I also thought about how much I would have enjoyed seeing Rome with Tom. We had planned to honeymoon in Paris, where the sights would have been equally magnificent. Still, standing outside the Farnese Palace on a sunny morning, I could hear his voice in my ear. "We won't build that big a place in Alpine, Emma. It'd outshine Ed's Casa de Bronska." I'd laugh and nestle my head against Tom's shoulder. He'd put his arm around me and we'd cross the square, heading for the market in the Campo de' Fiori where executions had been held long ago.

Tom had been executed, though in today's context his murder was termed an assassination. I suppose it didn't matter what it was called. Tom was still dead. Yet I felt him beside me with every step I took on the city's ancient cobbles.

❉   ❉   ❉

A minute or two after I sat down, I saw Nat entering the restaurant. He spotted me at once and strode in his purposeful way to our table.

"Am I late?" he asked, discreetly glancing around the dining area.

"No, I just got here." I explained that we'd almost ended up next to Spencer Fleetwood and Rita Patricelli.

Nat frowned. "Requesting another table was wise. I prefer not to have eavesdroppers." His black eyes shifted in the direction of the two older women. They were obviously absorbed in their own conversation, which seemed fairly heavy. During my brief wait, I'd caught the words *probate, gold digger*, and *criminal goings-on*. Maybe there was a better story there than what Nat was going to tell me.

We accepted ice water but abstained from alcoholic beverages. I'd rarely seen the college president drink in public. Initially, I'd wondered if he had a problem, but as time went on and his wife, Justine, remained aloof from all but the most important academic occasions, I speculated that she might be one who drank. Or who couldn't drink anymore.

During our meal, we engaged in chitchat: state funding, scholarship donations, enrollment—nothing that hadn't already been published in the *Advocate*.

At last, Nat began to speak of the subject that was on his mind. By coincidence, the two older women were toting up their bill and getting ready to leave.

"I've come to trust you," Nat said, looking not at me but at his hands that were folded on the table. The admission was stated in a manner that indicated I should be thrilled to pieces. "You've treated the college fairly. You've also demonstrated good judgment and discretion."

"Those things are all part of my job," I declared in my most businesslike voice.

Nat finally raised his eyes. "That being said," he continued, "I want to share a situation with you that isn't for publication. At least not yet. It's bound to leak out in a short time."

The two old gals were still sorting out the bill, but at least it kept them occupied.

"So you want me to have the background?" I inquired, knowing that he also wanted to make sure I heard his side of the predicament first.

Nat nodded. He was a handsome man, aging better than most. His slightly wavy dark hair had silver streaks and the creases in his face made him look more mature rather than merely older.

"I've had two very interesting job offers recently," he said, his hands still folded. "Over the years, I've had other opportunities, but none that really challenged me. Both of the current inquiries do. One is at a four-year college in California, and the other is for a two-year school in upstate New York."

I could understand why the offers appealed to Nat Cardenas. His struggle to rise above the obstacles of his Hispanic ancestry and his impoverished youth was admirable. But I'd always sensed that he still felt he had more to prove.

"Congratulations," I said. "I'll file the job offers away until you decide if you're going to accept one of them."

Nat grimaced. "It's not that simple." He finally unclasped his hands and paused as the women at the next table finally rose from their chairs and departed. "Frankly, I'm not sure I intend to take either of them."

I expressed surprise. "The offers seem like a step up the academic ladder," I said.

"That's true," Nat allowed. "But there are other considerations." He cleared his throat. It was obvious that confiding in others was difficult for him. "As the first president of SCC, it was my responsibility to make this a viable educational institution. I like to think I've done that. We've grown in enrollment, faculty, and staff by thirty percent since the college opened almost five years ago. We've established five new programs. We've received endowments of . . ." He stopped, looking embarrassed. "You know all this. My point is that I take great pride in what we've done. Not," he added hastily, "that I did it alone. I've had a tremendous amount of help, from not only the personnel at the college, but the community itself."

I was beginning to drift. As I got older, I noticed that after a large lunch—as opposed to my usual fare from the Burger Barn or the Venison Inn—I often became sleepy. Nat was droning away as my eyes started to glaze over. Educators tend to run on. There was a point to this meeting, I was sure of that, but I wished he'd get to it before I nodded off.

". . . in good hands." There was appeal in Nat's dark eyes. "But once I'm gone, there's nothing I can do about it. It's up to the Board of Trustees."

I'd missed something. Frantically, I tried to retrieve a word or phrase from Nat that might give me a clue to what he'd been talking about. "In other words," I said, hoping I didn't sound as idiotic as I felt, "you lack confidence in your possible successor." Had Nat mentioned a name? Clea Bhuj, head of the Humanities Department? Shawna Beresford-Hall, the registrar? Karl Freeman, the high school principal? Crazy Eights Neffle, our local loony?

Nat frowned again. "It's a question of personality. It's important in this job to present the right image, not to mention reaching out to the state legislature in Olympia. Hans has done a good job as dean of students. He's an able administrator. But Hans doesn't possess leadership qualities. I would think the Board of Trustees could see that."

Hans. Hans Berenger. I'd omitted him from my quick list of potential candidates, probably for the very reason Nat didn't think he'd make a good president. Hans was austere and seemingly humorless. He'd always struck me as an automaton, quietly and efficiently going about his business with all the personality of a boulder. He was easy to forget, effortless to ignore.

"Hans does seem a bit of an introvert," I finally said. "How does he relate to students?"

Nat's expression was wry. "He doesn't. That is, he lets the counselors and the secretaries handle them. Remember," he added, assuming a more serious look, "Hans is first and foremost an administrator. As I mentioned, he's very good at it."

Hans was good at delegating, too, I presumed. "If you decide to leave, what makes you think the board would appoint Hans to your job?"

"There are seven trustees," Nat explained. "Kermit Cederberg from the bank, Doc Dewey, Jonathan Sibley, Jack Blackwell, Rita Patricelli from the chamber, Reverend Nielsen, and Mary Jane Bourgette."

I nodded. Mary Jane had filled the vacancy left by her brother, Einar Rasmussen Jr., who had been murdered just before the student union building was officially opened. Named for Einar, the Rasmussen Union Building was unofficially known as the RUB. To further the Rasmussen legacy, Einar Jr.'s aged and ornery mother, Thyra, had donated money to build a theater on the campus, which was duly named in her honor.

As for Mary Jane Rasmussen Bourgette, she was active in many charitable causes, mainly through our parish church, St. Mildred's. Her husband, Dick, had his own construction company and two of their sons owned a 1950s-style diner on River Road, while a daughter, Rosemary, was the county's prosecuting attorney.

Of the other board members, Jonathan Sibley was also an attorney, though in private practice. Jack Blackwell represented the timber industry, and Donald Nielsen was the pastor at Faith Lutheran Church.

"The current chairperson," Nat went on, lowering his voice almost to a whisper, "is Rita Patricelli. She and Hans are very close friends." He paused, undoubtedly noting my quizzical expression. But Nat didn't elaborate. "As head of the chamber, Rita has a great deal of influence. Kermit—or Stilts, as I believe he's called—along with Jack Blackwell, Mary Jane Bourgette, and Reverend Nielsen would probably follow her lead. They're all great civic boosters. I can't speak for the others."

Nor could I. I hardly knew Jonathan Sibley. My limited legal business had been with his partner, Marisa Foxx. As an attorney, Jonathan would literally keep his own counsel. I'd known Doc Dewey ever since I arrived in Alpine. He was a fine man and an excellent physician who'd do what he felt was best for the college and the community. My experiences with Reverend Nielsen were limited. Vida considered him a ninny, but she lacked religious tolerance for anyone except her fellow Presbyterians and considered some of them ninnies, too.

"But," I pointed out, "this is all irrelevant if you decide to stay on."

"Yes." Nat looked up as our waitress refilled our coffee cups. "Dessert?" he asked me.

I shook my head. A rich finale would put me asleep at my desk. Nat also abstained and requested the bill.

"My treat," he insisted. "You're right about my staying on. There are other reasons than loyalty why that could be the right decision. On the other hand, there are also considerations for leaving other than the obvious."

"How does Justine feel about a move?" I inquired, wondering if my query was a touchy subject.

Nat didn't elude my gaze. "My wife is basically a city person." He smiled slightly. "I'm sure you can understand that, coming from the city yourself."

His reply struck me as somewhat vague. "So you're saying she's for it?"

Nat accepted the faux leather folder from the waitress and slipped his credit card inside. "I'm saying she wouldn't mind. But she insists that I have to do what's best for both of us."

"I see," I remarked, though I felt as if I were sitting in fog. "How soon do you have to make up your mind?"

"March twelfth," Nat replied. "That is, I have to let the people in upstate New York know by then. I have until April first to respond to the California offer."

I nodded. "In other words, your suitor schools want things settled by spring break."

"Yes." Nat looked up as the waitress made another stop at our table, this time with the credit card and the receipt. My host added on the tip and scribbled his name before thanking the young woman who was a Burleson or an Olsen or the possessor of some other Scandinavian surname. "I know," Nat continued after the waitress had again departed, "you'll keep this to yourself for the time being. But I felt obligated to inform you that there may be some news coming out of the college fairly soon."

Nat was right. But the big news that was coming from the campus turned out to be very different.

A few flakes were fluttering down when I left the office just after five. The rehearsal was slated for six-thirty. I'd just have time to eat, change, and call my son, Adam, in Alaska, where he was serving as pastor to an Inuit community near Nome.

I was proud of Adam for following in his uncle's footsteps. The two of them had been close during the years that my son had grown into manhood. With his father *in absentia*, it had been only natural for Adam to look up to Ben as his role model. Tom had his own two children to raise. When I'd discovered that his wife and I had both gotten pregnant about the same time, I'd cut Tom out of my life. My son and his father didn't meet until Adam was in college. They'd gotten along quite well, all things considered, and Adam had been so pleased that his parents were finally going to get married that he'd asked us to wait until after his ordination so that he and Ben could concelebrate the ceremony. It had seemed like a fairy tale—until it turned into a nightmare.

Erk. Squawk. Ping. Zlezlezle. Buzzz. The radio-relayed connection between Alpine and Mary's Igloo was worse than usual. Just as I thought I was going to suffer a hearing loss, I heard Adam's very faint "Hello?"

"Mom here!" I shouted.

Then came the usual delay. ". . . can't . . . you," he said.

"I can't hear you, either," I replied, guessing at what he meant. "Later?"

Ten, fifteen seconds passed, with more odd noises interjected. "Tomorrow night?" said Adam.

"Yes. You okay?"

I waited. Adam spoke, but all I could catch was sporadic monosyllables.

Since he was alive and able to answer the phone, I assumed he hadn't been attacked by a walrus or swallowed by a whale.

"Love you!" I yelled, and hung up.

While waiting for my chicken breast and rice to cook, I sorted through the mail, which yielded nothing but ads and a couple of bills. I considered fortifying myself with a bourbon and water but decided it was unwise to show up for the rehearsal with liquor on my breath. Feeling virtuous, I decided my reward would be not staying for more than one act. It was a public relations appearance, after all, since the real news would be the performance and its reception by the audience. I didn't dare play drama critic if I wanted to remain alive and well in Alpine.

Exchanging one pair of slacks and a heavy sweater for another, I ventured out into the night. There were still a few flakes fluttering down, but no sign of a serious snowfall as yet. That was another good reason to leave early. I didn't want to get snowed in.

A private parking area had been roped off by what was known as the Thyra Rasmussen Theater. There were several cars already parked in the lot. I pulled in across from Ed's Range Rover. He used to have two Mercedes sedans but had traded one in for the Rover the previous fall. Ed claimed that he and Shirley wanted a different kind of vehicle, but my theory was that the Bronskys had trashed the other Mercedes so thoroughly that no one in the overweight family could fit inside. It was easier to sell it than to clean it.

Discreetly, I made my way into the auditorium and stood about halfway down the side aisle. A dozen people milled around onstage, while another dozen sat in the first and second rows. The set was a diner, complete with a view into the kitchen, a half-dozen stools at the counter, and four tables with a requisite number of chairs. A green neon sign above the open kitchen spelled out EMERALD CAFÉ. The floor was yellow. I was beginning to get the idea.

I'd only been in the theater twice, for the O'Neill play and for commencement. The seats were covered in serviceable red fabric and fairly comfortable. There was a small balcony and a much smaller orchestra pit. Dark blue draperies had been hung on the walls and the curtain matched the red seats. The ambience was simple but serviceable.

I recognized most of the people who were involved in the production. My not-so-good neighbor, Destiny Parsons, had her long prematurely gray hair haphazardly tucked into a bun. Hans Berenger's tall, thin frame looked as rigid as ever, and his comb-over didn't enhance his appearance. Rita Patricelli paced nervously at one side of the stage. Deputy Dustin Fong stood off to the other side, looking as if he wished he were somewhere else. Mayor Baugh, who appeared to be campaigning, was shaking hands with several of the other participants, including Dr. Jim Medved, the Reverend Poole, Coach Rip Ridley, and Clea Bhuj, the head of the Humanities Division, who had the lead role of Dorothy Oz. I barely knew Clea, a dark-haired woman who was inclined to wear large quantities of gold bangles and, upon occasion, a sari.

"A Who's Who of Alpine," murmured a mellow voice behind me.

I gave a start, then turned to face Spencer Fleetwood. "You scared me. I was concentrating on who really is who—in the play."

"It's more like a Whose Zoo," Spence said, still in his soft, mellow radio mode. "How were you spared? I'm not sure how I got roped into this."

"You've got the voice to be the narrator," I replied. "I have no dramatic talent."

Spence chuckled. There had been a time when I'd thought of him as my archenemy. There had also been a time—though brief—when I thought he was the incarnation of evil. And though we remained rivals, we'd called a truce. In fact, we had tried some joint promotional ventures, including an on-line Web site that had begun to show dividends for both the *Advocate* and KSKY.

"I'd rather see you playing the waitress part than Rita," Spence remarked. "You're a lot better-looking, and she can't act, either."

"Who can in this bunch?" I inquired, not immune to the compliment but unwilling to acknowledge it.

"Well . . ." Spence studied the figures both onstage and in the front rows. Like most radio personalities, he knew a few things about drama. "Clea's not too bad, though she doesn't project well. If Nat Cardenas would let go a little, he'd be okay. At least he knows his lines. Fuzzy, of course, hams it up, but that's not all bad, because he'll get some laughs, intentional and otherwise. The best of the bunch is Rey Fernandez. It's not just because he looks the part of an itinerant worker, but he's actually got some talent."

I didn't know Rey Fernandez. He was an older student who'd enrolled at SCC for fall quarter. I could spot him easily, however, if only because I knew the others. Rey was maybe thirty, average height, but with a muscular build and a dark mustache that gave him a rakish look.

"I should introduce myself," I noted. "By the way, how's Roger doing?"

Spence's hawklike features grew enigmatic. "That depends."

"On what?" I asked, fruitlessly scanning the auditorium for my favorite future candidate for the FBI's Most Wanted list.

Spence winced. "I hate to say it, but the kid may have talent. He's undisciplined, of course."

"You're telling me," I murmured, as the cast appeared to be assembling for the rehearsal's start. "How come they're not in costume? Or are they?"

"Some of the wardrobe got held up by the snow," Spence replied as we moved closer to the front. "Several characters—like Ed and Dustin—can wear their own clothes. It saves on production costs. Excuse me, Emma. I have to get up on that stool at the side of the stage and become the narrator."

A certain amount of scrambling for places ensued. The curtain closed, the houselights dimmed, and Destiny Parsons strode into the orchestra pit. A spotlight lurched around the front of the stage, apparently trying to find Spence. Finally, he was revealed, sitting on the stool, reading from a large green- and gold-covered book, and wearing his usual garb of slacks, open shirt, and V-necked cashmere sweater.

"There once was a small town called Evergreen," Spence began in his mellifluous voice, "a close-knit community high on a mountainside and deep in the forest."

So far, so good. I sat in the second row, three seats from the aisle. The rest of the auditorium was deserted. Or so I thought until I heard a voice in my ear:

"Goodness!" Vida exclaimed. "I thought I was going to be late. Buck called from Palm Springs. He talked my ear off."

Buck Bardeen was Vida's longtime companion. He spent part of the winter in the California desert, where he golfed and got together with his children and grandchildren. Vida and Buck had been through some rough turf recently but appeared to have made up. While Vida might interrogate everybody else about their personal lives, she was reticent when it came to her own.

"I didn't know you were coming," I said under my breath, hoping Vida would take the hint and tone down her customary stage whisper, which probably could be heard out in the parking lot.

Holding on to her faux sable pillbox, she plopped down next to me. "I didn't want to miss Roger in rehearsal," she said, still loud enough to block out Spence's narration and evoke a sharp "Shush!" from Destiny Parsons.

"Twaddle," Vida responded, though she did drop her voice. "The curtain's not even up yet."

The words were barely out of her mouth when Spence stopped reading. The spotlight on him went down, and the curtain rose slowly, revealing Hans Berenger in the kitchen, an unlighted cigar in his mouth, a spatula in his left hand, and a chef's hat covering his comb-over. Rita Patricelli was trying to look harried—and not doing a bad job of it, since she often seemed that way at the Chamber of Commerce. Rita was taking orders from Fuzzy Baugh and Jim Medved, who sat at a table to the left of the stage. Two of the counter stools were occupied by Ed and Rip. They had their backs to the house, and their backsides were pretty amazing. Coach Ridley's rear was part muscle, since he had played pro football for the Chicago Bears. Ed, however, was just plain fat, since the only muscle he seemed to exercise was his mouth.

The opening line belonged to Fuzzy, who laid it on thick with his original Louisiana accent.

"Ah don't know 'bout this new bidness, Dane," he declared. "Evahgreen sure can use some ec-o-nom-ic in-put, but more timbah cuttin' isn't the way."

"Oh, good grief!" Vida gasped, fortunately to herself.

"You're right, Leroy," our town veterinarian responded. "I've fought against any kind of development that . . ." Jim stopped. "That would . . ." He stopped again, looking helplessly at Destiny. "I'm sorry. I blanked on what comes next."

" '. . . development that would hurt the environment,' " Destiny said from the pit.

Jim nodded. "Got it." He paused before continuing with his lines. "You're one of the few builders around here with a conscience, Leroy. You care about people. You care about animals."

"Like you say," Fuzzy replied with three big nods, "animals got rights, too."

Coach Ridley swerved around on the stool. "Like getting

shot with my .22 every fall. That's the only right those critters have as far as I'm concerned. What else has an out-of-work logger got to do around here?"

Ed didn't budge. He appeared to be eating. He probably was.

"Hey!" Jim jumped up from his chair, accidentally knocking it over. "Sorry," he apologized to Destiny. "I'll try that again." He sat back down, got up again, and repeated his line: "Hey!" The chair stayed put.

"Dear me." Vida looked pained but leaned closer. "I'm sure this will all turn out very well tomorrow night. Don't they always say that a bad rehearsal means a fine performance?"

I kept my mouth shut.

Rip slid off his stool and advanced on Jim. "You want a piece of me?" He shook his fists. "Come on, Animal Boy. Let's have at it!"

Jim held up a hand. "I won't fight you. I don't believe in violence."

Rip clumsily waved his arms. "Awww! You're just a shickenchit!"

"Hold it!" Destiny called. "Let's hear that line again, Coach."

Rip looked puzzled.

"The line is 'chickenshit!' " Destiny shouted. "You read it backward."

"Oh." Rip looked embarrassed.

"Goodness," Vida whispered. "I certainly hope there's not much of that kind of language in this play. I wouldn't want Roger exposed to such things."

Again, I kept my mouth shut. The real problem was keeping my eyes open. In the next ten minutes, there were several screwups with delivery, inflection, blocking, and lighting. At last, Clea Bhuj made her entrance along with a large English sheepdog called Dodo. Clea's petite figure was encased in tight denim jeans and a clingy red mock-turtleneck sweater. I assumed her costume hadn't arrived, either. As Dorothy Oz, it had to be something in a blue-and-white check. Instead of a basket, Clea carried a backpack.

"Where am I?" she asked in a wistful voice.

Hans Berenger removed the cigar from his mouth. "You're in Evergreen," he said somewhat stiffly, then made an attempt to give Clea a hard stare. "Are you lost or are you one of those druggies? We don't care much for druggies around here."

"Oh, no," Clea replied in a breathless tone that I guessed was intended to convey shock. "I got off the bus to go to the rest room and it was gone when I—"

"Stop right there!" Destiny commanded. "Clea, they won't be able to hear you past the third row."

"I should have sat farther back," I murmured. "Maybe then I couldn't hear any of it."

"Hush!" Vida snapped. "Roger may be about to come onstage."

But Roger wasn't. After an hour, I couldn't stand it anymore. The cast members were still slogging their way through Act One. Despite Vida's pleas for me to stay, I told her I was expecting a call from Adam. It might even be true; maybe my son would make another attempt to connect with me.

But he didn't. I contented myself with reading a book on the Civil War and eating microwave popcorn. As I headed for bed around eleven-thirty, I figured the rehearsal was probably still going on. I hoped the actual performance would be much shorter.

Unfortunately, my wish would be granted.

THREE

FRIDAY GOT OFF TO A BAD START. ADMITTEDLY, I'M NOT AT MY best in the morning. All my working life I've found it difficult to rise early. During the years I was employed by *The Oregonian* in Portland, the job began at nine. When I purchased the *Advocate* and became my own boss, I figured I could adjust my schedule to what suited me. However, the previous owner, Marius Vandeventer, had always opened up at eight. Residents of Alpine don't like change. The inherited staff members—especially Vida—wanted to keep to the original hours despite the fact that there's no daily deadline pressure on a weekly. The rest of the town also preferred the status quo. If they had classified ads to drop off or items to submit, they found it more convenient to drop by on their way to work. Thus, I was stuck with the early opening and could only cope by consuming massive doses of caffeine.

It had snowed a couple of inches during the night, but because the temperature still hovered in the low twenties there was no new ice to make driving dangerous. But the weather wasn't what made me extra grumpy. I was digging in my big handbag for my keys when I happened to look out the window to see Destiny Parsons standing on her front steps across the street and clapping her hands. Sure enough, her wretched dog was once again decorating the snow in my yard. I didn't know if the applause was for Azbug's success or merely to urge the mutt on. In any event, I yanked open the door and marched outside.

"Hey!" I yelled. "Beat it!"

Destiny leaned forward. "Are you speaking to me?"

"I'm speaking to your dog," I called back. "Would you please stop sending him over to my yard?"

"It's a she, not a he," Destiny shouted as the fox terrier trotted back across the street. No doubt the mutt wore a smug expression. "Azbug goes where she goes."

"Then she'd better not go here anymore," I retorted. "If she does, I'll take a broom to her."

"How dare you!" Destiny drew herself up to her full height and glared in my direction. "If you do that, I'll report you to the SPCA!"

"Then I'll report you to the sheriff for harassment!" I shouted. "Meanwhile, get yourself a shovel and a bag and clean up your critter's mess! If I have to do it, I'll dump it on your porch!" Furious, I turned around and stomped back into the living room, slamming the door behind me.

I peeked outside. Azbug had joined Destiny. The big bitch and the little bitch went into their house. I started toward the fireplace to get the ash shovel but stopped at the edge of the hearth. Maybe Destiny would remove Azbug's deposit later. I'd give her the benefit of the doubt. Better her than me. I went out to the car and backed down the driveway. As I pulled onto Fir Street, there was no sign of activity across the street. Maybe Destiny couldn't find a shovel.

By noon, my temper had cooled down and the weather had warmed up. I rarely watch the TV forecasts. A more accurate prediction came from going outside and sensing what meteorological changes were in store for Alpine. Crossing Front Street to the Burger Barn, I thought it felt like more snow.

Milo Dodge agreed with me. He was headed in the same

direction, coming from his office two blocks down from the *Advocate*.

"The state patrol is issuing a traffic advisory for later in the day," he said as we entered the restaurant. "The big snow they expected earlier still may hit by tonight."

"Before or after the play?" I asked, looking for an empty booth.

Milo apparently didn't realize I was being facetious. "No telling." To my surprise, he started in the direction of the counter.

"Hey," I said, grabbing at the sleeve of his regulation parka, "there's a vacant booth toward the back."

"Huh?" Milo turned slowly. "Oh." He hesitated. "Okay."

As I led the way, the sheriff couldn't see the annoyance on my face. After we sat down, I asked him the burning question:

"What's with you lately? Ordinarily, if we bump into each other on the way to lunch, we always eat together. Have I done something to piss you off?"

Milo stared at me without expression. "No."

"Then why were you going to sit at the counter?"

He shrugged. "Habit, I guess."

"Not when you're with me."

"I wasn't with you. I mean, we didn't . . ." His hazel eyes wavered. "I had my mind on something else."

"Like what?"

He shrugged again. "Oh . . . work."

When it came to "work" with the sheriff, it often translated into "news." "Is it something I should know about?"

"No."

My response had to go on hold as our server appeared. Both Milo and I stared. Instead of the usual young, blond waitress of Scandinavian descent, Rita Patricelli stood at our table.

"Are you ready to order?" she asked as if she'd never seen us before.

Milo turned his coffee mug right-side up. "Coffee here, Rita. What's this?" he asked, waving a big hand at her Burger Barn waitress uniform. "Did you quit the chamber?"

"No, sir," Rita replied meekly. "Would you care to order your entrée now?"

Looking baffled, Milo nodded. "Sure. Cheeseburger, fries, green salad. I don't get it." He stared at Rita again.

Rita leaned closer. "I'm getting into my part for the play tonight. Destiny thought I should try being a waitress for a few hours to get the feel for my character of Angela." She straightened up. "And you, miss?" Rita said to me.

I ordered the Friday fish and chips special with coleslaw and a pineapple malt. Rita moved briskly to the kitchen counter, where she slid our order into a metal clip.

"I suppose I should make an appearance to show SkyCo's law enforcement support," Milo said. "Not to mention that Dustin Fong would get his feelings hurt if I was a no-show."

I hadn't seen Milo's deputy after the rehearsal started. In proofing the playbills earlier in the day I'd noticed that he was playing the part of Kevin Chang, an attorney. Dustin would probably do all right if he maintained his usual professional, somewhat stoic manner.

"Want to go with me?" I asked in what I hoped was a casual voice.

Rita had returned with the coffeepot for Milo. He didn't answer until she was gone. I got the impression he was grateful for the interruption. "I probably should take the Cherokee Chief," he said at last. "If more snow comes and we get some accidents around here, I may have to leave early. I wouldn't want you to be stuck at the playhouse."

I considered sulking but reminded myself that I was a mature middle-aged woman. I'd get mad instead. After all, my day had started out with a flare of temper. Why should I stop now?

"Fine," I snapped. "What next, we pretend we don't know

each other? You've been acting like a real jerk for the past . . ." I had to stop to think how long it had been since Milo had become standoffish. ". . . Four, five months? What did I do, snub you at Harvey's Hardware because I didn't see you from behind the Weed-Eater display?"

Milo grimaced, then began rearranging the salt and pepper shakers, a longtime habit of his. "Forget it. It's no big deal."

I leaned across the table, keeping my voice down. "No, I won't forget it, not as long as you keep putting me at a distance. I thought we were friends again. We went through this once before, after our official breakup. But after Tom died, we picked up where we'd left off, and I was happy about that. We even slept together a couple of times. And then"—I snapped my fingers, hoping that the Nordby brothers across the aisle wouldn't notice—"poof! You started acting as if I were a contagious disease."

Milo's gaze also roamed toward the Nordby brothers, but they were engaged in a serious conversation, too. Trout and Skunk, as they were known, owned the local GM dealership. They weren't talking car sales, though. Rather, I had caught the words *Martin Creek*, *too cold*, *too high*, *off-color*, and *hopeless*. I knew they referred to steelhead fishing and apparently not having any luck. Milo probably heard them, too, and wished he could join them. Typical male that he is, the sheriff would prefer discussing the elusive seagoing trout rather than a relationship with any mere woman.

"Okay," he finally said, passing a hand over his long face as if he wished he could make himself disappear. "You're the one I thought was being kind of strange lately. I figured you had somebody else on the line."

I almost smiled. The analogy revealed what Milo was really thinking about. "Me?" I was surprised. "Who? I'm not seeing anybody."

Our orders arrived, courtesy of Rita, who remained in character. "May I bring you anything else?" she inquired politely.

We both said we had everything we needed.

Rita suddenly switched gears. "You two look like you need a lot of things," she snarled, then leaned forward and literally got in the sheriff's startled face. "If I catch you screwing some slut in the rest room again, I'll see you never come in here again!"

I must have looked as shocked as Milo. Before either of us could say anything, Rita straightened up and smiled a bit sheepishly. "Sorry," she said, "but I'm rehearsing my back talk to one of the characters in the play."

"You seem to have it down pat," I responded, feeling relieved.

"You bet your sweet ass I do, chicky." Rita turned around on her rubber-soled shoes and screeched off like a car on two wheels.

It took a moment for Milo to regain his aplomb. "What," he asked, still keeping his voice down, "about Max Froland? Didn't you go out with him?"

"Once," I retorted. "As you well know. He passed out during our dinner at Le Gourmand, and you and the rest of the emergency crew had to haul him away to the hospital. Of course, he was grieving over his father's death at the time."

"I thought you dated him after that," Milo said.

I shook my head. "He called once or twice, but we never got together. Do you really think he'd drive all the way up here from Seattle in the winter to see me?"

Milo shrugged again. "He might."

"He didn't." I waited, but the sheriff seemed focused on his cheeseburger. "That's it?"

"Unh." He pointed to his mouth, where he was chewing the cheeseburger. "You and Fleetwood seem pretty friendly since he got his radio station blown up."

"He had a lot more happen to him than that," I replied. "I'll admit, it changed him a bit. He's not nearly so obnoxious and arrogant. But our relationship is strictly business."

"Like going to Seattle together before Christmas to hear some concert?"

"The Messiah?" I scowled at Milo. "Would you have wanted to go with me?"

"Isn't that the one with all the *hallelujahs*?"

"That's it."

"Probably not. You know me. I'm not much for highbrow music."

"I know," I said. That was one of the problems with our relationship. Milo didn't care for many of the cultural activities I enjoyed. Our only common interest was baseball, and spring training had barely gotten under way.

"So you invited Fleetwood to go with you." He made the statement without inflection.

"He invited me." The conversation was getting more stupid by the second. "He'd gotten two free tickets from one of his buddies at a Seattle classical FM station. I'd mentioned something about not having heard *The Messiah* in concert for over twenty years, so he asked if I'd like to go with him."

"Mmm." Milo was chewing French fries.

I knew what he was thinking. After a late dinner at El Gaucho, Spence and I had stayed over. We'd had separate rooms at the downtown Marriott. I refused to mention that fact. Milo's attitude still annoyed me, and I wasn't going to give him the satisfaction of supplying an answer to the question he wouldn't ask. I'd gone to Mass at the cathedral that Sunday morning before we headed back to Alpine. My absence from St. Mildred's had been a source of gossip. Furthermore, Vida had used our attendance at the concert for one of her "Scene Around Town" items. No doubt people had conjectured for days.

"Well," Milo finally said, "I hope you don't think I'm sticking my nose in your business. That is," he went on, his long frame squirming a bit, "I was kind of curious."

I couldn't help but laugh. "No kidding."

He smiled faintly. "Guess I sounded pretty weird."

Rita stopped to refill Milo's coffee mug. "If you'd lay off the booze," she said to me, "you wouldn't wake up in the gutter every morning. No wonder you can't get a job, scumbag."

I received this latest bit of acting talent with a fixed smile. After Rita had stomped off again, I responded to Milo's remark. "You sounded suspicious—just like a lawman."

"Sorry. I didn't mean it that way." Milo finished his salad and reached for his Marlboro Lights. "My treat today," he said, picking up the bill that Rita had left on the table when she stopped with the coffeepot. "Should I tip her?"

The sheriff isn't cheap, but he's careful with money. "You mean because she's not really a waitress?" I shrugged. "Why not use phony money?"

Milo, however, decided he should make a gesture. Maybe, I thought, it'd help her acting. I had to admit, she'd sounded fairly convincing when she'd called me a scumbag.

"Speaking of the play," Milo said, reaching for his wallet, "what do you think about Destiny Parsons?"

I eyed the sheriff curiously. "In what way?"

"Oh . . ." He paused, putting down two ones and a couple of quarters. "When this *Outcast* stuff is over, I thought I might ask her out to dinner. You know, to thank her for reviving the dramatic club thing."

I wore a face of stone and fought to keep my mouth shut.

"I haven't socialized much lately," Milo went on, tapping his cigarette into the plastic ashtray. "She seems like a decent woman. You must know her pretty well. Not bad-looking, either, although she could use some meat on her bones. She lives across the street from you, right?"

"Yes." The stone face was cracking. If, after over two years of not dating, Milo found Destiny attractive, I should be happy for him. But he had a poor track history with women, including his ex-wife. And me, for that matter. At least—unlike some of the others—I'd never wanted to hurt him. I had anyway, but that was different. There would have been even more pain in store for

Milo if we'd continued our romantic attachment. "Destiny's a good choice if you like shoveling dog crap."

Milo was taken aback. "Huh?" he said around the cigarette that he'd stuck in his mouth while he stood up and put on his parka. "What do you mean?"

"Never mind." I turned away and tromped toward the entrance. I still didn't think much of his taste in women.

※　　※　　※

Ben had managed to get us tickets to a production of Don Giovanni *at the Rome Opera House. The seats were in the third balcony and off to the side, but it was a fabulous production. All of the singers were in marvelous voice. It was a traditional setting, unlike some of the* Dons *I've read about in the last few years. On my feet and clapping so hard that my hands hurt for the next hour, I shouted cheers and shed some tears along with the rest of the audience.*

Rome. Mozart. The venerable opera house. I hadn't felt so exhilarated in years. Maybe I'd finally detected a pulse.

※　　※　　※

I remembered that wondrous night as I drove to the Thyra Rasmussen Theater. Making comparisons would only put me in a bad mood. Rome was then; Alpine was now. My temper had settled down during the afternoon. All I had to do for the rest of the evening was sit in my seat and try not to doze off.

It wasn't hard to spot Vida in the lobby, since she stood well over six feet in her black suede pumps and a maroon satin hat with long matching feathers springing out of a garnet clasp. She was wearing a three-quarter black mouton coat I'd never seen before, but I estimated that it had been in her closet since before the Korean War. I would have approached her, but she was surrounded by not only Roger's parents, Ted and Amy Hibbert, but several others. Buck's brother, Henry Bardeen, Grace Grundle, and Dot and Durwood Parker completed her coterie.

Except for smiles and nods as I passed through the throng, I tried to keep a low profile. But I was stopped in my tracks by gasps and squeals behind me. At five-foot-four, I was too short to see over the people who stood between the entrance and me.

But the theatergoers parted to make way for the newcomer. Using two canes adorned with Egyptian temple dogs, Thyra Rasmussen moved slowly, painfully, and proudly across the lobby. The woman who had built the theater must have been close to a hundred. She had been a tall, handsome woman in her younger days and had ruled Snohomish like an empress. Despite the tragedies that had befallen her family in recent years—including the death of her husband, Einar Sr., a year ago—she still lived in the big Victorian-era family home on Avenue B. Thyra was accompanied by her surviving son, Harold, and his wife, Gladys. Mary Jane Rasmussen Bourgette and her husband, Dick, were nowhere to be seen. When Mary Jane married a Catholic, the senior Rasmussens had cut her out of their lives. It was said that Mary Jane's appointment to Einar Jr.'s position on the Board of Trustees had been looked upon with great disfavor by her mother and had almost put a crimp in the plans to build the theater.

If Vida's attire went back half a century, Thyra's dated from the post–World War One era. She wore a long black taffeta grown with what looked like a brown sable cape. Her turban was wreathed in pearls, as was her neck. Indeed, the necklace's triple strands hung below her waist. Black kidskin gloves crept above her elbows, with a pearl-and-diamond bracelet on her left wrist. The only items that didn't go with her costume were a pair of soft carpet slippers.

Thyra's sharp gaze flashed around the lobby as if her eyes were taking photographs. The eagle glance set briefly on Vida, then darted away. The two women had a history, dating back to an unpleasant encounter between Thyra and Vida's mother involving homegrown gourds. No truce had ever been called. Vida looked fit to spit.

Just beyond her nemesis, Thyra stopped, lifted her chin, and addressed the crowd. "Do you all *love* the living theater?" she called out in her surprisingly strong voice.

We'd damned well better, I thought as nervous affirmatives mingled with heartier endorsements.

Leaning on her canes, Thyra studied the gathering more closely. "The theater is life," she proclaimed. "Life is a theater." She paused. "I was an actress many years ago, before my marriage to Mr. Rasmussen. He encouraged me to continue with my career, but I felt I should be a homemaker. Those were the old days, when a woman stayed home and raised her family." There was a sneer on her face as she stopped again and took a deep breath. "But the theater was in my blood. Through this wonderful building and upon this handsome stage I can vicariously relive my golden days before an audience."

"Oh, good grief!" It was Vida, and I could hear her stage whisper from fifteen feet away.

If Thyra heard her, she ignored the remark. Resting one cane against her skirt, she raised a gloved hand. "As is said at the beginning of *I Pagliacci, 'Andiam. Incominciate!'* "

Thyra's Italian phrase to begin the show couldn't help but remind me of Rome, at least in a weird kind of way. She was a little like the Forum, ancient, degenerating, and yet imposing. Vida, however, was glaring at the old lady as if she were debris floating on the Tiber.

Accompanied by Harold and Gladys, Thyra made her way from the lobby. The Rasmussen contingent had been joined by Irene Baugh, the mayor's long-suffering wife, and, in a rare public appearance, Justine Cardenas, Nat's elegant, if aloof, spouse.

As seasoned journalists are apt to do when they want only

to observe, I slipped around the edge of the throng and entered the auditorium through a side aisle. Except apparently for Thyra Rasmussen and her devotees, who were moving into the third row center, seats weren't reserved. I sat two-thirds of the way back and four seats over. Nobody was yet sitting in the row, so I concentrated on reading the cast of characters one more time:

THE OUTCAST
Written and Directed by
Destiny Parsons

Narrator	Spencer Fleetwood
Leroy Billingsate, *developer*	Fuzzy Baugh
Dane Olmquist, *animal rights activist*	Jim Medved
Ted Owens, *unemployed logger*	Rip Ridley
Dorothy Oz, *a lost young woman*	Clea Bhuj
Otto Meeks, *café owner*	Hans Berenger
Angela D'Amato, *waitress*	Rita Patricelli
Alex Garcia, *itinerant worker*	Rey Fernandez
John Brown, *sheriff*	Nat Cardenas
Jamie Jejune, *teenager*	Roger Hibbert
Kevin Chang, *attorney*	Dustin Fong
Gabriel, *an angel*	Otis Poole
Chester White, *café customer*	Ed Bronsky
Dodo, *a dog*	Dodo

I'd finished reading the credits, the list of donors, and the ads—including our own—when Milo arrived, about two minutes before curtain time. The row I was in had filled up, mostly with students. The sheriff moved in behind me, one seat over. Reaching out with a long arm, he tapped me on the shoulder.

"It's starting to snow," he said, nodding at Vida, who was coming my way with the Hibberts.

"Great." I wondered if Thyra had been carried in by her family members. Carpet slippers weren't suitable for snow-covered ground. "Very hard?"

"Not yet," Milo replied, looking uncomfortable in his seat. I guessed that there wasn't sufficient room for his long legs. He was wearing a shirt and tie under his heavy nonregulation jacket. Somehow, formality didn't suit the sheriff. In all the years I'd known him, I'd only seen him dressed up about four times. "It's supposed to get heavier later in the evening," Milo went on, shrugging out of the big brown parka. "I had to call Sam Heppner and Dwight Gould in to keep track of the highway and the side roads. They're pissed. They wanted to watch Dustin act."

Vida sat down next to Milo with Amy and Ted in the next two seats by the aisle. "Goodness!" she exclaimed. "I never thought I'd see Queen Thyra in Alpine, theater or not. I swear she hasn't left Snohomish in thirty years. And those slippers! Couldn't she put a pair of galoshes over them?"

The auditorium was filling up. Leo had told me that the premiere was a sellout and that sales were going well for the next three performances. All profits would be plowed back into the theater, since no one was getting paid.

Vida's mind was running parallel with mine. "I wonder if Thyra expects to make money out of this. I wouldn't be surprised if she took some off the top. To paraphrase the Duchess of Windsor, 'No woman can be too mean or too rich.' "

I expressed my doubts about Thyra dipping into the theater's fund. "But to quote the Duchess," I said as I saw Scott Chamoud creeping near the stage to take pictures, "the old girl is also thin."

"Piffle," said Vida as the doors were closed and the houselights began to dim. "She's not just thin, she's scrawny. She always was. Now she's more so."

The audience grew silent except for someone behind Vida

who asked politely if she'd please remove her hat. The request was ignored.

Spence began his narration. He was a professional, and I had to admit that he raised the bar for the performers who followed. When he finished and the café interior was revealed, the audience burst into spontaneous applause. It was, in fact, a fine set. The program gave credit to students and a couple of volunteers from Jack Blackwell's mill.

It also seemed that the actors, who were now in costume, looked more credible. Certainly the theatergoers thought so. They seemed caught up in the drama, gasping at the confrontation between Coach Ridley and Jim Medved, sighing at Clea Bhuj's bewilderment, laughing at Rita Patricelli's hard-boiled comebacks to her customers, and the sight of Dodo the dog seemed to make everybody feel warm and fuzzy. Just like Dodo.

Meanwhile, Ed sat on his stool and ate. He couldn't help but give a convincing performance.

Halfway through the act, the person behind Vida again asked if she'd remove her hat. The second request wasn't quite as polite as the first. Vida paid no attention.

A few minutes later, after Clea had expressed her desire to go home to the city, the person whose view was marred by Vida's hat—and possibly by Milo's head—spoke sharply if not loudly:

"Ma'am, please take off that thing you've got on your head. With those foot-high feathers, it looks like a dead bird."

Everyone within earshot turned to stare, including me. I didn't recognize the young man. In fact, I could hardly see him with Vida's hat and the sheriff's head in the way. I guessed that he might be a college student. Whoever he was, he didn't know Vida or Milo.

"This," Vida said in her stage whisper, "is a special occasion hat. And this play is, I believe, a special occasion. I'm not taking it off."

"Vida," I heard Milo say, "lose the damned hat or I'll have to arrest you and the bozo behind us for disturbing the peace."

"You wouldn't dare!" Vida retorted. "Mind your manners, Milo!"

"Hey." Milo sounded conciliatory. "This play's a big deal for Alpine, right? You want to ruin it for everybody?"

I was staring straight ahead, trying to focus on the introduction of a new character, Rey Fernandez as Alex Garcia, itinerant worker. Vida hadn't responded. Rey was lamenting the fate of the Poor.

Vida emitted a huge sigh. "Oh, very well," she said. "I can adjust the feathers. It's a shame," she huffed, "you can't shout *boorish* in a crowded theater!"

I waited a couple of moments, then discreetly turned enough to see Vida, who had pulled each of the feathers down and to the side. She looked like a lop-eared rabbit.

Clea spoke of the Homeless in the city and how she longed to return so that she could help them. Rey countered with the burden of moving from town to town, trying to find work in the forests and the fields. As Clea began to realize that the big city wasn't the only entity with social problems, the curtain came down.

Vida remained in her seat during the intermission, but I got up to stretch my legs and use the rest room. Justine Cardenas was washing her hands when I approached the triple sinks. She must have seen me in the mirror but didn't acknowledge my presence.

"Hi, Justine," I said, sounding overly friendly. "How are you? Does Nat come on in Act Two?"

"Oh, hello, Emma," the college president's wife responded as if I'd just materialized out of the drain. "I'm well, thank you. Yes, Nat appears as the sheriff in the second act. I understand there's more violence between Coach Ridley and Dr. Medved. Oh, and Rey Fernandez. Then the runaway youth arrives."

Roger. "I'm getting the impression that Rey and Jim Medved and Fuzzy Baugh are modeled on the Tin Woodsman, the Lion, and the Scarecrow. Is that right?"

"Not precisely," Justine said in her carefully modulated voice. "Jim is in fact the Scarecrow, Nat is the Tin Woodsman, and Hans Berenger is the Lion. The mayor is the Wizard."

"Ah." It made sense. Fuzzy would have to play a wizard. It'd go down well with the voters.

Justine offered me a cool smile and glided away, every highlighted hair in place, every line of her expensive Donna Karan ensemble in perfect order. She was replaced at the sink by the small and disheveled city librarian, Edna Mae Dalrymple.

"I can't quite figure this play out," she declared. "Are loggers supposed to be bad?"

"I'm sure Rip Ridley will somehow redeem himself," I said.

"I hope so," Edna Mae replied, her brow furrowed. "I realize that the timber industry evokes some poor images, but that's what built Alpine. Originally, I mean. Oops!" She dropped her paper towel and bent to pick it up. "Besides, Mr. Blackwell certainly wouldn't want to give logging a bad name."

Early on in the second act, Edna Mae was proved right. Hans Berenger, as café owner Otto Meeks, began to timorously defend the logging industry. Jim chided him while Fuzzy rode the fence. Rip Ridley declared that Hans should put his money—or something—where his mouth was. Hans, being a cowardly lion, backed off, saying that he didn't want to offend any of his customers. Business was bad.

The play whined on, back and forth between the issues of jobs and the environment. Clea seemed to be reaching some kind of enlightenment, but she sure was taking her time about it. Then, just as I was fighting the urge to nod off, Roger appeared. He was dressed much as he was in real life, with baggy jeans, a T-shirt emblazoned with RUNNIN' REBELS, and a backpack that I figured usually contained several snacks and a couple of X-rated videos instead of school texts and notebooks. He had, however, lost a bit of weight since I'd last seen him. Or maybe he'd grown taller instead of just wider.

Vida poked me. "Doesn't Roger look wonderful?"

"He looks the part," I whispered in a noncommittal tone.

Hans addressed the runaway teen: "What are you doing here, sonny? I don't think I've seen you before in Evergreen."

Roger had assumed a certain swagger. He turned to Hans, who remained behind the serving counter. "Fuck you!" Roger shouted. "Fuck all of you!"

Vida gasped. I turned slightly in my seat. "Very convincing," I said under my breath. *Practice, practice, practice.* Roger was smirking at the audience, who had uttered some shocked reactions of their own. Even logging towns have standards when it comes to vulgarity. What's fit for the big city's ears is often unacceptable to small towners.

"Really!" Vida seemed to be hyperventilating. "Really now!"

"Pipe down, Vida," Milo said. "Everybody's staring at you. You don't want to take the attention away from Roger, do you?"

Milo, who shared my opinion of Vida's grandson, had used the correct tactic. I could sense that Vida was still fuming, but her mutterings had become inaudible, perhaps at the urging of her daughter Amy. After all, this was Roger's big moment in the sun.

To be fair, Roger wasn't bad. In fact, he was surprisingly good. He had the monologue that closed the act, describing the wretched circumstances that had made him run away from home and his horrendous experiences living on the city's streets. Of course he was called upon to use language that no doubt made his grandmother—among others—wince, but the applause was generous when the curtain fell.

I stood up and turned to Vida and the Hibberts. Amy and Ted exhibited great pride and no alarm over their son's dialogue. Vida, however, looked upset.

"I don't see why," she declared, "Destiny Parsons had to use foul language. It's not necessary. What's worse, Roger seems to be the one who says most of it. Except for Rip Ridley, of course. He's certainly not setting a good example for his high school students and the boys on the football team."

"The play's about real life, Mother, especially in the city," Amy said quietly. "I should have warned you, since Ted and I've heard Roger rehearsing. He's worked very hard to make his part believable."

"He's done a fine job of it," I asserted, wondering if this was the first time I'd ever had a word of praise for Roger. "Maybe he's found his niche." Certainly he was good at yelling obscenities.

"I still don't like it one bit," Vida stated. "I'm going to write an article about it for my page this coming week."

I hesitated. "It's called freedom of speech, Vida," I said. "If you really want to do that, then I'll write one, too, presenting the other side of the issue. We can run the pieces on the editorial page."

Vida glared at me from behind her big glasses. "Do you want us to squabble in public? And what must the Reverend Poole think? Surely he can't appear in the play and condone such vulgarity!"

It was useless to argue with Vida. "We won't squabble," I said, "here or in the *Advocate*. We have different opinions, that's all. Excuse me," I went on, moving down the aisle. "Speaking of the paper, I want to see how Scott's doing with the pictures."

Scott was doing fine, both with his camera and with his hands. He was caressing the shoulders of Tamara Rostova, his ladylove of the past three years. With her dark beauty and tall, angular figure, Tamara looked more like a ballet dancer than a college professor. Nor did she resemble a *Tammy*, as Scott called her. I used *Tamara* when we conversed.

"I think I've got some good stuff so far," Scott informed me.

"I'm sure you do," I replied. "Maybe you've taken some good pictures, too."

Scott was still young enough to look embarrassed. But he

didn't let go of Tamara, who was a few years older than her suitor and much more worldly.

"Scott needs a pay raise," Tamara declared pleasantly enough. "We're thinking about marriage down the road."

"I was thinking the same thing," I admitted, appreciating Tamara's candor. "About raises, I mean. Our ad revenue is up since we've been doing some co-op promotions with KSKY. Am I right in assuming you'd stay in Alpine?"

Scott looked to Tamara for the answer. "That depends," she said, raising a slender hand to her forehead and assuming a dramatic pose that suggested she was peering into the future. "I've been thinking about moving on to a larger school. I like the diversity of a city."

Recalling Scott's comment about becoming a freelance photographer, I tried not to look disappointed. I liked more diversity, too, but I seemed to be stuck in Alpine. The disappointment was accompanied by a pang of envy. There was a wider world out there, and I was missing it.

The gong sounded for the start of the third and final act. I resumed my seat, noting that Vida still looked somewhat grim.

The act began as the others did, with Spence's narration. Destiny's script compelled him to summarize what had gone before and muse on the obvious themes. It seemed redundant, as if the play couldn't stand on its own.

But it certainly could talk. Preach, argue, lecture, sermonize, moralize—all in the name of Why Can't We Be Nice to One Another? Clea had come to realize that a small town wasn't so different from a big city.

"We're all human," she proclaimed as Otis Poole smiled benignly from a swing that had been lowered a few feet from the stage. "Where *is* home? Could it be in the heart?"

I stifled a yawn. I could swear I heard Milo snoring. It certainly sounded like him, and I should know. For one brief moment, I had an urge to reach behind me and take his hand.

I didn't catch exactly what happened next except that Rip Ridley and Rey Fernandez were suddenly confronting each other. Rip held a steak knife and was shouting something about "wetbacks" and "foreign bastards." Clea tried to intervene but was held back by Jim Medved, who didn't want her—or Dodo—to get hurt. Hans Berenger came slowly out from the kitchen area, doing his best to look scared yet brave. The lion apparently had gotten a dose of courage.

Nat Cardenas, playing the sheriff, raced in from stage left. He ordered the combatants to stop fighting. They ignored him. As Rip lunged with the knife to attack a struggling Rey, Nat pulled his gun. Rip started to bring the knife down, but Hans charged into the melee, apparently in an attempt to shield Rey, who was wielding a beer bottle.

Fumbling slightly, Nat pulled a gun out of his holster. "Stop!" he cried. "Stop, or I'll shoot!" The trio continued wrestling around the stage, knocking over tables and chairs, and evoking screams from Clea and Rita. Everyone else looked appropriately horrified—except Dodo, who was piddling on the floor. Ed actually stopped eating and turned around.

Nat fired two shots. Hans fell to the ground, motionless. Acrid smoke filtered out into the first few rows of the auditorium. I heard someone cough loudly and dramatically. Maybe it was Thyra Rasmussen, doing some acting of her own.

"Violence!" Clea exclaimed, a hand to her cheek. "Guns!" She whirled on Nat. "See what you've done? You've killed an innocent man! He was only trying to help!"

Nat, doing his best to look dismayed, tossed the gun aside. Dodo scampered over to sniff at the barrel.

Then everyone got into it, denouncing firearms, prejudice, hunger, famine, war, plague, locusts, and whatever else was screwing up the human race. Rip repented, embracing Rey. The Reverend Poole descended once more, offering a blessing. Ed finally spoke:

"Amen!" he shouted. And belched.

Mercifully, the curtain descended. I felt stiff as a board. The rest of the audience seemed enthusiastic, however, and applauded with gusto, finally erupting into a standing ovation.

I stood up, too, if only to stretch. Milo apparently had woken up, since he, too, was on his feet. Vida was applauding madly and shouting, "Roger! Roger! Roger!"

The curtain stayed down. There was no sign of the actors eagerly taking their curtain calls. The applause and cheers began to fade. Finally, as curious voices started to fill the theater, Spence came out from behind the curtain.

"Ladies and gentlemen," he said, his usually mellifluous voice uncertain, "there's been an accident. Would you please remain inside the auditorium?"

FOUR

Some of the audience members had already made their exit, but those who remained were stunned into silence. Spence disappeared into the wings as the houselights came up. Worried voices began to hum all over the auditorium. Suddenly I saw Dustin Fong, still costumed as an attorney in a three-piece suit, hurry past me and lean toward Milo.

"We need you, sir," Dustin said softly but urgently. "Will you come backstage?" He leaned closer to his boss, saying something I couldn't hear.

Wordlessly if clumsily, Milo edged past the Hibberts. Vida was already in the aisle, grasping Dustin by the lapels of his dark suit coat.

"What's going on?" she demanded. "Who had an accident? Is it Roger? Has something happened to my darling?"

"Roger's fine," Dustin replied.

Milo attempted to elbow Vida out of the way. "We have to do our job. Let go, Vida."

She obeyed but followed the sheriff and his deputy down the aisle. "Press!" she cried. "Coming through!"

Naturally, I had to follow her. Vida was right: We were indeed the press. And our rival was already behind-the-scenes, gathering the story for his sign-off newscast at midnight.

I couldn't see Scott anywhere, but Thyra Rasmussen was easy to spot. She was standing in the middle of the far aisle clinging to her canes and shouting at her son, Harold, to take her backstage. Harold seemed reluctant. His wife, Gladys, dithered at his side.

The area near the stage had become clogged with curious patrons. Milo exerted his authority, both professional and physical:

"Step aside. Move. Break it up here."

I felt like a running back, moving quickly in the wake of a hard-hitting blocker. Two blockers if I included Vida, whose pushing and shoving were almost as effective as the sheriff's less vigorous efforts.

We went through a side door, then up some concrete steps. From there I could see the stage from the wings. It appeared that the entire cast, along with Destiny Parsons and some young people who were probably stagehands and lighting techs, had assembled amid the shambles that was now the café set.

I moved closer, still behind Milo, Vida, and Dustin. I could see stricken looks on the faces of several people, especially Nat, Destiny, Fuzzy, and Jim. Rita was slumped in one of the café chairs, sobbing hysterically while Reverend Poole tried to console her. As Milo and Dustin moved into the circle, the sheriff motioned for Vida and me to stay back. Vida didn't look as if she was willing to cooperate, but I grabbed her coat sleeve.

"Just wait. I have an awful feeling about this," I murmured.

Milo also asked the others to move away from the center of the stage. Through the curtains I could hear the audience's voices rise to a crescendo. Visions of Alpine theatergoers storming the stage like French peasants attacking the Bastille flitted through my mind's eye.

But reality came crashing down like a sandbag let loose from the flies. Peering around Vida, who was now holding Roger in a fierce embrace, I saw Hans Berenger still lying on the stage. A small pool of blood oozed over the boards. Hans hadn't moved an inch since Nat had fired his gun.

"Damn!" I said under my breath, and crossed myself. It wasn't the first time I'd seen a body. But this time I steeled myself and put distance between Hans's inert form and my emotions. I'd sworn that after having Tom die in my arms there was almost nothing that could ever wound me again.

"Okay." Milo rose from his kneeling position. "You're right," he said to Dustin. "Berenger's dead."

The confirmation of what the others must have already suspected elicited more sobs and groans. The sheriff and his deputy conferred in voices so low that only the deceased could have heard them.

"Listen up," Milo said after he and Dustin apparently had plotted their next moves. "An ambulance is on the way, along with a couple of our other deputies. Dr. Sung should be here any minute."

"Where's Doc Dewey?" Fuzzy asked with no sign of his southern drawl.

Milo shrugged. "Out of town, I guess. Ms. Parsons told Dustin that Doc and his wife are—were—coming to the final performance." He glanced down at the body. "It looks like Doc will miss it."

"Ohmigod!" Destiny shrieked. "How could this happen to me?"

Rita's head jerked up, her face a blotchy tearstained mass. "You callous bitch! *How could this happen to Hans?*"

Another voice was heard from: "How could this happen in my theater?" Thyra Rasmussen was moving slowly toward the stage. "Don't tell me those bullets were real?"

Destiny whirled around, green eyes snapping with fury. "They weren't, you meddling old bat! Do you think I'm crazy?"

Thyra didn't give an inch. "I think you're careless. And stupid. I'm sorry I ever permitted you to use my facility."

It was hard to know who to root for. But Milo intervened.

"Come on, let's calm down. I want this stage cleared as of now. The immediate backstage area, too. This is all a crime scene." He looked at Spence, who was holding on to Dodo and scratching the dog behind the ears. "Hey, Fleetwood, go out into the auditorium and ask everybody to leave their names and phone numbers. Then they can go home. I'll have Sam Heppner help you with the list when he gets here."

Spence handed the dog over to his owner. Dodo seemed like the only cast or crew member who was unaffected by the tragedy. When Jim took the dog, his hands were trembling; Spence looked pale, despite what I'd always guessed was an artificial tan.

Four feet away from where I stood, Milo was speaking with Thyra. "You should go home, too, Mrs. Rasmussen. We could be in for a long night."

"Nonsense!" Thyra snapped. "This is my theater and I'm not leaving. Harold and Gladys can wait outside or wherever they want, but I intend to remain here with the rest of this sorry little bunch."

The sheriff didn't argue. "Okay, let's have you all move . . ." He glanced around, then pointed to Destiny. "Where's a good place?"

Destiny looked blank before finally gesturing in the direction of heavy double doors behind the stage. "The workshop."

Milo nodded once. "Okay, let's move. We'll wait there for Dr. Sung."

Slowly, warily, the group began to shuffle from the stage. Even Thyra, plying her canes, went with them. Vida, Roger, and I remained.

"Get the kid out of here," Milo ordered.

Vida bridled. "He's staying with me!"

"Yeah!" Roger chimed in. "Fuck you!"

"Roger!" Vida slapped a hand over her grandson's mouth. "See here, young man," she admonished, "don't ever let me hear you talk like that again!"

Roger pushed her hand away. "Hey, Grams, chill. I'm still in character."

Vida looked as if she wanted to believe him. Milo ignored Roger's rude response and turned his back on us. "Go get his parents," he called over his shoulder. "They can all go backstage, too."

To my surprise, Vida gave in. Maybe she'd had too many shocks for one evening. Now I was alone with Milo, Dustin, and the late Hans Berenger. "So what do you think happened?" I inquired.

Milo gave me an ironic look. "Somebody put real bullets in the gun. That's what happened. Maybe it was an accident, maybe not."

"But not Nat's fault?"

"Not necessarily." Milo looked away into the wings as Elvis Sung hurried toward us.

"Thanks, Doc, for getting here so fast," the sheriff said. "Here's the victim. He's been shot at least once."

Dr. Sung was still in his thirties, a native Hawaiian of Korean descent who hated hot weather. The more it rained, the better he liked it. I figured he must be ecstatic when it snowed.

But I was wrong. "I almost didn't make it," Dr. Sung said, putting on a pair of white latex gloves. "It's bad out there, even with four-wheel drive."

"How bad?" the sheriff asked.

"We've gotten a good four inches in the last couple of hours," Dr. Sung answered, kneeling next to Hans. "More up at the summit." The doctor paused for a moment as he began examining the corpse. "I hope Doc Dewey can make it back from Seattle tonight. I need him in the ER." Elvis Sung had peeled away Hans's bloody apron and T-shirt to study the wound. "They closed Stevens Pass from Index to Leavenworth about an hour ago. Christ." Sung moved enough to let Milo and Dustin have a look. I hung back. "I can only see one bullet hole," Sung said, "entering under the left armpit and probably puncturing the lung and maybe the heart. We'll know more when Doc Dewey does the official autopsy." He gazed up into the flies. "Maybe I should try Doc's cell phone again. He was out of range the last time I called."

Milo grimaced. "So where's the other slug?"

Dustin pointed toward the kitchen area of the set. "Maybe back there, sir. Nat Cardenas fired twice, in rapid succession. The other bullet must have gone that way. I bagged the gun as soon as I realized Mr. Berenger had really been shot."

"Good," Milo said absently, looking to the rear of the stage. "What kind of gun is it?"

"A Smith & Wesson .38 Special revolver," Dustin replied. "It's old, but well maintained. It may be a service pistol from the Second World War. The gun belongs to Dr. Medved."

Sam, Dwight, and the medics arrived all at once, griping about the weather.

"Why does somebody have to get killed during a freaking blizzard?" Sam demanded, wielding a camera to take photos of the crime scene. "And how does some college prof get himself shot during a play?" He stared at Dustin as if it were the young deputy's fault for taking part in the fatal theatrics.

"You're lucky we came at all," declared Vic Thorstensen, one of the medics. "We've been on the run all night, what with so many morons not knowing how to drive in a snowstorm. Why can't they stay home? Then we could, too."

Dr. Sung, who was of medium height but built like a weight lifter, cocked his head to one side. "Guess what, Vic? We don't need you. We need an ambulance. Unless," he added in a musing manner that was becoming familiar, "you want to cart the corpse to the morgue." He turned to Milo. "Or does the deceased stay put for a while?"

Sam was still taking pictures. Milo didn't answer right away, but when he did, he gave Elvis Sung a thumbs-up gesture. "We've seen enough. You finished, Sam?"

Sam nodded.

"Go ahead," Milo said to the medics. "Take him away."

"Sure," Del Amundson, the other EMT, shot back. "Maybe we can pick up a couple of stiffs out on River Road while we're at it. Somebody just called in to say they thought they saw a car floating in the Sky. If it gets too crowded, we can always dump some of 'em off in a snowbank. They'll keep."

Elvis Sung held up his hands. "Just go. Take our body with you, then check out the river. I'll meet you at the clinic."

"Upstairs or in the basement?" Vic asked as Del rolled a gurney to center stage.

"Upstairs," Elvis answered. "I'll be in the ER, not the morgue. I can't do anything for Berenger."

As the two medics removed the corpse, I looked again for Scott and Tamara. They were nowhere to be seen. I began to suspect that they'd left after the curtain fell. No doubt they had plans of their own for the rest of the night. I couldn't blame Scott, but it meant we were without a photographer. We couldn't use any of Sam's photos—they were too graphic. Nor would he let us borrow county property to take some shots of our own. Maybe someone in the cast had a camera. Vida wasn't as good as Scott, but she was better than I was. "Remove the lens cap" was about the only instruction I got right, and upon occasion I'd forgotten even that.

Sam Heppner had gone to help Spence take down names and addresses. In the relative quiet behind the curtain I could hear the anxious buzz of conversation in the auditorium. I hoped the three hundred–plus attendees could be dispatched quickly. Nobody wanted to spend the night snowed in on campus.

The body was taken away, a pathetic bundle moving at what struck me as unseemly speed through the backstage area and out through a rear exit. As the door remained open for a few seconds, I could see the snow coming down, driven by a howling north wind. I began to wonder if I'd be stuck at the college.

Milo had cut Dustin from the herd, telling him to join the other cast and crew members. "You're a witness, Dustman," the sheriff said with a grimace. "For now, you're one of them, not one of us. Sorry."

Dustin, however, understood. He headed for the workshop, where the double doors now stood open. I trailed along, watching Dustin sit down on a stool between Destiny Parsons and Reverend Poole. Some of the twenty or so people who waited on the law's whim seemed to have recovered their nerve. Others, like Rita, Nat, Destiny, and Jim, still appeared visibly shaken. Thyra Rasmussen refused a folding chair. She leaned on her canes and glared at Milo. Dodo was now asleep under the vet's stool.

"Emma, Vida," Milo said, "you're out of here. Roger's folks can stay because he's a minor." Forestalling any lip from either of us, he made a sharp gesture with his thumb. "Beat it. Now."

Vida wasn't going quietly. "Amy and Ted can go home. I'll stay with Roger."

But the sheriff was firm. Vida was out; the Hibberts were in. In her splayfooted manner, my House & Home editor stomped angrily to join me by the exit. We left just as Sam Heppner returned from the auditorium. Spence wasn't with him, no doubt already hightailing it to the radio station to make the deadline for his midnight newscast.

"Really!" Vida exclaimed as we got outside. "How dare Milo behave in such a high-handed fashion?"

"He's conducting a possible murder investigation," I said loudly, my voice being swallowed up in the swirling snow and wind. "Damn it, this is bad! Did you bring your car?"

"Yes!" Vida shouted back at me as she held on to her hat. The feathers were blown backward, making it look as if she were about to take off. "Amy and Ted had to come early with Roger. If we're careful, we'll be fine. Go slow, Emma."

"I hardly intend to drive like a maniac," I replied, then remembered that I hadn't asked anybody if they had a camera. Too late. Milo wouldn't allow pictures during an interview.

"I'm still mad," Vida declared loudly as she trudged through a path that had apparently been made by the medics and the deputies. "My car's right over here at the edge of the parking lot."

My car wasn't. I realized that I'd have to walk all the way around the theater. I'd be better off going inside and leaving through the main entrance. Without another word, I watched Vida disappear from view.

Fortunately, the rear door was unlocked. I wondered if it had been that way during the play. If so, anyone could have entered the theater and tampered with the .38 special. Of course, I thought, it could have been some sort of accident. I didn't know which was worse, especially for Nat, who had fired the fatal bullet.

No eyes were on me as I quietly entered the backstage area. The temptation to eavesdrop was great. I hesitated by a pile of stage flats near the workshop's open doors. Stepping behind the disassembled scenery, I tried to hear what was being said some thirty feet away.

Milo had his back to me and his laconic voice was low. I could hear Destiny, however. She was speaking in high-pitch, verging on hysteria.

"It was an artistic decision," she declared, "a social statement! I had to use a gun to point out how dangerous they are!"

"You sure as hell did that," Rip Ridley said in an angry voice. "I could have been shot, too! So could anybody else onstage!"

Milo stepped in to stop the argument. "Hold it," he ordered

in a voice I could hear. "Cut the crap, everybody. Speak when you're spoken to." He lowered his voice to pose another question I couldn't make out.

But I could hear Destiny's response: "Not just *anybody* could get at the gun. I mean, not without being seen. It was right there in the prop box by the wings until Nat made his entrance in Act Two."

I moved cautiously to the other end of the flats, hoping to hear better. Admittedly, I felt foolish, like Lois Lane on the trail of the big story. If I needed rescuing, I'd be lucky to get Clark Kent, let alone Superman.

But Milo's queries were now partially audible. It sounded as if he'd asked Nat about wearing the gun during intermission.

"The gun was in the belt holster," Nat replied, his educator's voice modulating each word and carrying across the backstage area. "I never took it off once I put it on." He glanced down at his hip. The now-empty holster was still there. Nat regarded it with revulsion.

"So . . . long did . . . sit . . . prop box?" Milo inquired.

There was a pause. I leaned around the side of the flats to see who would respond.

"About two hours." The speaker was Boots Overholt, whose grandparents owned a farm on the edge of town. I vaguely recalled that he had enrolled at the college the previous fall. Apparently, he was one of the stagehands or techs.

"You were . . . of props?" Milo asked.

Boots nodded. He looked like a future farmer, with a forelock of blond hair and a sparse, close-cropped beard. "I put everything out there about seven, including the gun. We wanted to use a starter gun, but Ryan Talliaferro—he coaches track—wouldn't let us borrow his."

Ryan taught English but, like many of the faculty members, wore a couple of extra hats. One of them could have been a dunce cap for marrying Carla, our former reporter. I suspected that since taking on his scatterbrained bride Ryan had learned the hard way about lending items. While working at the *Advocate* Carla had borrowed many things from her fellow staffers. Rarely, if ever, did she bother to return them, and often, when pressed, admitted that she'd lost whatever she'd been loaned.

Milo spoke again. "Where . . . been . . . ?"

"Dr. Medved had it," Boots replied.

Jim nodded. "That's right. I'd brought it from home. We used a water pistol in rehearsal."

"Did . . . it loaded?"

"Never. It was my father's," Jim explained, his thin face still ashen. "He served in Europe. I kept it locked in the safe at the office."

"Who loaded it with blanks?" Milo asked, raising his voice.

"I did," Boots answered, looking miserable. "Honest, they *were* blanks. I hunt, I know what real bullets look like."

Apparently, the sheriff didn't doubt a fellow sportsman's word. "So how long did the gun sit in the box for periods when nobody was around?"

"Never," Destiny said emphatically.

"Bullshit!" Rip shouted. "What about the first intermission? Half the cast and crew went outside to smoke and freeze their goodies. I was standing all alone by that damned box. I could have switched blanks for bullets and nobody would've been the wiser. But," he added hastily, "I didn't."

Several voices were raised. Destiny showered abuse on the coach. Rita was screaming, "I knew it! I knew it!" Rey asserted that there were other opportunities.

"Before Cardenas went on," Rey declared after the others had shut up, "everybody was onstage except him and the reverend and the kid. The crew wasn't anywhere near the prop box. Neither were you, Destiny."

"How do you know?" Destiny demanded.

Rey sneered at his director. "Remember the blocking? I was

at the far left of the stage, almost in the wings. I could see the box from there."

"Okay." Milo sounded weary. "Cut the arguing." He stretched his neck and arms. "We'll stop here. You can go now before you get snowed in, but don't leave town. Not that you probably could with this weather. We'll be calling you in separately starting tomorrow morning."

Words of relief mingled with expressions of protest. Nat Cardenas took the floor, addressing his faculty members and students. "Let's be cooperative," he urged them. "Let's share our knowledge—however limited—with Sheriff Dodge and his deputies. But we mustn't run our mouths off in the larger community. This," he said, sounding even more earnest, "is to be kept within the school. We have a reputation to guard and people to protect."

I wondered what he meant by the last part. Nat wasn't finished, however, as it appeared that educators couldn't cut short their lectures under any circumstances. Milo and his deputies had come out of the workshop and were standing between me and the stairs that led to the auditorium. I was trying to figure out how to reach the front door before I was spotted. Thyra Rasmussen, accompanied by her son and his wife, who'd come backstage to fetch her, had left with her head high, as if in defiance of Milo, scandal, and Death itself.

Hoping no one would notice, I decided on an end run. I crept out from behind the scenery flats to join the rest of the small exodus that included Roger and his parents, the Reverend Poole, and Ed Bronsky. Naturally, Ed saw me as soon as I crossed the floor.

"Emma!" he shouted. "You still here? I thought you'd gone. Have you seen Shirley and the kids?"

I hadn't. But Milo had seen me. He looked away from Sam and Dwight and Dustin to call my name. "Emma! Get your butt over here!"

Obedience meant I'd have to listen to the sheriff berate me for eavesdropping. I smiled and shook my head, pushing at Ed to keep moving.

"Don't you want to talk to Dodge?" Ed inquired in surprise.

"Not now. Walk, Ed. Hurry up."

Ed hesitated, so I gave him another shove. "Okay, okay, I'm going. Hey," he said over his shoulder as he started down the steps, "how was my performance?"

I suppressed a sigh. Ed was being his usual crass and egocentric self. Nothing seemed to shake him except when they ran out of pork chops at the Grocery Basket. "Very believable, Ed," I replied as I heard Milo shout my name one last time. "What were you eating in Acts One, Two, and Three?"

"Cold cuts, mostly," Ed replied. "Hans couldn't actually cook onstage. He probably doesn't know how. *Didn't,* I mean. Too bad about the accident. Do you suppose they'll be able to find somebody to take Hans's place? He didn't have an understudy except for some college kid. Actually, I know his part pretty well. I could do it."

"I can't imagine they'd want to continue," I said as we reached the almost empty auditorium.

"Hey, hey, hey," Ed said, poking a pudgy forefinger at me. "The show must go on, right? Ah. There's the gang." He waved like a windmill at his family.

I held back. It was almost midnight, and I was beat. A chinwag with the Bronsky clan was the last thing I needed. Luckily, they waddled off, leaving the auditorium virtually deserted.

To my relief, someone had been shoveling the parking lot. My dark green Honda sat in isolation, though there were still at least a dozen parked cars closer to the theater. A couple of them were occupied by drivers who were having problems starting up. No doubt the sheriff and his deputies wouldn't abandon them.

The Honda's engine purred nicely. My windshield wipers could barely keep up with the constant fall of snow. I drove slowly—but not slow enough to get stuck—toward the road that led from the campus. I was almost there when someone pounded at my window. Startled, I gently hit the brake and looked to see who it was.

"Emma!" cried Destiny. "My car won't start! Can you give me a ride home?"

I hesitated. If Destiny Parsons had lived anywhere but across the street from me, I'd have told her she'd better ask Milo for help. But she was a neighbor, if not a very good one.

I nodded and gestured toward the passenger door. Destiny, scowling mightily, got in and brushed snow from her knit hat and wool coat.

"Thanks." She was shivering. "Just what I need right now—a starter that won't start."

"You're sure it's the starter? Could it be the battery?" I inquired, though I didn't give a damn. My focus was on following the tread marks that led to the Burl Creek Road.

"Cal Vickers at the Texaco station warned me about the starter earlier this week when I bought a new battery," Destiny replied in a bitter voice. "I should have had the thing fixed, but I was so involved with the play that I didn't want to take time out for anything else."

"Cars can be a problem," I remarked. So far, the Honda ran well, as had the Lexus. It had been my old and much-loved Jaguar that kept me broke. Despite its constant need for repair, I still missed it.

Destiny kept quiet until I reached the road. With all the theater traffic, it was drivable. "I feel like I'm living in a nightmare," she finally said. "How could that have happened?"

I assumed "that" was the death of Hans Berenger. "It does seem incredible," I allowed. But after Tom had been shot to death, there was nothing that could shock me anymore. Life was damned cruel. "I scarcely knew Hans. Did he have a family?"

Destiny shook her head. Her graying hair hung in wet ten-drils from under the knit cap. Though I didn't think she was much more than forty, she looked old and haggard. The hair didn't help hide her age; the disaster clearly weighed her down. She had well-defined features, which, under different circum-stances and after a serious makeover, might render her suffi-ciently attractive to spark Milo's interest. Or maybe the sheriff had grown desperate.

"I think Hans was divorced," Destiny said. "He never men-tioned having children. If his parents are still alive, they'll have to be notified. Damn. I suppose I should do it."

"Maybe Nat Cardenas will," I answered. "He's the college president. It should be his responsibility. Did you know Hans well?"

"No," Destiny replied rather abruptly. "That is, I've only been at SCC for less than two years. Hans has been here some-what longer. I probably spoke more with him in the past few weeks than I have since I arrived in Alpine."

"I've heard he was standoffish," I said, cautiously taking a curve near the fish hatchery road. Up ahead, I saw the taillights of another vehicle through the swirling snow. I hoped the driver knew what he or she was doing. A sudden stop could put us both in trouble. "I was surprised he took a role in the play."

"So was I." Destiny kept looking straight again. I didn't take my eyes off the road, but I assumed she was still grim-faced.

I could now see the car ahead. It was Ed's Range Rover mov-ing along at a proper pace. Despite the snow, I was able to read his vanity plate: MR PIG. The name was taken from the short-lived animated Japanese TV series based on Ed's self-published autobiography. The plate on Shirley's Mercedes read: MRS PIG.

I was waiting for Destiny to mention her dog, Azbug, and possibly apologize for letting the mutt use my front yard as a bathroom. This was the ideal time for Destiny to make amends, since I was doing her a favor. I was disappointed, however. She said nothing. We continued in silence until we reached Alpine Way. There the driving was much easier, because the street had been plowed since the new snow started falling. But when I turned off onto Fir, I saw that we were literally at the end of the road. The accumulation was almost half a foot deep and, because of the north wind, was piled even higher on the right-hand side of the street.

"I'm afraid we'll have to leave the car and walk the rest of the way," I told Destiny.

My passenger still said nothing. I parked the car as best I could in front of Jim Medved's animal clinic. We still had almost five blocks to go. I could hardly blame Destiny for not wanting to chat. We needed all the oxygen we could get just to keep going. Heads down and feet deep into the soft stuff, we trudged along past the RV park, some converted condos, and finally the small individual homes that lined Fir Street. The south side of the block where I lived had no real end—my property sloped up into the forest that climbed the face of Tonga Ridge.

The temperature wasn't that cold—thirty degrees, maybe—but the wind felt raw against my face. Briefly I fretted over chilblains and frostbite. But not out loud. We forged ahead in silence, except for the storm's howl and a crackling power line somewhere nearby.

It must have taken ten minutes to walk the five blocks. We parted company with only a couple of grunts. I stopped to catch my breath, while Destiny made her way to her door. It was easy enough for her, but the snow had drifted over my mailbox and filled my walk and driveway. I plunged ahead, feeling the chill wind in the marrow of my bones. All I wanted was warmth. Primeval Emma, fighting the elements.

The scream seemed to come from over the mountains and down through the trees. I stood stock-still, trying to listen despite the howling wind. I heard a second scream. It was close, I realized, and turned to look back across the street.

Destiny Parsons was standing on her front porch. The light was on, but I could scarcely see her through the heavy snow. I blinked and brushed the flakes from my eyes. She was holding something in her arms. A coat? A blanket?

"Destiny?" I shouted into the wind.

"It's my dog!" she shrieked. "It's Azbug! She's dead!"

FIVE

MAYBE I WAS BECOMING AS CALLOUS AS ED. I DON'T HATE DOGS;
I don't dislike animals. Adam had a dog for almost nine years,
but the poor pooch got run over by the milkman the day my son
entered seventh grade. We never had the heart to get a replacement for Goofy. Yet as I stared across the street at Destiny with
her beloved Azbug I felt only a twinge of sympathy.

"What happened to him? *Her,* I mean?" I called back.

But Destiny was too overcome to answer. She just stood there,
holding the dog in her arms.

"Damn," I muttered, heaving a sigh and starting toward her
house.

Destiny didn't appear to see me until I was at the bottom of
the two steps that led to her small porch. She was still wearing
her coat, but the front door was wide open. I assumed she'd
found Azbug as soon as she got inside. "Emma?" Her voice was
choked.

"Right. Emma. We shouldn't stand out in the cold."

She didn't seem to hear me, either. Her teeth were chattering
and tears ran down her pale cheeks. The tears might freeze if she
stayed outdoors much longer.

I grabbed her by the upper arm. "Come on, let's go."

She obeyed like a robot, tripping over the threshold. I closed the door behind us and looked around. We were in the living room, where a single torchère burned in one corner. I guided her to the brown leather sofa. Some of the fabric at each end had been torn away, probably by the late Azbug.

Destiny sat down but didn't surrender the dog. I perched on a matching leather ottoman. "What happened to Azbug?" I asked.

The answer was slow—and difficult—in coming: "Her . . . neck's . . . broken."

In spite of myself, I winced. "You mean . . . she had an accident or . . ." I couldn't say the words aloud.

"I found her on the back porch," Destiny said, her eyes finally coming into focus. Gently, she stroked the animal's fur. "I called to her as soon as I got in the house, but there was no answer. Then I looked out back. Azbug shouldn't have gone outside. She never does at night and in bad weather."

"But she can, even when you're not home?"

Destiny used the back of one hand to wipe away the tears. "Yes. It's a doggy door, like a cat's door, but bigger. I had to install it when I taught night classes fall quarter. There were days when I couldn't get home to let her out. But if she went out, she came right back in. Azbug was always waiting for me." She turned just enough to look at the telephone on the side table. "Should I call the sheriff?"

I considered how much Milo already had on his plate. "Wait until morning," I cautioned. "I doubt that he can send anybody tonight."

"Why not?" Destiny demanded, a spark of life surfacing in her green eyes.

For a moment I simply stared at her. "Because," I said. "Hans Berenger. The weather. Traffic accidents."

"Oh." Destiny hung her head. "Of course. Hans."

It occurred to me that if anyone might be a suspect in Azbug's death, it was me. Apparently, Destiny's thought processes hadn't gotten that far. "Could your dog have fallen in the snow and broken its neck?"

Destiny eyed me with disdain. "Hardly. That would be a freak accident. Azbug wasn't a clumsy dog. Someone," she went on, her voice rising, "did this deliberately. I wouldn't put it past those kids who live next door to you."

"The Nelsons?" They weren't my favorite neighbors, either. Their kids, who were now well into their teens, had always caused me grief.

"Yes." Destiny, who was still petting Azbug, looked self-righteous. "Or that cat woman next to me. What's her name? Holmgren?"

"Edith Holmgren." A few years ago, I'd taken in a friend's Siamese cats that drove me nuts. I'd managed to dump them on Edith, who already had a feline menagerie that numbered close to a dozen. "I can't see her doing such a thing—unless your dog bothered her cats."

"Azbug never bothered anybody," Destiny asserted.

That was a lie, I thought, but didn't argue. "Is there anything I can do?"

Destiny shook her head. "I'll have to wait until morning. I can't bury Azbug in this weather, but maybe Jim Medved can keep her until the snow melts."

"That sounds like a plan," I remarked as I slid off of the ottoman and stood up. "Unless you need something, I'll go home now."

"Fine." Destiny didn't look at me but kept her eyes on the dog.

I, however, made a quick perusal of the living room. There were at least three framed photographs of dogs, presumably Azbug, since they all looked alike. There was a doggy bed near the hearth, complete with matching plaid blankets and pillow. The andirons were fox terriers, a glass figurine—Steuben, maybe—of a fox terrier resided on the mantel, and the pattern of the drapes was fox terriers rampant. The carpet was littered with doggy toys and pigs' ears.

Without another word, I left Destiny to mourn.

I was so worn out that night that I slept until almost ten. The phone rang just as I was coming out of the bathroom. It was Ben, calling from his cinder-block parish office in Tuba City, Arizona.

"Hey," he said in his crackling voice, "I hear you got more snow. I saw it on the Weather Channel. Are you marooned yet?"

"Give me a minute," I replied, taking the cordless phone out into the living room. "I'm not awake yet. Let me look."

Opening the front drapes, I looked out onto a world of white. The snow had stopped, but at least another six inches had piled up, high enough to partially block my view.

"Yes," I said, "I'm marooned. Are you satisfied?"

"We've got rain," Ben said cheerfully. "A real gully washer. Eight inches in less than two hours. Thunder and lightning, too. It woke me up."

Yawning, I turned toward the kitchen. "Did anybody drown?"

"Luckily, no," Ben replied, sounding somewhat more somber. "But there may have been some loss of livestock."

"You got off easier than we did," I said.

"What do you mean?" Now my brother's voice conveyed a hint of alarm. "Are you okay?"

"Yes, I'm fine." I always set up the coffeemaker before I go to bed, thus eliminating the need to think in the morning. Clicking on the switch, I regaled Ben with the shooting story.

"I'll offer a Mass for the guy," Ben said after I'd finished. "Thursday, maybe. The other days are taken. The Santiago family had three members die in a car wreck six years ago. This week is the anniversary of their deaths. They always offer up a bunch of Masses for the repose of their kinsmen's souls. Last week, I said one for our folks."

I winced. Ben was far more conscientious than I was when it came to remembering the date that our parents had died in a car wreck on the way home from his ordination. Of course the twentieth of each month had twice the significance for him. But that was no excuse. They'd died in May over thirty years ago, and except for the day and the month itself, I tried not to dwell on their loss.

"I guess you were always a better son than I was a daughter," I said wistfully.

"Bullshit," Ben retorted. "I'm in the prayer business, remember? Do you think whatshisname—you better tell me again so I can write it down—got shot by accident?"

"Hans Berenger," I said, then spelled it out. "I don't know, Ben. It could have been. I've heard some pretty weird tales about how people manage to shoot somebody or themselves with the gun that wasn't loaded. Let's face it: people in this county own guns. I own one myself."

"Dad's?"

"Yes."

"He had two," Ben replied. "I've got the other one. It comes in handy for shooting rattlesnakes."

"Have you ever killed one?"

"No." Ben paused. "But I'm ready."

I managed my first smile of the day. "Same here. Every so often we get a bear or a cougar coming into town. There were two cougars, in fact, while you and I were in Italy. They were in the cul-de-sac just down the street from my house."

"Did somebody shoot them?" Ben asked.

"No," I said, pouring a mug of coffee. "One of the forest rangers used tranquilizer darts. But a year or so ago, Dwight Gould had to kill a very angry bear that made its way onto the playfield at the middle school. That was scary. But accidents do happen," I went on. "A couple of years ago Milo sponsored a gun safety class. He brought in an expert from Seattle who started his lecture with the standard 'the gun is always loaded' bit. Then he checked his weapon and assured everyone that *his* gun wasn't loaded. To prove the point, he took aim at the ceiling, pulled the trigger . . . and blew out the lights."

Ben laughed. "Milo must have blown up, too. I assume the guy hasn't been asked back."

"No, but you can imagine how embarrassed he was. Darla Puckett fainted and they had to send for the medics."

"So you're hoping this one was an accident," Ben remarked.

"Of course. Do you think I'm a ghoul?"

"No," Ben responded, "but murder makes good headlines. Besides, Birchwood or whatever his name is at the radio station beat you on the actual shooting. If it's an accident, it's the end of the story. But if it's not . . ." Ben let the sentence trail away.

"For a priest," I retorted, "you're pretty damned harsh."

"No, I'm not," Ben asserted. "I'm realistic. That's why I'm a pretty damned good priest."

"Not to mention modest," I snapped.

"Honest. Modesty has nothing to do with it." Ben cleared his throat. "Hey, these days with all the problems in the priesthood, I have to give myself a pep talk now and then."

I'd put two teaspoons of sugar in my coffee. The combination of caffeine and glucose began to revive me. "You started out as a good man. Ergo, you ought to be a good priest."

"I started out as a naive kid," Ben replied. "I was still a teenager when I entered the seminary. That was the way it was done thirty-five years ago. I'm glad it's not like that now. Adam got a taste of the world before he decided he had a vocation. That's good. I had to learn by doing . . . or not doing. Hey—got to run. I'm saying a noon Mass at the public health hospital. Stay warm, stay dry, stay put. And for God's sake, stay safe." Ben hung up.

I didn't have much choice but to remain inside. I wondered how the tin roof was holding up at the newspaper office. If Kip

MacDuff could cover the six blocks between his house and the *Advocate*, he'd check on the building's status. Visions of the roof caving in and leaks in my cubbyhole deep enough to require waders flitted through my mind's eye. But there was nothing I could do about it except hope for the best.

Coffee in hand, I strolled to the front window and looked across the street to Destiny's house. I almost expected to see a black crepe wreath on the door. But all was quiet; all was white. Like me, the pristine snow in her yard and driveway revealed that she, too, was stuck. With Azbug. Destiny wouldn't dream of putting her dog outside. Maybe the fox terrier was lying in state.

The thought made me grimace. I should call to see how Destiny was doing. We certainly weren't friends, but we were neighbors. Instead, I returned to the kitchen and made breakfast. Discovering that I was famished, I went to the trouble of fixing Swedish pancakes, ham, and a fried egg. Fortunately, I'd grocery-shopped Wednesday on my way home from work. The larder was fairly full.

A little after eleven, I called Milo on his cell phone. I didn't know if he'd made it into work or was marooned at home in the Icicle Creek development.

The sheriff, sounding grumpy, answered on the third ring. "You bet your ass I'm at work," he snarled. "I rode the snowplow in. If you weren't still hunkered down in your cutesy log cabin, you'd see that Front and some of the other streets are open."

"I don't want to see," I retorted. "Have you taken a look at the *Advocate*?"

"What do you mean?" Milo asked, sounding puzzled. "It's been out since Wednesday."

"I meant the building, not the paper," I said in an impatient tone.

"Oh. Yeah, well, since I didn't notice anything, I guess it's still there. If you were brave, you'd walk down and have a look for yourself."

"I'm not that brave." Or foolish. Breaking a leg or getting frostbite would definitely hamper the next edition. "I want to build a fire and read a good book. I hear there's a best-seller out about a sinister sheriff."

"I hope you already got it. I don't see you getting your tootsies cold going out in the snow. And by the way," Milo added, "it's just barely under thirty degrees. Now that it's stopped snowing and the wind's died down, it feels like spring."

"I don't see any sun," I pointed out. "The clouds are still gray and close in."

"Whatever. Why'd you call?"

"To have a pleasant chat with Sheriff Dodge," I said. "Would you please put him on the line?"

"Okay, okay, so I'm not in a real good mood." He paused, maybe to check his emotional barometer. "Well?"

"Did you find the other bullet?"

"Yeah, we found it fairly easy," Milo answered, actually in a more agreeable voice. "It was lodged in the counter between the stools. Bronsky's lucky he didn't get it in the ass."

"It's hard to miss a sedentary target," I murmured, "especially one that's so large. Have you started your interviews?"

"Not yet. Everybody's stuck except for Jim Medved. He's coming in on his snowmobile. We're going to have to ferry people here or see them at home." The sheriff sighed heavily. "This is a bitch. Say, did you hear about Destiny and her poor dog?"

I told Milo that I not only knew, I'd been there. "How's she doing?" I inquired.

"She's pretty shook up," Milo said. "I'll try to get up there later. Jim's picking the dog up after he gets through here."

Ordinarily, I'd have asked the sheriff to stop in for coffee or a drink. But he annoyed me. How, I wondered, could he take time out from investigating a suspicious death to call on Destiny Parsons? Then I remembered that she was a witness, and a major one as director of the ill-fated play. Maybe I should cut Milo some slack.

But I didn't. "You'll need Jim's snowmobile to get here," I said.

"We've got one," Milo replied. "We stretched the budget last winter. The only thing is, I don't know how to run it."

"Why can't Jim show you?"

"Guess he'll have to. Say," Milo went on, "I should get a statement from you. You're a trained observer, right?"

"I'll be darned. So I am."

The sheriff ignored my sarcasm. "You saw what happened. Maybe I'll stop by after I see Destiny."

"I'll leave a light in the window," I said. "That way, if you run amok with the snowmobile, you'll know how to avoid hitting my little log cabin. Why don't you take lessons from Durwood Parker? He used to drive a snowmobile before you benched him after he took out the Kiwanis Club ice sculpture in Old Mill Park."

"That's how we got the snowmobile," Milo said. "We bought it from Durwood in exchange for a fat reckless driving ticket."

Durwood, who was a retired pharmacist and the original owner of the local drugstore that still bore his name, was the worst driver in Alpine. It was a miracle that he'd never done serious damage to anyone, including himself. His license had been suspended for years.

"You could always ski up here," I remarked.

"I haven't skied in ten years," Milo said. "My knees won't take it anymore."

Yet another reminder that Milo and I weren't getting any younger. We were growing old, but not together.

❋ ❋ ❋

I've always liked history. But maybe I'm shallow. Ben had seen the Roman Forum before, so I went without him, joining a tour group led by a hyper young woman who spoke four languages and kept screaming at us to stay together, move along, listen up. I'd felt as if I were in third grade.

From our guide's rapid-fire English I learned that there had been several forums, built by different emperors, and that serious disintegration didn't start until a great fire in the ninth century. Almost a millennium passed before restoration was begun.

But the place still looked like a wreck to me. Broken columns, decaying marble, grass and moss creeping everywhere, with nary a bathroom in sight. The names of the great emperors rolled by—Julius Caesar, Augustus, Trajan, Hadrian. They'd had a long run. But they were all dead, some for over two thousand years. What was left of the Forum seemed a symbol of life's futility. I felt depressed again.

But I finally found a bathroom.

❋ ❋ ❋

Vida was not depressed. When she called me about half an hour after I got through talking to Milo, my House & Home editor was in high gear.

"Imagine!" she shrieked in my ear. "Roger couldn't settle down last night until almost three in the morning! Can you think how hard this has been on him? Why, he might have been shot, too! He'll have nightmares for months!"

"It's pretty hard on Hans, too," I noted. "Have you found out if he has family?"

"No one around here," Vida retorted, indicating that if the deceased had survivors somewhere other than in Alpine, they might as well not exist. "According to Stella Magruder, Hans and Rita Patricelli were romantically involved. Stella does Rita's hair—every week Rita has hers touched up, can you believe it?—and they had plans to go to Hawaii over spring break."

I recalled Rita's hysterical reaction to Hans's death. "I'd heard they were seeing each other, but I didn't know it was serious."

"Maybe, maybe not," Vida responded. "You never know with people's morals these days. But Rita certainly was upset. My niece, Marje Blatt, told me she had to be sedated last night and one of the Patricellis had to stay with her."

As usual, Vida's grapevine was working well.

"Furthermore, Amy told me that Roger said Destiny and Hans did not get along *at all* and that she—Destiny—would never have cast Hans in the part except for pressure from Clea Bhuj. Destiny and Hans fought the whole time."

"Wasn't Roger cast at the last minute?" I asked.

"Yes," Vida replied, "but he'd been 'hanging out'—as the young say—with Davin. They're friends, you see. And of course with Roger's interest in the theater, he attended most of the rehearsals. That's how he knew Davin's part so well."

I still couldn't see Roger bitten by the acting bug. Maybe, I mused, someone was handing out not just parts but also marijuana. "Why was Clea so insistent on Hans being in the play?"

"I've no idea," Vida said, sounding miffed with herself. "Campus politics, maybe. Hans was dean of students, Clea is head of the Humanities Division. I understand that the so-called Ivory Tower is fraught with political maneuvering. Wouldn't you think that *teaching* would be enough?"

"It probably has something to do with *eating*," I said. "College professors don't get rich, not even the administrators. And don't forget power. In a small world like a college campus, power can be a heady thing."

"Really," Vida sniffed. "I can't think why. I mean it isn't like government or some large corporation."

"Power's power," I said, looking out of the window and noting that icicles were forming. Maybe it was starting to thaw. "Let's face it," I went on, remembering Nat Cardenas's offers from other schools. "SCC is a small college. It may be a jumping-off place for ambitious educators."

"Nonsense!" Vida snapped. "Why would anyone want to leave Alpine? Larger schools are usually in larger cities. Think of all the problems there must be in a place like Seattle or . . ." I was sure she was shuddering. ". . . Los Angeles."

"The pay's better in California, I hear." I wasn't ready yet to break Nat's confidence. "Do you really think Nat would shoot a colleague over a job issue?"

"No. No, of course not," Vida said in a more reasonable tone. "But isn't that the point of the investigation? To find out if someone intentionally put real bullets in Jim's gun?"

"I suppose it is," I allowed. "But was Hans the one who was supposed to get shot?"

"Yes," Vida stated. "I read the script after I got home last night. I picked up a copy at the theater when we were backstage. The character of the café owner was supposed to be an innocent victim of gun violence. Surely you noticed that no one acted surprised when Hans fell to the ground."

"That's true." Thus, Hans was the intended victim all along. But obviously he wasn't supposed to die. "Say, did you hear anything about the car that was supposedly floating in the Sky last night or did the medics make that up?" I'd forgotten to ask Milo. His interest in Destiny had gotten me sidetracked.

"What car?" Vida's reaction was swift.

I explained what Del Amundson had said after she had left. "I didn't listen to the radio this morning," I confessed. "I couldn't bear to hear Spence gloating over his latest scoop."

"He doesn't usually work on weekends," Vida said. "He lets

those college students take over for him. Not," she added hastily, "that I listen to KSKY very often."

I don't believe Vida when she insists that she ignores the competition. Never ever would she turn down a news source, not even if Hitler were the disc jockey, playing German military marches between newsbreaks.

"Besides," she continued, "I didn't have time. I was too worried about Roger and then I got on the phone. I'll have to call my nephew, Billy. He wasn't scheduled for duty this weekend, but with everything happening around here, Milo probably has all his deputies on the job."

Bill Blatt was yet another one of Vida's blood-related sources. Since she hadn't yet mentioned Destiny's dead dog, I decided to relay the one piece of news I possessed.

"Dogs!" Vida exclaimed. "Noisy creatures. But not as bad as cats. Cats are so spoiled. And they don't *do* anything. I'm perfectly satisfied with Cupcake. A canary is a most enjoyable pet. Which," she added on a darker note, "is another reason I think it's wise for Buck to have his own place. He has a dog, you know."

"I didn't," I said. "You mean he's found somewhere to live in town?"

"Yes," Vida replied. "He'll be moving in when he gets back from Palm Springs. It's a small house near Burl Creek. It needs work, but he's handy."

Vida and Buck had almost parted ways last fall when she refused to let him move in with her after he sold his home down the highway at Gold Bar. She had argued that not only would people talk, but that she needed all three bedrooms—one for her, one for Roger when he stayed over, and one for her hats. Buck, naturally, had failed to understand.

"By the way," I asked, "do you know where Hans Berenger lived?"

"An apartment," Vida answered promptly, "in the same building where Leo lives. But someone—now who was it? I don't recall—told me that he'd bought some property not far from the campus. Maybe he intended to build. Really, I must dash. I want to phone Amy and see how Roger's doing this afternoon. It's so difficult not to be able to get out and about."

It seemed to me that Vida was keeping very busy at home. Despite my misgivings, I flipped on the radio. It was almost two o'clock and time for the news.

A canned commercial for McDonald's was airing, but as soon as it finished, an unfamiliar voice filled the airways. "This is Rey Fernandez, with the news from your favorite station, KSKY, the voice of Skykomish County."

I should have recognized Rey, but he sounded very different from the itinerant worker he'd portrayed in *The Outcast*. The whining Hispanic accent was gone, replaced by a smooth baritone. He sounded almost professional.

"The investigation of the death of Hans Berenger, Skykomish Community College dean of students, continues today as witnesses undergo interrogation by Sheriff Milo Dodge. It has yet to be determined if the fatal shooting of Berenger, age forty-eight, will be ruled an accidental homicide."

Rey continued with some of the details, then switched to the weather, which, as anybody with eyes could see, wasn't good: "The forecast for Skykomish County predicts temperatures slightly above freezing by late this afternoon. Tonight may bring freezing rain, with winds up to ten miles per hour. Look for a break in the weather by tomorrow, with higher temperatures and more rain."

That meant slush, great big piles of it, but only if it didn't get colder and freeze everything into dangerous ice. It also meant that the river would rise.

Rey said as much, then segued to the floating car story.

"Sheriff's deputies are still seeking the driver of a nineteen-ninety-nine Mitsubishi Galant that plunged into the Skykomish River around midnight. Divers have been brought in from Snohomish County to help with the search. It's not known whether anyone was actually in the vehicle when it went into the river not far from Anderson's Auto Supply and the steel bridge into town."

Rey broke for a couple of commercials before returning with regional, national, and international news. I turned off the radio when he got to the first story out of Olympia, the state capital. By the time we received the information from the wire service Monday, it would be old news. Over the weekend, everything I wanted to know was happening here in Alpine.

I wasn't alone in seeking the local angle, however. The phone rang as soon as I stepped out into the carport to check the thermometer. The caller identified himself as Rolf Fisher from the Associated Press. The name was familiar. I'd spoken with him a few times concerning other news items originating out of Skykomish County.

"We got wind of your drama disaster," Rolf said in a voice that had some kind of New York accent. "Can you fill me in?"

I went on the defensive: "Why me?"

"Sheriff Dodge isn't talking," Rolf replied. "Neither is the college president. Come on, Emma. We're in the same business."

I hedged. "How did you hear about it?"

"We picked it up from your local radio station this morning," Rolf replied. "KSKY doesn't have much of a signal, but one of our guys went steelheading early up on the Sky near Sultan. He managed to get it on his car radio."

"Then you know as much as I do," I said, noting that it was thirty-four degrees in the shelter of the carport. "We're snowbound. I haven't been able to get out today and Sheriff Dodge is hampered in his interviews by the weather."

"You didn't happen to be in the audience, did you?" Rolf asked.

Emma Lord, eyewitness reporter. I didn't much like scooping myself. "I saw what everybody else saw, which is what got reported on KSKY. Talk to Spencer Fleetwood, the station owner. He was there, too. He was actually in the play." Let Spence take the heat. He already had the story.

"We did," Rolf responded, sounding impatient. "He gave us the party line, too. What is this, some kind of cover-up?"

"Are you kidding?" I'd come back inside and was taking a jug of apple cider out of the fridge. "Why would we do that? We simply don't know anything yet."

"You know," Rolf said, sounding amused, "you small towners are all alike. You take care of your own. You barricade yourselves up in the woods or out on the farms and do everything but build a moat around yourselves. What's the point?"

"What's *your* point?" I snapped.

Rolf uttered a little laugh. "My point is getting a news story, same as yours. It's not my fault that the *Gazette* or the *Bugle* or whatever your paper is called happens to be a weekly. I've got a deadline to meet. It's one thing if some logger bashes in another logger's head in a tavern brawl. But this is different, in case you haven't noticed. Some guy gets whacked in plain sight of several hundred people and nobody even knows he's dead until he doesn't get up for his curtain call. That, lady, is news."

I didn't like the lecture and I hadn't liked being called a small towner. I still felt like a city girl inside. Rolf Fisher was making me mad.

"Don't call me, I'll call you," I said, and banged down the phone.

Five minutes later, I berated myself for being childish. Rolf was doing his job, and it was the same as mine. I'd treated a colleague badly. Maybe I should call him back and apologize.

But before I could make up my mind, I saw the snowplow coming down Fir Street. Milo was driving and he had a passenger with him.

The plow stopped in front of my house. Or rather, it stopped in the middle of the street, where the sheriff got out, and loped his way through the snow that had piled up in Destiny Parsons's front yard. Jim Medved, lugging an animal carrier, followed in Milo's tracks. Azbug's body was about to be removed.

A dead man, a dead dog, I thought to myself, watching the sheriff and the vet go inside Destiny's house. I couldn't see her, but I knew she was there. It bothered me that Destiny seemed more distraught over the death of her pet than the possible murder of her colleague. Human beings should always come first in the hierarchy.

And accidents did happen.

I found no comfort in the thought.

SIX

FOR THE NEXT HALF HOUR I BUSIED MYSELF WITH CHORES BUT KEPT an eye on the Parsons house. I'd built a fire from some of the dry logs I keep under a tarp in the carport. If I had to be stuck inside, I wanted to be cozy.

The snowplow stayed put in the middle of the street. It wasn't blocking traffic because there wasn't any, except for the couple on skis who were making their way through the intersection at Fir and Fourth. Most of Alpine seemed hunkered down, even as the icicles began to drip from the eaves.

I saw Jim leave, trudging through the snow and carrying Azbug away. His clinic was six blocks from my doorstep. Apparently, he'd decided he could walk. Fox terriers aren't heavy dogs.

Milo didn't reappear for almost another half hour. By that time, it was close to four-thirty. I wasn't exactly posted at the front window, but I happened to look up from my laptop, on which I'd been writing a letter to my friend, Mavis Marley Fulkerston, in Portland. The sheriff was heading my way.

"How's the bereaved dog owner?" I asked as he stamped his feet on the porch.

"Not good," Milo replied. "She rescued that dog from the pound and raised her from a puppy. She was like a kid to Destiny."

I tried to look sympathetic. "I gather Destiny has never had children."

"She was married once, a long time ago." Milo began the task of removing his parka. Puddles formed on my carpet, but I ignored them. They'd dry. "No kids, I guess."

"Are you on duty or do you want a drink?" I asked as Milo spread out in my easy chair.

"I'm here to take your formal statement," he replied, "but I wouldn't turn down a shot of Scotch. It'll keep me warm."

In the kitchen, I made two quick, short drinks—Milo's Scotch, my bourbon. When I came back into the living room, the sheriff was nodding off.

He jumped when I approached him with his glass. "Jeez!" he exclaimed. "I was practically asleep. That fire feels good."

Sometimes it was hard to stay mad at Milo. He looked so comfortable in that easy chair with his long legs stuck out so far that they almost reached under the coffee table in front of the sofa. He was rubbing his eyes and brushing the graying sandy hair from his forehead. The familiar way he was lounging meant that with any luck, I'd find at least a dollar in change that had fallen out of his pocket. I was trying to be unsentimental, but it wasn't easy. The sheriff always looked so at home in my living room.

"How are the interviews going?" I inquired, getting Milo an ashtray before I sat down on the sofa.

"What you'd expect," he answered, pausing to light a cigarette. "Everybody still seems in a state of shock, including Dustin. I've only talked to him, Cardenas, Fleetwood, Medved, and Destiny so far. The rest of my guys have done some interviews with audience members over the phone. Oh . . ." He stopped to take a sip of his drink. ". . . I paid a courtesy call on Old Lady Rasmussen this afternoon. They couldn't get back to Snohomish, so she's up at the ski lodge."

"In the imperial suite," I remarked. "If they had one."

"She's driving Henry Bardeen nuts," Milo said with a sardonic smile. "Henry's had his share of pains in the ass over the years, but he swears Thyra's the worst."

Henry was the ski lodge's longtime manager and the younger brother of Buck Bardeen, Vida's dear friend. "You can't blame Thyra for being upset," I said. "Killing off a cast member isn't good publicity for your theater."

Milo nodded. "The old girl blames Destiny. Carelessness, that's what Mrs. R. calls it. Hell, she may be right."

"I suppose," I mused, "you can't have a murder without a motive. Does Hans Berenger have a lurid past or have you had time to check?"

"I had Nat Cardenas fax me Berenger's résumé," Milo replied, flicking ash from the end of his cigarette. "You must have gotten the same dope for the paper. Don't you always do a story on new faculty members?"

"I think Scott did that one," I said. "This is—I mean was—Hans's third or fourth year at SCC. Frankly, I don't remember what the story said except that he was originally from the Midwest."

"Chicago," Milo said, and frowned. "What does that mean? People say they're from Chicago or L.A. or New York, and then you find out that they really came from some suburb you never even heard of. Seattle's getting like that. I met a guy at the firing range in Yakima last fall and he told me he was from Seattle. Turned out he was forty-two years old, grew up on the Eastside in Issaquah twenty minutes from the city, and hadn't ever seen the Space Needle except from an airplane."

Milo had a particular dislike for Seattle's eastern suburbs. His ex-wife had moved to Bellevue with their children after the divorce. Tricia—or Old Mulehide, as Milo called her—had remarried almost as soon as the decree had become final. Her second husband was, in fact, a schoolteacher. Maybe the sheriff wasn't trying as hard as he could to find out who might have wanted to kill Hans Berenger. Maybe he was trying to get some vicarious revenge on the profession.

"You digress," I said. "Refresh my memory about Hans's background."

Milo made a face. "I can't remember all that stuff about his degrees. He got a doctorate of some kind from Wisconsin, moved to Southern California, and later took a job in the Bay Area. Anyway, he came up here about four years ago. He was dean of students at some two-year school in the Bay Area. Cardenas hired Berenger because he'd had experience as a dean."

"Not married?"

"Widowed," Milo replied. "His wife died while they were still living in California. Some kind of accident. No mention of kids."

"It sounds as if he wanted to get away from big cities," I noted. "From Chicago to Wisconsin to Southern and Northern California to here. Does it sound as if he's been running away?"

"Could be," Milo allowed. "The wife's death probably had that effect on him."

"She must have been fairly young," I said, noticing that Milo's glass was empty. "Do you want a refill?"

Milo shook his head. "Can you write down what you saw before I take off?"

I shrugged. "There's not much to write. I saw what the rest of the audience saw—what you saw, too. The fight broke out, Hans tried to break it up, Nat entered . . ." I stopped and retrieved my laptop from the other end of the sofa. "Here. I always do better when I type. It'll just take a minute. Do you want me to print it out or bring it by Monday?"

"Monday's fine," Milo said, looking at the fire and yawning. "It's just routine. You know me, I like to cover all the bases."

By the book, that was our sheriff. I finished the three paragraphs and closed the laptop. "Are you sure you can stay awake for the rest of the day?"

Milo grimaced. "It was one hell of a short night. It's thawing out there, and that damned snowplow's hard enough to drive without steering it through slushy stuff. I still have a couple of people to talk to." He extinguished his cigarette and stood up.

"Who?"

"Rita Patricelli and Clea Bhuj," Milo replied, getting into his parka. "I hear Rita's been seeing Hans. Seems like an odd couple to me."

"Rita certainly fell apart last night," I said. "Whatever happened to her ex?"

Milo looked puzzled. "Haines? Wasn't that his name? She used to go by it when she first came back to Alpine." The sheriff shrugged. "I think she left him behind in Seattle. I don't think I ever met the guy. He wasn't from here."

"By the way," I said as Milo opened the door, "Vida mentioned that Clea was responsible for Hans being cast in the play. Maybe he's been playing the field. Clea's single, isn't she?"

But I was mistaken. "She's got a husband in Everett," Milo said. "They sort of commute back and forth. He works for the city over there. Dustin told me he has to live in Everett to keep his job. It's some kind of rule they've got."

"Oh." I'd begun to realize how little I knew of SCC's faculty despite the fact that the college had now been around for several years. It was strange, really. Many of the instructors were in my peer group, and most undoubtedly had more wide-ranging interests than their bowling scores or how many half racks they should lay in for the weekend. Yet I hadn't gone out of my way to make friends, and when it came to interviews, I usually handed off the assignments to Scott or Vida. It was an old story for me. All my life, I'd built so many fences to protect myself that there were few to mend and no one to help me rend them.

Under deepening clouds of gray, Milo went off into the melting snow. I hadn't pried about his meeting with Destiny. Was that because I didn't care?

I made myself another drink and tried to think of other things.

One of those things that came to mind that evening was the car that had gone into the Sky. Around eight, I turned the radio on. But Saturday nights were devoted to Big Band music, with only a few commercial breaks. Spence's theory was that KSKY could be piped into the local taverns so the patrons could trip the light fantastic toe. Assuming, of course, that they could still stand up, let alone dance. I didn't wait for the sign-off news at midnight. By eleven-thirty, I was fast asleep.

By one-fifteen, I was wide awake. The bedroom seemed to shake, and at first I thought we were having an earthquake. Then a bright light filled the bedroom and I heard a whirring noise. The room stopped vibrating; the light and the noise grew fainter by the second. If I'd been in the city, I would have sworn it was a helicopter. But nobody that I knew of in Alpine— including the sheriff—owned any type of aircraft.

Without bothering to put on a robe, I went to the window and pulled up the shade. Sure enough, I could see blinking white lights and a single beam through the mixed snow and rain. The copter was circling above the south side of town, searching my neighborhood and the nearby woods.

I picked up the phone from the nightstand and called the sheriff's office. A weary Jack Mullins answered on the fourth ring.

"Go back to bed, Emma," he said tartly. "Are your doors locked?"

"Yes," I replied, struggling to put a robe on over my shivering body, "but I'm not going back to bed until you tell me what's going on. Where'd that copter come from?"

Jack heaved a sigh. "The state patrol. We borrowed it. We're looking for somebody, okay?"

"No kidding. Is he armed and dangerous?"

"Hang up now, Emma."

"Where's Milo?"

"In the copter. Good night, Emma." Jack hung up.

I was still looking out the window. The aircraft hovered over First Hill before starting to turn back toward the residential area. I felt frustrated and wondered if I should call the state patrol. They might be more helpful than Deputy Mullins.

Before I could make up my mind, the phone rang. Even as I reached for the receiver, I knew it would be Vida. The copter was now in her vicinity, on Tyee Street, a block away from the middle school.

"My nephew Billy won't come to the phone," Vida declared without any preamble. "He's working, but he's out of the office. Since he can't fly a helicopter, where in the world is he and what's he doing?"

I didn't have a chance to conjecture. Vida rattled on. "Imagine! A helicopter hovering over Alpine during the night! What can it mean? Is Milo chasing Hans Berenger's killer?"

The thought had crossed my mind. "Maybe." The sheriff had had eight hours to discover the perp. If there really was a perp. "It could be something unrelated. Grace Grundle may have reported another prowler."

"Milo wouldn't bother getting a helicopter for that," Vida scoffed. "The last time Grace phoned in with one of her fright attacks, it turned out to be the mailman. Marlow Whipp, in fact. He'd forgotten to drop off her cat toy catalog and knew she'd be upset if it didn't come on time. Besides, who'd be prowling around in this weather?"

Vida had a point. "I talked to Jack Mullins," I said. "He virtually hung up on me."

"This is most aggravating," Vida asserted. "It's no way to treat the press. I've a mind to march right down to the sheriff's office."

"Don't," I warned.

"Why not?" She paused. "Roger left his sled here a year or two ago. He said sleds were for kiddies. He wanted a luge. Maybe I could—"

"Don't even think about it," I interrupted.

"Why not? It's straight downhill to Front Street. I'd merely have to walk a few blocks to the sheriff's." She sighed. "If only Buck were back in town. He's an air force colonel. He'd be able to sort all this out."

"Please don't," I begged. "It's too dangerous."

"You think I can't ride a sled?"

"I think you won't be able to see," I warned Vida. "The weather's awful, the snow may be melting, but it's still piled high, and you might run into a car once you hit Front Street. They plowed down there."

"You fuss too much," Vida said. "I should go now."

Vida clicked off. She should go where? To the sheriff's? Back to bed? To call someone else? I paced around the house. Maybe I should try Vida's number. If she was on the phone, I'd know she was safe at home. If she didn't answer . . . I couldn't think about that possibility. Nor was there anything I could do about it.

But there was. I should be the one who was hell-bent on getting the news. I was twenty years younger than Vida; I was the editor and the publisher of *The Alpine Advocate*. By nature, Vida was snoopier than I was. But she shouldn't be more professional. When it came to risking a neck, it was mine that had to be on the block.

I picked up the phone in the living room and dialed Vida's number. She didn't answer on the first three rings, which alarmed me. But then I heard her impatient voice.

"Yes? Who is this?" she demanded.

"It's me: Emma. What are you doing?"

"Getting dressed. Then," she went on in a vexed tone, "I'm going to look for Roger's sled. It's somewhere in the basement."

"Don't. I'm already on my way." It wasn't quite true, but I had to forestall her.

"So? We'll both go. How are you getting there?"

"I'm using Adam's skis," I replied. "He had to get a different kind when he was assigned to Alaska."

"You don't know how to ski," Vida declared.

"I'm not turning out for an Olympic downhill race. If I can walk, I can ski. And if I can't ski, I can still walk."

"You're being foolish," Vida admonished.

It seemed as if we'd reversed roles. Vida was now the one urging caution. But that was good. I'd taken over the news gathering, which was my responsibility.

Getting Adam's skis out of his closet was no easy task. In the past few years his visits had been depressingly infrequent, and the result was that I used his former space for storage. I had to move at least six boxes, a broken lamp, and the vacuum cleaner before I could reach the skis. After much exertion, I managed to free not only the skis but also the poles. It was only then that I realized I needed boots. Adam had taken his with him, and they wouldn't have fit me anyway. Stumped, I stood in the middle of his room and wondered what to do next.

I was still mulling when I heard the helicopter in the distance. Whoever was lost had not been found. Frustrated, I looked through the window. The copter was out of sight. Maybe the search had been called off. I went back to the living room and dialed the sheriff's office.

Jack answered again. "You're a pesky little devil," he said, sounding more like his usual jovial self. "Okay, just because we belong to the same church and we're going to nap through Mass later this morning, I'll let you in on a secret. The copter has landed in that cul-de-sac down the street from your little log cabin."

"Really?" No wonder it had disappeared so fast. "Why?"

"Ah . . . that's where I stop being helpful. Why don't you trot down there and see for yourself?"

"Why don't I? Or," I added, "are you trying to tell me you don't know why the copter's in Ms. Lord's neighborhood?"

"You choose. Bundle up, Emma. It's cold outside."

I bundled. That was the easy part. I got out my flashlight and turned it on. It didn't work. The thing required four D batteries, and I only had two in the drawer. Cursing myself, I ventured out into what was now sleet. The snow had gotten so soft that I sank with every step and was soaked through to my midsection by the time I got off my own property. It might be above freezing, but Jack was right—it was definitely cold outside. At least there wasn't much wind, but it certainly was dark. No lamps glowed from behind windows, and streetlights are a luxury afforded only to the blocks in or near the downtown area. But after going—slowly, arduously—about twenty feet along Fir, I could literally see a light in the clearing. In another ten feet I could hear voices.

Finally, I saw the copter, sitting like a big bug on ground that had obviously been cleared for its landing. Nearby I saw Milo, Sam Heppner, Bill Blatt, and a grim-faced man I didn't recognize who was probably a state patrol helicopter pilot.

Milo spotted me but kept talking to the other men. Grateful to be on firm soil, I hurried toward the foursome.

"Hi," I said, tugging at Milo's sleeve. "What's up?"

Milo looked down on me with a pained expression. "What the hell are you doing out here in the middle of the night?"

"I'm a journalist, remember? We don't keep regular hours."

"Who does?" Milo responded with a weary sigh.

"So why are we here?" I kept my tone light.

Milo glanced at the copter, then at the disgruntled pilot, and finally looked back at me. "We knew there was a state patrol copter in the vicinity, looking for stranded cars. We asked for help searching for the guy who was driving the car that went into the river."

I was flummoxed. "Why are you searching aboveground?"

The sheriff's expression indicated he thought I was a moron. "Because the guy didn't go into the river, the car did."

"Can you explain that?" I inquired.

"Sure. He either jumped out of the car before it hit the river or let it roll."

"How do you know this, since you haven't found him?" I gestured at the copter. "Or is this just another one of those crazy law enforcement larks?"

"Don't aggravate me," Milo warned, with a scowl on his long face. "It turns out this jerk showed up at Mugs Ahoy, bragging about how he dumped his car in the river and wasn't that just the funniest thing anybody ever did? Abe Loomis, the owner, called us because he knew we had divers brought in. I sent Sam and Bill over there, and as soon as they walked in the son of a bitch jumped off the bar stool and ran out the back way. My guys lost track of him about three blocks away. I didn't like the sound of it, so I asked if the state patrol copter could fly over as long as they were in the area. We've got enough on our plate as it is." Milo's voice had turned defensive, and he shot a quick glance at the pilot, who still looked out of sorts. "The only problem," the sheriff went on, speaking closer to my ear, "is that this prick is pissed off for sending him on what he calls a wild-goose chase. Screw him. He knows we don't have much in the way of resources here."

I was still puzzled. "What do you want to arrest the driver for? Escaping from death?"

Milo remained peeved. "The car's registered to a woman in Seattle. We can't locate her. She's not in the book. And any time a guy takes one look at a couple of cops and runs off, we get suspicious."

"Oh. Of course." I'd assumed the car belonged to the missing man. It was stupid of me. I've told myself a hundred times never to assume anything. "But you've called off the search?"

Milo nodded. "Visibility is next to zero. We thought we might be able to sight him in town and even in the forest where the trees aren't so thick. But we've gone all over the immediate area with no luck. Maybe he found some shelter or he's hiding in the woods. Either way, we can't do much now. So the pilot's right." Milo looked glum. "We wasted his time."

"And yours," I pointed out. "I take it you were in the copter, too?"

Milo nodded again. "It's my job."

I held out my hands, which were encased in big leather gloves. "It's my job, too. Being here, I mean."

"I know." Awkwardly he patted me on the shoulder.

"Have you got an APB on the guy?" I asked.

"Yeah," Milo replied. "Early to mid-twenties, short dark beard, full head of curly dark hair, average height and build, wearing a heavy brown jacket and jeans. We tried to get it on KSKY, but nobody answered."

"That's not surprising," I said, squinting at Milo through the sleet. "Spence uses canned music and commercials Saturday nights. The only one there is the engineer. Maybe he was in the can."

"Swell." Milo paused. "You want a ride home on the snowplow?"

I wasn't proud. It was a hard, chilling rain and I was shivering. "Sure. Who's driving?"

"Me. Hold on." He went back to confer with his deputies and the pilot. I assumed Milo was making some sort of apology, since handshakes were given all around. A moment later, the pilot was getting back into the copter. The sheriff and his men backed away. The copter lights went on and the rotors started to turn. The whirlybird slowly lifted off the ground, creating a

wicked breeze. Now I could see the snowplow parked on the opposite edge of the clearing.

Milo waited until the copter's noise began to fade a bit. "I
think we can all get aboard," he shouted. "Come on, let's go!"

As I approached, Sam and Dwight made deferential gestures
toward me by touching their wool watch caps. Sizing up the
plow, Milo looked apologetic.

"I guess you're going to have to sit on my lap, Emma.
There's not as much room as I thought."

"I could walk," I offered, brushing at the sleet that was ob-
scuring my vision. "It's not even a block to my house."

Milo shook his head. "Walking in this stuff is pretty damned
rugged. You're already soaked."

"So are you," I noted. "Hey, it's three in the morning. What
else have I got to do? Give me a ride and I'll make us a strong,
hot drink."

Milo brightened. "Sounds good. We're off-duty. How about
it, guys?"

"Sure," Sam said.

"Thanks, Ms. Lord," Bill replied.

And off we went. It was a bumpy ride. I felt stuffed, rather
than seated, in Milo's lap. He kept bumping my face with his fore-
arms, making me feel like I'd had a rough day at the dentist's.

But we arrived at the front porch in one piece. Having driven
straight through the front yard, Milo promised to plow my driveway on the way out. I immediately started a new fire, then went
into the bedroom to change clothes. Five minutes later, I had the
teakettle on. Fortunately, I still had some buttered rum mix left
over from the holidays.

"Hits the spot," Milo announced after the first big swig. His
deputies echoed his sentiments.

The fire had caught and was burning brightly. The scene
seemed ironically cheerful. I hated to break the spell by bringing
up the subject of murder. But I did it anyway.

"Any luck finding out if Hans was shot by accident?" I asked.

Milo frowned. "Not yet. We still haven't talked to everybody. As usual, the witness who talks the most is the one who doesn't really have much to say."

"Who?" I inquired.

Milo made a face at Bill Blatt. "Bill's cousin Roger. He's eating all this up. Roger wants to play detective."

That came as no surprise. "I should have guessed," I said.

Bill, however, defended the family honor. "Hey, don't knock the kid too much. Unlike a lot of teenagers, Roger notices things."

I supposed it figured, being Vida's grandson. Maybe Roger had inherited Grams's heightened sense of curiosity.

Milo didn't look impressed. "Maybe he does, but saying that he saw a bushy-haired stranger backstage during the play sounds like his imagination got the better of him."

I hated to give Roger the benefit of a doubt. But for once, I had to. The description of Roger's stranger sounded eerily like the man who was missing from the car that had taken a dive into the Skykomish River.

SEVEN

MILO DIDN'T AGREE WITH MY REACTION. "WHEN I TALKED TO Roger earlier in the evening, we didn't have a description of the guy. We didn't even know if he was still alive. And 'bushy-haired stranger' is about as big a cliché as there is."

I wasn't convinced. I figured Bill Blatt wasn't, either, but he wouldn't contradict his boss in front of an outsider. "Exactly what did Roger say about the stranger?" I asked.

Milo sighed before holding out his empty mug. "How about a refill before we visit Fantasy Island?"

"Okay." I looked to Bill and Sam, but they declined.

I decided I might as well join Milo in a second round. I wasn't sure I could get back to sleep, and what was worse, I was starting to get hungry.

"So tell me Roger's story," I said after sitting back down on the sofa next to Sam.

Milo scratched his head. "I took a formal statement. Roger was wandering around backstage during the second act. Hanging out, he said, mainly with Rey Fernandez and the other college students who were doing the technical stuff. Rey was showing him a field template for the stage lighting. When Rey finished,

Roger happened to look toward the rear exit. He says he saw somebody he didn't recognize, but he didn't think much of it at the time because the students who worked as techs during rehearsals weren't always the same ones. Later, before Roger made his entrance again in the last act, he saw the same guy, just kind of looking around. Then Roger went onstage. He says he didn't see the guy again but had to wonder what he was doing there. Roger thinks he's probably our suspect." Milo made a face.

"Well," I blurted, "he could be. Aren't you going to take Roger seriously?"

"Nobody else saw the guy," Milo responded, reaching into his pocket. "Dammit!" he swore. "My cigarettes are wet." The sheriff gave me a look of appeal.

I got up. "Okay, so I've got a pack stashed in the kitchen—just to prove I don't need them anymore. Hold on."

If there was one big impediment to my stop-smoking campaign, it was Milo. I returned with the pack—from which I'd removed a couple of cigarettes in weak moments—and handed it over. But not before I took one for myself.

"Damn you," I said. "Why can't you corrupt your deputies and make them smoke, too?"

Milo chuckled. "Jack and Dwight smoke. Unfortunately, they're not here."

"I quit," Sam said, "six years ago last month. I haven't had a cigarette since that New Year's Day at eleven-oh-eight in the evening." He winced as he concluded the sentence. Probably he still longed for a cigarette, but I admired his self-discipline and said as much.

Milo was chuckling again. "I know of a guy up in Whatcom County who died a while back because he stopped smoking. He got so mean that his wife finally blew him away with his hunting rifle."

The mood in the living room had shifted, becoming anecdotal and unrelated to our current crimes. After another half hour,

Milo said it was time to go. The trio left at a few minutes after four. I went into the kitchen and made scrambled eggs and toast. By four-thirty, I was back in bed. To my surprise, I fell asleep almost immediately and didn't wake up until the alarm went off at nine.

My body wanted to stay in bed; my soul told me to move my rear end and get ready for Mass. Wisely I listened to my soul. I could always nap during Dennis Kelly's well-constructed but often soporific homily. Father Den is very bright, and if he hadn't possessed a religious vocation he could have been an engineer or an architect. Every phrase is perfectly shaped; every word is in the right place. He says it takes him the entire week to prepare for each Sunday sermon. But he's not a speaker; he's a thinker. Despite this, he's a wonderful priest and a surprisingly good conversationalist.

To my great relief, the streets had been plowed and the snow was still melting. There was plenty of slush and rivulets of water. I hadn't checked the thermometer before I left, but the temperature had to be well above freezing. There was no snow in the rain, just a steady gray downpour, as I drove the four blocks to St. Mildred's.

Jack Mullins was seated across the aisle from me. We nodded at each other. Jack looked as tired as I felt. His wife, Nina, appeared as perky as she always does.

Father Den, however, veered from the norm. He had, he declared, put aside the homily he'd intended to give and spoke instead of the recent tragedy at the theater. While I wondered if some of the parishioners might have the feeling that our priest was going to deliver the usual knee-jerk rant against guns, I knew better. Dennis Kelly's father had been a career military man. He'd taught his son to respect weapons, rather than fear them. God didn't put guns in people's hands. It was evil intent— or rank stupidity—that wreaked havoc.

So Father Den spoke of the randomness of death and how

God doesn't choose whether you live or die. Human beings have free will, and they possess flaws. What men and women do isn't dictated by the Creator. And no one knows when the last hour will come. The young think they are immortal. The not-so-young believe they still have time to change their lives. People suffer from many faults, perhaps the greatest of which is self-delusion and a denial of our mortality.

We all stayed awake.

The most dreaded part of the Sunday ritual always came after Mass, when I inevitably encountered Ed and Shirley Bronsky and their brood.

"Hey, hey!" Ed called, coming toward me in his cashmere overcoat with the mink collar. "You want an eyewitness interview for the paper?"

I did, but not necessarily from Ed.

"I could write it up myself," he volunteered before I could respond. "You know—'in his own words.' Readers love that stuff. And I could use it in the second volume of my autobiography, *Mr. Ed Gets Wed*."

I succeeded in keeping a straight face. Ed's sequel supposedly was based on his family life, so that he could share his philosophy for becoming a successful husband and father. I thought that *Mr. Ed Gets Fed* would be more appropriate, but I never said so. To be fair, Ed and Shirley seemed as happy as if they had good sense—to quote Vida—and their five children had turned out well enough. So far.

And, in fact, Ed's idea for the newspaper article wasn't all that bad. At least I wouldn't have to write it—merely edit it, as I had been coerced into doing with the original *Mr. Ed* manuscript. I dreaded the day that Ed would ask me to "just look over" the second installment.

Shirley, who was wearing enough Norwegian fox to cover a

colony of vixens, chimed in. "Ed's so clever. Not to mention ob-
servant. Milo came by Casa de Bronska yesterday while we were
having high tea."

I still kept a straight face. High tea at the Bronskys' pseudo-
villa consisted of double cheeseburgers and fries from McDonald's
instead of small sandwiches and light pastry. Maybe Saturday
had been an exception. I couldn't envision any of the Bronskys
tramping six blocks through the snow to the Golden Arches on
Front Street.

"What did you observe?" I asked Ed, recalling that he hadn't
mentioned anything to me when we were leaving the theater Friday night.

Ed assumed a thoughtful expression. "It's deep," he said. "Not
just what I saw, but what I sensed." He paused for what I presumed was dramatic effect. "Nuances. Feelings. Glances. Things
unsaid."

"Such as?" I tried to avoid looking exasperated.

"You'll read about it in my article. I'm going to go home
and work on it now. We got a new computer last week, so it may
take me a day or two," he explained. "Getting used to the latest
bells and whistles. It's top-of-the-line, beyond state-of-the-art."

Ed was beyond belief, but he hadn't lost his touch for clichés.
His advertising copy had reflected his lack of creativity. A ship-
ment of shoes at Barton's Bootery was always "fit for you!";
Platters in the Sky's latest CDs and tapes were "music to your
ears!"; at Alpine Intimates you could "build a firm foundation."
Fortunately for our revenue, advertisers and readers seemed to
like his work, a fact that had made me shake my head.

Ed and Shirley bounded off to join their family in the MR
PIG Range Rover. Since the kids had grown up—and out—they
all couldn't fit into the Mercedes sedan. I headed for my humble
Honda, nodding at Dick and Mary Jane Bourgette, who were
pulling out of the parking lot in their SUV.

Since the streets were drivable, I decided to go to the office and see if it was still in one piece. As I came down Fourth, I realized that I hadn't reckoned with the laws of gravity. Front Street, like most of Alpine's commercial section, was at the bottom of the river valley. The melting snow had gone downhill from the south side of Tonga Ridge and dumped almost a foot of water and slush into the main artery. The town's sewer system couldn't handle all of the excess. Except for a couple of trucks, there was no traffic on Front. I reversed at the intersection and parked on the steep side of Fourth, next to the Alpine Building.

Fortunately, I was wearing knee-high boots. I waded across Front Street to the *Advocate*. Feeling anxious, I unlocked the front door and went inside. The reception area looked fine, everything in its proper place, as Ginny Erlandson had left it Friday afternoon.

The newsroom and the back shop were also unharmed. So far, so good. I'd saved my office for last, fearing the worst.

My fears were justified. An inch of water covered most of the floor, almost but not quite reaching the newsroom door. The floors are uneven, as most are in the earthquake-prone Northwest. Everything that I'd left on my desk and file cabinets was soaked. Another half-dozen large leaks had developed in the roof, and melting snow dripped everywhere. I managed to find three buckets and a basin, but they weren't enough. Harvey's Hardware was closed—like most Alpine businesses whose owners adhered to the policy that "if you can't make it in six, you won't make it in seven."

I called Kip MacDuff and told him about the situation. There was the hint of reprimand in my voice, and Kip heard it. "Gosh, Emma," he said. "I should have gotten around to fixing those leaks sooner. You say we got more?"

I assured him we did. Kip promised to come right down and bring more buckets. I suggested that he also bring a bunch of towels or heavy rags. Maybe we could wipe up most of the standing water.

While I waited for Kip, I wielded the office mop and used what rags I could find along with an entire package of paper towels. When he arrived twenty minutes later, I'd made considerable headway. Luckily, the damage that had been done wasn't serious. Nothing on my desk or the other surfaces was irreplaceable.

Kip brought some pieces of plywood along with the buckets and towels. "For now, I'll have to close the leaks from inside," he informed me. "It won't look pretty, but it should work. I'll get the roof materials from Harvey's tomorrow." He smiled sheepishly, looking much younger than his twenty-six years. "I really feel bad about this. I guess being a married man has distracted me."

I smiled back. "It's not the worst thing that could happen. I'll get out of your way. I think I'll walk over to the river. It should be running high."

"It is," Kip replied. "They're talking about flooding." His ruddy face turned somber. "We may be in for it here at the paper. We were lucky before when the Sky went over its banks. The water never got past Railroad Avenue on this side."

I remembered all too well. I went out through the back shop and saw that there definitely was cause for alarm. Across Railroad Avenue and the train tracks a dozen people were lugging sandbags where the river would crest. The water was roiling gray, already carrying brush and branches as it swept through town. Hearing the whistle of a freight train, I hurried to the other side of the tracks. Milo was there, talking to Wes Amundson, one of the park rangers and a cousin of Medic Del.

Between the roar of the river and the rumble of the approaching freight, I merely waved. The Burlington–Northern Santa Fe always slows to a crawl when it comes through Alpine. But on this rainy Sunday with the threat of flooding, the train inched its

way past the warehouses, the water tower, and the other buildings along Railroad Avenue.

It was a long freight, a doubleheader with maybe sixty cars,
heading east. I didn't speak until the caboose was well down
the line.

"How bad is it?" I asked Milo and Wes.

Wes frowned. "Bad enough. They're predicting the Sky will
go over its banks here around four o'clock this afternoon. We
may get a break if it stops raining or at least lets up. The state
meteorologist's office says that could happen." He looked sky-
ward. "See? The clouds are beginning to lift a little."

Frankly, I couldn't tell. "I'll take your word for it."

The work crew, which seemed to consist mostly of college-
age kids, had halted their efforts. Boots Overholt, who had been
the prop man at the fateful play, came toward us.

"We've run out of sandbags," he announced. "What do we
do now?"

Wes informed the young man that there were more on the
way, coming from Monroe. "They're sending what they can
spare," the ranger said. "The river's rising down there, too."

The Sky flows westward along Highway 2 until it joins the
Snoqualmie where they both go into the Snohomish River and
finally to Puget Sound near Everett. Most of the corridor from
the summit of Stevens Pass was endangered.

Milo slapped Wes on the back. "Good luck. Let me know
if we can help." The sheriff turned to me. "You had breakfast
yet?"

"Sort of," I replied. "If you call coffee and toast breakfast."

Nudging at my elbow, Milo pointed the way to the rear of
the Venison Inn. "I've had coffee, but that's it. I didn't get up until an hour or so ago. I heard the river was rising, so I came to
check it out."

Explaining our minor flood at the office, I told Milo I'd
meet him at the restaurant in a few minutes. I found Kip stand-

ing on my desk and nailing the last of the plywood to the ceiling. When he'd finished, we cleared up the last of the mess before I called Scott. He didn't pick up, which figured, so I dialed Tamara's number. Scott answered the phone. I told him he should come down to the river and take some photos.

"They're getting more sandbags," I told him, "so right now nothing much is going on. The Sky's supposed to go over its banks around four. We'll need pictures of that, too."

Scott didn't sound pleased, but he agreed to break up his Sunday afternoon for the sake of our readership. I left Kip to lock up and plodded down the street to the Venison Inn.

Milo was already eating a waffle, eggs, and sausage. "Take a seat," he said after swallowing a mouthful of food. "I was too damned hungry to wait."

"That's okay," I assured him, not bothering to look at the menu. "How are the interviews going?"

Milo stared at me. "What interviews? I told you, I only got up a little after ten."

"Lucky you," I remarked as a waitress approached to take my order. "I've accomplished many things already today," I added after the waitress left. "I feel very virtuous. Who's left on your list?"

"Mostly students," Milo replied. "Don't worry, I'm not dragging my feet. For one thing, old Thyra keeps calling the office to nag us. She even called me at home before I left this morning. She's a real pain in the butt."

"Is she still at the ski lodge?"

Milo shook his head. "Probably not. They were going to try to get back to Snohomish. As long as they chain up they should be fine."

"Explain something to me," I said, picking up the mug of coffee that the waitress had just poured. "Where did the real bullets come from? Were they Jim's?"

Milo shook his head again. "The gun belonged to his dad,

who died about four years ago. Moose Medved—his real name
was Marvin or Mervin or something like that—had served as an
MP in World War Two. He'd guarded German prisoners in Europe, and he brought back his own gun—the .38—and a couple
of Lugers he'd gotten from the Germans. Jim inherited them after
Moose died, but he's no gun fancier. On the other hand, he felt
he should keep the ones that'd belonged to his dad. If there was
ammo with the .38, he didn't save it. Jim swears the gun wasn't
loaded when he brought it to the performance. They'd used a
water pistol in the rehearsals."

I didn't speak until after the waitress delivered my pancakes,
eggs, and hamburger steak. "Did anyone know what kind of
gun Jim was bringing?"

"Oh, yeah," Milo said, pouring more syrup on his waffle.
"Jim knew the German guns were Lugers, but he didn't remember offhand what the American gun was. Rip Ridley gave him a
bad time about that, so before Jim came to the next rehearsal,
he checked. He told everybody who was around at the time that
it was a Smith & Wesson .38 special."

"That was when?" I asked.

"About three weeks ago, a couple of days after they started
rehearsing."

I grew thoughtful as I ate my pancakes. "So if someone had
planned to turn the gun into a lethal weapon, they had plenty of
time to prepare."

"Right." Milo added extra salt and pepper to what was left
of his eggs. Then, while I tried not to wince, he doused his sausage with more catsup. "It's too damned bad that Talliaferro
didn't let them use his starter pistol. Hell, Rip should have gotten one from the high school. Nobody's turning out for track in
this weather."

"Who got the blanks that were supposed to be used?"

"Destiny. She bought them at Harvey's Hardware last week."

I grew silent again, staring at the Venison Inn's refurbished gray walls. The place had lost its character since the remodeling in the fall. It was clean but bland. "Who was supposed to load the blanks?"

"Boots Overholt," Milo answered after eating the last bite of waffle. "He says he did, before the play started."

"I really don't know Boots," I admitted. "He was just a kid when I moved here. I know his dad, Ellsworth, and I've driven past their farm a million times. I didn't even recognize Boots when I saw him at the theater."

Milo nodded toward the door. "Here's your big chance. Boots just came in." The sheriff waved a hand, summoning Boots to our table. "His real name is Gregory," Milo murmured as his cell phone went off.

By the time Boots reached us, Milo was answering his call. The fair-haired young man looked at me in an uncertain way. I guess he didn't recognize me any more than I'd recognized him.

"Hi," I said, putting out a hand. "I'm Emma Lord, otherwise known as the newspaper witch."

Boots deferentially shook my hand. I half expected him to tug at his forelock and say, "Ah, shucks, ma'am." Instead, he smiled shyly and allowed that it was nice to meet me.

With an irritated expression, Milo clicked off the phone and started to get out of the booth. "Excuse me. That was Thyra Rasmussen. She's still at the ski lodge, raising hell. She wants to see me. I'd better go. I'll get my bill up front."

"Have a seat," I said to Boots when Milo had stalked away. "Are you taking a break from the sandbags?"

Boots looked as if he felt unworthy of taking the place vacated by the sheriff, but after a moment's hesitation he sat down. "Yes. They told us the stuff from Monroe wouldn't get here until around one. It's just a little after noon now, so I thought I'd get something to eat. I've been out on the river since six." He spoke rapidly, nervously twisting his hands on the table. When the waitress returned, he asked for the special. I suspected he had no idea what it was, but he'd ordered it because he didn't want to have to concentrate.

"Hey," I said softly, "I'm not here on business. Don't worry about what you say to me. It's off-the-record."

Boots seemed puzzled. "How do you mean?"

He might be a farm boy, but I thought he must watch TV. "It means that whatever we talk about isn't going to be printed in the paper." I smiled in reassurance. "But of course I'm curious about the shooting Friday night."

Boots winced and looked away. "I feel like it's all my fault."

I pushed my empty plate away. "From what I've heard, it's not. You weren't expected to guard that prop box with your life, were you?"

"I couldn't," Boots said with a helpless expression. "During intermission especially, I had to check stuff onstage. You know . . . like making sure Mr. Bronsky had food on his plate."

Maybe there was some way that Milo could arrest Ed as an accessory in the death of Hans Berenger. But I put such evil thoughts aside and asked instead when Boots thought someone might have had unobserved access to the prop box.

"Unobserved?" Boots stared at me with dark blue eyes. "You mean nobody could see what was happening with the box?"

I nodded. "It wouldn't take a pro more than a few seconds to remove the blanks and substitute real bullets. Even someone not used to guns could work pretty fast. I'll bet it didn't take you long to put in the blanks."

"No. No, it didn't." Boots shook his head. "I guess somebody might be able to do that without being noticed. We had a real zoo backstage. The spotlights weren't always following the right actors, some of the people were having trouble remembering their lines, a couple of pieces of stage furniture weren't in the right places, the blocking—or whatever you call moving around onstage—was wrong, Mr. Berenger didn't have all his kitchen props, Professor Parsons was afraid the pulleys wouldn't work when Reverend Poole came down from heaven. It was crazy."

His rapid-fire recital went by me so fast that I could barely sort out the incidents. One remained fixed in my mind. "What happened to Hans's kitchen props?"

Boots paused to examine the special that had just been placed before him. It was a huge omelet with mushrooms peeking out, Swiss cheese oozing onto the plate, and an occasional chive. The toast and hashed browns were on separate plates. Boots seemed overwhelmed.

"Gosh," he said. "I thought I'd get ham and eggs."

"Maybe there's ham in the omelet," I pointed out. "You've certainly got eggs."

"Yeah." He uttered a nervous little laugh. "Oh, well."

"The kitchen props?" I urged.

Boots had taken his first bite of omelet. He chewed slowly before nodding approval. "This is good. I don't think there's any ham, though."

I smiled and waited for the answer to my question. If Boots remembered what it was.

He did. "The kitchen part of the set was supposed to have three frying pans, and there was only one. He didn't have enough coffee mugs, either. I don't know where they went."

That struck me as the least of the evening's problems. "Did you help Nat Cardenas with his holster and gun?"

"Nope. He said he could do it himself. I kind of kept my distance from him the whole time. He's kind of standoffish."

Nat, of course, would be guarding his dignity. "Did you see anyone backstage who didn't belong there?"

"Nope," Boots repeated. "I know most of the stagehands and techs. I have classes with them. That's how we all got to help with the play—it was required as part of the course. We take drama from Professor Parsons."

"Someone mentioned seeing a bushy-haired stranger," I remarked.

Boots, who was chewing on toast, shook his head. " 'Course," he said after he'd swallowed, "there could've been somebody. Like I told you, the place was a zoo, especially between acts." He paused. "There was the dog."

"The dog?" I echoed.

Boots nodded again. "Dodo. Dr. Medved's dog. If Dr. Medved was doing something else, he couldn't watch the dog. Don't get me wrong, Dodo's pretty well behaved. Professor Bhuj tried to keep an eye on him, since he was supposed to be her dog—in the play, I mean—but she had other stuff to do, too. Hey!" Boots became animated. "There she is now!" He waved enthusiastically.

I was beginning to feel as if I were in a play, too. Names were dropped; people appeared. Of course it wasn't that strange, given that most of the town's residents had been holed up inside the previous day. Only three restaurants in Alpine served a full breakfast, unless you counted McDonald's Egg McMuffins or Starbucks' pastry.

Clea Bhuj came down the aisle, wearing a self-possessed smile and a fur-trimmed parka. I'd met her a few times and always marveled at her delicate dark beauty. Her parents had emigrated from Bombay shortly after their marriage. Clea had been born and raised in California.

"Ms. Lord," Clea said, holding out a gloved hand to me. "How nice. I haven't seen you in months." She turned to Boots, leaned down, and brushed his cheek with a kiss. "May I?" Clea pointed to the space next to the young man.

"Please!" Boots had bumped his legs on the table as he tried to stand like a gentleman. He blushed but kept smiling and gazed adoringly at Professor Bhuj.

"I couldn't stand staying indoors another minute," Clea announced, flipping back the parka's fur-lined hood. "Ordinarily, I would have left town for the weekend, but I couldn't because of the weather."

I wasn't sure if it was tactful to bring up the subject of a husband, but I did anyway, if in a veiled manner. "I understand you commute to Everett," I said.

"Usually," Clea replied, apparently at ease with my comment. "Sometimes Allan comes here." She smiled again. "He's my husband. He works for the port in Everett."

"Yes," I said. "I heard something about your commute the other day. It's a pain during the winter, isn't it?"

Clea sighed as Boots helped her out of the parka. "It is. But I guess it could be worse. I understand the last two winters haven't been so severe in Alpine. Until now. I hope the river doesn't flood. That could be awful." She patted Boots's arm. "I think it's terrific that you and some of the other students have volunteered to help. Whose idea was it?"

"Um . . ." Boots was blushing anew. "President Cardenas called a bunch of us."

"And you responded." Clea smiled some more. She had the whitest, most perfect teeth I'd ever seen. If she hadn't seemed so pleasant, I would have hated her. "That's very brave. You never know when the river will rise."

"Gosh, no," Boots said, frowning. "When I was a kid, I saw it come all of a sudden in a big roar through the valley. Our whole farm was flooded."

Clea nodded. "That's what I mean. Rivers are unpredictable." She turned to me. "It must be frustrating, Ms. Lord. The paper coming out on Wednesdays means you can't always get on top of breaking news."

I couldn't help but utter a lame little laugh. "How right you are. Unfortunately, most people in Alpine don't realize that we even have a deadline. For example, they'll bring stories in on a Thursday that just have to be in the paper for the weekend."

Clea nodded in sympathy. "It shouldn't be that hard to understand when they get the paper only once a week. It's doubly hard for the students. *The Iron Goat* comes out every two weeks. Believe me, I've had to let Carla Talliaferro cry on my shoulder many times, between stories the paper has missed and . . . other problems."

I could well imagine some of the "problems" Carla had had as adviser to the college newspaper, beginning with its name. Since the high school nickname was the Buckers, some of the students had thought they should keep the logging tradition and call the paper *The Sawyer*. But the more environmentally inclined, particularly among the faculty, had asserted that the name was inappropriate. There had been much debate, spilling over into the town. Timber industry people had picketed the school for a week, but finally a compromise was reached with *The Iron Goat*, a tribute to the nickname for the Great Northern Railroad, the forerunner of our current freight and Amtrak trains.

"I know about some of the situations Carla's encountered," I said. "Of course, being a faculty adviser isn't easy."

"Sometimes not," Clea allowed. "I do get to hear my share of complaints as head of Humanities. Carla, of course, is in our department. She's so vivacious. She must have been a joy to have on the *Advocate*."

If "joy" was running a picture of Reverend Poole upside down or stating that the people Doc Dewey performed autopsies on "were usually dead," then joy had abounded during Carla's tenure at the paper. Thus, I merely smiled and remarked how nice it was that with a young son Carla could work part-time on campus with her husband, Ryan.

"That's true," said Clea, her perfect mouth turning down. "I wish I had that kind of situation. But," she added with another pat for Boots, "there are plenty of compensations. Especially the students."

I put on my most sympathetic face. "How are you holding up, Clea? May I call you that?" I was at sea about whether to call her Professor or Doctor or Your Royal Highness.

"Please do," she replied quickly. "I'll call you . . . Emma, correct?"

"Yes. I don't mean to pry, but I understand that you and Hans Berenger were not only colleagues, but friends."

For a moment, I thought Clea's face shut down. Certainly she was devoid of expression before looking away. "We were both, of course. It's helpful to be on good terms with the dean of students. Being adversaries only results in doing harm to the students and the programs. I've always tried to maintain good relationships with my colleagues."

That wasn't the answer to my original question. "So his death must have hit you quite hard."

"Naturally." Clea looked me in the eye with a mournful expression. "It will be terribly hard to replace Hans. He was an outstanding administrator."

That still wasn't the answer I'd expected. Clea, after all, had badgered Destiny into giving Hans a role in the play. Maybe Clea was merely sucking up to the dean of students. I sensed that under that charming facade she was a political creature.

"Do you believe it must have been an accident?" I inquired after waiting for Clea to order dry whole wheat toast, imitation scrambled eggs, and coffee.

"I try to eat healthy foods," she declared, avoiding a look at what was still left of Boots's gut-busting omelet. "Of course, when you're younger, you can afford to splurge occasionally."

I put the conversation back on track. "I was wondering if you felt that Hans's death was a genuine accident."

"I . . ." She stopped, darting a quick glance at Boots, who had been watching her with pathetic admiration. No wonder he hadn't finished his breakfast. "I have to assume it was. Who on earth would want to kill Hans?" Clea gave a good imitation of a shudder. "I'm sure Boots didn't load real bullets into Dr. Medved's gun. I suppose what happened was that someone else accidentally switched them later in the evening."

"Why," I asked, "would anyone do that?"

Clea sadly shook her head. "You've no idea what sort of confusion reigned before and even during the play. After all, we're amateurs. Someone gave Rey Fernandez the wrong headsets, so he couldn't communicate from the stage to his lighting people in the booth. Dodo was running loose and at one point we couldn't find him anywhere. I mislaid my backpack—Dorothy's backpack, that is. Coach Ripley had to walk off a leg cramp. It was very stressful."

Clea seemed adept at avoiding direct questions. I surrendered. "I'm sure it was," I agreed, sliding out of the booth with bill in hand. "The performing arts are like that. Stressful, I mean." I made my farewells, paid the bill at the register, and went out into the heavy rain.

Confusion seemed to be the key word when it came to what was going on backstage before and during the play. Maybe that could lead to an accident. Or maybe it provided camouflage for premeditated murder.

There had also been confusion—if choreographed—onstage.

That was when I began to wonder if Hans Berenger had actually been the intended victim.

EIGHT

I had stood on the banks of the Tiber River in Rome, a quarter of a mile from Hadrian's Tomb. It was a cool autumn day, with a pale sun reflected off the river's placid waters. I'd gazed upstream at the ancient stone and granite edifice I knew better by another name, Castel Sant' Angelo. It is from there that Floria Tosca leaps to her death in Puccini's opera. Her lover has been shot to death, and she cannot live without him.

For a few moments, I'd reflected on fiction and fact. What was life going to be like without Tom? Then I recalled the other reason—maybe the more imperative one— for Tosca's suicide: She had murdered the villainous chief of police. His death would be avenged by underlings who were chasing Tosca to the edge of the parapet. It was a no-brainer. Under different circumstances, she probably would have muddled through, plunging back into her successful career as an opera singer. Publishing the Advocate *wasn't as glamorous as singing Mozart and Monteverdi, but it was my vocation. I, too, had talent—I'd studied; I'd trained; I'd honed my writing talent over the years. I, too, had an audience and a responsibility to serve it. Suicide is not only morally wrong; it's a gyp. It takes away not only a life but also a gift that serves others.*

❋   ❋   ❋

THE SKYKOMISH IN FEBRUARY WAS NOT PLACID LIKE THE TIBER IN October. Rome was almost three thousand years old; Alpine had yet to celebrate its centennial. The Tiber's surroundings had been civilized for over two millennia; the Sky tumbled among old growth forest and rugged mountainsides. In a little over a decade I'd seen the river change course, cut new channels, erode its banks, take trees and even buildings into its churning waters. The rivers of the West were peculiarly American—changeable and individualistic. I would rather live by any stream, large or small, than a lake or the sea. Somehow, despite the danger, I find hope in rivers.

"It's higher," I said to Wes Amundson as we stood in front of the public storage building. "No new sandbags yet?"

Wes glanced at his watch, which bore the U.S. Forest Service logo. "I don't expect them until after one. We've got a half hour to go."

At least sixty Alpiners lined the river. There were small children and large dogs. Most of the adults and some of the older kids were trying to help, though there was nothing much they could do except pile odd-lot pieces of barricade behind the sandbags. I looked around for Scott but I couldn't see him. I hoped he'd come along in time to get pictures that would tell the story better than words.

"What about those houses on the other side of the river?" I asked. "Will they be evacuated before the river crests?"

"We've already warned them," Wes replied. "They can see for themselves. Some of the folks have already gotten out. But nobody's leaving town in this weather."

I studied the small frame houses that dated from the 1930s.

They'd been built by one of the logging companies for their employees in the days when there was good money in risking life and limb harvesting the forest. The company had been gone for almost twenty years, and the real estate had been sold off. Still, there were at least a few old-timers who lived there. Loggers don't like change. They have pride in their dying profession. Working in the woods isn't just a job. Often logging has been handed down from father to son. They're like clergymen whose religion has been outlawed by the state. They'd rather give up a chance for a better life doing something else than forsake their vocation.

There was no reason for me to stand around waiting for the river to flood. It wasn't as cold as it had been, but it was very wet and generally miserable. I returned to the office to find it deserted. The leaks had been stopped. Kip had done his job.

Instead of going home, I drove to Vida's house on Tyee Street. Her car wasn't there. She'd probably attended services at First Presbyterian before going on to her daughter's home in The Pines development on the other side of town. Maybe I should crash the family party. I didn't like dropping in unexpectedly, so I used my cell phone to call first.

Not surprisingly, Vida answered. "I've been trying to call you," she said before I could utter more than a peep. "What's happening with the investigation? Does Milo know anything yet? He interviewed Roger yesterday—very helpful, I'm sure—but being Milo, and so tight-lipped, Roger and his parents didn't learn anything. My nephew Billy won't—or can't—pass on anything of interest. I'm very frustrated. Where are you?"

I informed Vida that I was sitting in my car in front of the *Advocate*. She asked if the office was underwater. I said not yet.

"It could happen any hour," she declared in ominous tones. "I wonder if I should remove my recipe files."

Since Vida never used notes and kept everything tucked inside her brain, the recipes were the only background she retained in her desk. Frankly, she'd be lost without them. While Vida regularly dispensed meals both simple and exotic, she couldn't cook to save her life. When it came to something as uncomplicated as spaghetti, she put a whole new meaning into *al dente*. Her pasta was so undercooked that a diner risked a broken tooth. It was more like *a dental*, as in a trip to visit Dr. Starr.

"Don't worry about any files," I said. "I doubt it'll get too bad."

"Then come over here right away," Vida commanded. "We must catch up, and I'm staying on for dinner." I heard a voice in the background before Vida spoke again. "Oh, yes—Amy says you're invited, too."

Since it was still early afternoon, I politely declined the invitation, not being keen on staying cooped up in the Hibbert house with Roger for at least four hours. But I did agree to drive straight over.

The Pines is an upscale neighborhood, at least as upscale as Alpine gets—not, of course, counting the Bronsky villa at the other end of town. I arrived to find Vida and the three Hibberts playing Monopoly.

"Look!" Vida exclaimed, pointing to the board. "Roger has both Boardwalk and Park Place! He's building hotels. As usual, he's beating us soundly." She beamed favorably at her grandson, who ducked his head and stuffed his face with cheese balls.

"I surrender!" Ted exclaimed genially as he landed smack on Park Place. "Here, Son, take everything I've got."

Roger slapped money and mortgaged property next to his own fortune. "You're all wiped," he declared. "Give." He held out his beefy hands to his mother and grandmother.

"So cleverly done," Vida said in congratulations as she rose from her chair at the dining room table. "Really, Roger, you're going to become quite a capitalist someday."

Roger scowled at his grandmother. "I want to be an actor. I want to make action movies."

I slid onto the chair that Vida had vacated. "I think that's fascinating," I said. "I didn't know until the other day that you had acting aspirations, Roger."

"Yeah." His small eyes were wary. I'd always sensed that he considered me the Enemy.

"I had an uncle who was an actor," I said. It was true, though Great-Uncle Andy had performed only in amateur theatricals and since he'd lived in Ohio before I was born, the only thing I knew about his acting career was that he'd once played King Lear in a gunnysack.

But Roger evinced no interest in my uncle. Instead, he took another handful of cheese balls, got up from his chair, and wandered into the living room, where Ted had turned on an NBA basketball game. Vida and Amy were putting the Monopoly pieces away. Doggedly I followed Roger.

"Sonics and Lakers," I remarked, standing by Ted's easy chair. Roger was sprawled on the floor, chin on fists, clearly bent on ignoring me. He looked not unlike a beached whale.

"Right," Ted responded.

"Shoot! Three! Three!" Roger exclaimed as one of the Sonics fired a rim rattler from just outside the three-point line. "Awright!" Roger shook a fist as the ball went in.

The teams moved to the other end of the court. "Good D!" I cried, trying to ingratiate myself with the surly kid.

"Yeah, yeah!" Roger shouted. "Foul Shaq!"

"Good plan," I remarked. "He can't make free throws."

Roger didn't respond to my comment. Ted, however, chuckled. "Shaq's like a big cedar," he said. "Have a seat. Make yourself comfortable."

"I should be talking to Vida," I replied. "I'll wait for half time. There's only a couple of minutes to go. I'll just sit here." I dropped down on my haunches next to Roger.

Time-out. Roger shifted restlessly in front of the TV set.

"I guess they're still looking for the bushy-haired stranger you saw at the theater," I said, stretching the manhunt story to emphasize Roger's importance.

He finally turned to look at me. "Yeah? Well, they'd better find that dude. He's a pile of vile."

"You mean because you think he's responsible for Professor Berenger's death?"

"Hell, yes," Roger asserted.

"Son," Ted put in, "mind your language."

I smiled faintly before asking Roger another question: "Do you think you could pick the man out of a lineup?"

"Sure," Roger said, though his attention was focused on three buxom beauties in bikinis peddling beer in a commercial.

"What did you see him doing backstage?"

"Huh?" He paused until the bikini-clad girls gave way to a pair of agile old duffers in an arthritis ad. "The guy was like . . . lurking. You know. Like hanging out, only he was looking around to see if anybody was watching him."

"Furtive?"

"Yeah. Furtive." Roger turned the word over on his tongue as if it were some strange new taste.

"You'd never seen him before?"

"Nope."

The game had resumed. Ted cleared his throat. "Okay, Son, let's see if we can cut it to under ten points before the half."

Apparently, that was my cue to stop interrogating Roger and keep my trap shut. It took five minutes to finish what had become a ninety-second quarter. A parade of free throws and a couple of twenty-second time-outs slowed the game to a crawl.

When the half finally ended, Roger got up and left the room. Maybe Vida had had better luck quizzing her grandson. Wherever Roger had gone, it wasn't into the kitchen. Mother and daughter were seated in the inglenook, drinking tea.

"Where've you been?" Vida asked. "You disappeared after Roger's Monopoly victory."

I explained that I'd joined the guys to catch a basketball game.

Vida saw through the ruse. "Did you question Roger? Did he say anything I couldn't already have told you?"

I shook my head and sat down next to Amy, who had scooted closer to the wall to make room for me. "He hardly said anything. He was watching the game."

"Tea?" Amy interjected.

"I can get it myself," I said. "It's easier for me to get up."

"The cups and saucers are in that cupboard to the left of the stove," Amy informed me. "Would you mind terribly turning the teakettle back on? It's full."

"Sure." The request had been meekly made. Amy and her sisters, Beth and Meg, looked like their mother but had few of her personality traits. I assumed they took after the late Mr. Runkel, who had died several years before I arrived in Alpine.

"I assume you believe Roger," Vida remarked when I sat down again.

I hesitated even as Vida's gray eyes bored into my face. "Why would he lie?" To me, the answer was obvious: The kid wanted to be in the limelight.

Vida, however, took my comment seriously. "I can't think of anyone Roger might want to protect. He's still in high school. He doesn't know many of the college students or faculty."

"What about the townspeople?" I asked. "Like Rita Patricelli and the Reverend Poole and Dr. Medved and Mayor Baugh and Coach Ridley?"

Vida looked askance. "You can't be serious. None of those people could possibly be responsible for what happened to Hans Berenger. Unless . . ." She let her gaze roam around the kitchen's geranium-patterned wallpaper.

"Unless what? Give, Vida," I urged.

Amy was watching both of us with somber interest. I wondered how often she'd seen someone dare to challenge her mother.

Vida sighed. "The only two people you mentioned—and I

notice you left out Ed, who is too lazy and too dim-witted to plot a murder—that Roger knows well are Dr. Medved and Coach Ridley. I'm certainly not saying I think either of them is a killer, but Roger has such a vivid imagination. He might be afraid for them." She looked fondly at Amy. "You know how our dear boy loves his pets. Jim Medved has always done the best he could for them, including Waldo the Snake."

"Yes," Amy said a bit grimly. "Even Waldo."

"Thus," Vida continued, "Roger is fond of Jim. Grateful."

I glanced at Amy, who didn't look so grateful. Maybe it was because of the snake. Or the ferrets. Or perhaps the three pet rats that became twelve and then twenty-seven and finally over fifty in number before Ted insisted on getting rid of them by scaring Roger with threats of Black Plague.

"As for Coach Ridley," Vida resumed, "toward the end of the football season, he started Roger in the last two games, against Sultan and Monroe. Roger was thrilled."

With a one-and-seven record at that point, Rip had thrown in the towel. I gazed at each woman in turn. "Do either of you think Jim or Rip would have a motive for murdering Hans Berenger?"

To my surprise, Vida said it was possible. "Jim wanted the college to train veterinarian assistants. Nat Cardenas—and I understand Hans Berenger as well—insisted there wasn't money in the budget for such a program. As for Rip, he's wanted to quit his coaching jobs at the high school for some time. What with budget cuts, he and Linda Grant are the only coaches for the high school sports teams. Rip and Dixie"—at this point, Vida shuddered—"have even talked of moving away from Alpine if Rip got the right offer. He asked the college for a job in their athletic department, but neither Nat nor anyone else in administration wants to expand beyond intramurals. They're very firm about emphasizing the academic and vocational programs."

I seemed to be out of the loop when it came to college gossip, though I was aware of the de-emphasis on sports. I wondered which of Vida's many relatives worked at or attended the school. Obviously, she had a pipeline into the campus.

I shook my head. "Those aren't motives for murder. Granted, Rip has an explosive temper and Jim is sufficiently methodical to figure out a scheme to kill somebody. What I'm wondering is if—assuming we're dealing with a homicide—Hans was the intended victim."

Amy let out a little gasp. I sensed that her mother didn't let her in on the sleuthing Vida and I had occasionally done to seek truth and justice for our readers.

Vida sipped her tea before responding. "I see what you mean. Such a rumpus in that scene. Everyone moving around the stage. Except Ed, of course."

"The bullet could have been meant for Rip or Jim or even Rey Fernandez as well as for Hans," I pointed out.

"How gruesome!" Amy exclaimed. "Excuse me, Emma, I should ask if Ted or Roger need anything while they're watching the game."

I got up and Amy got out.

"She's squeamish," Vida declared when Amy had left the kitchen. "She was always the most impressionable of our girls. Not to mention that the thought of Roger being in danger must disturb her. It certainly upsets me."

I was confused. "Danger? From who? We're not sure if there *is* a killer. Do you really believe Roger saw a bushy-haired stranger?"

Vida shifted uneasily on the seat cushion. "I can't make up my mind. Either Roger invented this person to draw attention away from Rip and Jim, or he actually saw someone who didn't belong. After all, the sheriff is searching for a stranger, bushy-haired or not."

I frowned. "The APB describes the driver of the car as having a full head of curly hair."

"Oh?" Vida sat up straight, giving me an owlish look from behind her big orange-rimmed glasses. "Well, now! I didn't hear the APB."

I was relating everything I'd done and heard since I'd last spoken to Vida when Amy returned, looking timorous.

"Are you sure you won't stay for dinner, Emma?" she asked. "We're eating around five. On Sundays, we always eat earlier."

The kitchen clock, which was shaped like a coffeepot, informed me that it was a few minutes after three. Knowing that after my late breakfast but no lunch, I'd start getting hungry around four and having nothing better to do, I acquiesced. Thus far, Roger had proved bearable. It was about time. He was graduating from high school in June. Assuming he could forge his name on a diploma.

Vida was looking displeased.

"Unless," I added hastily to Amy, "you don't have enough for a guest."

"Oh, no," she assured me. "I have plenty. I bought a big roast on sale at the Grocery Basket. It's just a matter of adding more beans and potatoes and carrots."

"Of course you're welcome to stay, Emma," Vida put in. "But I am surprised that you didn't update me until now. I feel like an outsider."

"I told you," I said. "I haven't had a chance. For a Sunday, it's been a busy day."

Vida turned to Amy, who was removing the roast from the refrigerator. "Do you need help?"

"Oh, no, Mother," Amy replied a trifle too hastily. "I can manage just fine."

"Then," Vida declared, getting up, "Emma and I are going out for a while. We'll be back well before five."

Dutifully I followed Vida to the front door. Roger had reappeared in the living room, watching the Sonics with Ted. A glimpse at the score informed me that Seattle was down by fifteen. Roger ignored us, but Ted looked up.

"You leaving?" he asked us.

"Only for a bit," Vida replied.

We got into my car, which was blocking Vida's Buick in the driveway. The rain was still coming down, though not as hard. Puddles of melting snow were everywhere. If the temperature dropped to freezing during the night, we could be in for big trouble in the morning.

"Where are we wading?" I inquired of Vida after reversing cautiously down the sloping drive.

"The river," Vida replied. "Go down by the old mill site and Ptarmigan Tract."

I obeyed. It was a short drive, covering only about three blocks. We got out of the car by Alpine Auto Supply, just west of the bridge, which had been closed off. Ptarmigan Tract was on the north side of the river, some fifty feet from where we stood. The river was running high and fast, reaching the sandbags that lined its banks. Some thirty residents were milling around, looking worried.

Vida hailed Rip and Dixie Ridley, who lived in the development.

"So terrifying!" Vida shouted above the roar of the current. "Have you taken precautions?"

Rip cupped his ear. "Huh?"

Vida moved closer and repeated the question.

"What can we do?" Dixie responded, her round pink face plainly showing her distress. "We sent the kids to some friends who live higher up, on Cascade Street."

"This has been one hell of a weekend," Rip said angrily. He glanced at Vida. "Excuse the language. But I can't remember a worse time, except when the Buckers bottomed out three years ago by losing twenty-one games in a row."

"Very unfortunate," Vida murmured, though I doubted that Rip and Dixie heard her over the rushing river. She raised her voice. "Were you and Hans close?"

Rip looked startled. "Berenger? I hardly knew the guy. I don't think I'd exchanged more than ten words with him until we started doing the play. He wasn't what I'd call friendly. Why do you ask?"

Vida attempted to look apologetic. "I was merely trying to gauge the depth of your grief."

"Oh." Rip wore a sheepish expression. "It's a hell of a thing, him getting shot. Sure, I feel bad about it. But to be honest, I'm sorrier about Vince."

"Vince?" Vida echoed. "Who is Vince?"

"My hunting dog," Rip answered as Dixie patted his wide shoulder. "I named him for Vince Lombardi because, like the coach, he's always a winner, especially when it comes to lowland waterfowl."

"What happened to him?" I asked, feeling, as I often do, like Vida's dim-witted sidekick.

Rip shook his head. "He got attacked by a cougar the other day. He'll be okay, but he may not ever be able to hunt. His left hind leg got pretty torn up. I'm going to have to get another dog before hunting season starts this year."

The current was propelling more brush and debris over the banks. Rusty tin cans, a fishing boot, rags that may have once been clothing, a chunk of tire tread, a tennis ball—all decorated the sandbags. The river itself was inching closer to flood stage. Volunteers and gawkers alike began moving farther away. But they didn't leave. I had seen a rushing river rise so fast that it swept up everything in its path—trees, buildings, people. I wondered if we should all take to the high ground.

Wes Amundson and Dustin Fong were talking to each other at the other end of the auto supply building. Another man, who had just gotten out of a truck marked U.S. ARMY CORPS OF ENGI-NEERS, had joined them. I assumed they were assessing the potential danger.

Vida, however, seemed to be ignoring Nature's wrath. "Why," she demanded of Rip, "are you certain that Hans was killed accidentally?"

Rip shrugged. "Because if somebody wanted to kill him, why take that kind of chance? It'd be too damned complicated. Why not shoot him some dark night on campus?"

The coach had a point. It would be less risky to hide in the heavily forested college grounds. Berenger was an administrator. He probably worked long hours.

"Was Nat Cardenas aiming at Hans?" I asked, realizing that while the wind was still strong, the rain had turned into a mere drizzle. Maybe Alpine would be spared. For now.

"Yes," Rip said. "That was one of the messages in the play. Destiny had a pretty big agenda. In Hans's case, his shooting was to show how innocent people get hurt—even killed—when they try to be peacemakers. Or some damned thing."

Vida was wagging a finger at Rip. "Do you swear like that in front of your high school students?"

"Swear?" Rip looked genuinely puzzled. "When did I swear?"

"Ooooh!" Vida swept off her glasses and began to rub her eyes, a sure sign of ultimate frustration. "Really, you don't even realize what a poor example you're setting for young people!"

"Jeez, Vida," Rip said in a peevish voice. "Do you honestly think kids these days don't know every swearword in the book by the time they're eight years old? A *damn* or a *hell* once in a while is pretty tame stuff."

"That doesn't mean it's right," Vida shot back. She wiped the rain from her glasses and put them back on. "Swearing is swearing. You can't expect youngsters to discriminate between the bad words and the very bad words. When Roger stays with me, I don't allow him to watch TV shows with foul language. To my knowledge, Amy and Ted don't swear, and heaven knows I don't. I couldn't believe my ears when I heard my grandson say a certain four-letter word in public Friday night."

Rip turned away. I knew he was trying to suppress his mirth. Dixie, however, smiled kindly at Vida. "It was in the script. He had to say it. After the performance was over—well, maybe he was still in his part. Sometimes, after rehearsals, Rip was still playing a surly logger when he came home. That's acting, Vida dear. It's all make-believe."

Dixie was right, up to a point.

But Hans Berenger wasn't pretending to be dead.

NINE

WE DIDN'T GET MUCH MORE INFORMATION OUT OF RIP RIDLEY. Apparently tired of Vida's reprimands, he walked off to talk to Wes, Dustin, and the man from the Army Engineers truck, who had been joined by another colleague.

Though the river was still threatening to go over its banks, the rain was diminishing by the minute. Dixie had been greeted by one of her neighbors, a woman I recognized only by sight. Vida would know, of course, but I didn't ask. Instead, we started back to my Honda.

We'd barely taken a couple of steps when I spotted Scott Chamoud farther upriver by the bridge. He had his camera and was talking to Jack Mullins. Vida and I took a detour to check in with Scott.

"Got anything?" I asked Scott after we'd greeted the two men.

Scott nodded. "They just closed Highway 2 east of Skykomish. Deception Creek went over the road at the falls. Jack and Bill had to rescue a couple of cross-country skiers. I went with them." He tapped his camera. "I got it all right here, including a really great shot of the water bursting up against the bridge over the creek."

"Skiers?" Vida was aghast. "In this kind of weather?"

"They started out Friday afternoon," Jack put in. Since I'd seen him at Mass he'd changed from his civvies into his regulation all-weather gear. "They got lost during the snowstorm but had some camping stuff with them. They finally found the creek this morning and were following it down to the highway when it flooded. We took them to the hospital. They're pretty weak and beat-up."

Deception Creek was a mile or so from Alpine. "What about the other streams?" I inquired. "Burl and Icicle especially. They go right through town."

"They're high," Jack replied, "but not quite at flood stage. We've asked residents to be prepared for the worst." His expression was ironic. "Dodge's house is only thirty feet from Icicle. I told him he should have bought a boat when Warren Wells tried to sell him one last spring."

Vida surveyed the river's churning gray mass. The water hadn't yet flowed over the steel grids that formed the driving lanes, but the onrushing current had flung all sorts of debris that blocked passage.

"The rain's letting up," she finally said. "The worst of it may be over."

"Let's hope so," Jack said in an uncharacteristically earnest voice. "But it's still February. Chances are, we'll get more snow before the end of the month. It wouldn't be unusual to have a couple of big storms in March, either."

I turned to Scott. "Follow up on those skiers. If all their fingers and toes don't fall off from frostbite, it could make for a feel-good story. We could use one around here."

"Will do," Scott said, flashing me his killer grin. He looked beyond me. "Here comes Mr. Radio."

"Here goes Ms. Newspaper," I said, not in the mood to talk to Spencer Fleetwood.

Vida and I headed back to the Honda.

"We must talk to Rita Patricelli," Vida declared as our boots squelched and squeaked in the slush. "I suspect she knew Hans better than anyone else." Vida glanced at her watch. "We have time to drop by. Dinner won't be ready for an hour."

Unlike me, Vida didn't mind appearing unannounced. But I still had qualms. "Are you sure? Rita was pretty upset."

"All the more reason," Vida retorted as we got into the car. "We can console her. Besides, I must learn who's making the funeral arrangements. We don't know if Hans will be buried before the paper comes out. Tsk, tsk."

After her mother's death a few years earlier, Rita had moved into the family home on Tyee Street, about three blocks from Vida. The Patricellis had raised a large family, and the last time I'd been inside, Polly Patricelli had still been alive. The house had been dark and musty, a rabbit warren of a place filled with worn furniture and enough religious artwork to fill a dozen rectories.

We were met at the door by her brother, Pete, who, like Rita, had put on some weight in recent years. Maybe they'd eaten too many of Pete's large deluxe pies from his Itsa Bitsa Pizza Parlor.

Vida inquired after Rita.

Pete frowned. "She's in bed. She had to have a sedative to calm her down the other night. I don't know when I've seen her so upset."

"Goodness," Vida said softly as she edged across the threshold. "Have you been staying with her the past two days?"

"Off and on," Pete replied, stepping back as the relentless tide that was Vida made it as far as the living room entrance. "I slept over Friday. Our daughter, Marina, stayed with her last night."

"You poor man!" Vida cried, linking her arm through Pete's and leading him to the sofa. "I had no idea Rita was so disturbed! Were she and Hans engaged?"

"Ah . . ." Pete had no choice except to sit down next to Vida, who had all but pulled him onto the sofa. "Well . . . not exactly. But they were . . . uh . . . seeing each other."

I sank down into a soft leather armchair. I barely recognized the living room. The heavy drapes were gone, along with the worn carpets, the religious paintings, and the old furniture. The only thing that seemed the same was the fireplace, though the statues of saints had been replaced by a glass deer with two fawns and an artificial flower arrangement. Rita hadn't shown much flair in redecorating, but at least the house didn't look like a mausoleum.

"What's going on?" The voice came from the second doorway off the hall where Rita stood looking disheveled and surly.

Pete seemed embarrassed. "We have company. Mrs. Runkel and Ms. Lord dropped by to see how you're feeling."

Clutching her pink bathrobe and wearing matching slippers, Rita looked as if she'd be more pleased to see a couple of armed assassins.

"I'm fine," she snapped, standing in front of the fireplace. "I was suffering from shock, that's all. I'm going to work tomorrow."

"Now that's spunk," Vida declared. "I've always said you're a strong person."

As far as I knew, Vida had never said any such thing. She had a number of opinions of Rita, but none of them favorable.

"Really." Rita didn't look convinced. "As far as I'm concerned," she went on, turning toward her brother, "you can go home. If I get hungry, I'll fix some eggs."

Pete started to rise from the sofa, maybe to prove that Vida hadn't nailed him to the cushions. "You sure?"

Rita nodded once. "I appreciate your help, Pete. But I'm fine. I've just never seen somebody killed right in front of me before."

Rita's words evoked images of Tom dying in my arms. If she'd cared for Hans even a fraction of how much I'd loved Tom, I sympathized with her wholeheartedly. But Vida had the floor. I kept quiet.

With a commiserating look for Rita, Vida uttered a mournful sigh. "How true. How sad. And to think that over three hundred people were there to witness such a terrible thing."

Rita took a step toward Vida. "Are you saying I'm the only wimp who was in the theater Friday night?"

Vida clucked her tongue. "You know I'm not. Some people are more sensitive than others. Obviously, you were more deeply affected by the tragedy. Your reaction is most admirable."

Pete had gone out into the kitchen. Rita remained standing, arms folded and hands tucked inside the bathrobe's sleeves. "Vida, I never know *what* you're saying," Rita asserted. "Sometimes I think you speak with—what's the expression?—forked tongue?"

"Oh, Rita!" Vida's expression was shocked. "Would I have come to call if I hadn't been worried about you? And," she added hastily, apparently remembering my mute presence, "Emma as well. Tell me, when are they holding poor Hans's services?"

"They aren't," Rita snapped. "Hans wouldn't have wanted a funeral. He wasn't religious."

"I see." Vida seemed downcast. "So sad when there's no service. Are you making the arrangements?"

Rita shook her head. "The college is handling it. As soon as . . . the body is released by the sheriff, there'll be cremation in San Diego. That's where his wife's ashes are."

"That's so," Vida remarked, though I doubted that she was aware of the aforementioned spouse. "How sad that they both died young. She wasn't more than thirtysomething, was she?"

Rita scowled at Vida. "Julia was thirty-five. You knew about her?"

Vida nodded vaguely. "So tragic."

"Accidents happen." Rita's tone was glib, but she lowered her gaze. "Anyway, that's all I can tell you. Check with Cardenas for the details if you're going to write up an obituary."

"Of course," Vida responded. "Hans was part of the community. He'd been here for some time."

"Excuse me," I said, all but raising my hand to be recognized. "What kind of accident was it? The one that killed Mrs. Berenger, I mean."

Rita shook her head again. "I don't know. Hans couldn't talk about it. Julia was a topic to be avoided."

"No children?" I inquired.

"No." Rita's lips grew tight.

"If you're sure you're all right," Vida began as she stood up, "we'll go. But if there's anything we can do for—"

"There isn't," Rita broke in. "I'll be fine."

I pulled myself out of the deep leather chair. "By the way, did you notice anybody backstage Friday night who didn't seem to belong?"

Rita hesitated. "Now that you mention it, there was some guy I hadn't seen before," she said. "Fairly young, dark. I didn't pay much attention. I was already in my part."

Vida had stopped in the doorway between the living room and the hall. "Did you tell the sheriff?"

"No. It didn't seem important. I figured he was a college student. Frankly, I didn't know most of the kids who were involved in the play." She frowned. "What are you saying? This guy was an outsider? How come? You think a hit man showed up to kill Hans? That's crazy."

"Not exactly," Vida said with a sharp glance for me, "but it would appear that only you and one other person took note of this man. Would you describe him as 'bushy-haired'?"

Rita came close to cracking a smile. "He *had* hair," she said. "It was dark. But *bushy* might be pushing it."

"Did you notice what he was doing?" I asked. "Or recall exactly when you saw him?"

"Right before the play started," Rita answered, "but I didn't pay much attention. He was just hanging around, I think. As I mentioned, I was into my part as Angela the waitress."

"Of course." Vida gave Rita her Cheshire cat smile. "Most interesting. You take care of yourself, Rita."

"Well," I remarked when we were back in the car, "Roger's credibility may be improving."

"Twaddle," Vida retorted. "I never doubted him. Do you think he'd make something up?"

"You said yourself he might have misguidedly been trying to protect Jim or Rip."

"That doesn't seem to be the case, does it?" Vida was smug. We'd reached Alpine Way before Vida spoke again. "Hans had a scar."

"He did?"

Vida nodded. "On his forehead. I noticed it when he was hired and the college sent us a publicity photo. You couldn't see it from the audience Friday. Stage makeup would hide it."

It took me a minute to figure out what Vida was getting at. "Are you saying that Hans and his wife—Julia—were in an auto accident and he survived, but she didn't? That maybe the accident was Hans's fault and he felt guilty about her death?"

"Or merely surviving," Vida replied as we turned off Alpine Way to enter The Pines. "Often, survivors have a terrible sense of guilt when they're involved in a fatal tragedy. They can't understand why they're still alive and the other person—especially a loved one—is dead."

"You're jumping to conclusions," I noted. "Hans may have fallen off his bike when he was ten. You don't know how he got that scar."

"Admittedly," Vida said as we pulled into the Hibberts' sloping driveway. "But it's a thought."

It was the kind of thought I would have easily dismissed. Except that it came from Vida.

I must confess that I didn't sparkle as a dinner guest. Vida was full of praise for Roger's powers of observation; Amy chattered on about whether or not she should host the family Easter dinner, since the holiday fell early and who knew what the weather might be like in Alpine at the end of March? Ted, when he got a word in edgewise, commented on a study he was doing with the department of forestry for better harvesting of timber. Roger's contribution consisted mostly of grunts and belches.

The rain had stopped by the time I went home at a little before seven. My log cabin looked dark and forlorn. But I could get the Honda into the carport, which meant I didn't have to wade through the puddles and rivulets that had taken over my property.

I'd changed into my robe and was looking through the TV schedule when I heard someone at the door. A squint through the peephole showed Spencer Fleetwood standing on the porch.

"I'm not wearing my hostess gown," I said as I let him in.

Spence shrugged. "No problem. Except that's one ugly bathrobe."

"Thanks," I said with a grimace. He was right. I had two robes. The other one was lush crimson velvet that hung in sensuous folds from a mandarin collar. I hadn't worn it since Tom died. The robe I was wearing had seen much service. The cuffs were frayed; the hem sagged in places; the once electric blue fabric had suffered a serious power outage. But if it was good enough to wear in front of Milo Dodge, it was more than good enough for Spencer Fleetwood.

"Have a seat," I said, waving at the nearest easy chair. "Can I get you something to drink? A hot buttered rum, maybe?" I still had a dab of the mix left in the fridge.

"That sounds just right," Spence replied, sitting down and maneuvering the chair closer to the fire I'd built as soon as I got home.

In the kitchen I took a shortcut, using the microwave instead of waiting for the teakettle to heat. Three minutes later, I was settled back on the sofa, mug in hand.

"Is the smoking lamp lit?" Spence asked, pulling out a pack of his expensive imported cigarettes.

"Oh . . . sure." I reached into the end-table drawer to retrieve the ashtray I kept for Milo. And for me, in my weaker moments.

Spence proffered the gold-on-black cigarette box, but I declined. "How come you're not at the station?" I asked.

"The river's dropping," he said, batting at the cigarette smoke to send it in the direction of the fireplace. "Rey Fernandez is in charge for this shift. It's getting colder, so nobody expects any big problems until the morning commute programming. I'll take over then."

"That's good news for now," I said, keeping an eye on a cedar log that was throwing sparks onto the hearth. "But if it freezes up, driving's going to be awful in the morning."

"Highway 2's still closed," Spence noted. "A bunch of skiers got stranded at the summit. The Red Cross sent a couple of buses from Wenatchee to take them out on the eastern slope, via Leavenworth and Blewett Pass to I-90."

"Anybody from around here?" I inquired.

Spence shook his head. "City types. Not attuned to nature like the locals."

I sipped my hot buttered rum and looked straight at Spence. "You didn't come here to discuss the weather."

Spence flashed his white, white teeth in the grin that always made him look slightly feral. "Right. I came to gossip."

"Huh?" I was surprised.

"Look." He set the cigarette in the ashtray and leaned forward, hands on knees. *Mr. Earnest,* I thought. What now? "I assume," he continued in his full, mellow radio voice, "you're doing your usual 'let's-get-to-the-bottom-of-this' sleuthing with regards to Hans Berenger's death."

"Journalists always seek Truth," I said, deliberately sounding pompous.

"Right, right." His expression was amused. "I don't have that luxury. Just keeping the station on the air takes up most of my time and energy. In many ways, I'm a one-man operation. And, of course, I don't have Vida Runkel."

"True," I conceded.

"Which is why I'm here." Spence turned his head to clear his throat, no doubt an acquired habit from not making extraneous noises into a microphone. "Having been present when Berenger was shot, I feel an obligation to help sort this out. But I can't focus on it. So my contribution is to give you what information I have. It may be worthless. The he said/she said stuff isn't my forte anyway. That's women's work. Females seem to have a knack for sorting out the wheat from the chaff."

I think it was a compliment. "So who said what?"

Spence sat back in the chair and took a puff on his cigarette. "Let's start with generalities. Rehearsals were often rife with contentiousness. I've done amateur theatrics before, and there's always chaos and disagreement and warring personalities. But this was different. There was an undertone I couldn't quite pin down."

Ed had made a similar statement, but I hadn't taken him seriously. Maybe he had sensed something gone awry. If so, I trusted Spence's interpretation more than I did Ed's. "No outright animosities?" I asked.

"Oh, yes, there were plenty of those." Spence paused for a quaff from his drink. "Destiny fought with almost everybody except Reverend Poole. And Nat Cardenas. I suppose she didn't dare challenge him because he's the boss. But it was clear that Cardenas wasn't comfortable being in the play. I assume he felt he had to do it to promote the college."

"It seemed beneath his dignity," I allowed.

"That script was beneath Dodo's dignity," Spence said. "Even a dog shouldn't have had to perform in that piece of junk."

"Other than blatant self-promotion, why did *you* do it?"

He chuckled. "Vanity."

His candor surprised me. "No kidding."

"Rey Fernandez asked if I'd like to be the narrator," Spence explained. "Destiny had mentioned the idea to him. I hadn't read the script yet. I decided that if a narrator was required, they might as well have a pro. Who else?"

The question was so artlessly posed that I had to smile. "Well, you're definitely that."

Spence shrugged. "I was ripe for the picking. After all the troubles with my family and the station getting blown up, I needed to do something off-the-wall. At the time, it seemed like a welcome diversion."

I softened at Spence's reference to the tragedies he'd lived and relived the previous September. I'd seen a different side of him then. Vulnerable. Guilt-ridden. Close to the breaking point. But ultimately, undaunted. "I understand," I said quietly.

"Yes." He stared at me for a long moment. "Yes. You do."

The silence that fell between us was painful but not awkward. Spence broke it by tapping the coffee table and making a *rat-tat-tat* noise. "And now back to the news," he said in his radio voice.

I smiled. "I'm all ears."

"So we've got all these actors and techs and hangers-on at the rehearsals. Some of Destiny's students didn't take an active part, but they had to attend all the pre-performance doings in order to get credit for the course. That's how Rey got roped in, though he figured he'd enjoy it. He's serious about going into radio or TV someday. So Destiny's being a control freak, which doesn't sit well with the cast members. It's clear that she and Hans can't stand each other, but then Hans isn't—wasn't—Mr.

Lovable." Spence was delivering his information as if he were racing the hands of a big clock in the studio. "The only two people Hans didn't seem to despise were Rita and Cardenas. He even snubbed the reverend and the mayor. At one point, the ornery S.O.B. tried to kick Dodo. He and Medved got into it over that, but Jim's your basic nonviolent type and I doubt Hans was used to taking disagreements out into the alley."

Spence paused for breath and another sip of his grog.

"I heard Clea insisted that Hans have a part in the play," I put in. "Do you know why?"

"Why she insisted or why he agreed to do it?" Spence frowned. "Campus politics on her part. Perversity on his. I heard he wanted to play the sheriff, but Nat outranked him on the faculty A-list."

"None of this sounds like a motive for murder," I remarked.

"No. It sounds like ordinary pettiness and backbiting." Spence lit another cigarette. "But sometimes those traits are symptomatic of deeper, more sinister feelings."

"Are you saying you don't think Hans's death an accident?"

Spence exhaled and shook his head. "God, no. Jim Medved is meticulous, careful. He'd never put real bullets into that gun. Thus, the shooting of Hans Berenger was premeditated murder."

I had the frightening feeling that Spence was right and repressed a shudder. But there remained the problem of the victim. "So it was Hans who was meant to die? In the play, I mean."

Spence's expression was wry. "Of course. They didn't ad-lib the last part of the performance. In rehearsals, Destiny kept reminding Nat to aim in Hans's direction, though not straight at him. Even blanks can do damage. But in the heat of the performance, Nat turned into a real sharpshooter."

"So everyone involved knew Hans would get shot," I mused, then leaned forward to check Spence's mug. "I'm out of buttered rum mix. Can I get you something else?"

"No thanks. I should be on my way, just in case the temperature drops fast and ice starts to form."

When Spence rebuilt the station last fall, he'd also erected a small house on the same property. I'd never been inside, but the boxlike exterior was unimaginative and austere. Basically, it was a wood-frame structure that replicated the concrete radio headquarters. It struck me that Spence hadn't wanted a home, just a place to eat and sleep.

I asked him if he'd seen the phantom stranger. Spence evinced mild surprise. "Not that I recall," he said, "but I was busy when I wasn't onstage. Studying my lines, helping the techs, especially the sound guys—a giraffe could've showed up and I might not have noticed."

"What about Rita?" I asked, suddenly recalling her lunch with Spence at the ski lodge.

He chuckled. "I was wondering when you'd get to that. How was your tête-à-tête with Nat Cardenas?"

"Touché," I responded. "It was all campus politics sandwiched in between self-glorification and feigned humility."

"Sounds about right," Spence murmured. "Rita was doing her Chamber of Commerce thing, and I was trying to get some co-op ads out of her. Putting noncompeting members under one umbrella, as in all the car-related businesses or services such as insurance, investments, and so forth. She hedged. Rita has no vision."

"That was it?"

Spence's dark eyes twinkled. "Up until she nudged me with her knee."

"True or false?"

"True. I ignored the nudge and asked how Hans was getting along. The knee went away, but the question didn't faze her. She said he was fine—couldn't I tell that from being around him at rehearsals? I said not really, he wasn't an outgoing kind of guy. Rita said he was deep." Spence stopped and grinned. "I told you there would be a he said/she said thing somewhere."

"What else did Rita say?" I prompted.

"She insisted that Hans was a very positive person. In fact, he was going to buy a farm this side of Gold Bar."

I was incredulous. "A farm?"

Spence nodded once.

"With pigs and chickens?"

He shrugged. "I didn't ask. Farmer Hans didn't sound right to me."

I agreed. "Was this to be their honeymoon hideaway?"

Spence shrugged again.

"It's close to Alpine," I said. "Fifteen miles, more or less."

"Depending on how far off the highway it is." Spence didn't seem much interested. Of course, with Hans dead, it was a moot point.

Yet I couldn't quite leave it alone. "A farm," I muttered as Spence stood up and started to put on his hooded fleece-lined jacket. "Property's no longer so cheap along that part of the Stevens Pass corridor."

"Ah!" He wagged a finger at me. "You really are sleuthing, aren't you?"

"I'm seeking Truth," I said with a straight face.

"Go for it." He opened the door himself. A heavy fog was settling in over the town. Damp, cold air rushed inside the house. Spence moved onto the porch and stopped. "I've never understood if you're helping Dodge or competing with him. Which is it?"

"Good question," I retorted. "I'll let you seek that particular Truth."

Spence opened his mouth to say something, thought better of it, and started on his way. He didn't speak again until he was at the door of his Beamer.

"Actually," he called out to me, "you figure it out. Thanks for the hospitality. And tune in tomorrow to KSKY for all the news that's not fit to print until Wednesday."

Black ice was the first obstacle to overcome Monday morning. It took me twenty-five minutes instead of the usual five to negotiate the Honda through what was left of the snow and the few clear patches of pavement. I could have walked, but I feared falling down. If an accident was going to happen, I wanted some automotive armor to protect me.

My usual parking place in front of the *Advocate* was taken. In fact, the black Lincoln Town Car took up two places, despite the diagonal white stripes that had been cleared of snow and slush on Front Street. I found a spot toward the end of the block. As long I was that far from the front entrance, I walked toward the river to see how much it had dropped overnight.

The current no longer reached the sandbags. I estimated that the Sky had gone down almost a foot in the past sixteen hours. The thermometer in my carport had registered at just above thirty-two degrees when I left home.

The fog hadn't completely lifted, but I knew that ominous clouds hid overhead.

When I entered the *Advocate* building through the rear entrance, I heard something else that was ominous: A shrill female voice resounded from the newsroom. Vida retorted in anger. With a heavy sigh, I opened the door to see who was causing the commotion.

With the aid of her sticks Thyra Rasmussen stood near Vida's desk. An embarrassed Henry Bardeen hovered by the main door. Vida was also on her feet, fists on hips. Scott wasn't there; Leo was pretending that he wasn't.

"I repeat," Vida said, perhaps as much for my benefit as for Thyra's, "no one dictates what's printed in the *Advocate*." Her voice rose again. "Especially no one from Snohomish."

"Be that way," Thyra snarled. "You're very stupid if you think leaving out *my* response to what happened in *my* theater is good journalism. It's censorship, that's what it is."

I realized that the Lincoln Town Car parked haphazardly in

front of the office belonged to the ski lodge. It was rarely used, being reserved for a few VIPs who came to ski at the summit and stayed at the lodge.

"Hold it," I interjected. "What's the problem?"

Thyra jerked around to stare at me. "You. Vida's stooge. Didn't you just hear what I said?"

"I did. Do you have a written statement?"

"Certainly." Thyra waved one of her sticks at Vida's desk. "She has it."

Vida picked up the single sheet of paper and tossed it in Thyra's direction. "I don't want it."

Thyra scowled at the floor where the paper lay near one of her sticks. Then, as Henry hurried to pick up the statement, Thyra turned to me. "You see? Do you call that journalism? Do you call that wretched woman a journalist?"

"I call her my House & Home editor," I replied quietly. "Unless your statement contains recipes or pruning tips, you should not have given it to Vida. You should have given it to me."

As if on cue, Henry thrust the paper at me. "Here, Emma. If you'd been here, I'm sure Mrs. Rasmussen would've—"

I cut the ski lodge manager off with a wave of my hand. "That's fine, Henry. I'm sorry I was late. Driving was treacherous."

"I know," Henry replied with a swift, hostile glance at Thyra. "We had to come all the way from the lodge."

I looked at the single-spaced typewritten page.

"Mrs. Rasmussen dictated her statement to Heather," Henry said, referring to his daughter.

I nodded. "I'll read through this and decide how to use it," I said to Thyra, then avoided Vida's blazing stare. "Thank you both for going to so much trouble."

"No trouble at all," Thyra retorted. "When Mr. Rasmussen and I had a real chauffeur, he knew how to drive in any kind of weather."

"Easy to do when he's driving a horse and buggy," Vida said in an angry voice. "Don't you dare leave here until you apologize, Thyra Rasmussen!"

Thyra's head snapped back. "For what? For saying you're not a journalist? It's true, isn't it? The only reason Marius Vandeventer hired you was because you had all the dirt on everybody in this silly little town. And he felt sorry for you because your crazy fool of a husband had gotten himself killed and left you with those three ugly daughters."

The old girl had gone too far. Vida came out from behind her desk to stand within six inches of the other woman. "See here, you miserable hag, if you want to discuss children and grandchildren, let's start with yours. Take Einar Jr., for example, who lies six feet under because—"

Thyra let go of the sticks and put her hands to her ears. "Stop!" she screamed. "Stop, stop, stop!" Her face turned purple and she crumpled to the floor before Henry could catch her.

"My God!" Henry cried, on his knees. "Mrs. Rasmussen, are you all right?"

Leo finally emerged from behind his computer and gazed at the old lady's motionless form. Vida stood in place, her face rigid and her fists clenched at her sides.

"She's faking," Vida said, barely moving her lips.

"I don't think so," Leo said, reaching for the phone. "If you ask me, Vida, I think you just killed her."

TEN

LEO DIALED 911 BUT INFORMED THE OPERATOR THAT THYRA RAS-
mussen was dead as a dodo. Henry, who was schooled in first
aid as part of his responsibilities in caring for guests at the ski
lodge, had already pronounced Thyra beyond help. Beth Raf-
ferty, who handled the county's emergency calls, told Leo it
would be best to call Al Driggers at the mortuary.

"I'm guessing apoplexy," Vida said, returning to her usual
spot. "It would be most fitting. But don't phone Al. Thyra
wouldn't want him to touch her. Try Dawson-Purdy or whatever
they call themselves nowadays in Snohomish."

"What about her son and his wife?" I said. "Shouldn't we
notify them?"

Vida looked at her watch. "Yes—it's only nine o'clock. Harold and Gladys should still be sober." A malevolent gleam sur-
faced in her gray eyes. "I'll call them myself."

"It's not Dawson and Purdy anymore," Leo said, looking up
from the Snohomish County directory. "It's called Purdy and
Walters with Dawson."

"That sounds rather complicated," Vida declared. "For all I
care, you can tell the dog pound to pick her up."

I, too, was growing impatient. "We can't leave her here lying in the middle of the newsroom floor. On any other Monday, a half-dozen people would've trooped in here by now."

At that moment, both Scott and Ginny came through the door. Scott stopped in his tracks and Ginny let out a little cry.

"Don't worry," Vida said to them. "She's harmless. Now."

Leo explained what had happened, while Henry spoke to me in low tones. "I feel responsible. I should never have agreed to bring her here. It's a wonder we didn't both get killed coming down that narrow, winding road from the lodge."

"People don't—didn't—say no to Thyra," I reminded him. "The problem is, she has to be moved. Pronto."

Henry studied his surroundings. "Do you have an extra room? Storage, perhaps?"

"Holy Mother of God," I murmured. "Not really."

Leo, who had finished his recapitulation for my other staffers, swiveled around in his chair to look at Henry. "Why not put her in the Town Car? Seriously, there's a certain dignity to one of those babies. If it was good enough to bring her here, it's good enough to take her away."

Vida, looking rather gleeful, hung up the phone. "That was the bereaved son. They'll drive down from Sultan to make the arrangements in Snohomish and have the funeral home there collect the body at the ski lodge."

"Good," I said. "Meanwhile—"

"Leo's right," Henry interrupted, apparently having been lost in thought. "If he and Scott can help me, we'll put Mrs. Rasmussen in the car."

"The trunk would be better," Vida remarked.

I ignored her. "Then go ahead. Kip MacDuff should be here, but he was going to the computer store to get some new software this morning."

"We'll manage," Henry assured me. The three men immediately began their sorry task.

"It's awful," Ginny said with a shudder. "I've never seen a person who just died. Except Uncle Cord, of course."

I'd never asked Ginny about Uncle Cord, whose name was only mentioned in the most morose situations. I wasn't going to ask her now. She filled her coffee mug and returned to the front office.

It didn't take long to gather up Thyra's body. Scott and Henry carried her out of the room while Leo took her sticks. The emerald eyes of the Egyptian temple dog handles seemed to spit green fire. The old lady had a purse, but because she'd needed to free her hands, it was on a long slim chain around her neck. I said a silent prayer before facing Vida.

"You really are hard-hearted sometimes," I declared.

Vida looked me straight in the eye. "That woman spent a lifetime causing misery for other people. You know that's so. And frankly, your lack of support just now didn't help my disposition."

I was taken aback. "What do you mean?"

"You were far too polite with her after she insulted me. Then, when she and I truly got into it, you just stood there like a cedar stump."

"I never had a chance to get a word in edgewise," I asserted. "Before Thyra collapsed, I was trying to keep a lid on things, if only to get rid of her."

Vida, chin on palm, looked away. "Perhaps."

"Hey, come on," I said. "I walk in the door and hear what sounds like a couple of dueling harpies. For all I knew, there was an innocent bystander or two in the newsroom. How would you like a 'Scene Around Town' item for your gossip column that was about a scene here in the *Advocate*?"

Vida sighed. She was looking at me again and her expression was less agitated. "You see? Thyra was nothing but a troublemaker. Even in death, she causes trouble between the two of us."

I smiled wanly at Vida. "No, she doesn't. Let's forget about it. We've got work to do."

As the old-timers in Alpine would say, "Talk's cheap, but it takes money to buy good whiskey." I was in no mood to settle in at the desk as if this were any other Monday morning. A woman had died just a few yards from my swivel chair. Even now, with my office door open, I could see Leo and Scott crossing the spot on the floor where Thyra Rasmussen had so recently expired.

"Damn!" I murmured, forcing myself to look at the items on my desk. Thyra was old; she was mean; she was probably the most self-centered woman I'd ever met. She hadn't mellowed over the years, but I've never believed that people do. They soften a bit around the edges, maybe. But basically, they become more of what they always were. If Thyra had really died of apoplexy because she couldn't get her own way, that seemed an appropriate way for her to exit this world. Vida had been unkind and callous, but she and her mother had suffered at Thyra's grasping hands. Still, I hated to think that Vida might believe she'd finally gotten her revenge on the old bag.

But I'd been right the first time: There was definitely work to be done. My conscience prodded me to call Spencer Fleetwood and tell him about the death in our newsroom. The irony of being scooped on my own premises rankled. I'd wait to see if he could ferret out the story by himself, like any good journalist.

It was impossible to erase the image of Thyra Rasmussen's corpse, but I had to finish the tasks at hand. At the top of the agenda was tending to the phone calls that Ginny had taken before I arrived. The first was from Mayor Baugh. Grimacing, I called him back at his office in the courthouse.

"We dodged a bullet," Fuzzy announced, using a phrase that seemed typically inappropriate, considering the recent shooting death. "The flood danger seems to have abated."

"For now," I hedged. "What can I do for you?"

There was a slight pause. "I was right there most of the time."

"Where?"

"At the river." Fuzzy cleared his throat. "Indeed, that handsome young man who works for you was kind enough to take some pictures of me helping with the sandbags."

Gasbag meets Sandbag, I thought. It would make a great cutline. Except we couldn't use it. Obviously, the mayor wanted to take credit for sparing the town from a watery grave.

"I haven't seen any of the photos yet," I said in a noncommittal voice. "We should have a full front page, between Hans Berenger's death and the flood danger." I didn't mention Thyra. The last thing I wanted was to have Fuzzy poking around the office and asking a trillion questions.

"Well," the mayor drawled, "just make sure when you choose your pictures that you give credit where credit is due."

"I always try," I replied, again sounding noncommittal.

"I know you do, Miss Emma. By the way, did I see a very fine Town Car pull up by the newspaper? The window in the second-floor men's room looks out on your headquarters, don't you know?"

"I didn't know that," I said. "I've never been in the men's room at the courthouse."

Fuzzy chuckled, all warm marmalade trickling over a baked yam. "Now who could be riding around Alpine in such a fancy automobile?" he inquired.

"You know that Town Car as well as I do," I retorted. To distract him, I went on the attack: "Say, Fuzzy, do you really think Hans Berenger's death was murder?"

"What?" The mayor was taken aback, as I'd intended. "Now, Emma, you know that in my position I can't take controversial stands. It wouldn't be right for me to say what I think."

"Oh," I said, feigning disappointment. "I thought you'd

want to make a statement. You know—as the community's civic leader."

The appeal to Fuzzy's vanity worked. Sort of. "Why, yes indeed," he replied. "A statement. Though not controversial. Let me think."

I considered starting a Dickens novel and waiting for Fuzzy to interrupt Chapter Three before he issued his official words on the Berenger death. But he surprised me.

"It is with great regret," he began slowly, "that as mayor of this fine community, I mourn the loss of an outstanding educator in the untimely demise of Hans Berenger. He leaves behind him a . . ." Fuzzy paused. "What's the word? Like inheritance."

I was briefly stumped. "You mean *legacy*?" I finally offered.

"Yes, yes, a legacy of helping young people go out into the world better equipped to meet the challenges of the twentieth century. How's that?"

"Fine, Fuzzy, but it's the twenty-first century."

"Oh. So it is. My, how time flies!"

As a statement, it would have to do. "Did you know Hans very well?" I asked after entering Fuzzy's quote on my computer.

"Well now, I can't rightly say we were *close*. Hans wasn't one to seek out new friends. Though," the mayor added hastily, "I would have been happy to call him a friend. Educators are special people. The future of this fine city and this great nation rests on the shoulders of the Young. I've said it before and I'll say it again. You may use that as well, Emma."

I already had, possibly a half-dozen times when I'd been stuck covering the mayor's speeches at civic occasions. "Thanks, Fuzzy. I appreciate your . . . input."

"Life's a funny old thing," Fuzzy said in a musing tone. "When one door closes, another one opens."

"What?"

The mayor chuckled. "It seems strange. You see, Hans had

put in a bid on some property down the highway a piece." He stopped speaking, then lowered his soft southern voice to a point where I could barely hear him. "This is off the record now, you understand, Emma darlin'?"

I assured him I did, though I knew I was in for one of the mayor's long-winded spiels.

"Hans was looking to buy some land and so were we. Now don't get me wrong—my bride and I don't plan on moving from Alpine. But Irene gets a notion now and then to do something besides being Mrs. Mayor. She's the boss, as I always tell folks. 'The mayor's mayor'—that's what I call my Irene."

My ear was getting sore and I had other things to do. "So what does she have in mind?" I prodded.

"Puppies," Fuzzy responded. "You know how she's always loved our doggies, Mutt and Jeff. Well, they're up in years now—and so are we." The mayor chuckled some more. "Anyway, the Kruegers down the road are selling out and moving to Arizona. They've had their property on the market since right after Thanksgiving, but there wasn't any action until lately. I can't think why they'd want to sell out, but they say Arizona will be better for their arthritis."

I vaguely recalled the Kruegers' name. There was a sign on the highway at their gate that read: KRUEGERS' KENNELS, with a drawing of a Labrador retriever. At least that's what I'd guessed as the animal's breed, not being a dog lover.

"I never knew if they were breeders or boarders," I remarked. "I think Carla did a story on them several years ago, but I don't remember much about it." Except, of course, for the clumsy writing that had implied that Mrs. Krueger was a bitch. Carla had somehow gotten the female owner and the female dog confused in her sentence structure.

"For many years, the Kruegers bred dogs as well as boarded them," Fuzzy explained, "but when they hit their eighties about four years ago, they concentrated on the breeding. German shepherds, to be exact, with some of their pooches included in the sale. Anyway, that's right up Irene's street, since that's what Mutt and Jeff are. We were all set to buy the place when poor old Hans upped his offer. Now I guess the coast is—sadly—clear."

Irene's desire to branch out was understandable. If nothing else, it would get her away from Fuzzy on a regular basis. "I'd heard it was a farm," I said.

"It was, way back," Fuzzy informed me. "Marty Krueger's dad raised dairy cows. But when Marty and Jan took over the place, Jan wanted to turn it into a doggy spot. She's like Irene, crazy about the pooches."

"Let me know when you actually buy the property," I said. "Vida would probably like to do a story for her page."

"I most certainly will," Fuzzy promised. "You good folks will be the first to hear."

"Thanks," I said, looking up as Milo Dodge arrived to rescue me. "The sheriff's here, Fuzzy. I'd better talk to him."

After hanging up, I rubbed at my tired ear and tried to smile at Milo.

"Fuzzy," I said.

The sheriff needed no further explanation.

"What's up?" he asked, sitting down across from me. "A call came through from here for the medics, but it was canceled. Did somebody fall into a snowbank?"

I brushed my long bangs out of my eyes. "Thyra Rasmussen dropped dead in the newsroom."

Milo looked flabbergasted. "No shit!"

I nodded for emphasis. "She was beyond help. Henry Bardeen took her away in the ski lodge's Town Car."

The sheriff had turned around in his visitor's chair, staring out into the newsroom as if he could see Thyra falling to the floor. "Jesus! What happened?"

Keeping my voice down so that Vida's antenna-like ears

couldn't hear, I related the sad story. "Thyra must have been close to a hundred," I concluded. "Between the quarrel this morning and the disaster at her theater Friday night, I suspect she was at the end of her tether."

Milo had turned back to face me. "Not to mention all the family troubles she's had in recent years. I would've thought she'd consider the college campus bad luck after her son got murdered in the RUB. I kind of wondered why she decided to build a theater on the campus."

Einar Rasmussen Jr. had been stabbed to death in the student union building that bore his name. The fledgling college had wanted to honor him for his generous donations. But despite the tragedy and the havoc it had raised with other Rasmussen family members, Thyra was tough as a bull cook's steak. Somehow, she had managed to rebound.

"The old girl was gutsy, I'll grant her that," I remarked, tossing Fuzzy's phone memo into the wastebasket. "What's new on the homicide and missing persons front?"

Milo looked pained. "Not a hell of a lot. We checked with the car's owner, who told us it'd been stolen sometime Friday, which makes sense."

"Where was it stolen?" I asked.

"At the Alderwood Mall north of Seattle," Milo replied. "The woman—her name's Allison Burke—wasn't in the Seattle directory because she lives a couple of miles past the city limits, in what's now called Shoreline. Naturally, she's mad as hell."

"But doesn't know who might have stolen the car?"

Milo gave me a withering look. "Hell, no. The Shoreline cops and the King County sheriff's office are working on the case, but nobody expects much to come of it. As for our APB, it's turned up a big fat zero except for the usual cranks, who say they saw a bushy-haired stranger sitting on a telephone pole or soaking in their bathtub."

"You figure he's left the area?"

Milo shrugged. "What else? He steals a car, goes for a joyride, runs off the road into the river, stops for a beer, and gets chased by the cops. Would you stick around and wait for the Welcome Wagon?"

I frowned. "Hold it, Milo. What if he's the guy who showed up at the theater Friday night? As it turns out, Roger isn't the only one who saw someone he didn't recognize. And why would a car thief take a so-called sixty-mile joyride up Highway 2 during the dead of winter? Why turn off at Alpine? Wouldn't you figure he had a purpose?"

The sheriff's expression was droll. "He was running out of gas. The gauge registered on E."

I shook my head. "It still doesn't make sense. I think the driver came to Alpine for a purpose. Have you checked with King and Snohomish counties to see if someone matching that description has been reported as missing?"

Milo looked annoyed, as he always did when I hinted he might be derelict in his duties. "Hell, yes. There are at least two dozen young dark-haired white males missing from those highly populated counties. I doubt that our guy is among them. Let's face it, he's only been gone from wherever he belonged for two full days. If anybody cares enough to notice, they'd probably figure he'd taken off for the weekend."

The sheriff had a point. "Okay," I said with a sigh, "I'll buy that. But if he's got a job, his employer may want to know where he is."

"For all we know," Milo said, standing up, "he's at work right now."

I was silent for a moment. "He wasn't in the car when it went over the bank, was he?"

"No."

"Was he trying to ditch it or did he forget to set the hand brake?"

"How should I know?" Milo rubbed at the back of his head.

"Jeez, Emma, quit playing detective. Don't you have a news-paper to put out?"

I did. "Sorry," I said halfheartedly. "I'm just trying to get things clear in my mind before I start writing. Having a corpse decorate the office has put me off my feed."

Milo was backing out of my cubbyhole, lowering his head so that his Smokey the Bear hat didn't get knocked off. He glanced over his shoulder. "That'll do it to you." He rapped his knuckles on the door frame. "See you around."

I went back to work. Shortly before eleven o'clock, Spencer Fleetwood showed up. Instead of coming directly to see me, he stopped at Vida's desk. I assumed he'd heard about Thyra. The next thing I knew, he had a microphone in front of my House & Home editor and appeared to be interviewing her. Grimacing, I started to get up, thought better of it, and pretended to be deeply absorbed in my weekly editorial.

Half an hour later, Spence was still there. Maybe it was a live hookup. Once again, I considered going into the newsroom, but Scott arrived with the proof sheets of the photos he'd taken over the weekend. There were some excellent shots of the near-flood, the damaged Mitsubishi that had gone into the river, the audience gathering for the play, but, alas, nothing after the final curtain. Sheepishly Scott admitted that he and Tamara had ducked out as the curtain fell. But somewhat to my chagrin, Scott had taken pictures of Thyra Rasmussen being loaded into Henry's Town Car. One shot focused on legs encased in black cotton stock-ings and black shoes with silver buckles. Fittingly enough, she reminded me of the Wicked Witch from *The Wizard of Oz*.

"I don't know about using these," I said. "It might be bad taste."

Scott shrugged. "Why are these shots any different from photos of people lying in their caskets? They get run all the time in the dailies."

I allowed that that was true. "At least she isn't under a house in Kansas and Henry Bardeen doesn't look like a Munchkin," I noted. "Thank God Vida isn't standing over her making a victory sign." I glanced out into the newsroom. Vida and Spence were both on their feet. Spence was putting his equipment away; Vida was donning her coat. They left together. An ominous feeling crept over me. I must have shivered, because Scott looked alarmed.

"You okay, Emma? Have you caught a chill?"

I attempted a smile. "I'm fine. Was Spence doing a remote broadcast?"

Scott made a face. "I'm afraid so. I thought about butting in, but since you stayed in your office, I figured it was okay."

"It is. I can't stop him from doing his job."

For the next ten minutes, Scott and I marked our choices for the upcoming issue. We'd have plenty of photos, some of which required at least three columns by six inches for maximum effect. We'd need more advertising to support what undoubtedly would be an extra four pages. As soon as Scott left, I scanned the newsroom for Leo. He wasn't there. It was going on noon, so maybe he'd left for lunch. Once again pushing the long bangs off my forehead, I decided to see if Stella Magruder would give me a quick trim.

The snow was still melting as I braved the slush to cross Front Street and walk two blocks to the Clemans Building, where Stella's Styling Salon is located. Just before noon, the beauty parlor was deserted except for Stella herself and Janet Driggers, Al's wife. Stella was putting the finishing touches on Janet when I arrived.

"Damn!" Janet cried when I came through the door. "I'm caught! Now everybody in Alpine will know I get my hair highlighted! Honest, Emma, I've always been a natural redhead. More or less."

I grinned at Janet, who was never one to withhold her feelings or her often ribald thoughts.

Stella patted her own short curls, which were currently strawberry blond. "I did my own last week. Doesn't this shade have more pep?"

"It's nice," I said, though I'd never colored my hair and was afraid that if I did it'd all fall out. "You both look good."

Janet paused to admire herself in the hand mirror Stella had given her. "I'm hot, baby. Al had better watch out. I'm in a dominatrix mood. Bring on the heavy metal!"

I never wanted to know what went on in the Driggers bedroom. Al was so straitlaced and lifeless, he appeared to use his own embalming fluid. But Janet was wont to depict him as Super Stud.

She returned the mirror to Stella and eyed me with her usual lively curiosity. "I hear Vida took Thyra Whoozits out this morning. Did they actually exchange blows?"

I shook my head. "They had an argument, that's all."

"Damn!" Janet pounded the chair's armrest. "Darlene Adcock told me that Edna Mae Dalrymple heard from Francine Wells that Vida tried to strangle the old bitch. Oops!" She put a hand over her mouth while mischief danced in her green eyes. "Sorry. Shouldn't speak ill of the dead. But I'm told Thyra was a real horror story. It was probably because she wasn't getting any."

"She was close to a hundred," I noted.

"So?" Janet allowed Stella to remove the salon's protective cape from around her shoulders. "Hey, use it or lose it. That's what I tell Al. Or," she added in a lower voice, "in his case, find it or wind it."

I didn't want to know what she meant. In any case, she switched gears faster than a NASCAR driver. "And wouldn't you know it?" Janet's pretty face turned peevish as she brushed off a few stray hairs and rose from the chair. "Al and I didn't make it to the play Friday night. Not that we haven't seen enough corpses in our time. But we certainly missed some real excitement."

"It wasn't that exciting for the audience," I pointed out. "Most of us didn't realize what had happened until well after the curtain came down and about a third of the crowd had left. Does Al have the body?"

"To do what?" Janet's fine eyebrows went up.

I rarely found Janet's bawdy remarks annoying, but for once I had to rein in my impatience. "You know what I mean. Who's handling the arrangements?"

Janet's very sharp. She sensed my exasperation and grew serious. "Not yet. The M.E. in Everett is supposed to release Hans this afternoon. As usual, they had a busy weekend. The weather took out a lot of people over in SnoCo."

"So Hans will be sent back here?" I asked.

Janet shrugged. "I suppose. Frankly, nobody's officially contacted Al yet."

Stella, who'd been sweeping up Janet's clipped tresses, leaned on her broom. "I thought maybe Rita Patricelli would be in charge. Weren't they pretty tight at one point?"

"We haven't heard from Rita," Janet said as she slipped into her all-weather coat. "She's a flake, if you ask me. She tried to talk Al into some kind of co-op ad under the heading of Services— right next to Estate Planning and Roto-Rooter."

I assumed Janet referred to the advertising package Spence had proposed to the chamber. But it was Stella who'd caught my attention. "What," I asked her, "do you mean by 'tight at one point'? Had they broken up recently?"

Stella put the broom aside and accepted Janet's credit card. "I did Rita's hair for the play. She wanted what she called a 'waitress cut'—whatever that is. Anyway, I gathered she and Hans were on the outs. It had something to do with an investment he was making."

I waited for Stella and Janet to complete their transaction. After Janet had left with a breezy "Keep on truckin'—or something like that!" I indicated my shrubby bangs.

"Just a trim," I said. "I may let the rest of it grow."

"You'll be sorry," Stella said but proceeded to oblige my latest coiffure whim.

"I'm sleuthing," I confessed. "Did Hans's investment involve buying some property west of town?"

"I think so," Stella replied, critically eyeing my image in the mirror. "Frankly, I don't always listen to my clients when they ramble on about their personal lives. I'm getting too old to hold everybody's hand. I learned way back that if you give advice, they don't really want it. They just want to natter on about their problems. So I keep my mouth shut and sometimes my ears, too." She cut off a good half inch of hair.

"More," I said. "My hair grows so fast."

"Besides," Stella continued, "I was so busy last week, helping with the makeup and hair for the play. Frankly, I'm still beat. If we weren't shorthanded on Mondays, I wouldn't have come in today."

Taking my cue from Stella, I was only half listening. It sounded to me as if the breakup—if that's what it was—had happened last week. That made sense. Rita and Hans had still been seeing each other when the play was cast. Hans must have made his offer on the Krueger property in the last few days. If there'd been no activity for almost three months and he'd outbid Fuzzy Baugh, I would've expected the Kruegers to snap up Hans's proposal. And since the romantic breakup was so recent, it'd account for Rita's distress. Regrets, perhaps, or guilt. Maybe even genuine sorrow.

But I sensed that Stella was a dead end as far as Rita and Hans were concerned. "I don't suppose," I said in a musing tone, "that you heard anything at the theater that might indicate somebody had it in for Hans."

"Ha!" Stella grinned at our images. "How about everybody?"

I stared at Stella's reflection. "Really?"

"Pretty much." She went back to work, fluffing up the rest of my hair. "Don't tell me you haven't heard?"

"Heard what?"

Stella stood back to admire her work, then gave me the hand mirror. "About the death threats," she said. "Hans had received at least two in the months before he was shot."

ELEVEN

"YOU'RE NOT KIDDING, ARE YOU?" I SAID TO STELLA.

She shook her head. "I heard it from Tamara Rostova. You know, Scott's girlfriend."

"Yes, of course." I pronounced myself improved, if not in appearance, at least in vision. "What did Tamara say?"

"She went short a couple of weeks ago," Stella said, once again wielding the broom. "I tried to talk her out of it—she has such gorgeous raven hair. It's the real deal, no tint, no dye, no color of any kind except what God gave her. But she was tired of dealing with it. Anyway, she told me that Hans has—had—his office across from hers and one afternoon she heard him let out a terrible groan. That made my ears prick up. No personal woes for Tamara, just juicy gossip. She thought Hans was sick, and ran to see what was wrong. Tamara said he collected himself right away, but she said he looked really queer and his face had turned white. He seemed anxious to get rid of her. She noticed he had what looked like a letter on his desk that he tried to cover with his hands. Tamara's farsighted. She could see just a few words on the sheet of paper—'You are going to DIE Friday.' *DIE* was in capital letters, so it was hard to miss. She did her best to get him to open up, but he got really rude and told her to mind her own business. She finally left and he locked the door behind her."

"Has Tamara told the sheriff this?" I inquired, now on my feet.

Stella shrugged. "I don't know. What's more to the point, why didn't Hans tell the sheriff? Or did he?"

"Not that I know of," I said, aware that Milo didn't always share his information with me. More to the point, I wondered if Tamara had told Scott. "You said two death threats. What about the other one?"

We had progressed to the front desk. "That one I heard about from Clea Bhuj. Now there's another woman with wonderful black hair. She keeps it long but needs an occasional trim. Clea mentioned a faculty party during the holidays where—you'll *never* guess who this was—Justine Cardenas was overheard to say that Hans would die first before she'd . . . allow something-or-other."

"Justine?" I wouldn't have guessed it. "That *is* incredible. Justine is one of the most self-controlled women I've ever met."

"I guess something riled her up," Stella said, refusing the five-dollar bill I proffered for the trim. "I'll clip you next time. Ha-ha. Clea also mentioned that the party got a little tense after that and pretty soon everyone went home."

"Where was the festive gathering?" I asked.

"At the Cardenas house in The Pines." Stella was putting on her coat. "You want to grab a bite with me at the Burger Barn?"

I was tempted but suddenly discovered I craved a very rare beef dip sandwich from the Venison Inn. The Burger Barn didn't serve them. "Thanks," I said, "but I'm headed in the other direction."

We parted ways at Third and Front, where she went on to the Burger Barn and I crossed the street to the Venison Inn. Since the restaurant's renovation, the owners had installed a hostess for the lunch and dinner hours. Sunny Rhodes, part-time Avon lady and wife of the evening shift's bartender, greeted me with her glued-on sunny smile.

"I'm not sure I have a table for one," she said, still smiling despite the crease in her high forehead. "We're really busy today. I guess everybody wanted to eat out after the bad weather over the weekend. Would you mind sitting in the bar?"

"No," I replied. "That's fine." Briefly I considered confronting her about the *Advocate*'s policy regarding her son, Davin, and his bike accident. But all I could think of was rare beef.

Sunny's smile had turned mischievous. "Tip me five bucks and I'll find you a good spot for the floor show."

"The last floor show I saw in here was Jake and Betsy O'Toole arguing over the dent she put in their new Chrysler," I remarked. The owner of the Grocery Basket and his wife were famous for their public feuds, which had little effect on their devotion to each other. Quarreling for the O'Tooles seemed to be some kind of ritual, even a variation of lovemaking.

Sunny handed me a menu and sent me on my way. Halfway through the restaurant I saw Vida and Spence sitting at a window table. I considered going over to greet them, but I thought better of it. They seemed like an odd couple. I wondered what was going on between them. To add to my astonishment, Milo was sitting in a back booth with Destiny Parsons. I felt like the odd woman out as I walked into the bar's comparative darkness.

But not for long. Leo was sitting at a small table eating a pork sandwich and reading *Sports Weekly*. Automatically I looked to see if he had a cocktail glass. Years ago, Leo's personal problems had been caused by alcohol. Though he had quit his heavy drinking after he came to work for me, I still fretted over the possibility that one day he'd again free-fall off the wagon.

But Leo had only a small glass of beer on the table.

"May I?" I asked, giving him a slight start.

"Hey . . . sure. Take a seat." He folded the paper and slipped it under his chair. "You get frozen out of the dining room, too?"

I said I did.

"What's up with Vida and Mr. Radio?" Leo inquired.

"Good question," I said, putting the menu aside, since I already knew what I wanted. "Were you in the newsroom when Spence did the remote interview with Vida about an hour ago?"

Leo shook his head. "I was out hustling, earning my keep, raking in revenue."

"Which reminds me," I said before launching into our need to support four extra pages.

Leo liked the idea of the co-op ads. "The only problem is, we already do them. The churches, the home services, the real estate. Spence's concept is only an expansion that, I gather, he hasn't been able to sell. We couldn't do it, either. You can only stretch so far."

I hadn't quite thought it through. "You're right," I agreed. "But we still need more advertising this week. And yes, I know it's short notice. But what about weather-related products? There must be burst pipes and basement floods and—"

"I'm all over it," Leo interrupted as the waitress came to take my order. "I can't guarantee four pages' worth, but I'll try."

I knew he would. "Thanks, Leo." I smiled kindly at my ad manager. "Do you ever get tired of badgering the same old advertisers in the same old town for the same old paper?"

The lines in Leo's leathery face grew deeper. "Sure. Don't you? Same people, same kinds of stories, same type of editorials. Same crackpots. I'm getting closer to retirement—if I want to. You're lagging a few years behind me. Why are you still here?"

I sighed. "I think about it sometimes. Maybe I'm afraid to change."

Leo finished his entrée. "You made a big change thirteen years ago. That took guts."

If it hadn't been for the unexpected windfall I'd received when my long-ago ex-fiancé died and left me a quarter of a million dollars from his Boeing life insurance policy I probably wouldn't have made any changes, let alone moved out of Portland. Don and I had parted ways in college and hadn't been in touch since. When his wife, Ruth, discovered I would get his benefits, she was furious. I didn't blame her. But Don, who had been a highly creative think-tank guy, never paid much attention to life's little details. Such as deleting my name as beneficiary. Luckily, Ruth had inherited a nice nest egg from Boeing stock and hadn't been left destitute. They'd had two children and she later married a dentist. I didn't feel guilty about using the insurance money to buy the *Advocate*. Had it not been for that fluke, I probably would still be at *The Oregonian*, covering Portland news and writing what an editor had once described as "sprightly features."

"You're not a small-town girl," Leo pointed out as he lighted a cigarette.

"You're not a small-town guy," I retorted. "You're from L.A."

Leo gave me his off-center grin. "Why do you think I'm not there anymore? I mean, besides the obvious, which is that Tom Cavanaugh recommended me for the job as my last chance to crawl out of the gutter. I've always felt it was L.A. that drove me to drink. After I hit thirty, I wasn't up to the pace. One thing led to another. . . ." He spread his hands in a helpless gesture. "You saved me, babe. I owe you."

"No, you don't," I replied. "You saved yourself."

He shrugged. "Whatever. I wouldn't recommend that you move to L.A.—but your old hometown of Seattle seems like the right place for you. You miss it, don't you?"

"Yes. But it's been thirty years since I lived there. It's changed. Maybe I have, too."

He exhaled and shrugged again. "I shouldn't have brought it up."

"You didn't," I said, pausing as my food arrived. "I did. Maybe it's all rhetorical. We're both still here."

There was an unusual glint in Leo's brown eyes. "Yes. Does that give you a clue to the answer?"

The question put me off. "How do you mean?"

"Never mind." He laughed. "Gotta run," he said, digging into his pocket for his wallet. "Must save paper, must make revenue, must hold local merchants' heads underwater."

When I returned to the office just after one, it wasn't Leo who was uppermost in my mind. Vida was acting strange. She was pleasant but in a bogus kind of way. Her attitude was not unlike her manner when interviewing people she considered fools and nitwits, which covered most of Alpine's residents. She even hummed.

I asked about her lunch with Spence. "Interesting," she replied, and hummed a bit.

"In what way?" I prodded.

"In many ways," she said, making crop marks on a photo of Darlene and Harvey Adcock, who had recently spent two weeks in Palm Springs. "Perhaps I've underestimated his professionalism."

I pressed on. "Why is that?"

"Oh . . ." She stared up at the small window above her desk. "Just generally." She hummed some more.

I gave up. As falsely chipper as she seemed, it was better than the callousness and hostility she'd exhibited in the morning. But neither mood was the real Vida. I tried not to worry about that, either.

Instead, I stewed over Milo's apparent brick wall in the murder investigation. I wanted to bring up the alleged death threats, but I'd already insinuated that I didn't think he was covering all the bases. Finally, at a little after four, I walked down the street to call on him.

The sheriff had just returned from the barbershop. When Jack Mullins admitted me, Milo was using the reflection on his computer monitor to guide a comb through his freshly cut hair.

"Am I getting bald?" he asked, not looking up.

"Definitely," I said.

He looked up to stare at me. "Really? Can you tell?"

I sat down in his visitor's chair. "Ask the barber. He'd know."

"I already did. He said I wasn't." Milo scowled. "Maybe he just wanted to make me feel good."

I laughed. "You're not getting bald. I was kidding. You're going gray, but you're entitled to do that."

"Jeez." His broad shoulders slumped. "You scared me." He looked back at the screen. "Do you think it's too short?"

"Too short for what?" It wasn't like Milo to be concerned with his appearance. I wondered if Destiny Parsons was the cause for his about-face.

"Come on, Emma." Milo was getting exasperated. "I'm serious."

"You look fine. It's the same haircut you've had ever since I met you. Why the big fuss?"

Milo shrugged. "No reason. I just wondered. So many guys my age have lost most of their hair."

"Then you're lucky," I pointed out. As Milo put his comb away, enlightenment dawned. "If there was a reason, would it be Destiny Parsons?"

The sheriff looked affronted. "Of course not. Why would it be?"

"You two looked very cozy today at the Venison Inn."

The sheriff gazed into his coffee mug, then poured the dregs in a potted fern that his receptionist, Toni Andreas, had given him for Christmas. "I happened to run into Destiny at the restaurant. I figured maybe she'd open up more about the murder in a more casual setting."

"Did she?"

"Not really," Milo admitted. "I guess she's told me everything she knows."

"Including the death threats Hans got?"

Milo's hazel eyes narrowed. "What the hell are you talking about?"

"What I just said. Death threats. Two of them." I leaned back in the chair, feeling smug. "One written, one verbal. Didn't Hans report them to you?" I asked in an innocent voice.

Angrily the sheriff used his long legs to push himself and his chair back from the desk. "Goddamn it, Emma, you'd better not be giving me a wild-assed tale you overheard from some moron like Crazy Eights Neffel."

Since Crazy Eights was the town's premier nut job, Milo knew darned well I wouldn't believe Crazy Eights if he told me I was Emma Lord. "I'm not kidding this time," I said in my most severe tone, and had to bite my tongue to keep from admitting that I'd heard it at the beauty parlor. In Milo's opinion, that would be almost as bad as quoting Crazy Eights. "Admittedly, I learned about the threats secondhand. But the first one came from Tamara Rostova. The second, from Clea Bhuj."

Milo's face grew dark. "Neither of them said anything of the sort to me." He paused. "Come to think of it, I didn't interview Tamara. She wasn't part of the play."

"No, she wasn't," I allowed. "But Clea was."

"Then why didn't she tell me that Hans's life had been threatened?" Milo demanded.

"I can only guess," I said, and went on to explain that Justine Cardenas had made the threat at a faculty Christmas party. "Since it was Justine and she's the boss's wife, I suspect Clea was intimidated. It was probably one of those threats that people say and don't really mean. The letter that Tamara saw was another matter."

Milo sighed heavily after I finished my full recital. "I suppose Berenger destroyed the letter Tamara saw. I wonder if that was the only one he got."

"It must have been delivered to him at the college," I said.

"It could have come in the interoffice mail. I thought maybe Destiny had confided in you."

The remark obviously stung Milo, but he didn't jump me for it. Instead, he thought for a moment before responding. "Destiny might not have overheard Justine at the party. And I don't see how she'd know about the letter. That seems to be Tamara's dirty little secret."

I rose from the chair. "You think I'm being a pill and maybe I am," I said, "but I wanted to let you know what I heard. Which reminds me, Rita and Hans broke up shortly before opening night."

The sheriff ran his big hand down his face. "Great."

"Do you want to hear why?"

"Sure." Milo pulled the chair back up to his desk and lit a cigarette. "Tell me that Hans was cheating on Rita with Janet Driggers. Or Justine Cardenas. Or how about Vida?"

I told him, of course, about the Krueger sale.

"So," he mused, "Fuzzy Baugh arranged to have Hans knocked off to get Irene her dog patch."

I kind of liked the idea. But I didn't say so. "You know yourself, Milo, that a breakup quarrel is often the tip of the iceberg."

"Right." He gave me a sharp look. "There was a time or two when I felt the captain of the *Titanic* myself. Go away, Emma. I'm still on the job."

I went. Back at the office, I did phone interviews with some of the residents whose homes had been most endangered by the near-flood. When I finished, it was after five. Everybody had left except Kip MacDuff, who was installing the new software. Computer-savvy as he was, Kip had encountered some problems. Since I'm lucky if I can turn on my PC every morning, I didn't offer advice.

Driving home was much easier than going to work. The snow continued to melt on the streets, but not at an alarming rate that might cause the river to rise again.

I felt at loose ends that evening. If Milo had interviewed only the faculty members who were directly involved in *The Outcast*, maybe he should question some of the other hundred-plus people who worked at the college. And maybe he would, if he had the time and the manpower. Since Hans's murder, I'd spoken only with Destiny and Clea. Not Nat Cardenas and certainly not his wife, Justine. Of the students, I'd talked to Boots Overholt but not Rey Fernandez.

I made a list. As far as the rest of the cast was concerned, I could cross off Rip Ridley, Rita Patricelli, Fuzzy Baugh, and Roger. I'd chatted with all of them since the tragedy. I also put a line through Dustin Fong's name. Being a law officer, he would have told Milo everything he knew. That left Rev. Otis Poole and Dr. Jim Medved. Maybe I should make some phone calls.

I skipped the Reverend Poole, knowing that he conducted a prayer service Monday nights. It wouldn't be wise to call Nat and Justine at home. They could cut me off at will. Rey was probably sitting in for Spence at KSKY. That left Jim Medved.

His wife, Sherry, answered. Sherry was a former Washington State University cheerleader who still had more energy than the law allowed.

"Emma!" she exclaimed. "How are you? I keep meaning to stop by the newspaper office just to say hi, but darn—I always seem to be on the run. Are you calling about the women's shelter? I've been putting in some long hours there, but it's so-o-o rewarding. I can't believe there are so many battered women in Skykomish County. Would you believe we've even gotten some poor darlings from King and Chelan counties?"

She had to stop for breath, allowing me to tell her that I was actually calling for her husband. After another burst of nuclear-sized energy, Sherry handed the phone over to Jim.

"Did you find a stray?" Jim asked in a far more subdued voice.

"Just stray questions," I replied, hearing the wind suddenly swoop down through the chimney. I explained that I was trying to put together a cohesive story on Hans's shooting. "I know this is painful, Jim, but I still have to interview the people involved."

"I was certainly that," he broke in, his tone bitter. "I feel as if I might as well have fired that cursed gun myself."

"Since Nat did the firing, I'm sure he feels just as awful as you do," I noted.

"Maybe. Nat's a cold fish." He paused. "Sorry. That wasn't kind. Let's say he shows a cold exterior. Maybe he's torn up inside."

"Nat's extremely disciplined," I said, having always felt that Nat's public face was carefully cultivated. "I'll keep this short, Jim. Did you buy the blanks?"

"Yes," he answered, "from Harvey's Hardware. He had to special-order them. They didn't come in until last Monday."

"Did you check them out?"

"How do you mean?"

"Did you look at them to make sure they were blanks?"

"Of course." Jim sounded a bit put off by my query. "I opened them as soon as I got back to the office. They looked like real bullets, but they weren't. The box was marked BLANKS in several places."

"Was it sealed?"

Jim paused. "Yes. There was some tape. You know, just ordinary Scotch tape."

"You never let the box out of your sight after you got it?"

"I can't say that." Jim cleared his throat. "I put it in my desk. That night I took it home and put it with the .38."

"Which was where?"

"In a drawer of our bedroom dresser."

It sounded safe enough. Except for the time when the blanks were at Jim's office. "Who," I inquired, "had appointments that day?"

"Ohhh. . . ." Jim stopped to think. "You know, so much has happened, I can't remember off the top of my head. I'd have to look at my appointment book tomorrow. Is there any hurry?"

"Tuesday is our deadline," I reminded Jim. "Can you call me at the paper?"

"I'll try," Jim said. "Is that all?"

I led Jim through the hours before and during the play. His account jibed with what I'd already heard. The bottom line, of course, was that the gun had been left unattended at various times, despite Boots Overholt's best efforts at tending the prop box. Jim hadn't fired the gun during rehearsals. There were only a dozen cartridges in the box. With four performances scheduled, he couldn't waste them.

After hanging up, I could hear the wind in the evergreens that flanked the south side of my house. The weather must be changing. I stepped out the front door to check the clouds. They were moving swiftly to the west. Perhaps the skies were finally clearing. Or more clouds were moving in from the Cascades. You could never be sure in western Washington.

By ten o'clock, the wind was still blowing. I estimated the gusts to be somewhere in the vicinity of fifty miles an hour. I could hear garbage can lids clattering and tree branches snapping. The lights flickered several times. A power outage was likely.

Sure enough, the house was plunged in darkness just before I turned on the eleven o'clock TV news. I lit the candles I kept on the mantel but didn't bother to stoke up the fireplace. It was almost time for bed.

Assuming mine wasn't the only household without electricity, I again went to the front porch. The town seemed to have vanished. While the wind was still blowing hard, the sky had cleared. I could see stars and a half moon over Mount Baldy.

Once my eyes grew accustomed to the darkness, I could also

see something move across the street at Destiny Parsons's house. It was human. It looked more like a man than a woman. Whoever he was, his progress was impeded by the wind as he walked slowly toward the street.

I stepped back off the porch but continued to watch. Maybe I wanted to make sure the man wasn't Milo. But this guy was shorter and seemed younger as well. He stopped near the street and began to wrestle with something that was lying on the ground. It was Destiny's mailbox, which apparently had blown over. The man struggled to upright it and resettle it in the ground. He finally accomplished his task and started back into the house.

Watching him make his plodding way to the porch, I saw that he was wearing a heavy jacket, jeans, and a watch cap. At one point, he turned so that I could see his profile. He had a beard.

He matched the description of the man who had driven the Mitsubishi into the river and fled from the police.

TWELVE

I picked up the phone to call Milo, but the line was dead. I felt frustrated, but only for a moment. Modern technology would save me. Getting my cell phone out of my purse, I attempted to reach Milo the twenty-first-century way. Wireless. Not relying on landlines that could be blown down at Mother Nature's whim.

But I met defeat. Getting a recorded message that informed me the call could not go through, I realized that I wasn't the only one in Alpine who was thinking high tech.

Maybe I was overreacting. Occasionally I'd seen young people arrive at Destiny's house. I'd assumed they were students. But they came early in the evening and never stayed late. I couldn't rule out the possibility that Destiny had taken a student lover. That would explain his midnight presence.

Still, I wasn't satisfied. My inability to reach Milo frustrated me further until I came up with another, much older, idea. The Good Neighbor Policy would be practiced. Removing my robe, I dressed hurriedly and left the house. The wind seemed to have abated, at least temporarily. I had little trouble crossing the street, barely enough time to rehearse my speech describing my concern for Destiny, who had already suffered enough lately and shouldn't be left alone at such a time.

I poked the bell but couldn't hear it ring inside the house. Maybe it was very soft; maybe it was broken. I knocked on the door. I knocked again, louder. After the third try, I went around to the back and resumed knocking. After a half-dozen tries, I gave up. But before I could go down the three steps that led to the walkway, I heard the door open behind me.

Destiny's voice was sharp: "Who is it?"

"Emma," I replied, turning around. "Are you okay?"

Destiny was in her bathrobe. "Of course. Why wouldn't I be?"

I waved a hand at the sky. "The wind. The power failure. I just thought I'd check to see if—"

"I'm fine. I was in bed. What's the big deal? This isn't the first power failure we've had around here."

"No, but it's—"

"Thanks for checking. Good night." She slammed the door.

So much for the Good Neighbor Policy. Apparently, I'd qualified for the Nosy Neighbor Award instead.

I tried to reach Milo again but had no luck. It was going on midnight, but since I was already dressed, I decided to drive to his house in Icicle Creek. It took me fifteen minutes. While there was virtually no traffic, the moon had slipped behind Baldy, making visibility poor. Obstacles—tree branches, garbage cans, cardboard cartons, even *Advocate* delivery boxes—littered the streets. I didn't dare go faster than five miles an hour.

Milo was up when I arrived, and talking on his cell phone. He looked startled to see me but let me in without disconnecting his call. As I wandered around his kitchen and bumped into various objects, I realized that he was on the line with the PUD, trying to determine when power would be restored.

"Shit!" he exclaimed, finally dumping the phone on the

kitchen counter. "They don't know jack!" He was silent for a moment, fingering his long chin. At last he looked at me as if he only now realized I was present. "What's with you? Did your house blow down?"

"No, but I think—maybe—I know where your missing man is."

"What?" Milo rubbed at his eyes. "Come into the living room. I've got a couple of Coleman lanterns in there."

Everything else he owned seemed to be in the living room, too. The place was as cluttered as I'd ever seen it. The sheriff wasn't much of a housekeeper at best, and he'd certainly been busy the last few days. Before I sat down, I removed an empty pizza box, a *TV Guide*, and a box of pretzels from an armchair.

"You won't want to hear this," I began, "but I have to tell you." I proceeded to describe who and what I'd seen at Destiny's house. I also told Milo about my futile visit.

Milo, who was wearing a tattered pair of khaki pants and a Mariners sweatshirt, looked skeptical. "You didn't get within thirty feet of this guy. Could you pick him out of a lineup?"

"Only if the other men didn't have beards," I admitted. "But that hardly means you should ignore him."

"How many times have you seen young guys at Destiny's house?" he asked, lighting a cigarette.

I grimaced. "A few times." Like ten or more. "She has students come over for discussions or coaching or whatever, I think. But I usually hear them leave—if I hear them at all—before ten."

Milo smoked and thought. "Hell. Maybe it's worth a shot." He retrieved his cell phone from the kitchen. "Sam and Dustin are on duty tonight. I'll send them. You want a drink or something?"

I shook my head. Milo finished his call, went back to the kitchen, and returned with a shot of Scotch. "This could be a long night," he muttered. "Let's hope you're wrong."

I didn't comment. After a long pause, I mentioned that I should head home.

"Better wait," Milo cautioned. "If you're right about the guy at Destiny's house, you don't want to be around if things get dicey."

"On the contrary," I said, standing up, "that's exactly where I want to be. I'm a journalist, remember?"

The sheriff also got to his feet. "Emma . . ."

"Spare me," I said with a wave of my hand. "I have to follow my nose for news."

Milo blocked my passage. "You don't want to get your nose shot off, do you?"

I jabbed at his chest, right in the middle of the Mariners' compass logo. "Move it, Lawman. I've got work to do."

Milo grabbed my wrist. "Slow down." He looked into my face. It wasn't the stern, stubborn, or commanding expression I'd expected. Yet I knew this look equally well. It was desire, yearning, loneliness, maybe even a touch of hope.

"Milo . . ." I sounded forlorn.

To my surprise, he let go and stepped back. "Go ahead. Just be careful. And stay inside."

I promised that I would. With a tentative smile, I left.

But not without regrets.

It was going on one o'clock when I got home. To my surprise, the sheriff's patrol car was parked in front of my house. As I slowly pulled into the driveway, I noticed that Sam and Dustin appeared to be in the vehicle. There was no one in the backseat.

I got out of the Honda; they exited their car and headed toward me.

"Knock, knock, nobody home across the street," Sam said in his dour manner. "Nobody suspicious, that is. Mind if we come in?"

"Of course not," I replied. "Coffee?"

"No, thanks," Sam said. Apparently, Dustin agreed or merely deferred to his senior officer. "Just wanted to let you know what happened," Sam went on. "Dodge told us you were on your way home."

I was about to suggest we leave the kitchen for the living room where I could relight one of my candles when suddenly the electricity went on.

"Thank goodness," I breathed. "Have a seat."

But Sam refused that offer, too. "We have to get going. Lots of debris to clear, more than the road crew can handle." He took out a wrinkled handkerchief and blew his nose. "Got a damned cold from all this crazy weather. Wouldn't you know it?" He blew his nose again.

"Are you okay, Ms. Lord?" Dustin inquired while Sam got his sinuses under control.

"I'm fine," I said with a smile. Dustin Fong could be the poster boy for Your Kindly Law Officer. "So Destiny didn't answer the door?"

Sam took over again. "Eventually. She was madder than a wet cat. We told her we'd gotten a report of a prowler in the neighborhood. Finally she let us search the house, but no luck. She told us she'd had company earlier, one of her students, Boots Overholt. He'd left around midnight."

"I don't believe her," I declared, realizing that Destiny would blame me for the deputies' intrusion. "The man I saw wasn't Boots. Yes, Boots has a beard, but he's taller. And he drives a pickup, which I didn't see parked outside her house. In fact, I didn't see any vehicle at her place."

Stuffing the handkerchief in his back pocket, Sam shrugged. "We'll check with Boots tomorrow. Anyway, the neighborhood is safe. Except for the damned weather."

On that note, the deputies left.

❄   ❄   ❄

When I finally got to sleep, I dreamed of Italy. At St. Peter's Basilica in Rome I saw Michelangelo's Pietà. *It is, of course,*

*magnificent. And yet, as I studied the sorrowful face of the
Virgin Mary holding her dead Son in her arms, all I could
think of was how I'd felt when I looked at Tom and realized he'd been killed. What happened after that I'm not
really sure. I was so shocked, so stupefied, so incredulous,
that my memory has obliterated the details. I think I fell on
his body until someone—I don't recall who—pulled me
off. I know I fainted at one point. I tried to remember the
sequence of events as I stood behind the rail that separates
the admirers—and nutcases—from Michelangelo's masterpiece. Nothing more came back to me. My only emotion
was grief, not for the Blessed Mother or her Divine Son but
for me.*

*That was wrong. It wasn't the effect that Michelangelo
had sought to convey.*

But I couldn't help taking it personally.

❄　　❄　　❄

Tuesday. Deadline. Pressure. Loose ends. I never get over the
sense of panic that always hits me around eleven in the morning.
It was no different on this last Tuesday of February. In fact, it
was worse. We had plenty of news, but much of it was incom-
plete, which meant that in the next few days we'd probably get
scooped again by KSKY and possibly even the met dailies.

It was exactly eleven when Rolf Fisher called from the Associated Press. "I heard you got another body up there," he said.
"Did that Snohomish *grande dame* really croak in your office?"

"Yes, she did. I didn't kill her. Natural causes."

"What did she do, just keel over?"

"That's right," I said. "She was almost a hundred."

"Bad timing for you," Rolf noted.

"Don't rub it in," I snapped. "Why aren't you calling her relatives? Or somebody in Snohomish?"

Rolf sniggered. "You don't remember me, do you?"

"From when? Last week, when you called about Hans Berenger?"

"No. From the AP cocktail party right before Thanksgiving. It was held up in the Columbia Tower. You were there, so was I. You lost an earring in the crab dip."

"I got it out," I said.

"I thought you were cute. You reached into the dip to retrieve your earring, then you wiped your hand off on the tablecloth. You blushed."

"I never blush." I didn't remember Rolf Fisher. I'd met at least two dozen people at the party. Several of them had known Tom. We'd talked about him. That was all I recalled, except for the lost earring. And that the crab dip was heavenly. I wanted to change the subject. "Are you still following up on the Berenger murder?"

"Sure. What've you got for me?"

"Ask Sheriff. Dodge," I retorted. "He's in charge of the investigation, not me."

"Has Dodge found the guy who drove the stolen car into the Sky?"

"Ask him." I paused. "I'm hanging up now."

"I still think you're cute."

I pressed the disconnect button.

Vida was still in an odd mood, but since she was being pleasant I didn't confront her. Just before noon she received the information she needed for the story on Thyra Rasmussen. Thyra would've been 100 years old on March 11. She probably thought the century mark would be her final triumph over her many adversaries. The funeral was to be held Friday in Snohomish at the same Lutheran church from which Einar Sr. and Einar Jr. had been given their sacred send-offs. I knew Vida wouldn't miss the service for the world and that there was a faint possibility she'd dance on Thyra's grave.

I was about to run over to the Burger Barn for takeout when Jim Medved called.

"I checked my appointments for last Monday," he said. "We'd scheduled ten patients for the afternoon, after I brought the blanks back to the office. I assume you want the owners' names, not the animals'."

"Right," I said dryly. "Fido and Fluffy wouldn't mean much to me."

Jim ran down the list, which included Grace Grundle, who probably had a standing appointment with one or more of her pampered cats. The only other names that jumped out at me were Destiny Parsons's and Rip Ridley's.

"Destiny had a well-dog appointment for Azbug," Jim said sadly. "The dog was in excellent health. What a shame she was killed."

"What about Rip?" I inquired. "Was that because of the cougar attack on Vince?"

Jim nodded. "Rip's bringing him in this afternoon for a check-back. That's really a shame, but those cougars get bolder and bolder. It's not all their fault. Their habitat keeps shrinking. Oh!" He snapped his fingers. "We had a couple of drop-ins who aren't in the book. Edna Mae Dalrymple came in with her parakeet, Pretty Boy, and Boots Overholt brought a lame goat from his folks' farm."

I thanked Jim, then studied the names I'd written down. Destiny, Rip, and Boots had all been involved in the play. Somehow, I couldn't see Rip and Boots as killers. But despite my dislike of Destiny, she didn't fit the role, either. On the other hand, I was aware that under certain circumstances just about anyone can be driven to take a human life. Shaking my head, I left to get lunch.

Milo came into the Burger Barn while I was waiting for my standard order of a hamburger, French fries, and a vanilla malt. I'd already spoken with him on the phone earlier. He'd checked up on Destiny's story that Boots had been at her house. The young man had assured Milo that it was true. Boots often went there so Destiny could help him with his interest in the theater. Apparently, he was serious about it, especially the technical side. Or maybe he was just tired of goats.

"What about Hans's background?" I inquired, noting that the sheriff also ordered takeout.

"I only had a résumé until this morning. Cardenas sent Berenger's complete file over around ten," the sheriff replied with a nod at Ginny's husband, Rick Erlandson, and his Bank of Alpine colleague Stilts Cederberg. "I've gone through it. Standard stuff. Forty-eight years old. Born in Winnetka, Illinois, outside of Chicago, attended Northwestern University and Wisconsin. Taught high school in Appleton, married, moved to San Diego, worked at a community college, widowed, a year later left for the Bay Area, taught at another community college until three years ago, when he accepted the dean of students job at SCC."

"An odd choice," I remarked as my order arrived on the counter.

Milo frowned. "How so?"

"For one thing, the pay's better in California," I pointed out. "For another, Hans sounds like a city guy. Chicago, San Diego, the Bay Area."

Milo seemed defensive. I suspected that like other Alpiners, he felt that any implied criticism of the town was incomprehensible. "What about Appleton, Wisconsin?"

"His first job," I said. "He had to start somewhere."

"Maybe he liked the outdoors," Milo said.

"Oh?" I collected my white paper bag with its red barn logo. "Did he?"

Milo didn't meet my gaze. "Well . . . Not that I know of. But he was a quiet guy. Maybe he didn't talk about how he used his spare time. And," he continued, now looking me in the eye, "he was buying property. He wanted some space. You couldn't buy the Kruegers' four acres near a big city for twice the price."

I allowed that Milo was right. But Hans Berenger, Nature Lover, didn't fit with my perception of the man. I paid up front and waited there for Milo to get his lunch. When we were outside, where a pale sun hung directly overhead, I asked if he knew how Hans's wife had died.

"I put that question to Nat Cardenas," the sheriff replied. "He said Hans didn't like talking about it, even six or seven years since her death."

"Did she have a name?"

Milo made a face. "Yeah, sure. What was it? Julia or Julie or something like that. Hans met her in graduate school. She was a marine biologist. I suppose that's why they moved to San Diego. She'd be right by the ocean."

"There's marine life in the Great Lakes," I noted dryly.

"What? Oh . . . right."

We started across the street, which was now bare and dry. Reminders of the windstorm were everywhere. Two saplings that had been put into planters along Front Street lay uprooted on the sidewalk by the dry cleaner's. A couple of letters on the Whistling Marmot Movie Theater were missing—*The Gladiator* now starred Russell C ow . Parker's Pharmacy had lost its pestle-and-mortar sign.

Back in the newsroom, I mentioned these items to Vida for her "Scene Around" column. Of course she already had them.

By three-thirty, Leo had enough advertising—barely—to justify sixteen pages instead of our usual twelve. He'd talked Thyra's son and daughter-in-law into paying for a quarter-page photo of the deceased in exchange for an obit of equal size.

Vida wasn't happy about that. "A half page devoted to a

woman who didn't even live in Alpine? That's ridiculous! I suppose I'll have to write it." An evil gleam suddenly showed in her gray eyes. "Well, why not?"

"I'll do it," I volunteered. "I've got my stories just about done."

Vida scowled at Thyra's photograph. "Look at this picture! It must have been taken in the twenties! Thyra has bee-sting lips."

"Selling photo space is the new thing in obits," Leo said. "They do it all the time in the met dailies. More often than not, the photo submitted is from the deceased's earlier years. I'm wondering if we shouldn't start charging, too. Thyra sets a precedent."

"Wouldn't you know it," Vida muttered, sounding more like herself. "But I don't think it's a good idea to make local folks pay. It'll create bad feelings. It's almost like charging for having lived in Alpine. That's certainly not right."

Leo shrugged. "It was only a thought."

I didn't say that the decision was up to me, not Vida or Leo. Instead, I asked Leo if he'd gotten to know Hans while they lived in the same apartment building.

"I hardly ever saw him," Leo replied as Vida handed him Thyra's photo. "He seemed to leave early and come home late. I figured him for a workaholic. I don't think I talked to him a half-dozen times."

I considered Leo's words. "What's your rent, Leo? I'm not snooping. I'm trying to figure something out."

Leo grinned. "Like my next raise?"

I grinned back. "Not exactly."

"Three-seventy-five," he said, then added with a straight face, "but that doesn't include pool privileges."

There was no pool at the venerable three-story apartment house on Pine Street. "Do you think Hans paid about the same?"

"Probably," Leo replied. "He was on the third floor, above me. Those are all one-bedroom units like mine."

"Do you know the asking price for the Krueger property?"

"Two hundred and ninety thousand," Vida put in. She simpered a bit. "I checked it out with Doukas Realty."

"They haven't advertised the place in the *Advocate*," Leo noted.

"The Kruegers only listed it with Doukas on Monday," Vida said. "They were trying to sell it on their own, without spending money on brokers or advertising. Fuzzy's cheap. I suspect his bid was so low that they decided to have a professional handle the sale now that Hans is out of the picture."

Vida was probably right. "So how much did Hans make at the college?" I mused. "Forty, fifty grand?"

"Somewhere in there," Leo said. "I seem to remember that when Cardenas was hired on he got seventy-five as president. That was several years ago, but the state legislature has been stingy with education."

It was no wonder that Nat was considering other offers. "Fifty grand isn't bad for a single person," I remarked, "but where would Hans get the money to make a down payment on the Krueger property? A loan from the bank or the teachers' credit union?"

"Down payment my foot," Vida said. "The Kruegers want to cash out. They're buying some fancy-pants condo near Phoenix."

Leo rubbed the back of his head. "Wow."

"Rita doesn't have the money," Vida went on. "The Patricellis have always been poor. Pete's done fairly well with his pizza parlor, but I understand Rita had to settle a large sum on her ex-husband, who had an aversion to work."

"Insurance," Leo said. "Maybe Hans's wife had a big insurance policy."

Naturally, I thought back to Don. Boeing had been generous with its benefits in those days. "I wonder who Mrs. Berenger worked for," I said. "Her employer might have had substantial benefits."

Leo eyed me with suspicion. "You're thinking Hans bumped off the wife to collect her big bucks insurance?"

"No, no," I assured him. "I'm thinking that may be where he got the money to buy property here."

"Could be," Leo replied. "Even a six-figure policy wouldn't get you much land in the Bay Area."

Writing up Thyra's obit took nearly half an hour. The funeral home in Snohomish had provided not only bare facts but some news clippings from the weekly *Tribune* as well. Thyra had had a finger in every possible pie, though the funeral director termed the SCC theater as "her crowning glory." To placate Vida, I omitted that phrase.

Ironically, by four-thirty we seemed to be ahead of schedule for our five o'clock deadline. All I had to do was proofread Scott's and Vida's articles. I did some minor editing on Scott's stories, but as usual I didn't touch Vida's section, except for a couple of minor typos. Vida's conversion—*surrender* would have been more apt—to semimodernity had been to replace her battered upright with an electric typewriter. Finding replacement parts for her old Remington had become virtually impossible, so she'd been forced to abandon it. But she refused to make the complete leap into the computer age. I had to humor her, though her recalcitrance drove Kip crazy.

Everything was ready for Kip at ten to five. Vida, Scott, and Leo went home. I lingered, thumbing through the college handbook. The hierarchy seemed clear: President Cardenas, Dean of Students Berenger, Registrar Shawna Beresford-Hall, and then the division heads, including Clea Bhuj for Humanities. But what I was really looking for was some way of getting a private chat with Nat and Justine Cardenas.

The idea struck me at a few minutes after five, and I don't know why I hadn't thought of it sooner. We had no follow-up on how the students, staff, and faculty reacted to a murder on campus. I rushed into the back shop to ask Kip how long he could hold a six-inch space open for me.

"We don't have any space," Kip said. "We're jammed as it is. That half page for Mrs. Rasmussen filled whatever holes we had."

I studied the layout, page by page. "Here," I said, pointing to Vida's feature on Darlene and Harvey Adcock's trip to Palm Springs. "This can be cut. As usual, Vida has overwritten a travel story. Take out the last four grafs, starting where Darlene talks about coming home to all the snow last Wednesday and rambles on about preferring Alpine's climate to the desert's. Okay?"

Kit shrugged. "It's okay by me, but Vida won't like it. How soon can you get your new stuff in?"

"I'm not sure I can get it at all," I admitted. "I'm going to call Nat and Justine right away."

Justine answered in her cool, controlled voice. I apologized for not phoning sooner, for being negligent, for not acting with sensitivity, and for being alive in general.

Justine remained distant. "Nat got home only minutes ago. He's exhausted. Couldn't you make it some other time?"

I explained about our deadline. "It would be a disservice to the college to run the story next week. Your students and faculty need to heal. I'm sure Nat has spoken to them and done his best, but sometimes a public forum is more effective. It touches the entire community."

The positive publicity angle apparently struck a chord with Justine. "Well . . . it *has* been a very difficult time. When did you want to stop by?"

"I can come now," I said. "That way, I won't interfere with your dinner hour."

Justine agreed that would be best. Fifteen minutes later, I was at their pseudo-Colonial house in The Pines. To my surprise, a black wreath hung on the front door. Justine, wearing tweed slacks and what looked like an expensive black cashmere sweater, ushered me inside.

"Nat and I are having a cocktail," she said. "It helps him unwind. Would you care for something?"

I was tempted but politely refused. I didn't want to waste their time—or mine. Justine offered me an armchair with a muslin seat. The Queen Anne and Chippendale style of furnishings included both a highboy and a lowboy. I could picture Justine carefully choosing the pieces to reflect America's Colonial era. It struck me that she had deliberately obliterated Nat's Hispanic background. The result was sterile, as if nobody actually lived in the house, or at least in the living room. I'd have preferred a couple of piñatas hanging from the ceiling.

Nat looked properly academic in his dark blue shirt, gray sweater-vest, and black trousers. To add to the illusion, he put down a copy of Petrarch's *Canzoniere* before rising to greet me.

"Thank you for coming," he said, shaking my hand. "Justine explained your mission. You're right—it's time and past time that I made a full public statement. I was still in shock when your Mr. Chamoud telephoned for my reaction Monday."

The quote Scott had used stated that the college president "mourned the loss of an exceptionally able colleague who had made an indelible impression on Skykomish Community College students."

Nat sat down again and I resumed my place in the uncomfortable armchair. "I made some notes before you arrived," he continued, reaching for a tablet on a cherrywood end table next to the double settee that looked like two of my chairs glued together. I couldn't imagine that the settee was very comfortable, either. There was no sofa. I wondered if Justine had chosen the furniture with yet another motive in mind—guests squirming in discomfort won't stay long.

" 'I particularly regret,' " Nat began, reading from his notes, " 'that I was the instrument in Professor Berenger's untimely death. No matter how innocent my actions may have been, I will bear the burden of guilt for the rest of my life.' " He glanced at me. "How does that sound so far?"

"Fine," I said.

He went back to the notes. " 'It is possible that foul play was involved. However, I want to assure the college and the community that the campus is a safe haven. No student or parent should feel ill at ease about our academic environment. We are dedicated to excellence in education. However, we must remember that there are always areas in higher education that we can improve. The state legislature should keep in mind that the future of this country rests on the quality of teaching our young people. Even now, as the legislators meet in Olympia, I would urge them to consider not cuts but additional funding to the budgets for our two- and four-year institutions.' "

He put the tablet aside while I worked at keeping a receptive expression. At least Nat hadn't suggested that we put up a billboard showing Hans's bleeding body and urging the legislature to act before any more faculty members got shot to death in a student play.

"Do you want me to type this out?" Nat inquired, pointing to the tablet.

"No. No, that's fine. I'm sure I can read your notes, especially after having heard you voice your thoughts so . . . eloquently."

Nat sipped at his drink. "Good." He reached over to the end table and tore off the top sheet. "It's a single page only. I wanted to be brief."

From my experience, most educators don't know the meaning of *brief* unless they're teaching law. Nat stood up to hand me the paper, which I felt was his way of dismissing me.

But I wasn't done yet. In fact, the statement wasn't really what I'd come for. It was only an excuse.

"There's been some talk about a stranger showing up at the

theater Friday night," I said as Nat stood in front of me. "Did you see anyone you didn't know?"

Nat shifted his stance but remained in place. "Is this the person that the police are looking for?"

"It might be," I said, "but there's no direct connection so far. The descriptions of the person who was at the play and the one who drove the stolen car into the river seem to match."

"Hmm." Nat ran a hand through his graying dark hair before finally returning to the settee. "I didn't see him." He turned to his wife. "Did you, Justine?"

"Of course not," Justine asserted, fondling her cocktail glass. "I didn't come backstage until after the play was over."

Nat gave her a curious look. "Oh. I guess I . . ." He stopped and smiled affably. "I was thinking of the night before, at the rehearsal."

"Yes." Justine's brittle manner seemed to crack just a bit. "I was backstage Thursday night, not Friday."

Nat smiled sadly. "When something like this happens, you tend to lose track of time. The tragedy seems as if it took place weeks ago, not mere days."

"Do you know who's handling the arrangements for Hans?" I inquired.

Nat shook his head. "Hans never mentioned any next of kin. I understand Al Driggers has been trying to track down any Berengers who might be related to Hans. He's concentrated on the Chicago area, but as of this afternoon, he'd had no luck."

"That's very sad," I remarked. "Have you contacted his previous places of employment?"

"Have *I*?" Nat seemed put off by the question. He probably felt that such dog work was beneath him. "I assume that's part of Al's responsibility."

Justine, cocktail glass in hand, stood up. "We mustn't keep you from your deadline."

"Yes," I said, rising from my uncomfortable chair and wondering when back spasms would begin. "I must head for the office."

I noticed that Justine's Chippendale side chair was upholstered with a handsome piece of needlepoint. Feeling an obligation to say something flattering about their house, I commented on the beauty of the seat covering. A spray of red roses with lush green leaves lay against a white background. The detail was amazing.

"Thank you," Justine said, her sharp features softening almost imperceptibly. "I did it myself. Needlepoint is my hobby."

"Ah!" I exclaimed, seeing the small, precise initials JBC in the bottom right corner. "You signed it."

"I sign all my pieces," Justine replied. "It was our children's idea. Since they both live so far away, they wanted to show off their mother's needlework. I made a set of dining room chair covers for each of them—a dozen in all, and every one is different."

"You do lovely work," I enthused. I decided that the way to Justine's heart was through her needle and thread.

"You're very kind." Justine edged toward the door. "I'm working on a footstool cover right now," she added.

We were on the threshold. I gestured at the wreath. "Did you make that?"

"Yes." Her face assumed its usual cool expression. "I enjoy other crafts, too, but my passion is needlework."

"It's very handsome," I said. "And such a beautiful way to mourn."

The cool expression became absolutely stony. "Yes," she said. "Good night, Emma."

THIRTEEN

I FELT AS IF I'D MADE SOME KIND OF GAFFE, BUT MY MISINTERPRE-
tation of the wreath's purpose had definitely been a conversation killer. Just when I'd detected a tiny slit in Justine's armor,
she'd soldered it shut. Maybe it didn't matter. We would never
be bosom buddies.

It took only a few minutes to type up Nat's statement and
hand it off to Kip. I cringed at Nat's lobbying tactic, but the
words were his, not mine. Indeed, I almost didn't blame him for
taking every opportunity to goose the legislators in Olympia.

Pub Day dawned, Crank Day for the *Advocate*. I tried to put
myself in a forgiving state of mind by attending 8:00 A.M. Ash
Wednesday services at St. Mildred's. Knowing that his parishioners had to get to work, Father Kelly whipped through the
liturgy and distribution of ashes. There would be a second service in the evening that would probably run closer to an hour. As
it was, I managed to get to the office shortly after eight-thirty.

Vida was again somewhat unlike herself and humming un-
recognizable tunes. After listening to phone calls telling me I
was a radical, a reactionary, and a Roman pawn of the pope, I
invited Vida to step into my cubbyhole.

"Are you all right?" I asked point-blank. "You seem a bit off lately."

"Off?" She bristled at the question. "What do you mean, 'off'?"

"I mean, you're kind of . . . not like yourself," I said.

She puffed up like a grouse. "Honestly, Emma, I've no idea what you're talking about."

"You're not still mad at me for throwing Thyra out of the office?"

"Heavens, no." She shook her head vigorously; the unruly gray curls went every which way. "That's in the past."

"Good," I said, though I retained some doubts. Vida definitely holds grudges. "Is Buck back from California yet?"

"Not until the end of the month." She eyed me shrewdly. "Did you think I was lovesick?"

"No, of course not." I smiled at Vida. "I just wanted to make sure everything was okay. How's Roger? Has he recovered from the trauma of Hans's murder?" The query was a peace-making gesture. I suspected that Roger was glorying in his role as a witness to homicide.

"Roger's doing very well, though I don't see how he manages such a brave face," Vida replied solemnly. "I suggested to Rip Ridley that they bring in a grief counselor at the high school to help Roger move on with his life. Rip said he'd think about it. Being an ex–football player, Rip is somewhat callous."

I didn't explore Vida's rationale about Rip, nor did I voice my opinion that after talking to Roger a grief counselor would need counseling—or at least consoling. "Just so Roger is doing okay," I said.

Vida rose from her chair. "He's managing, poor darling." Her sympathetic expression changed abruptly and there was a glint in her eyes. "If you really want to know, tune in KSKY at seven tonight."

"What do you mean?" I asked in surprise.

The glint shone brighter. "Remember. Seven o'clock."

Vida exited my office, humming.

Later that afternoon, I phoned Driggers Funeral Home. Al answered, so I assumed Janet was working at the travel agency. The woman has so much energy that she holds down two jobs, and when the death business is slow she moves on to Sky Travel. As Janet puts it, either way she's sending people somewhere.

"I don't know yet," Al said in frustration when I asked what he was going to do with Hans's body. "I called at least a dozen Berengers in Illinois and they'd never heard of him. Rita Patricelli insists Hans never mentioned any relatives except his parents, who are deceased."

"What about his late wife's family?" I inquired.

There was a pause at the other end of the line. "I never thought of that. Hunh. You're right. I could check Illinois vital statistics for a marriage license issued . . . when?"

I thought back to Milo's recapitulation of Hans's career. "More than ten years ago," I finally said. "If I were you, I'd check Wisconsin as well. Hans met his wife, Julia, while he was attending graduate school in Madison. Do you have her maiden name?"

"No." Al sounded mournful. "Wouldn't you know it? Here I am, stuck with an unclaimed body, and the weather's still bad. We're going to lose at least a couple more Alpiners in the next few weeks. I don't have that much storage space."

I pictured Al regarding his funeral home as some kind of human freezer. The concept made me shiver. It hadn't been so long ago that several bodies were found in the local meat locker.

"Let me know what you find out," I said. "If nothing comes of your inquiries, I can contact some of the local papers and we can run classified ads asking for anyone who knows—or knew—of a Hans Berenger in the Illinois-Wisconsin loop."

"That sounds like a lot of trouble," Al murmured. "Oh, well. It's all in a day's work."

I checked in with Milo via the phone. The forensic lab in Everett had gotten some prints off of the Mitsubishi and was running them through the FBI's database. The sheriff didn't expect to hear anything until tomorrow.

By five o'clock, the weather was again threatening snow. Al was right. We were still deep in winter. Driving the Honda into the carport, I once again wondered about enclosing the open structure. A few years earlier, I'd gone as far as getting some quotes, but the expenditure was beyond my means. Eventually, maybe. Meanwhile, I'd trust the Japanese car's durability.

I was finishing my Lenten dinner of scrambled eggs and canned fruit when I turned on the TV to watch a college hoops game. March madness was almost upon us, and I didn't want to be completely ignorant of the teams that might be contending for the NCAA basketball title.

I managed to catch the end of a close Michigan–Michigan State game, watching a parade to the free-throw line. A time-out was called. I happened to glance at my watch and noted that it was a couple of minutes before seven. Suddenly I remembered what Vida had said about turning on KSKY. I quickly shut off the TV before clicking on the radio. Spence was just concluding an ad for the Grocery Basket.

"And now, stay tuned for the big event we promised you on KSKY," he said, his usual mellow tone injected with enthusiasm. "For the first time, we are proud to present that super source of news in Alpine, our oracle of the airwaves, the woman who knows all and is willing to tell it—may I present Vida Runkel with our new weekly program, *Vida's Cupboard.*"

My jaw dropped. I could hardly believe my ears. But I had to—Vida's familiar, if somewhat reedier, voice was coming from my radio.

"A very pleasant evening to all of you in Alpine and Skykomish County. I can't even begin to tell you how delighted I am to have my very own fifteen minutes of fame, courtesy of Spencer Fleetwood and KSKY. Let's start right in with some of the news we weren't able to fit into *The Alpine Advocate* this week. Unfortunately, there wasn't space for the conclusion of my article about Darlene and Harvey Adcock's recent jaunt to Palm Springs. While the couple had an enjoyable time in California, Darlene emphasized how much she preferred the weather here in Alpine to . . ."

No wonder Vida had been acting so strangely. My first reaction was wrath. I felt betrayed. The seeds of hostility between the printed word and the electronic media had been sown in my college days. Rivalry between the two communications groups starts early and lasts a lifetime. My reaction was that Vida had gone over to the Enemy. I recalled Spence's remark that he didn't have time to sleuth—and he didn't have Vida. Well, he had her now. I glared at the radio.

But I listened. Vida was talking about the upcoming christening of a new baby at the Presbyterian church. We didn't have room to run more than the basic facts about such events. She went on to offer a recipe for Darla Puckett's upside-down banana cream pie. That would be filler—as well as filling—for the *Advocate*. I began to wonder what I'd have done if Spence had offered me my own program. It would be good advertising—which was what Vida was doing. Maybe I shouldn't be angry. But I still was, even as she stopped for a commercial break on behalf of the Upper Crust Bakery.

Vida's Cupboard, I mused. At least it wasn't called *Vida's Drawers.*

Vida returned to the airwaves, her voice sounding more normal. Apparently, a technical adjustment had been made.

"Now, dear listeners and fellow Alpiners," she announced in her most exuberant tone, "you're in for a very special treat. My first guest on KSKY is someone I hold near and dear. May I proudly present my grandson, Roger Hibbert. Welcome, Roger. It's my pleasure as a journalist and a grandmother to have you on our inaugural program."

Please don't ask Roger to define inaugural was my first mean thought.

"Roger," Vida said in her warmest voice, "you are one of those rare teenagers who knows precisely what they want to do with their life. Tell us why you've chosen acting as your future career."

Roger didn't answer immediately. I could picture Vida smiling fondly and pinching his cheek. The lull was broken by a clawing sound and a couple of squeaks. I guessed that Roger was fiddling with the equipment.

"It was when Davin fell down," Roger finally replied, sounding slightly less sullen than usual.

"You refer to Davin Rhodes, one of *The Alpine Advocate*'s outstanding carriers?"

Ah. A plug for the paper. Good.

"Yeah. Davin Rhodes. Rhodesy. Hey, what's up, Rhodesy? How's that hot sister of yours? Woo, woo!"

"Excuse me, Roger. We mustn't send personal messages over the air." She cleared her throat, probably to cover up the rattling noise her grandson was making with the equipment. "Now then." Vida must have been smiling her head off with encouragement for Roger dear. "Could you explain for us how Davin's accident made you realize you wanted to be an actor?"

A beat, another beat before Roger spoke. "He was in this play, like, at the college, and he couldn't, like, be in it 'cause his ankle hurt. So he, like, asked me to do it for him. So, like, I did."

"Now this was just two days before opening night," Vida said. "How was it possible for you to learn the lines so quickly? That was an amazing feat."

"Feet? I didn't have to, like, dance. But I did, like, have to run. That's why Rhodesy couldn't do it. He couldn't run with his ankle all bummed out."

I wondered if Vida was gritting her teeth. "I'm sorry, Roger, I didn't make myself clear. I meant how did you know the part so well?"

"I'd hung out with Rhodesy at rehearsals," Roger replied, sounding impatient. "He didn't, like, have to say a lot. So I kind of knew like what he had to say. When he said something."

"That's remarkable," Vida said. "Such a quick study. But since then, you've expressed a deep interest in acting. How do you explain that?"

Another pause. "Like acting's way cool. You know, like in the movies and TV. It'd be really cool to be an action hero, like Steven Seagal and Clint Eastwood. Except Clint's kind of old and gnarly now."

"Who knows? Maybe you can become the new Clint Eastvold."

"East*wood*, Grams. Jeez, don't you know—"

Vida laughed like a braying mule. "Oh, Roger, such a way to tease your grandmother. Aren't you the one?" She made a noise that sounded like clearing her throat. Or strangling herself. "On a more serious note, Roger, we all know about the terrible tragedy that occurred at opening night of *The Outcast*. Would it disturb you too much to discuss your reaction?"

"To what?"

"To Hans Berenger's untimely demise. *Shooting*, that is."

"Weird," Roger replied. "I mean, like, Otto—the guy in the play—was supposed to get shot, but not totally. After the curtain came down, we were all supposed to join hands to take our bows. We started to do it, but Otto—Professor Berenger—didn't get up. Professor Parsons yelled at him. So did Coach Ripley. Then Coach and Dr. Medved took a look at him—Professor Berenger—and said there was something wrong. The blood looked real, and Otto—I mean, Berenger—still didn't move. There was blood, but we had this cool stuff in what they call squids, and I thought, like, well, he's supposed to have blood from the squids."

"I think that's 'squibs,' Roger dear," Vida interjected. "Do go on."

"Whatever. Anyways, everybody went crazy, and that was when somebody—Coach, I think—told us he was really, really dead. I thought, *Oh, wow!* and tried to get a good look, but Ms. Patricelli was pitching a fit and everybody went, like, nuclear."

To my surprise, Roger's recollection was sufficiently articulate.

"Such a shock," Vida murmured into the microphone. "How have you coped with being involved in such a tragedy?"

"I chilled. I mean, like, the play was over, right? And the dude was dead. It was just like TV."

"So much violence. It's particularly dreadful when Hans was shot in front of a child." Vida's sigh quivered over the airwaves, along with some more scratching and scraping noises. "Thank you, Roger, for a most interesting eyewitness account. I'm sure everyone in our listening audience will agree that you are very brave. Spencer Fleetwood and I are both grateful to you for telling your story. That's all for now until next Wednesday at seven o'clock, when I'll be here to chat with Judy and Connie Dithers about their horses. So for now, I'm closing my cupboard"—a creaking sound and a gentle slam could be heard in the background—"until we meet again on the voice of Alpine, KSKY."

As soon as a canned commercial for Safeway began, the phone rang. I switched off the radio and grabbed the receiver, expecting Spencer Fleetwood to gloat over me.

But it was worse than that. "Hey, hey," shouted Ed Bronsky. "Why didn't Vida have me on her show? I was an eyewitness, too. I could've talked about my reaction and my new book, *Mr. Ed Gets Wed.* And how does Vida get her own program anyway? I'm the one with multimedia experience."

I hadn't made a drink before dinner, but I decided I needed

one now. "This is all a surprise to me, Ed," I responded, carrying the phone out into the kitchen. "Vida kept the program a secret. You might know she'd have Roger as her first guest."

"So what about next week?" Ed demanded. "The Dithers sisters? They don't talk, except to their horses. Everybody knows that."

I had to agree that Vida would be better off interviewing the horses than their owners. "I assume Spence may have lined up some of her guests. I'm sure he's acting as producer."

"Dumb. It's all dumb," Ed muttered. "I'll bet Fleetwood's got Vida hustling ads, too. Well, Vida doesn't know jack-squat about advertising. I do. How many years was I *The Man* when it came to advertising in this town?"

"But, Ed," I said, after taking a hefty swallow of bourbon and 7UP, "Are you implying you want to *work*?" He certainly hadn't worked very hard as *The Man*.

"Oh, no!" he gasped. "I don't mean *that*. I just mean I'd make a good interview. Gosh, think of everything I've done! Why do you think I'm writing volume two of my memoirs?"

Good question. But I ignored it. "Maybe she will interview you." *When Mr. Pig flies,* I thought. "This was only her first show."

"By the way," Ed went on, "sorry I didn't get my first-person account of the shooting done in time for this week's edition. It's running kind of long. You may want to use it in installments."

I'd forgotten about Ed's offer to write his own story. If he'd met deadline—and if we'd had room—I might have printed it. "Don't worry about it, Ed. You should concentrate on including it in your memoirs." I took another slug from my drink and forced myself to ask the question: "Did you come up with anything important that you might not have noticed at the time?"

"Well . . . no. I mean, I did a lot of reflecting. Studying personalities, replaying conversations in my head. You know the sort of stuff. I like to use my brain like a videotape."

Good idea. It doesn't work so well as a brain. "I see. But nothing new?"

"In a way." Ed paused. Maybe he was rewinding. "I didn't know whether or not to put in the part about the marijuana."

"What marijuana?"

"The marijuana some of the students smoked outside the theater. I didn't want to get anybody in trouble."

Ed probably didn't want to get himself in trouble by being a stool pigeon. "Kids will be kids," I remarked. "I don't necessarily approve and in fact I think it should be legalized, if only to cut down on the criminal activities that are involved."

"I don't know about that." Ed sounded a bit pompous. "Funny . . . I thought you could smell it."

"You can—it smells like broccoli that's boiled over onto the stove."

"You couldn't smell this stuff. I mean, it smelled, but not like I remembered. Of course," he added hastily, "I've never tried it. What kind of example would that be for our kids?"

Much better to let them watch Dad and Mom eat themselves into morbid obesity. "Are you sure it was pot? Users smoke other things these days, too."

"You mean . . . like *cocaine*?" Ed was aghast.

"Yes, among other things. Don't you remember the meth lab disaster last year?" I asked, referring to one of the sorrier episodes in Skykomish County.

"Gee. That's right. Well, I wouldn't name names."

"Did you recognize any of the students you saw?"

"Huh?" Ed seemed lost in thought. Or *reflection*, as he would say. "Oh . . . you mean who was doing it. I think so. They were off in the trees, by the college maintenance building. It wasn't just kids. Destiny Parsons was there once, so was Rey Fernandez and . . . I forget who else. There were a lot of students I never got to know. They were in and out."

"You didn't mention any of this to Milo?"

"No. Why should I? It didn't have anything to do with Berenger getting shot."

"Maybe not." Then again, maybe it did.

Alpine was beautiful when I woke up on Thursday morning. Two inches of new snow had fallen, covering all the slush and windstorm debris. The clouds had lifted; the air was crisp. I chided myself for not feeling invigorated.

As usual, Vida had arrived at the office before I did. It was her turn for the bakery run. The big, fat cinnamon rolls from the Upper Crust were still warm from the oven.

"Free," she announced, pointing at the tray next to the coffeepot. "They're a thank-you for having their commercial run during my program last night. They knew everyone would be listening."

Bold as brass and unrepentant. I narrowed my eyes at her. "Why didn't you tell me?"

She simpered a bit. "I wanted it to be a surprise. That's why the station didn't advertise in the paper. Spencer only did some on-air promotions, but he didn't use my name. What did you think?"

"I was annoyed," I admitted. "I still am. I'm not sure it's a good idea. It seems like a conflict of interest."

"Twaddle." Vida was definitely her old self this morning. "I wouldn't dream of using anything on KSKY that should go in the *Advocate*."

I believed her. "In that case, maybe I should consider it a good promotional ploy."

"Of course." She looked past me as Leo came through the door. "Well?"

Leo removed his snap-brim cap and sailed it across the room onto his desk. "Well what?"

"Didn't you hear my program?"

"What program?"

Vida jerked off her glasses and began to rub furiously at her eyes. "Ohhh . . . Leo, you're the most irksome man I've ever met!"

Laughing, Leo nudged Vida's shoulder. "Sure, I heard it. You were great, Duchess. Right up there with Larry King and Jerry Springer."

Vida stopped savaging her eyes to look up at Leo. "Who?"

"Never mind," Leo said, hanging his jacket on the back of his chair. "But why the hell didn't you tell us? Better yet, take out an ad in the *Advocate*?"

Vida blinked several times, then put her glasses on. "We will. I'll make sure Spencer puts one in next week."

Scott, Ginny, and Kip were all agog about Vida's radio debut. Obviously, they were more broad-minded than I was. Vida's phone began to ring. The first three calls sounded as if they had become members of her radio fan club. The next two seemed more like critics. Vida became defensive, even hostile. She hung up on somebody, so I retreated to my cubbyhole, coffee mug and cinnamon roll in hand.

I had to make a call of my own. "Milo," I said when I was put through to the sheriff, "what do you know about drug usage at the college?"

"It's there," Milo replied in his laconic manner. "Kids are going to smoke pot. As long as they aren't dealing, we ignore it."

"Somebody must be dealing," I declared, and related Ed's account.

"Ed." Milo spoke the name with disdain. "Since when did you trust Ed?"

"It's not a matter of trust," I pointed out. "Ed has absolutely no imagination, so he doesn't make things up. For all I know, the people he saw were smoking cigarettes, not drugs. But I'd figure that even Ed would be able to distinguish tobacco smoke from something else."

"So what? Did he see anybody dealing?"

"He didn't mention it," I replied.

"Why are you getting wound up over this deal?" Milo sounded impatient.

"We're missing something," I asserted.

"How do you mean?"

"Where's the motive for shooting Hans? We haven't found anything that indicates he has a dark past. His love life—such as it was—seems innocuous. He was a hard worker. He wasn't popular, but nobody apparently hated him. Why was he killed? Or was it really an accident?"

"Beats me," Milo said. "But the only way it could've been an accident was if he wasn't the intended victim." The sheriff sighed. "Look, you think I'm sitting on my dead butt. I'll admit we're stalled, but we're not giving up. Right now, we're checking out the possibility that the bullets were meant for Ridley or Fernandez. They were right in the middle of the so-called fight onstage."

I was slightly incredulous. "You're suggesting that some football player's folks wanted to shoot Rip because their kid didn't get enough playing time?"

"That's not as crazy as it sounds," Milo asserted. "You read about stuff like that in the paper and see it on TV. Little League parents attacking other parents or coaches, even killing them."

"What about Rey? Have you checked him out?"

"Sure," Milo replied. "He's from Fresno via Seattle. He came up here to take a construction job a couple of years ago. He liked the area, didn't like construction, and decided to go to college. He sounds serious about getting involved in radio or TV. Except for some speeding tickets, he's clean."

Everybody's innocent, I thought. How vexing. "Okay," I said in a plaintive tone. "I'll stop pestering you. For a while."

"Good," Milo said, sounding as if he meant it. "You've already gotten Destiny mad at me. That's just great. She's mad at you, too, by the—hang on."

The sheriff turned away from the receiver. I could hear another voice in the background. I thought it was Jack Mullins. I couldn't make out exactly what they were saying, but it was a good two minutes before Milo spoke to me again.

"We got a hit on our car thief," the sheriff said. "His name is Darryl Ivan Eckstrom. Last known address in Mountlake Terrace. That figures—it's close to the Alderwood Mall. He's been picked up a couple of times for auto theft and once for dealing crack. He got off on a technicality."

"Someone may be dealing crack to the college students," I said. "I take it you'll check that out and see if there's a connection between Eckstrom and anyone in Alpine?"

"Do you want my job?" Milo retorted. "You sound like you think you could do it better than I can."

"No," I began, "but there could be a link with the campus, since the locals have to get their drugs from—"

"Stick it, Emma." Milo was beyond being irked; he was mad. "And don't ask if Destiny knew this bird. She already told me loud and clear that nobody except Boots Overholt was at her house last night."

"I thought Eckstrom might have been enrolled at the college at some point," I remarked innocently.

"He's a high school dropout," Milo snarled.

"Yes, but some dropouts go to community colleges to get a GED. It's possible that Eckstrom—"

Milo interrupted. "I've got to go. I don't want you to think I'm still sitting on my dead butt."

On that surly note, Milo hung up.

I wondered if Al Driggers was making any progress on his search for information regarding Hans's late wife, Julia. I was about to do some surfing of my own on the Internet when Vida poked her head into my office.

"Was that Milo? Did he hear my program last night?" she asked.

"I didn't mention it," I admitted. "He was too busy being a jerk."

"Oh." Vida looked disappointed. "I must confess, I'm not thrilled over next week's interview with the Dithers sisters. That was Spencer's idea. I can't think why, but I felt I should humor him. After that, I plan to invite Pastor Purebeck from my church. For the Lenten season, you know. Contrary to what you Catholics may believe, we Presbyterians also acknowledge Lent."

"I never thought you didn't," I said. "I think having Pastor Purebeck on your show is a good idea."

"So that I don't offend," Vida went on, "I'm going to do a series for the paper on all the local pastors, including your Father Kelly. When I interview Pastor Purebeck, I'll have him expand on what he gives me for my House & Home page."

"Good."

But Vida wasn't done justifying herself. "I wouldn't have used the Adcocks if you hadn't cut the end of my vacation story off so abruptly."

"I had to," I replied. "I wanted to get Nat's statement into this week's edition."

"I don't know why," Vida remarked. "It was just more educator babble. Oh, well." In her splayfooted manner, she retreated to the newsroom.

I realized then that I wasn't mad at Vida anymore. The occasional spat between us always upset me. I knew she'd be annoyed by cutting the reference to Darlene Adcock's preference for the local weather. No other place, including Utopia, could ever come out ahead of Alpine, as far as Vida was concerned.

The smile I'd been wearing turned into a frown. Harvey and Darlene Adcock hadn't returned to Alpine until a week ago Wednesday. Jim Medved had bought the blanks for the .38 on the previous Monday at the hardware store. That meant someone other than Harvey had sold them to Jim.

I wanted to know who.

FOURTEEN

Julia Elizabeth Blair Berenger had been born April 12, 1963, in Milwaukee. She had married Hans Albert Berenger June 21, 1985, in that same city. On February 20, 1993, she had died in San Diego. I don't navigate the Internet very well, but after almost an hour I had found the information I was seeking and passed it on to Al Driggers and Milo.

At noon, I went to Harvey's Hardware and caught him just before he left for lunch. Harvey has two full-time employees, Verb Vancich and Warren Wells. He also uses some part-time employees, including the Peabody brothers, who are as strong as they are dim but make excellent lumberyard and delivery workers. Harvey also hires high school and college students as fill-ins.

"I keep a list of about ten kids," Harvey informed me, going behind the main counter. "It's often a last-minute call. Sickness or some other problem that my regulars can't anticipate. Let me see who came in a week ago Monday when I was in Palm Springs. Warren Wells would have made the contact." He was looking at a clipboard that apparently listed the number of hours each employee had put in. "Ah. Here we go. That would have been Davin Rhodes."

"Really." I tried to conceal my surprise. "I didn't know Davin worked here."

"He has—off and on—since before the holidays," Harvey explained. "He's laid up now, of course, with a bad ankle. But we needed some extra help for Christmas, and Davin was one of the high school students looking for some spending money." Harvey peered at me over his half glasses. "What's this all about, Emma? Am I in trouble over those darned blanks?"

"No, you're fine," I assured him. "Were you the one who originally ordered the blanks?"

"Yes. I did it the day before we left on vacation." Harvey glanced at the wildlife calendar on the bulletin board. "Darlene and I flew to Palm Springs February eighth. I put the order in February seventh. Do you want me to check it?"

I shook my head. "What I'd really like to know is who actually sold the blanks to Jim Medved."

Harvey, who is small and spare, stood on his tiptoes to look over the old-fashioned display cases. "Warren? You there?"

Warren Wells, who had remarried his first wife, Francine, after an interval of many years, came around from the nuts and bolts section. "What's up? Oh, hi, Emma. Francine told me that if I saw you to say she's got her spring line of Ellen Tracy in this week."

I smiled at Warren. "I'll have to wait for the markdowns," I said. Francine's Fine Apparel catered to the more upscale customers in Skykomish County. She also stocked items for the rest of us, or she wouldn't have survived.

Warren, who'd been in retail most of his life, had an infallible memory for customers as well as for merchandise. "A week ago Monday started out slow. The snow, I guess. Anyway, I took time out to run down the street to McDonald's. I left Davin in charge. Jim came in on his lunch break, so I missed him. What's the problem? You think we may have sold Jim real bullets?"

I grimaced. "A switch was made at some point," I added

with an apologetic expression, "though I'm sure it didn't happen here. I was curious, that's all."

I jumped as someone poked me in the back.

"If it isn't Lois Lane," Jack Mullins said with a grin. "Why do I have the feeling you're on the case?"

"Is that why you're here?" I retorted.

"Me?" Jack laughed. "No. I'm buying a space heater for Nina. My wife swears it's twenty below in our bedroom. I agree, but the space heater isn't going to warm things up."

Warren laughed out loud while Harvey chuckled discreetly. I shot Jack a dirty look. He was always giving Nina a bad time, at least when she wasn't around to defend herself.

"You'd be better off trying to figure out who wanted Hans Berenger dead," I asserted.

"Ah," Jack responded, "that's what I've been doing the last couple of hours. Dwight and I paid the Kruegers a visit. It seems they didn't like the cut of Berenger's jib. They thought there was something weird about the guy. They'd almost have preferred taking Fuzzy's lowball offer."

"Will they, now that Berenger's dead?"

"Not if they can help it."

"What was wrong with Berenger?" I inquired as Harvey moved away to help Skunk Nordby find nails and Warren led Alfred Cobb, one of our doddering county commissioners, toward power tools.

Jack had become serious. "The Kruegers couldn't put it into words. Berenger asked some odd questions, especially about security measures. Then, when Mrs. K. made some reference to Pasado's Safe Haven being down the road a ways, Berenger got flustered. It seemed peculiar to the Kruegers."

Pasado's Safe Haven was an animal shelter between Sultan and Monroe. It had been founded in memory of a much-loved donkey that had been tortured to death by a bunch of nasty teenagers.

"It seems peculiar to me," I declared. "Why would Hans act like that about a place that does so much good?"

"Damned if I know," Jack replied. "The Kruegers didn't, either. They didn't think Berenger had ever heard of it before. Maybe he hadn't. He wasn't around here that long." The deputy gave me another poke, this time in the upper arm. "Hey, got to find that space heater. Maybe it'll warm up my lovely wife. Ha-ha."

Jack moved along to the home appliance section. Feeling obligated to make a purchase, I restocked my battery supply and paid for it after Skunk Nordby had left with his bag of nails.

The giant cinnamon roll had filled me up, so I postponed lunch. The Chamber of Commerce office in the Alpine Building was on my way back to the office. Taking a chance that Rita might be in, I decided to pay her a call.

She was eating a tuna salad sandwich at her desk and looking as unpleasant as usual. "Now what?" she asked, licking mayonnaise off of her lower lip.

"Gee, aren't you ever glad to see me, Rita? Wouldn't you like to be in the news?"

"Cut the crap," she shot back. "You're here to ask me questions about Hans. Do you think I'm stupid?"

Ordinarily, that question was best avoided, but I wanted her cooperation. "Of course not. And yes, you're right. After all, you're the only one who seemed to know him well. Don't you want to find out why he was killed?"

"Isn't that up to Dodge?" she retorted.

"Sure. But our sheriff isn't always people-oriented. He's a just-the-facts-ma'am type. And," I added, trying to sound confidential, "he can't talk to women."

"You ought to know," Rita said. "Is that why you two broke up?"

I forced myself to remain civil. "Not really. Speaking of breaking up, why did you? With Hans, I mean."

She turned away, digging into a small bag of potato chips. *Crunch, crunch.* "We seemed to be going in different directions. I'm interested in a long-term relationship. Hans wasn't it."

"How do you mean, 'different directions'?"

Munch, munch. "We had different interests. Different goals. Don't get me wrong, I liked him. But I didn't see us going anywhere as a couple."

"I know what you mean." It sounded good. "Maybe," I allowed though it pained me to say so, "that was part of the problem with Milo and me." Girl talk. Sharing. Emma does *superficial.*

Scrunch, scrunch. "Men. It's all about them. I wanted a vine-covered cottage." Rita peered into the potato chip bag, saw it was empty, and tossed it into her wastebasket. "I mean, really. With garden statuary, maybe a statue of St. Francis or a cherub. Hans wanted land." She paused to eat the last of her sandwich.

"The Kruegers' land, I heard."

Rita nodded. "Right. That's a lot of land and a big house, not to mention a commute. No thanks. I like to garden, not farm."

"Hans was going to turn it into a working farm?" I inquired.

"No, not exactly," Rita replied. "He wanted to raise dogs, like the Kruegers did. I told him I didn't get it. He didn't even own a dog of his own."

"I don't think he could," I pointed out. "Not in an apartment."

"That's why he wanted to move, I guess," Rita said, wiping her hands on a paper napkin. "Personally, I don't like dogs, and I positively hate cats." She nodded at a pair of goldfish in a big bowl on top of a filing cabinet. Rita had named them Paulie Walnuts and Big Pussy after two cast members from *The Sopranos.* "Those are the kind of pets I like. No muss, no fuss."

"So that's why you ended it," I remarked.

"Pretty much." Rita frowned. "I think I'll take a break from men for a while. Alpine isn't exactly the place to meet somebody in my age group and who isn't as ugly as a pig's rear end." She suddenly brightened. "What about Fleetwood? He's eligible, isn't he? Don't you think he's kind of attractive?"

My long-standing rivalry with Spence disqualified me. "I suppose. He's not my type, though."

Rita's smile bordered on a sneer. "He's not rich, either."

The camaraderie we'd found briefly evaporated like drops of water on a hot stove. "That's unkind. I was never interested in Tom Cavanaugh's money." Before Rita could respond, I kept talking. "Which brings up another matter—where did Hans get the money to cash out the Kruegers?"

Rita shrugged. "He was a tightwad. We always went Dutch, unless I volunteered to pay. That ticked me off, too. He made more money than I did, plus he must have had some insurance from his wife. She worked for the state of California. I've heard they have good benefits."

"Someone told me Julia was a marine biologist. Was she killed in an accident of some kind?"

"Hans never talked about her," Rita said. "He didn't even have a picture of her. The only thing he ever told me was that she was very smart and something of a blond goddess." Rita's expression was rueful. "About the opposite of me. I wondered if he said that just to make me feel bad. Hans wasn't much for building a girl's ego."

"Did he ever mention getting a threatening letter at the college?"

Rita looked at me in disbelief. "Are you kidding? No. Did he?"

"I heard he did," I said, but like a good journalist I wasn't willing to reveal my source. I glanced at the big round clock on the wall behind Rita's desk. It was almost one o'clock. Watching Rita eat had stirred my hunger pangs.

"I'd better get going," I said, standing up. "You make Hans sound sort of like a pill. What did you like about him?"

It appeared that Rita had to think about that for a moment. "He was intelligent. He was devoted to his job. Reliable, I guess that's one of the things I liked. He didn't drink, he didn't smoke, he was a real straight arrow. And," she added with a wry little smile, "he was available."

The Desperation Game, I thought. I didn't like Rita much, but I felt sorry for her. Finding the right man—any man—after forty was no picnic.

It was just as well that I wasn't looking.

Or was I?

I'd applied myself to the job that afternoon, feeling as if I'd been spending too much time being a detective. The familiar routine always soothed me. I could zero in on the task at hand and block out everything else, including murder. Sometimes I could even stop thinking about Tom.

Milo was right—the investigation was his job, and he knew how to do it. But after four o'clock, when I'd completed a story on forest service road closures in the area, my mind went back to the murder of Hans Berenger.

I went into the newsroom to ask Scott if Tamara had a late-afternoon class. She didn't, he informed me. She spent the last hour or so grading papers and seeing students. Returning to my desk, I phoned Tamara.

"That letter!" she said when I asked her about the so-called threatening missive Hans had received shortly before his death. "He was a very unemotional man. But the letter—let me think— it was last Tuesday. Anyway, it really upset him. Not that I blame him for it, judging from what I saw. Imagine! Someone writing to say that he would die by Friday—and he did!"

Tamara's sense of drama had come to the fore. I could imagine her at her desk, making hand gestures and generally reenacting the incident. It was too bad she hadn't been cast in the play.

"But you heard nothing about any other letters to him?" I inquired. "Did anybody on the faculty know he'd been threatened before?"

"Before? You mean when Justine Cardenas went off on him at the faculty party?"

"Well . . . that, too."

"I don't think it was serious," Tamara replied before lowering her voice to almost a whisper. "I mean, can you imagine Mrs. Frosty Cold Cardenas seriously threatening someone? Frankly, I think she'd had too much to drink. The president's lady likes her liquor, if you ask me. Ohmigod!" Tamara exclaimed, still *sotto voce*. "What if my phone is bugged?"

"Doubtful," I said. "Frankly, I've wondered about Justine myself. When it comes to drinking, I mean."

"You have to," Tamara asserted. "What does she do all day in that fancy house? She has some woman from Index come in to clean for her every week. It isn't as if Mrs. C. goes out of her way to take part in the community unless she has to."

"She does needlepoint," I noted.

"Oh . . . yes, I think she was showing off some of her handiwork at the party. I suppose you have to be sober to get a needle into those little tiny holes. Personally, I hate crafts."

"What were Justine and Hans arguing about at the party?" I asked. "Something must have set her off."

"I don't know," Tamara answered, sounding disappointed with herself. "I only heard about that secondhand. It may have had something to do with Hans's work. I always thought he was ambitious."

"To get back to the letter," I said. "Did you talk about it with anyone else on campus?"

"Um . . . yes, I think I mentioned it the next day—that would've been Wednesday—to Clea Bhuj. She thought it must be a joke. But that's certainly not how Hans reacted. Besides, can you imagine anybody playing a joke on him? He had absolutely no sense of humor. I always thought if he really smiled his face would crack and the top of his head would fall off."

"Your office was across the hall from his, right?" I waited for Tamara's confirmation. "Did he usually keep his door open?"

"Not as a rule. But I figure he'd probably just come back from getting his mail and had forgotten to close the door. Maybe," Tamara continued, her voice rising with excitement, "he recognized the handwriting on the envelope and couldn't wait to see what the letter said."

"The letter was handwritten?"

"No, it was typed. But you know how sometimes you type a letter, but you address the envelope by hand."

"Yes, I do that myself." The truth was, I wasn't clever at printing envelopes on the computer. The addresses often came out upside-down or sideways. "Did you see an envelope?"

"No," Tamara admitted. "I wasn't there long enough to see much of anything except those words on the letter itself. He more or less threw me out."

Leo strutted past my door displaying a mock-up of a full-page ad for Nordby Brothers' GM March Madness sale. I nodded approval. "What did Clea think when you told her about the letter?" I said into the phone.

"She seemed shocked," Tamara replied. "Or pretended to be."

"Why do you say that?"

Tamara hesitated. "I don't like to gossip, but you're Scott's boss and he thinks you're wonderful. So I suppose it's all right to pass this on."

"Scott's wonderful, too," I remarked.

"Yes, he is, isn't he?" Tamara sighed in a dreamy sort of way. "Do you think I'm too old for him?"

"I don't know how old you are," I said. "Not yet sixty, I trust."

Tamara laughed merrily. "Oh, Ms. Lord! No, I'm five years older than Scott. I'll be thirty-four in August."

"That's not much of a difference," I said. "And please call

me Emma." We'd gotten off the track. "What were you going to say about Clea?"

"I don't think she liked Hans," Tamara said, the laughter gone. "It's nothing she ever mentioned, but it was her attitude. He could be very critical of how she ran the Humanities Division. Generally, he was a critical sort of person. But efficient. He did his job very well. Still, he wasn't one to hand out compliments—just criticism. 'Constructive criticism,' he would have called it. But it riled Clea, among others."

"I don't get it," I said. "I thought Clea insisted that Hans take a part in the play."

"She did," Tamara responded. "But I think she had kind of a mean motive for that. I was supposed to be the café owner and cook. Then Clea insisted that Destiny change the role for a man and that Hans should take the part. Destiny wasn't happy about it, but Clea's her division head, so she caved."

"I didn't realize you were in the original cast," I remarked.

"I never got that far," Tamara said with a little laugh. "I never even saw the script."

"You mentioned a 'mean motive' on Clea's part. Was she being mean to you or to Hans?"

"To Hans," Tamara replied. "I think she wanted him to make a fool of himself. You know, he was the greasy-spoon cook, and he didn't have very many lines. It was a far cry from his usual pompous, aloof self. I figure Clea thought she'd bring him down a peg, and in front of an audience, especially students."

Kip was standing in the door with what looked like software in his hand. I held up two fingers, indicating I'd be off the phone in a couple of minutes.

"That's an interesting theory," I noted. "Clea sounds like a bit of a conniver."

"She's clever," Tamara said. "I'm very careful around her. I think she likes to stir up trouble. It amuses her somehow."

"Some people are like that," I agreed. "Thanks for talking

to me. One of these days when I get organized, I'll invite you and Scott over for dinner."

"Sounds terrific," Tamara enthused.

On that convivial note, we hung up. Kip wanted to install the new software in my computer, which meant I had to vacate the desk. I went out into the newsroom, where Vida was using her two-fingered typing method to pound much harder than she needed on the electric typewriter.

"Ah!" She stopped typing and looked up. "You were certainly having a long phone conversation just now. Was it worth your while?"

I sat down next to her desk and related everything that Tamara had told me. I also caught her up on my visit to Harvey's Hardware and the Chamber of Commerce.

Vida ran a hand through her unmanageable curls. "I've been remiss. I can't believe I haven't become more involved in this Berenger situation. I've let myself become distracted with other things. Is there anything I don't know?"

"Oh, there's more," I assured Vida, and proceeded to fill her in on the driver of the stolen car, his connection to drugs, and anything else I could remember.

"It's almost five," she said. "Why don't you come home with me and I'll fix a lovely hot meal."

No, you won't, I thought, *at least not a meal that could be termed "lovely."* "That's too much work," I asserted. "Why don't we go to the diner for dinner?"

"Oh! What a good idea," Vida declared. "I haven't been there in some time. How soon do you want to leave?"

I told Vida I had to wait for Kip to show me how to use the new software.

"Software!" Vida exclaimed with a scowl. "Why do they call it that? It's not at all soft. From what I've seen of it, software looks like very small phonograph records. And this Windows business—what is that? I have yet to see a window on anybody's computer. Do they mean the screen? So why not call it a screen? Then there's that clicker thing they call a mouse. Does it look like a mouse? Certainly not. It makes no sense whatsoever. Why can't these computer people speak *English*? They have no respect for the language."

I didn't entirely disagree with Vida about the terminology, but I couldn't waste time with a vocabulary discussion. I had computer problems of my own, trying to comprehend what Kip was telling me about the new software. It took him almost half an hour to make a dent in my nontechnical brain, and even then, I had no confidence in my ability to remember his instructions.

When Vida and I headed for the diner in our separate cars, it was snowing again—soft, wet flakes drifting over the Honda's hood and windshield before evaporating on contact.

"It's best to come early," Vida declared as we slipped into a booth where the wall was decorated with photographs of James Dean, Marilyn Monroe, and Elvis Presley to evoke the 1950s. "Later in the evening, they turn the music up far too loud. All that rock and roll. It's almost as bad as what the children today think is so wonderful. Whatever happened to Big Bands?"

"The bands got smaller," I said. "We got bigger. Older, at any rate."

"You're too young to remember the Big Band era," Vida pointed out. "You had your own music. What did they call it when you were a teenager?"

"The Beatles," I replied. "Bob Dylan. All the protest songs and the folk music and the Rolling Stones and . . . Frankly, I wasn't really into popular music that much. In high school, I wasn't part of the 'in' group."

Emma, the Outsider. I'd always been that way. I still was, especially in Alpine, where you had to be born on Skykomish County soil to belong. I liked to think that my exclusion gave perspective to my writing.

"Like *The Outcast*," Vida murmured, "and here she comes."

I turned in the booth so I could see Destiny Parsons coming down the aisle. She caught my eye, looked startled—or irritated—and stopped.

"Hello, you two," she said, then glared at me. "I have to tell you, I didn't appreciate your prying the other night. I ended up with a couple of sheriff's deputies making my life miserable. But you probably already know that."

"I'd heard," I replied. "Look, I'm sorry. I had no intention of causing problems for you."

"Yes, you did," Destiny shot back, angrily loosening the plaid muffler she had wound around her neck. "You're a snoop." Her sharp gaze landed on Vida. "You, too. You're both snoops."

"It's our job," Vida said airily.

"That just gives you an excuse," Destiny countered. She turned back to me. "If I didn't know better, I'd think you were the one who killed my poor Azbug."

"I'd never do such a thing," I said hotly.

"I know you didn't," Destiny retorted, though there was no softening of her stance. "It was Hans Berenger who murdered my poor Azbug. Well, he got what he deserved, didn't he?"

Destiny stomped away, the tails of her muffler flying behind her like battle flags.

"Well now!" Vida exclaimed. "Is Destiny trying to incriminate herself? That dog's death could be a motive for murder."

"It could," I said in a thoughtful tone. "But Destiny isn't stupid. Why would she say something so mean about Hans if she'd killed him?"

"To throw us off the track," Vida replied, then gave a little shake of her head. "Besides, how does she know it was Hans who broke the dog's neck?"

I shrugged. "Beats me. Maybe she's guessing. She didn't like him, either."

"Nobody did, it seems," Vida remarked. "Except Rita."

"And even Rita had dumped him," I pointed out.

"Yes." Thoughtfully Vida fingered the menu. "Men. Women. Dogs."

"What?"

One of the younger Bourgette daughters, Teresa, known as Terri, arrived to take our order. Vida asked Terri to greet the Bourgette sons who had started the restaurant and were working in the kitchen. I inquired after the senior Bourgettes, Mary Jane and Dick.

"They're fine," Terri replied, "all things considered. Mom will feel better after Grandmother's funeral tomorrow. She ended up taking over the arrangements. Uncle Harold and Aunt Gladys don't cope very well in times of crisis."

"How typical," Vida declared. "Your poor mother was cut off by Thyra because she married a Catholic, and now Mary Jane is the one who has to take on the family responsibilities. Please send her my condolences."

I suspected that Vida's condolences were not for the death of Mary Jane's mother but for having to perform the tasks that should have been handled by Harold and Gladys.

Terri's brown eyes twinkled. She undoubtedly knew about the animosity between Vida and her grandmother. Indeed, because of Thyra's harsh treatment of Mary Jane and the old lady's refusal to acknowledge the existence of her daughter's family, Terri probably sided with Vida. "I'll do that. Mom and the Lutheran pastor in Snohomish have already had three huge arguments."

"I'm sure," Vida purred, "that your mother probably won. Lutherans can be so pigheaded. Catholics are more cunning."

I gave Vida the Evil Eye. "Don't you mean they're more clever?"

"No," Vida replied, unrepentant as always. "I believe I'll have the Audrey Hepburn shrimp Louie. There's an asterisk by it that says it's slimming."

"Got it," Terri replied, making a note on her order pad.

"But don't skimp on the Thousand Island dressing, please," Vida added. "So often with a Louie, you get halfway finished and there's nothing left to put on the rest of the greens. Oh, I'd like an extra hard-boiled egg or two. The entrée comes with rolls, I see. Would you mind bringing at least three? Rolls make such a nice addition to a salad."

I requested the Tony Curtis steak sandwich and fries with a side of Janet Leigh green salad.

"Woof, woof," I said after Terri had left. "What were you saying about dogs?"

"Oh. Dogs." Vida nodded once. "Yes. Hasn't it occurred to you that dogs play a large part in this Berenger business? Destiny believes—rightly or wrongly—that Hans killed her pet. Hans wanted to raise dogs on the Krueger property. Jim Medved's gun killed Hans, and Jim is a veterinarian. And Dodo, of course, was in the play."

"You have a point," I remarked, "but I assume you're not saying you think Dodo killed Hans?"

"Of course not," Vida said. "What I don't understand about the dog issue is that Hans didn't seem to like dogs. Let's assume Destiny is right—Hans did kill Azbomb or Aspirin or whatever the dog's name was. Didn't he also get into a ruckus with Jim Medved over Dodo?"

"That's true," I said. "I'd forgotten. I think Hans kicked Dodo at one point during rehearsals."

Vida put her fists on her hips and gave me a probing look. "Why would someone who treats animals badly be interested in raising them?"

I admitted I was stumped. "We could be misjudging Hans," I said. "We only have Destiny's word for it that Hans broke Azbug's neck. As for Dodo, he's a big and rather clumsy sheepdog. He may have bumped into Hans and knocked him down or caused some sort of minor injury. Hans may have been in a bad mood and overreacted."

"It sounds as if Hans was always in a bad mood," Vida asserted.

At that moment, Al and Janet Driggers came our way. I almost didn't recognize them. To my astonishment—and Vida's—Al was wearing a black leather jacket, jeans, T-shirt, and snap-brim leather cap. His usually straight, neat dark hair was tousled, and instead of his customary ramrod stance, he slouched. Even more amazing was Janet, wearing a blond wig and a knockoff of the white dress with the pleated skirt and low neckline that Marilyn Monroe had worn in *The Seven Year Itch*.

"Hey there!" Janet called as they approached our booth. "Anybody know where I can find a hot air vent to stand over?"

"Goodness!" Vida cried. "Aren't you freezing to death? It's thirty-two degrees outside!"

"Why do you think I'm looking for some hot air?" Janet asked in a breathy Monroe voice. She grabbed Al by his leather sleeve. "How do you like Marlon Brando here?"

"Very convincing," I murmured. "Do you always dress like this when you come to the Bourgettes' diner?"

Janet shook her head. The wig stayed firmly in place. "Don't you read your own ads? This is Fifties Celebrity Night. It doesn't start until eight, but we came early to get a good seat. I hear Fuzzy Baugh is dressing up as Jerry Lee Lewis."

I reached inside my purse to get out the cell phone. "I must call Scott. We'll want pictures."

Scott, however, knew about the event. He and Tamara were coming as Montgomery Clift and Elizabeth Taylor in *A Place in the Sun*. Scott was prepared to mix business with pleasure.

Janet had been twirling around, showing off a figure that was not quite up to Marilyn's standards but sufficiently sexy to cause several male diners to stop in their tracks and lean out of their seats.

"No, Janet," Vida was saying as I put the phone back into

my purse, "I don't believe we'll stay for the show. It'll be noisy—all that rock and roll."

"That's the fun of it," Janet replied. "We'll dance. Sing. Carry on." She grimaced. "And listen to Fuzzy play 'Great Balls of Fire' on the red piano in the bar. I hear Irene's doing a riff on Ingrid Bergman in *Anastasia*. You could've come as the Grand Duchess, Vida. Except you're a lot taller than Helen Hayes."

"I think not," Vida sniffed. "I've always found costume parties silly. People put on such outlandish clothes just to attract attention."

Janet was probably trying as hard as I was to keep a straight face. Vida was wearing a black-and-white fur hat that looked like a dead skunk.

"By the way," Al said, attempting to mumble like Marlon Brando, "thank you, Emma, for giving me the Berenger information." He paused to clear his throat. When he resumed speaking, he sounded like himself, which was a good thing, because I could barely understand his Brandoesque impression. "Unfortunately, none of the people we've contacted were related. Tomorrow, I'll try to find out more about Mrs. Berenger, but her maiden name of Blair is so common. I don't expect to have any luck."

"Start with the University of Wisconsin," I suggested. "Hans and Julia met there."

Al nodded solemnly. "I shall. That's a good idea."

It turned out to be both a better—and a worse—idea than I could ever have imagined.

FIFTEEN

AL AND JANET DRIGGERS LEFT US JUST AS OUR FOOD ARRIVED. Vida was full of smiles for Terri Bourgette, who had brought what looked like a pint of Thousand Island dressing.

"Why," I asked my House & Home editor, "didn't we have a story this week about the celebrity doings here? Leo knew about it because the Bourgettes took out an ad. Scott knew, too."

"Too many other things on our minds," Vida said, slathering a hot roll with butter. "Really, the last few days have been most eventful."

"That's no excuse," I declared. "We could have squeezed an inch or two in somewhere."

"Only if we'd deleted Thyra's ghastly photo," Vida responded.

"The Rasmussens bought that space," I pointed out. "In fact, I'll bet poor Mary Jane Bourgette ends up paying the bill, even though she would never have wanted to run the picture in the first place."

"That reminds me," Vida said, and looked faintly embarrassed. "I took a message for you while you were at lunch. Goodness, I'm at fault as much as the next one when it comes to oversights. Nat Cardenas has called an emergency meeting of the Board of Trustees for Saturday night. Seven-thirty, the conference room in the RUB. Mary Jane's a member, which is what spurred my recollection."

"Yes." I put my steak knife down. "But calling a meeting on a Saturday night? That's odd. Maybe they're in a hurry to fill Hans's position. I'd better attend instead of sending Scott."

"It's not open to the public," Vida said. "Curious, isn't it?"

"I don't recall a closed meeting of the trustees before now," I said. "I wonder if it's legal? They're a state institution."

"Perhaps you could challenge them. The press should never be shut out of important meetings."

And Vida should always be allowed to know what was going on, press or not. "I'll call Marisa Foxx tomorrow and find out," I said.

Vida speared two shrimp at once. "Isn't her law partner, Jonathan Sibley, a trustee? Surely he'd know whether it was legal."

"That doesn't mean he'd challenge Nat," I said. "Jonathan also represents the college."

Vida sighed. "It's all curious, isn't it?"

I had to agree.

We left the diner a little after seven, just as Lucy and Desi arrived along with Buddy Holly and a couple of Elvises. I'd been tempted to stay, but I didn't want to sit alone. I wished I'd had the nerve to call Milo and tell him I'd dress up like Grace Kelly if he'd come as Gary Cooper from *High Noon*. Tom would have done it. Milo would think I was nuts.

Instead, I went home and moped. Requiring company for my misery, I called Ben in Tuba City.

"You are a world champion pain in the ass," declared my brother. "Do you realize how much I spent on that dinner we had at Ristorante Camponeschi on the Piazza Farnese? As a missionary priest I took a vow of poverty, not stupidity. I guess I wasted my lira. I might as well have thrown it in the Trevi Fountain."

"I'm not moping about Tom," I retorted. "I mean, not in the usual way I mope about him. I just said that if he were here, he'd have gone with—"

"Stop. I heard you the first time. Furthermore, you look about as much like Grace Kelly as I look like George Clooney. What were you going to wear? Or did you plan to steal a vintage dress off of Thyra Rasmussen's corpse?"

"Ben!" I cried. "Sometimes I wonder why you became a priest. You seem a little short on compassion, if you ask me."

"I didn't ask," he shot back in his crackling voice. "And I've got plenty of compassion for those who really need it. You need a kick in the butt. If it's not Tom you're moping about it, what is it?"

I tried to rein in my temper. "I take it you've seen this week's edition of the *Advocate*?"

"I read it on-line this morning, right after I said Mass," Ben replied. "Sounds like you've got another big mess up there. Can't those people find something better to do than murder each other?"

"It's winter," I snapped. "They're bored."

"Are you sure Vida didn't strangle Thyra?"

"She was tempted," I admitted. "Maybe the recent deaths are why I feel glum. Oh, hell, Ben, I'm not glum so much as frustrated. Within four days, I see a college prof shot before my very eyes, then an old lady croaks in the middle of our newsroom. How much horror can one person take without being affected?"

There was a pause. "I see tragedy every day. We all do. Here it's a sense of hopelessness, poverty, disaffection, survival, loss of identity, conflict between the old ways and the modern world. It's a baby born with a serious heart defect, a husband beating his wife and his kids, young people leaving the reservation and ending up homeless on the streets of Phoenix or Flagstaff, an old man dying alone and not being found for two weeks. I feel like the little boy trying to put his finger in the dike. But I keep going because if I can plug up one hole, I'm doing something worthwhile. I'm asked if I feel good because I'm carrying out God's plan for me. Hell, I don't think God has a plan for me or anybody else. And how do I know that the thing I'm doing *is* the right thing? It may seem like it is, but in the long run, maybe it's not. I can help reconcile an unhappy couple and feel as if I've accomplished something that pleases God. But two years later, when the wife stabs the husband with a hunting knife, I realize it would've been better if I'd let them split up in the first place. Life's tough, Emma. It's supposed to be. You do what you believe is right at the time. You can't do a damned thing about what happens outside of your control. You suck it up and keep going."

"Gosh," I said in wonder. "You sound worse off than I do."

"No." Ben was emphatic. "No worse, no better. I just want to put things in perspective for you. Death—even violent death—isn't the worst thing that can happen. Death is part of life. It's the end of suffering." To my surprise, Ben chuckled. "You're not as upset over that Berenger guy and the old lady dying as you are about not being able to find out who committed murder. You're a writer. Every story has to have a beginning, a middle, and an end. You're frustrated because you're mired in the middle. But not all stories have an end. Maybe this is one of those that don't."

"Hunh," I said. "I called for compassion and got common sense instead."

"Often, it's the same."

"How true." I smiled into the receiver. "I'll hang up now and stop bothering you."

"You don't bother me," Ben responded. "You piss me off, but you don't bother me. Have you talked to Adam lately?"

"Not this week," I said. "He was going to Fairbanks for some meetings."

"I'll e-mail him over the weekend," Ben said. "Hey, I didn't mean to deliver a homily."

"You didn't," I replied. "You were giving your kid sister good advice."

"Really? All homilies should do that. It's what I try to do here. Short and sweet. Well, maybe not sweet. Say," he said, "speaking of church stuff, does Cardenas ever attend Mass?"

"Not that I know of, unless he goes to the Saturday five o'clock," I said. "I almost always go on Sunday. Why do you ask?"

"You told me once he was raised Catholic," Ben said. "I was just curious. What about his wife?"

"She's a WASP, through and through," I replied. "There was a 'Scene' item Vida did at Christmas about Justine donating flowers for Trinity Episcopal. But I don't know if Mrs. C. actually attends services there."

"How about Rita Patricelli?" Ben inquired.

"She's a C&E type," I said, referring to Catholics who only go to Mass at Christmas and Easter. "What is this, a poll of churchgoing Alpiners?"

"Not really," Ben replied. "A greater percentage of small-town residents attend church than big-city dwellers do. It's not a question of faith but of having something to do, somewhere to go, some place to socialize. Often it's a matter of conformity. Not to mention that you're a little short up there when it comes to minorities. As far as religion goes, it's a Christian community. Lutherans on top, Catholics on the bottom, and everybody else in the middle."

"That's true," I agreed. We don't have any Muslims and only a couple of Jews. I'm not sure what religion our small Asian population follows, except Dustin Fong, who's a Methodist. Carla Steinmetz Talliaferro shows up once in a while at St. Mildred's with her husband, Ryan, but I don't think she's ripe for conversion. In fact, I don't think she ever really practiced Judaism, much to her parents' sorrow."

"Why don't you call her?"

"What?" I frowned. "You want me to start converting Carla?"

"Of course not," Ben said. "But she advises the student news-paper, doesn't she? I remember some of the tales you used to tell when you worked on *The Mitre* at Blanchet and *The Daily* at the UDUB. Maybe Carla's got the lowdown on somebody at the college."

"Why didn't I think of that?" I mused aloud. "Except Carla is such a scatterbrain, I don't know if I could rely on anything she told me."

"I'm just trying to make you feel less frustrated," Ben as-serted. "Give it a shot. It's better than griping to me."

"I will," I said. "I think I'll do it now."

But Carla and Ryan had gone to Celebrity Night, according to their baby-sitter, who sounded faintly frantic.

"They promised not to be late," Debbie Gustavson said in a testy voice. "They'd better not be. I'm getting a cold and I have a social studies test tomorrow. Omar won't go to sleep and I can't study."

Omar was the Talliaferros' four-year-old son. Suddenly I heard a terrible crash in the background. Debbie let out a yelp. The phone let out a squawk. Apparently, she'd dropped the re-ceiver, but we were still connected. I could hear her shouting at Omar, who was either laughing or crying.

Apparently, the noise he was making was caused by plea-sure, not pain. Debbie was scolding him. After a noisy interlude, Debbie came back on the line.

"Omar pulled over his bookcase," she said in an angry voice. "It's a wonder he didn't kill himself." She sneezed twice, then began to cough. And cough and cough.

"Are you all right?" I asked.

More coughing, then several gasps. "Yeah . . . sort of. But I quit. I'm never going to sit this little brat again! I'm going to call the diner and tell Mr. and Mrs. Talliaferro to come home right now! I'm sick!"

"Wait, Debbie," I urged. "If you're really sick, I'll relieve you. Can you hold on for about fifteen minutes?"

"It'll take me that long to find Omar," she replied in a miserable voice. "I don't know where he is."

"I'll be there," I said, and after I hung up the phone I wondered if I'd lost my mind.

I hadn't yet undressed, so I got into the Honda and drove the short distance to the house Carla and Ryan had recently bought a mile from the college in Ptarmigan Tract. When Debbie came to the door, her nose and eyes were running and she looked as if she had a fever. Omar, however, was in fine fettle. He was standing on the dining room table, beating a metal wastebasket with a cooking spoon. *A Roger in the making,* I thought, and stepped aside as Debbie bolted through the front door and called out a muffled thank-you.

The house was a shambles, but that probably wasn't all Omar's fault. Carla had never been much for cleaning, and her desk at work had always been only slightly less cluttered than mine.

Upon seeing me, Omar stopped banging the spoon and stared with suspicious dark eyes. The only time I'd seen him in the past six months was during the holidays. He had Carla's dark coloring but his father's husky build.

"Are you a kidnapper?" Omar asked, backing away toward the edge of the table.

"I wouldn't dream of kidnapping you," I said. "Don't move or you'll fall."

Omar moved and fell. Luckily, the floor had plush new carpeting. The kid started to cry, but he sounded as if he was faking it. I tried to sit him up, but he punched me in the face.

"No! Go away! I don't like you!" Omar got up on his own and crawled under the table. "You can't catch me. Ha-ha."

"I don't want to catch you," I said. "Stay there. I'm going to sit down."

Which I did, on the Talliaferros' leather couch in the living room. I could see Omar watching me, but at least he was quiet. For the moment. It was almost nine-thirty. I wondered how late Carla and Ryan would stay out on a work night.

"I'm hungry." Omar kicked at one of the table legs. "I want cookies."

"Go get them," I replied.

"You get 'em," he retorted, kicking harder.

If Adam had ever said the same thing to me, I would have grabbed him by the feet of his footie-paws and given him the bum's rush into bed. But Omar wasn't Adam. The Talliaferro scion was obviously undisciplined.

I ignored the kid.

"I want cookies!" he cried

I picked up a copy of *People Magazine*.

Omar began to scream at the top of his lungs. I admired Gwyneth Paltrow's evening gown.

My ears were ringing from Omar's nonstop howling when Carla and Ryan came through the front door with Scott and Tamara behind them.

"Emma!" Carla exclaimed. "What are you doing here? Is Omar okay?"

"Ask him," I shouted over the kid's screams.

"Sweetheart!" Carla raced into the dining room and got down on her knees. "What's wrong, little love? Tell Mommy."

Ryan was looking bewildered. Scott and Tamara seemed embarrassed. While Omar demanded cookies, I explained my presence to the others. By the time I'd finished, Carla had brought the cookies from the kitchen and given them to her son, who decided he didn't want them after all. He crawled out from under the table, took one look at me, and said, "She's mean. Make her go away." Sticking his tongue out at me, he marched off to his bedroom.

Ryan thanked me for relieving Debbie Gustavson. "It's a

good thing you could come," he said, removing his cowboy hat. "Baby-sitters are really hard to find these days."

No kidding. "The fact is," I confessed, "I wanted to talk to Carla."

"Maybe we should go," Scott put in. He didn't evoke Montgomery Clift's troubled mystique, but he could give any handsome actor a run for his money.

"No," I said. "Since Tamara's here, I'd like to talk to her, too. Do you mind?"

Tamara, who resembled Audrey Hepburn more than Elizabeth Taylor, broke into a big smile. "You're investigating, aren't you, Ms. Lord? I mean, Emma."

"A journalist never stops working," I said with a self-deprecating expression.

Scott grimaced. "I've got to learn to be more like that."

"You're getting there," I responded.

Carla, who was dressed as a pioneer woman and wore a shoulder-length red wig, came out of Omar's bedroom. "The little guy's worn out. I can't understand why Debbie didn't put him to bed."

Ryan chuckled. "That'll be the day," he drawled.

I got it. He was supposed to be John Wayne. Despite the cowboy hat, the kerchief around his neck, and the toy guns in his holster, Ryan's average height and robust physique hadn't given me any clues.

"I'm going to make coffee nudges," Ryan said. "Do you want one, Emma?"

"Sure," I said. "Thanks."

Ryan went out to the kitchen. The rest of us sat down. Carla announced that she was Maureen O'Hara.

I didn't waste time getting to the point of my visit. "Carla, you must hear a lot of scuttlebutt at the college, especially from the students, since they're not as discreet as the faculty and staff. What do you know about Hans Berenger?"

Carla's big dark eyes widened. "How do you mean?"

"What was he like? How did you get along with him? What did other people on campus think about Hans?"

"I hardly knew him," Carla said. "One of the students interviewed Hans last fall. There were a couple of mistakes in the article, and Hans pitched a fit. He couldn't understand how we called him 'Hams' in the paper. Hadn't he ever heard of a *typo*? He also got mad because he said we misquoted him about his philosophy of education. Oh, then he insisted we'd gotten the curriculum screwed up." She clapped a hand to her wig. "Hans went on and on. He even criticized our spelling and punctuation and grammar. Finally, I told him that this was a learning experience for students, not a professional publication. Students need to express themselves in their own way. Some of them are really clever and insist on the freedom to write in their own style. So what difference did it make if our reporter wrote that Hans was 'planning to conference in Tacoma' or 'planning to *attend* a conference in Tacoma'? It means the same thing. Picky, picky, picky. You'd think Hans would've had better things to do than criticize the newspaper."

"Now, Carla," Ryan chided as he balanced a tray containing five steaming mugs, "the man's dead. He wasn't any worse than Destiny Parsons when she complained about being called 'Parsnips' in the paper."

Carla waved a dismissive hand. "They're all alike. Bitch, bitch, bitch. And I get blamed for everything. As I told Nat Cardenas a while ago, you can't make an omelet without cutting the cheese. Students learn from their mistakes."

Despite discreet snickers from the others, Carla's recital—as well as her mangled aphorism—had brought back painful memories. I couldn't help but glance at Scott and be thankful that he'd taken Carla's place. Scott might need a push to meet deadlines, but he could spell, punctuate, and type with a certain amount of accuracy.

"What about you, Ryan?" I asked, accepting a coffee nudge from him. "Did you have much to do with Hans?"

"Not really," Ryan replied, sitting down on the ottoman by Carla. "Hans wasn't a hands-on administrator. He was big on memos. Long memos. And he delegated. I don't want to criticize him now that he's dead, but Hans was really aloof. Nat Cardenas is warm and fuzzy by comparison. But Hans got the job done. He was especially good at keeping an eye on the budget."

"Which didn't make some of the faculty very happy," Tamara interjected. "I don't think he would have let Destiny put on her play if Thyra Rasmussen hadn't come through with funding for it. Hans wasn't open to new programs, and he felt the college should hire more part-timers." She gave Carla a sympathetic look. "Like you."

"Right." Carla curled her lip. "Part-timers don't make as much money and they don't get benefits. Plus, they can be let go anytime. Hans was just plain cheap. Last summer, when Hans and Coach Ridley got into it, I was hoping Rip would punch Hans out. But somehow, Rip held his temper."

"What were they quarreling about?" I asked. "The possibility of expanding the sports program?"

"Right," Carla repeated. "Hans didn't like sports. He didn't think they belonged on a two-year college campus. He got really mean about it, according to Rey Fernandez, who was there at the time."

"Nat must have backed Hans on his decision," I pointed out.

"Oh, he did," Ryan asserted. "Nat rules, no doubt about it. There were plenty of issues that both men agreed on, and sports was one of them. Rey told me that Coach Ridley would hardly even look at either Nat or Hans during the play rehearsals."

Rey. Rip. I'd only spoken to them briefly since the homicide. Rip had a temper and he was known to hold a grudge. But I couldn't see him planning a murder. He was the type to suddenly erupt and unscrew Hans's head from his shoulders. As for

Rey, I didn't really know him. But Spence did. Maybe he and I should talk.

I asked Ryan and Carla if they'd heard about threatening letters to Hans. Ryan didn't recall anything. Carla said she got threatening letters all the time. I understood and sympathized. But only Tamara seemed to know firsthand that Hans had been warned he would die on Friday.

Somehow, the conversation turned to campus politics in general. Tamara felt the emergency Board of Trustees meeting had been called to consider Hans's successor. Ryan suggested it might be a meeting for exploring ways to mend the college's image. Carla thought the trustees were going to plan an Easter egg hunt on campus.

What wasn't mentioned, however, seemed significant. Nobody brought up the possibility of Nat Cardenas accepting another position. The college's rumor mill must have broken down. I was surprised. Somebody must know about the offers that Nat had received.

Maybe that somebody had been Hans Berenger.

Friday morning I called Marisa Foxx. She informed me that it was perfectly legal for a state institution to hold a closed meeting.

"This is particularly true when they're dealing with personnel or property issues," Marisa said in her clear, calm voice. "They can't, however, keep decisions private. If the trustees hold a vote on something, they're required to go public."

I thanked Marisa and hung up. Meanwhile, I was anxious for an account of Thyra Rasmussen's funeral. It would be well into the afternoon before Vida returned. The funeral was at eleven, there was a reception to follow at the big old Victorian home in Snohomish, and the round-trip would take close to two hours.

Of course I had my own agenda that began when I phoned

Spence and asked if he could meet me for lunch. He couldn't, since he was going to be broadcasting until two o'clock, when Rey got finished with classes.

"How about dinner?" Spence inquired.

"The truth is," I said, "I want to talk to Rey. When's a good time?"

"God," Spence moaned, "my ego just deflated like a cheap tire. Why do you want to see Rey?"

"I'm sleuthing," I admitted.

"I suppose you're mad at me about Vida," Spence remarked.

"I'm trying not to be," I said. "But you'd better stick to the format of using only items that wouldn't go in the paper."

"I didn't hire Vida to scoop you," Spence assured me. "I can do that on our regular news broadcasts."

I sighed. "I know. But there's nothing I can do about that."

"Rey's on the air until eight," Spence informed me. "He takes an hour break between four and five. Come to the station then. He never strays very far. Are you considering him a suspect?" Spence's tone was good-natured, but I felt he had to be concerned.

"No, just a witness. I've tried to interview the people who were most closely involved," I explained. "Milo and his deputies have talked to everybody else."

"Got to get back to the mike," Spence said. "Good luck."

I went into the newsroom to check the AP wire. There was nothing pertinent to Alpine or Skykomish County, but I got an idea. It was off-the-wall and it would force me to humble myself, but I'd take the chance. Back in the cubbyhole, I dialed the number for Seattle's AP office.

"Rolf Fisher, please," I said to the operator.

"May I tell him who's calling?" the operator replied in a silky-smooth voice.

I gave my name. There was a pause before I heard Rolf speaking into my ear.

"Aha. You can't keep away from me, can you, Emma?"

"I see your face everywhere," I said in a tremulous tone. "In my dreams, on my computer screen, at the bottom of my recycling bin. Oh! Strange! I am haunted." In truth, I somehow pictured Rolf as short, dumpy, bald, and lacking in personal hygiene.

"No shit," Rolf replied. "What do you really want?"

"I want information," I said in my normal voice.

Rolf chuckled in a lecherous manner. "It'll cost you."

"It's already costing me, just to ask," I retorted. "Really, at the next newspaper meeting I'll buy you a drink, okay?"

"That's not much of an offer. Will you marry me?"

"You're already married," I said, though I had no idea if he was or not, since I didn't remember meeting him.

"No, I'm not," he replied, sounding serious. "My wife died of a brain tumor two years ago."

"Oh." I felt remorse. "I'm truly sorry."

Rolf didn't say anything.

But he'd given me a natural transition. "I'm calling about another man who was widowed," I said. "Have you done any follow-ups on the Berenger shooting?"

"If I had, you'd have seen them on the wire," Rolf replied, still solemn. "We won't run a story until an arrest is made. *If* it's made."

"I understand," I said. "What I want to find out is if you can check your files to see if there's a story—probably out of San Diego eight years ago come February—about Julia Blair Berenger, Hans's late wife. Nobody seems to know how she died. Hans never talked about it. I realize people often don't want to discuss a tragedy, but usually, if asked, they'll at least mention the cause of death. As you just did, Rolf."

"Yeah, that's true," Rolf allowed. "Okay, I'll check it out. It may take a while. I'm a busy man," he went on, sounding more like his cheeky self. "I've got all these hot babes chasing me around the office."

"Thanks, Rolf. I really appreciate it."

"No problem. When do we announce our engagement?"

"Let's wait until after we meet."

"Fair enough. I'm sending a big, wet kiss your way." He made a smacking sound and hung up.

Going on three o'clock, I hadn't heard anything from Milo, so I assumed there were no developments, or at least none that he was willing to share with me. I'd left a message for Rip Ridley at the high school but figured he wouldn't return my call until late afternoon. While Rip's main job was coaching football, he was also in charge of all the boys' sports programs. There was scarcely a day that he didn't have to be on hand after school for some kind of game or practice.

I was reminding Leo to make sure Spence bought an ad for *Vida's Cupboard* when the radio star herself staggered through the door.

"Aaargh!" she cried, leaning on the door frame. "It was too horrible! I feel as if I need an antidote! I've been poisoned with lies! Such nonsense from the pastor! So hypocritical and false!"

"That bad, huh, Duchess?" Leo remarked, taking a fresh pack of cigarettes out of his desk drawer. "Want a smoke?"

"Ack!" Vida exclaimed, making her unwieldy way across the room. "If I were a drinking woman, I'd have a drink. But I'm not. Is there hot water for tea?"

"There's the ticket," Leo said. "A good strong belt of Lipton's works wonders."

Vida glared at Leo. "It does for me."

I took her mug over to the big urn, poured water, and plopped in a tea bag. "Big turnout?" I asked innocently.

"Sufficient," Vida declared, removing her beribboned black felt hat. "Curiosity seekers, of course. The woman had no friends."

After adding creamer and plenty of sugar, I handed Vida her tea. "How were Harold and Gladys holding up?"

"They were being held up by two of the pallbearers," Vida

replied. "I believe they were both already drunk. Then Harold passed out shortly after we went back to the house for the reception. Gladys wouldn't stop crying. But the food was tolerable. It was catered, of course. Lovely salmon finger sandwiches and quite a tasty fruit salad, though I don't care for kiwi."

I sat on the edge of Vida's desk. "Did Mary Jane and Dick Bourgette come?"

Vida blew on her mug and nodded. "Very brave of them. Or at least charitable. Mary Jane was kind enough to give me a tour of the house. I'd never seen all of it. When you and I were there a few years ago, we were allowed only into Thyra's inner sanctum. But this time, I saw everything, including the ballroom on the third floor. I must say, there are some nice pieces of furniture, if you like that sort of overdone Victorian style, which I do not. But if the house and the furnishings are sold, they should fetch a very pretty price."

I made a face. "Which will go to Harold and Gladys, I presume."

"I suppose." Vida sighed. "Such a waste. That house would have been perfect for Mary Jane and Dick to have raised their children. They would have brought some joy to it, instead of all the misery that Thyra and Einar Sr. created."

Leo blew several smoke rings, a trick he knew Vida deplored. "I wouldn't be surprised if the old bat left everything to the college—or at least to the theater program."

For once, Vida didn't scold Leo for his smoking habits. "You know, you're right. I wouldn't be surprised, either. The estate will certainly be wasted on Harold and Gladys or any of the other wretched family members. Except Mary Jane, of course, but I'm sure she was never mentioned in the will. Oh," Vida said, narrowing her eyes at me, "I did manage to ask Mary Jane about the Board of Trustees meeting Saturday. She didn't know why it had been called but assumed it was to organize a search committee to find a replacement for Hans."

"That makes sense," I said as the phone rang in my office. "Be right back," I promised, hurrying to pick up the call before it trunked over to Ginny.

"It's your future husband here," Rolf Fisher said. "What kind of engagement ring do you want? Nothing too garish, I hope."

"I'm not into jewels," I replied. "Does this mean you found out something about the late Mrs. Berenger?"

"That it does," Rolf replied, sounding very pleased with himself. "I told those lascivious ladies here to take some long, cold showers. Thus, I had time to look into your query."

I felt a growing excitement, but not for the offer of Rolf's hand in marriage. "And?"

"I'll read the story to you," Rolf said. "It's fairly brief, and originated in the *San Diego Union-Tribune* eight years ago in February." He paused. "Dateline, San Diego, quote, 'A local woman was dead on arrival yesterday at Mercy Hospital after suffering more than two dozen bites by her three-year-old German shepherd. Julia Berenger, 33, was attacked when she arrived home from work shortly before 6 P.M. A neighbor, Eleanor Lacey, heard the victim's screams and called 911. Medics and other emergency personnel arrived within ten minutes but were unable to save Berenger. The dog was put down by a police officer who had been summoned to the scene. Berenger is survived by her husband, Hans, who wasn't home at the time of the incident. According to Lacey, the dog, whose name was Gus, had always seemed well behaved. The victim's widower, a professor at San Diego Mesa College, was in seclusion and unavailable for comment.' Unquote." Rolf took a deep breath. "Does that help?"

I winced. "It might." But at the moment, I didn't know how.

SIXTEEN

Dogs. They were barking in my brain. Kruegers' kennels, Azbug, Dodo, Vince, and now a German shepherd named Gus. The Kruegers had raised German shepherds. Why would Hans Berenger, whose wife had been killed by a dog of the same breed, want to raise them?

There could only be one reason, and it was so terrible that I didn't want to think of it. But I had to.

The phone rang. It was Rip Ridley.

"I'm taking a quick break from a run-through for tonight's basketball game," he said. "You want to come up and watch the Buckers review their offensive and defensive alignments against Arlington? It's an away game, so the buses leave at four."

That gave me less than half an hour to get to the high school and query the coach. But I agreed. I could go from the school to the radio station to meet with Rey Fernandez.

Rip was making sure each player knew who he was supposed to guard on defense. Like most gyms, the place smelled like sweat. When the coach saw me he walked over to the scorer's table. Most of the Buckers stood around and talked while the others practiced free throws.

"So what's going on?" Rip asked, snatching up an errant ball that had bounced our way.

I explained that I was still working on the Berenger story. "I thought maybe you—as well as some of the other witnesses—might have remembered something you'd forgotten to mention at the time. Has any detail—no matter how small—come to mind?"

Rip grinned. He wore a whistle around his neck and a hooded sweatshirt in the high school's green and brown colors. Since he'd begun losing his hair rather rapidly, Rip had shaved his head. His fair eyebrows were almost nonexistent and his skin had a pinkish hue. I was reminded of a cheerful baby. A very big baby, of course.

"I wish I could remember more," Rip replied. "If anything, I remember less." The grin disappeared. "I suppose I'm trying to forget the whole mess."

I nodded. "Let me ask a different question," I said. "What do you know about training dogs?"

"Me?" Rip shook his bald head. "Not that much. Vince—my dog—is a golden retriever. You don't train them to retrieve, because that's what they do. You just sort of coach them. If you've got a dog problem, talk to Medved."

"I will," I replied, "but I thought you might know something about what you can and what you can't do with dogs. Such as training them to kill."

"Jeez." Rip rubbed at his chin. "What brought that on?"

I shrugged. "Just a weird idea of mine." I raised my voice as Rip shouted criticism at his lanky center. "I'd better go," I said. "It's almost four. You have a team bus to catch."

"We'll make it," Rip said, glancing up at the big clock above one of the baskets. "There is one thing I do know about dogs in general. Whatever you train them for, it's better to start early. But the old saying, 'You can't teach an old dog new tricks,' isn't true. The main thing is that the dog has to recognize the owner as, in effect, the leader of the pack. If I'd gotten Vince when he was two or three years old, it would have taken me one hell of a long time for him to accept me as his new leader."

"Interesting," I murmured. "Oh . . . by the way, do you remember seeing Justine Cardenas backstage before or during the play Friday night?"

Rip grinned again. "The Ice Maiden? No, not that I recall."

I started to move down toward the home team's bench. "I don't suppose you have a favorite suspect as Hans's killer."

Rip caught another errant basketball and bounced it hard on the floor. "You bet I do. Me. I hated the bastard."

It was exactly four o'clock as I left the high school for the radio station. It was the second day of March, and the days were noticeably longer despite the low-hanging gray clouds. But there had been no snow all day and the forecast called for temperatures above freezing. I hoped the thaw would be slow, with no threat of flooding.

At KSKY, Rey Fernandez was in the tiny front office shuffling through a stack of CDs. He was expecting me and stood up when I came through the door.

"Canned goods," he said, pointing to the broadcast booth behind him. "I did five minutes of news at four, and now we've got some farmer's wife in Iowa telling our listeners how to prepare savory Lenten meals. I don't know where Spence got that one—tuna fish seems about the only seafood she ever heard of."

I sat down across the desk, noticing that the upholstered chair was almost new and far more comfortable than the rickety wooden ones we had at the *Advocate*. Again I went through my spiel about recollections of the tragedy and asked if Rey had anything new to add.

He didn't, though he gave the query some thought. "There was opportunity," he said. "That prop box wasn't guarded every minute, though Boots did his best. But there were just too many distractions. I was running around all over the place, trying to help out the techs. What's more, with those headphones on most of the time, I couldn't hear anything even in my immediate surroundings."

"You didn't see a bushy-haired stranger, I take it."

Rey laughed and shook his head. "That's not to say there wasn't one. I was in a zone."

I shifted uneasily in the chair. "Rey, what do you know about drug use among the college students?"

Rey stiffened. Even his black mustache seemed to bristle. "Small-town sentiment runs to racial profiling, I take it? Any Hispanic must know about drugs?"

I sighed. "You could be Polish or Pakistani and I'd still ask the question. You're older than most of the kids on campus and less likely to be intimidated by a snoopy reporter. Someone"—I neglected to mention that the someone was Ed, who was not always a reliable source—"saw you and some of the other students along with at least one faculty member smoking something strange outside of the theater."

"Good God!" Rey cried. "So Berenger's murder is connected to a few people having a toke? I don't believe it!" He ran a hand through his dark hair. "I thought you were more broad-minded than that."

"I am. I hope," I added. "No, I don't have any reason to think the murder and the drugs are related. But I'd like to know what a car thief who's also a drug dealer was doing in Alpine the night Hans was killed."

"Oh." Rey seemed to calm down a bit. "You mean the bushy-haired stranger?" He waited for me to nod my agreement, then waited a little longer. "Okay. Sure, there's pot on campus, there's pot all over town. Big deal. There's other stuff, too, and the students get some of it. So do faculty members and, for all I know, maybe the mayor and the county commissioners and the Baptist minister—Poole, isn't it?"

"I realize we're not living in a cocoon," I said. "Good Lord, we all know that after last year's meth lab mess."

"Right." Rey glanced at the clock. Four thirty-five. "I should get organized for the next segment. I wish I could be more help."

He seemed pleasant enough, but the dismissal struck me as abrupt. "I wasn't asking you to squeal on anybody," I declared.

Rey's smile was off-center. "I couldn't help you if you did." He returned to sorting the stack of CDs. "Good luck. Good-bye."

My abrupt departure allowed me to stop by the sheriff's office before Milo left for the day. When I arrived, he was in the reception area, leaning against the curving counter and eating popcorn.

"Have some," he offered. "Toni made it for us before she left early to see Dr. Starr. She had a toothache."

"Guess what?" I said after stuffing a handful of kernels in my mouth. "I know what happened to Hans's wife, Julia."

Milo cocked his head to one side. "What?"

Dwight Gould and Jack Mullins, who had been studying the latest copy of *Combat Handguns*, looked up from the other side of the counter.

"Julia was attacked by their dog and died from the wounds," I announced.

"Ugly," Jack said.

"That's bad," Dwight said.

"Are you sure?" Milo asked.

I scowled at him. "Of course I'm sure. I got it from someone at the Associated Press in Seattle who read me the original story from the San Diego newspaper."

Milo munched on his popcorn. "I'd really like to get a dog someday. The trouble is, I can't spend much time with an animal. And I don't hunt like I used to. I've always wanted a water spaniel."

"Milo!" I actually stamped my foot. "Doesn't this news mean something to you?"

"Like what?"

"Like . . ." I stopped. "Like why was Hans going to buy property? To raise dogs, the same kind that killed his wife?"

"Or train them *not* to kill?"

I considered the idea, then rejected it. "No. I'm thinking he trained their dog *to* kill."

Milo choked on his popcorn. "Jesus!" he exclaimed after pounding himself on the chest. "That's wild!"

"But it happens," I said quietly. "I've heard about such things, but most cases don't get to court. They're impossible to prove."

Milo took a swig from a can of Sprite. "Yeah, I've heard those stories myself. I thought maybe they were . . . what do you call them?"

"Urban legends?" I shrugged. "Maybe, maybe not."

"But even if it's true," Milo said, still looking dismayed, "what has it got to do with Hans getting shot eight years later in Alpine?"

"I'm not sure," I admitted.

Jack Mullins was shaking his head. "If it happened, it proves what a rotten S.O.B. Hans really was. No wonder Al Driggers can't get anyone to claim the body."

Dwight nodded solemnly. "You can train a dog to kill when you're not around. You have to use the right trigger. Like some regular habit of the victim's. You know—opening the liquor cabinet, putting on a gardening hat—whatever." Dwight grew even more somber. "If Berenger could do that to his wife, think what kind of other skulduggery he might've been up to. Or had on the drawing board."

"We're guessing," Milo said flatly. "That's no help."

I felt deflated. "Well, I thought I'd let you know."

"Thanks." Milo ate some more popcorn. "How do you know Berenger wasn't investigated?"

"I don't," I confessed, "but Cardenas is the cautious type.

At SCC, the dean of students is second in command. Nat would be pretty thorough in checking out a prospective hire."

"Probably." Milo was still looking thoughtful. "It's pretty weird, though. I wonder if Mrs. B. was rich."

"Money's always a good motive," Jack noted.

"Maybe I'll do some more checking," I said.

"Go ahead," Milo said. "Let me know if—" He stopped as his cell phone went off. "Dodge here," he said, turning away from the rest of us. "Right. . . . Sure. . . . No, it's your jurisdiction for now. . . . Good. . . . Here? . . . That makes sense. Who was the contact? . . . You're kidding me. . . . Yes, definitely get back to me. Thanks."

When the sheriff again looked at us, there was a glint of satisfaction in his hazel eyes. "That was SnoCo. They picked up Darryl Eckstrom this afternoon at a Lynnwood motel. He had about ten grand worth of crack cocaine with him. Eckstrom wants to cut a deal, so he's naming names, not just his suppliers but who he was dealing to. He handed over a list of about ten contacts. One of the names on that list was Hans Berenger."

It made sense, or so it seemed. Eckstrom hadn't yet served any prison time and would be a willing informant to keep from being put behind bars. The guy didn't sound very smart, but he'd be savvy enough to save himself. The way Milo figured it, Eckstrom had stolen a car, driven to Alpine last Friday night, and then skidded off the road and gone into the river. Or maybe he'd decided to ditch the Mitsubishi before he was picked up in it. He'd shown up backstage just long enough to exchange the blanks for bullets. Maybe, Milo said, Hans was trying to cheat him or get out of the deal. In any event, Nat Cardenas had involuntarily fired the shot that had killed Hans. Eckstrom had his revenge and an alibi. He'd probably been drinking at Mugs Ahoy when the murder was committed. Milo would wait until the

Snohomish County authorities were finished with Eckstrom before bringing him to Alpine for questioning.

"Drugs," Dwight said in disgust when Milo had finished. "These days, it always seems to come down to drugs."

Milo grabbed my arm. "Come on, let's go have a drink. Hell, I'll buy dinner. Jack, Dwight, meet us at the ski lodge when Dustin and Sam show up to relieve you."

"Can't," Dwight said with a doleful expression. "My wife's folks are coming for dinner."

Jack made a face. "I promised Nina I'd floss her teeth tonight. Or some damned thing."

Still holding my arm, Milo looked at me. "Emma?"

"Huh?" I'd only half heard the others. "Oh . . . sure. Shall I meet you there?"

"Ride with me," Milo said. "Maybe I'll even put on the siren."

I didn't want to puncture the sheriff's good mood. "Okay."

"I'll only be a few minutes," Milo promised, going behind the counter. "I've got some paperwork to do."

"That's fine," I said. "Is it all right if I borrow your computer out here? I want to look something up."

"Go ahead," Milo replied, and disappeared into his office.

I sat down at Toni Andreas's desk and keyed in the *San Diego Union-Tribune*. I clicked on the Archives icon and typed "Julia Blair Berenger" in the Search box. Four articles showed up. One of them was the story Rolf Fisher had read to me over the phone. Another was about pond research she was doing for the state. The third was a brief follow-up on her death but revealed nothing new. The fourth and final piece was her obituary.

It was standard fare, but I gaped at the list of survivors. Besides Hans, there was another name I knew, and it sent chills down my spine.

———

"We aren't talking business tonight," Milo declared after we got into his Grand Cherokee. "It's Friday, the case is wrapped up, and the baseball season is one month away. Let's think about the Mariners. It's going to be their year."

"Okay." My enthusiasm was halfhearted. It wasn't that I didn't want to talk about the Mariners, but I had something else on my mind. Maybe, I reflected as we turned off Alpine Way onto Tonga Road, there was no hurry to discuss the name I'd read in Julia Berenger's obituary. But I didn't really believe it. On the other hand, Milo deserved a break after his harrowing workweek.

Halfway through my bourbon and water, I managed to give the sheriff my full attention. He deserved it, especially since he'd offered to pick up the check. By the time we'd ordered our entrées as well as a second cocktail, he'd covered the pitching rotation and I'd assessed the bullpen. Milo ate a New York steak and I dined on halibut cheeks while considering the outfield, the catchers, and the bench. By the time his slice of chocolate decadence cake arrived along with my mocha, we were appraising the strengths and weaknesses of the other American League West teams. Midway through the Anaheim Angels, I set my coffee cup down and looked bleakly at Milo.

"What happened to the drugs?" I asked.

Milo scowled. "What?"

"I'm sorry," I said, "but the theory about Darryl Ivan Eckstrom has some holes in it. When did he have time to deliver the goods? If he came to Alpine to sell drugs to Hans Berenger, what happened to them? They weren't in the car, were they? Would Eckstrom head for a tavern in a town he didn't know with the drugs still on him?"

"The guy's stupid." Milo looked peeved. "Hell, Emma, you're going off on some tangent. I want to kick back."

I wasn't giving up. "Furthermore, why would Eckstrom write a threatening letter telling Hans he planned to kill him? And even if he did, why didn't Hans tell you? Look," I went on, taking a pen and a small notepad out of my purse. "Let's make a time line."

"Sheesh." Milo ran a hand across his brow. "What next, flip charts?"

"Bear with me. Please."

Milo didn't say anything. He ate the last bite of cake while I began to write. "Tuesday—letter," I scribbled. "DIE Friday," I added. "Hans had almost four days to alert you—or somebody else, like Cardenas—about the threat. Why didn't he act to protect himself?"

"Because," Milo said in a weary voice, "he didn't want anybody to know he was mixed up in drugs. How hard is that to figure out?"

The sheriff had a point. "Yes. Well, it still doesn't make sense. If Eckstrom came to the theater"—I paused to write: "Friday—play"—"why didn't Hans watch for the guy? Or get him out of the backstage area?"

"Maybe Berenger hadn't ever seen Eckstrom before," Milo said.

"Hmm. Maybe he hadn't." I frowned at my brief notes. "Oh, good God!" I exclaimed, and waved the notepad at Milo. A young couple at the next table stared. They looked like weekend skiers and probably didn't expect anyone in a small town to get excited. "It wasn't a death threat!"

The sheriff stopped in the act of lighting a cigarette. "Emma, have you gone nuts?"

I held up a hand in a pleading gesture. "Be patient, please. Tamara quoted the part of the letter she saw as saying 'you are going to DIE'—cap letters—'Friday.' Carla mentioned something last night about how sometimes people leave out a word, especially when they type. I think whoever wrote that letter to Hans meant to say, 'You are going to *meet* DIE Friday'."

Sadly Milo shook his head. "Poor Emma. She always seemed so sane."

I tapped the notepad. "*DIE* is capitalized because it's initials. Darryl Ivan Eckstrom." I sat back in my chair, waiting for Milo's response.

Milo smoked and stared at my notes. The young couple at the adjoining table was giving us dirty looks. Smoking wasn't allowed in the dining room. The sheriff invariably ignored such rules, which was probably the only time he ever bent a so-called law in his life.

"You could be right," he finally said as our server brought the bill. "So what? That doesn't change what happened."

But to me it did. The only problem was that I couldn't figure out how. "Okay," I said with a sigh. "I'll sleep on it."

Milo looked up from counting money. "I don't suppose you want company?"

I opened my mouth to say no. But Milo's eyes were begging me not to reject him. It had been a tough week for both of us. As always, it had been a lonely week.

I smiled. "Why not?"

Milo got lucky in more ways than one. For a fisherman, the only thing as good as sex and maybe sometimes better is an early-morning outing on the river. The Sky had held steady overnight, and although it was off-color, there was a chance of catching a steelhead. Like most ardent anglers, Milo carried his fishing gear in his vehicle. Thus, he left my bed and my house before first light. I didn't mind. I could sleep in.

We hadn't talked about crime or baseball that night. In fact, we didn't talk much at all. I finally woke up just before ten, with murder still on my mind. I wanted to discuss my theories with Vida, but she'd gone to Bellingham for a weekend visit with one of her other daughters.

As I stared out the front window, I felt antsy. There was still a foot of snow on the ground, but at least I didn't have to worry about Destiny Parsons's dog leaving unwanted additions to my property.

But I had other worries. There were so many disjointed thoughts and facts pecking at my brain that I had trouble concentrating on even the most routine of weekend household chores. One of the things that bothered me most was Hans Berenger, Drug Dealer. It didn't fit. According to Rita, Hans didn't drink, smoke, or, I was fairly sure, use drugs. "Straight arrow" was how she'd described him. So why was he meeting Darryl Eckstrom?

Then there was the name of the survivor in Julia Berenger's death notice. Maybe it was a coincidence. Maybe the person who had been listed wasn't the one I knew. Maybe I was beating my head against a brick wall.

I was washing the front window shortly after four o'clock when a car pulled up across the street. Roger emerged from the driver's side; Davin Rhodes limped out of the passenger seat. I dropped my cleaning rag and went outside.

"Roger!" I called. "Davin!"

The boys, who were heading for Destiny's house, stopped and looked not at me but at each other.

"Can I talk to you a minute?" I asked.

They moved back to the curb but no farther. It was still cold outside, but I didn't bother to grab a jacket. I crossed the street, noticing that the boys shifted around in a nervous manner.

"Hi, guys," I said. "Actually, it's Davin I wanted to see. I've got a question for you."

Davin cast me a wary look. "Like what?"

"Do you remember a week ago last Monday when you were working at Harvey's Hardware and you sold those blanks to Dr. Medved?"

Davin glanced at Roger. Roger shrugged.

"Yeah," Davin replied, "kind of. Why?"

"Had they been opened?" I inquired.

Davin wrinkled his pointy nose. "Opened?"

I nodded.

"They were in a box," Davin said. "They weren't like wrapped or anything. None of the ammo stuff comes that way."

"Where were the blanks kept?"

Davin was beginning to look more annoyed than suspicious. "On the shelf." He stopped and glanced again at Roger. Apparently "Rhodesy" couldn't speak without his chum's approval. "Wait. They weren't on the shelf. Mr. Adcock had to order them special. They were under the counter by the cash register."

"How long had they been there?" I asked, chafing my arms to keep warm.

"They just came in that morning," Davin replied. "An hour or two, maybe? I got there, like, around eleven. I cut study hall and lunch to work a couple of hours because Mr. Adcock was, like, gone. The store gets real busy around lunchtime."

"I see." What I saw was that there hadn't been much opportunity for anyone to tamper with the blanks at Harvey's Hardware. The timing would have to be perfect. "Okay, that's what I wanted to know. Thanks." I started to move away, then stopped. "Are you seeing Ms. Parsons about another play?"

Again Davin looked at Roger. But this time Davin didn't answer.

"Yeah," Roger said in his sullen manner. "Another play."

"What is it this time?" I inquired, hoping Destiny didn't have a filing cabinet full of her own scripts.

"Umm . . ." Roger stared at his shoes. "I forget." He slapped a hand on Davin's shoulder. "Come on, Rhodesy, we gotta go."

They went. I returned to the house but kept watching through the window. I sprayed and rubbed until my arm got tired. Fifteen minutes later, another vehicle pulled up. I recognized Boots

Overholt's truck. He got out, along with two other young men I didn't recognize. They, too, disappeared inside Destiny's house.

I went to the phone and dialed Milo's home number.

"Any luck?" I inquired.

"No, but it felt good to get out on the river," the sheriff replied. "I haven't been fishing for almost a month. I heard some guy say he caught a fourteen-pounder, though. Maybe I'll go out again tomorrow."

"Good for you," I said, forcing enthusiasm. "Do you feel like humoring me?"

"About what?" Milo's tone had become guarded.

Briefly I'd considered using feminine wiles, but I was aware I didn't have any. The direct approach had always worked best for me. "I was thinking of luring you back to my bed," I confessed, "and then somehow encouraging you to apologize to Destiny for having your guys search her house. But you'd know I was up to something, and anyway, that'd take too long. I think there's a pot party going on at Destiny's house, with minors involved."

"Jesus." Milo either sighed or exhaled. "Have you got it in for her or what?"

"Maybe I'm jealous."

The sheriff saw through even my most feeble attempt at womanly guile. "No, you're not. Besides, I couldn't get to first base with Destiny after that stunt you pulled trying to find the bushy-haired stranger at her place. She was really pissed at both of us."

"Fine," I snapped. "What about the underage pot party?"

"Emma—" Milo stopped. I knew he was about to say no, but maybe he hesitated because of our lovemaking the previous night. Or, more likely, he wanted me to stop nagging him. "Okay, I'll have Jack cruise by. He's working solo today. Our personnel schedule got all screwed up with the extra duty everybody had to pull last week."

I thanked Milo and went back to the window. Another car had parked near Destiny's house. Maybe I was being an alarmist, but journalists—like cops—have to play their hunches.

It was going on five o'clock when I left my post at the window. I usually close the drapes when it starts to get dark, but this evening I left them open. As I went into the carport to get wood for the fireplace, I saw Jack Mullins pull up in his deputy's car. Concealing myself behind the Honda, I watched Jack head for the front porch.

Only then did the enormity of what I'd done dawn on me. I clapped a hand to my head and leaned against the car's trunk. *Roger.* If he was caught smoking weed and Vida found out I'd tipped off the sheriff, she'd never forgive me. I'd been so involved with my theories and hunches that I hadn't bothered to think about long-term consequences.

It was too late. Jack was knocking on Destiny's door. In desperation, I ran down the driveway and shouted at him. He turned around and saw me.

"Emma? What's wrong?" Jack called out.

"Wait!" I hurried across the street. No one had yet answered the deputy's knock, though I heard a door slam somewhere nearby.

"What the hell's going on?" Jack demanded in an angry voice.

I was out of breath. "Just . . . hold on . . . a minute."

In the twilight shadows I could see at least two figures racing in the direction of the bushes behind Destiny's house. I hoped they were Roger and Davin.

"I think I've done something awful," I said in a miserable voice. "I may be wrong. I may—"

"Goddamn it," Jack swore, "you're stalling! Stand back! I'm going in!"

I didn't try to stop him. The debacle was all my fault. Jack was doing his duty, exactly what I'd asked the sheriff to have him do. I slipped behind Boots's pickup, shivering and upset. Jack was banging on the door with his flashlight, shouting, "Police! Open up!"

Destiny finally appeared, wearing silk pajamas and a nasty expression. "Mullins!" she cried. "What now?"

"It smells funny around here," Jack remarked in his customary impudent manner. He waved a hand at Destiny's attire. "Is this your hostess outfit?"

"You bet your butt it is," Destiny snapped. "It's a party, and you're not invited unless you've got a warrant." She started to close the door, but Jack put out his foot.

"All I want to know is if you've got any minors at your little get-together."

"Minors?" Destiny glared at Jack. "What do you mean? Under eighteen? No. I've got some students here. We're studying a script."

"What script?" Jack asked.

"*The Pajama Game,*" Destiny retorted.

"Ah." He surveyed Destiny's figure. "With real pajamas. Nice."

"Take a hike, Mullins," Destiny said, still trying to shut the door. "If you're here because the neighborhood crank tattled to her lover boy again, I'm going to sue for harassment." She stood on tiptoes to peer around the deputy. "I see you, Emma. And don't think I didn't see Dodge's Grand Cherokee at your place last night. I'm not the only one on the neighborhood watch."

Angrily I came out from behind the pickup. "Whatever we were doing," I called to her, "wasn't illegal!" I moved up the walkway. "Does the name Darryl Eckstrom mean anything to you?"

Destiny turned pale but held her ground. "Never heard of him."

"Shame on you, Destiny," I said from just below the porch steps. "You're a teacher. You should set a better example for your students."

"You ought to mind your own freaking business!" Destiny yelled. "Don't give me that holier-than-thou crap! You and your stupid little rag are a joke! Stop peddling that piece of junk and save the trees!"

"Stop writing plays and spare the audience!" I shot back. "You suck!"

"Ladies!" Jack, who was obviously trying not to laugh, held out his arms as if he were separating a couple of boxers. "Let's calm down." He looked at Destiny. "Go back to your P.J. game or whatever." His head swiveled in my direction. "Go home. Have a drink."

"A drink!" Destiny shouted. "What's the difference between getting drunk and smoking a joint, you damned hypocrite!"

"Hey!" Jack's tone was sharp. "Get back in the house," he ordered Destiny. "Get your ass across the street," he yelled at me. "Now! Both of you. Move!"

Destiny slammed the door; I stomped off, gritting my teeth. Jack followed me down the walk but stopped by his vehicle, apparently to make sure that Destiny and I wouldn't engage in a rematch. I didn't look back, but when I got inside I immediately went into the living room and closed the drapes. The phone rang just as I was going to collect the wood from the carport.

"It's me," Jack said. "I pulled into the cul-de-sac down the street. I'm going to wait a couple of minutes and then I'll hoof it to your place. I want to see who moves those vehicles in front of Destiny's house."

"A stakeout in my very own living room?" I said. "Come ahead. I'm building a fire."

Three minutes later, Jack knocked on my back door. He had cut through the woods and climbed over the neighbors' fence in order not to be seen in the street.

"Anybody leave yet?" he asked.

I told him I'd peeked through the drapes when I went into the living room to start the fire. "I'm guessing that Roger and

Davin—assuming they were the ones I saw running out the back way—are still hiding in the bushes. They probably want to make sure you're gone."

Jack removed his leather gloves and rubbed his hands together. "You got any coffee?"

"I can make some."

"Thanks." He remained at his post by the front window while I went into the kitchen. "There they are!" he called to me. "God, they look like a couple of spies from a B movie."

I hurried to join him. Sure enough, Roger and Davin were creeping along the side of Destiny's house, checking in every direction. Then they made a sudden run for it, jumped into the car, and roared off without bothering to turn on their headlights.

Jack laughed and shook his head. "Crazy kids. If I'd still been in the squad car I could've picked them up on a traffic violation."

"Would you have charged them with illegal possession?" I inquired.

Jack shook his head. "I couldn't. The stuff's probably still in Destiny's house. Jeez, Emma, if we charged everybody who smokes a little weed, Dodge would have to build an annex for the jail."

"So you did smell pot?"

"Oh, yeah. As soon as Destiny opened the door. Hang on— here come Boots Overholt and one of the Hedstroms and some kid I don't recognize. They're getting into the pickup, no rush, no panic."

"Keep me posted," I said, returning to the kitchen.

While I got out a pair of mugs and waited for the coffee to finish brewing, Jack reported that two girls and three more boys had left the Parsons house.

"I guess the party's over," he said as I brought the coffee into the living room. "The street's clear." Jack sat down in one of my armchairs. "So how are you going to maintain an armed truce with Destiny?"

Sitting on the sofa, I sighed. "That's up to her. As long as she doesn't make more trouble, I'll pretend she's not there."

Jack grimaced. "Maybe she won't be."

"What do you mean?"

Jack fingered his upper lip. "I should keep my mouth shut."

"About what?" I leaned forward. "Come on, Jack. You can't say something like that to a journalist and then turn into a clam."

Jack looked as if he'd gone to war with his conscience. "Sometimes," he finally said, "I'm not sure how fine the lines are drawn between public record and confidential information."

"The lines often wobble," I replied. "For instance, if a murderer tells Father Den, he can't break the seal of the confessional. But if a therapist or an M.D.—"

"I know all that," Jack interrupted. "Okay." He folded his hands tightly on his knee. "You were there yesterday when Dodge heard from SnoCo about Eckstrom's list of contacts. Dodge told you that Berenger was on it, right?"

"Yes. You were there, too."

"So if he gave you one name, why shouldn't you know about the others?"

I realized that Jack was stating his case for his benefit as much as for mine. "Right," I said.

"Today we got a fax from SnoCo with the full list," Jack said. "I called Milo about it over the phone. Has he mentioned it to you?"

I shook my head. "I didn't talk to him very long. I was in a hurry to get somebody to Destiny's house."

Jack nodded. "Dodge might not have told you anyway. He might have been embarrassed. But the other local name on Eckstrom's list was Destiny Parsons."

SEVENTEEN

"So Eckstrom was dealing to Destiny," I said. "That makes sense." I *had* seen Eckstrom at Destiny's house after all. Roger had probably spotted him at the theater but didn't recognize him. It wasn't likely that Roger or any of the other pot party invitees had ever met the dealer. Destiny wouldn't want any witnesses to an actual sale, especially young people who might be indiscreet.

Since Eckstrom didn't sound very bright, he may have thought the deal could be made during the play. Heedless or high, he apparently had ignored the problem of trying to sell drugs in front of an entire cast and crew. He also hadn't considered that Destiny would be preoccupied directing her masterpiece. So Eckstrom had left to wait for a better time.

The connection also explained why no large quantities of drugs were found in the car and why—aside from stupidity—Eckstrom wasn't afraid to go around town with marijuana on his person. For Destiny's cozy little gatherings her supplier could have put the stuff in a sandwich bag from the Grocery Basket.

What still didn't fit was Hans Berenger's name on Eckstrom's list. The man was multiflawed, but dealing or using drugs simply didn't seem like part of his personality profile. It was easier to envision him as a murderer, not a victim. But I didn't say so to Jack Mullins.

"Are you going to go after Destiny?" I asked.

Jack winced. "That's up to Dodge. Damn, but that man has had lousy luck with women. Why can't he find one who isn't screwed up?"

I stiffened. Jack noticed. "Oh, shit, Emma, I'm sorry," he said, getting red in the face. "I didn't mean *you*."

I smiled wryly. "But I *am* screwed up. I'm just not a crook."

❊   ❊   ❊

We said good-bye to Rome on a golden autumn day, the kind of afternoon that Botticelli and Raphael and Titian had been inspired by sun and sky. Our final tourist stop was St. Paul's Basilica. I tried to admire the portico's columns and the statuary that lined the roof, but the light was so bright that it was difficult to focus, even with sunglasses. I squinted upward, at the outline in the center of the magnificent structure. To me, the shape looked like a large T. *A* T *for Tom, I thought, and then I realized I was gazing at a cross. Of course it was a cross. What, in front of this holy place, was I thinking of? My priorities were in shambles. I couldn't look at Ben. I was too ashamed.*

❊   ❊   ❊

Jack was gone, I'd eaten chicken curry for dinner, and the long evening stretched before me. I made up my mind. There was only one thing to do. I was going to pay a call on Julia Blair Berenger's survivor.

It was foolish. It was rude. It was probably going to get me into trouble. Maybe I'd be thrown out into the night, like the unwanted guest I knew I would be.

I got no farther than the carport. Destiny was stomping

across the street. Seeing me, she took a detour and headed straight up the driveway instead of veering off to the front porch.

"It's time we had a talk," she declared, sounding strident. "My place or yours?"

"Mine's closer," I said, gesturing at the back door.

I let her go ahead of me. It didn't seem wise to turn my back on Destiny Parsons. The wind had come up again, and it blew the door shut behind us. Maybe March wasn't coming in like a lamb after all.

Destiny sat down at the kitchen table. I followed her lead but didn't offer coffee. This wasn't a social visit.

"Let's not mince words," she said. "You and I don't get along. It's too bad. I think everybody should get along. That's what my play was about."

I didn't say anything, though I could have pointed out that Destiny didn't seem to practice what she preached.

"You're in tight with the sheriff," she went on, then flipped her long gray hair away from her face and gave me a smile that was more of a sneer. "I'm not jealous. He's not my type. But I'm willing to strike a bargain with you."

This wasn't the conversation I'd expected. I sensed that the worst was yet to come. "What kind of bargain?"

Destiny tapped the table with a long, thin finger. "Kids— not just kids, of course—are going to smoke pot. It should be legalized. But since it's not, I figure that if young people are going to do it, they should have a safe haven. They shouldn't have to steal to get money to buy it and they shouldn't have to deal with criminals. You say I'm setting a bad example for students. I say I'm protecting them. I'd rather let them smoke the stuff in a safe environment than see them get mixed up in crime and ruin their futures."

Destiny had a point. "So what's the deal?" I retorted. "Am I supposed to host pot parties, too?"

Destiny looked at me as if I were the class moron. "Of

course not. All I want from you is to stop bitching about me to Dodge."

"My problem with you isn't personal," I asserted. "I'm trying to follow up on a story line that includes murder and drugs. You buy drugs. That's part of my investigative reporting. I'm looking for a tie-in with Darryl Eckstrom. You seem to be it."

Destiny looked faintly amused. "You're off the mark. I'm not worried about Dodge. The most he could charge me with is illegal possession. That's more trouble than it's worth. It's your meddling that drives me crazy. I want to live in peace. I want the whole world to live in peace."

It was a commendable thought but sadly, impractical. "So what's this bargain you're offering me?"

Again Destiny tapped the table. "I want everyone to know what a swine Hans Berenger really was."

"Are you saying Hans actually dealt drugs, too? Hard stuff, I mean."

Destiny leaned back in her chair. "Hardly. Hans abhorred drugs and anything else that might make people happy."

"But—" I stopped. It wouldn't be right to breach what I assumed was a confidence. Instead, I hedged. "I've heard something about Darryl Eckstrom coming to Alpine to meet Hans."

To my surprise, Destiny nodded. "Darryl came here for two purposes—to deliver pot to me and to see Hans about a much different kind of business arrangement. It's because of Darryl that Hans killed my poor Azbug. Hans had found out that I was letting students smoke weed at my house. He intended to tell Nat Cardenas, hoping I'd get fired. But I knew from Darryl what Hans was up to. I told him if he talked to Nat, I'd talk, too. Then Clea got into the act and insisted I use Hans in the play. I'm still not sure why, since I don't think she liked him, either. Anyway, Hans kept his mouth shut but got revenge by killing Azbug. A warning, too, I suppose."

"You're sure it was Hans?"

"Of course." Destiny's eyes narrowed. "He admitted it. He even boasted about it. I considered going to the sheriff but was afraid Hans would retaliate by tipping Dodge off about the kids and the pot."

"What about Boots Overholt?" I asked. "He wasn't at your house the night I saw Darryl Eckstrom, was he?"

Destiny looked faintly sheepish. "Boots didn't know what to do. He's got a huge crush on Clea Bhuj. He asked her advice, and she insisted that he owed his loyalty to the faculty, especially to me, since I'd helped him with some extra tutoring. Boots isn't exactly a genius, but he tries."

"I see." But I still didn't know why we two adversaries were sitting in my kitchen while the wind whirled through the ever-greens in my backyard. "Are you going to tell me what terrible thing Hans was doing that involved Darryl Eckstrom?"

"I certainly am." Destiny sat up straight. "I want you to put it in the paper. I want everyone to know." She took a deep breath. "Hans wanted to buy that dog place down the highway. If you've noticed, the house and kennels can't be seen from the road. It's very secluded, especially for someone like Hans who intended to breed and train German shepherds to be killers. After all, he'd done it once before."

I wasn't really shocked. My mind had already been traveling that route. Even Milo had allowed for the possibility. Not that there was anything he could do about it: Hans was dead, the property was still for sale, and Darryl Eckstrom was under arrest.

"I assume the dogs would serve as security," I said.

Destiny nodded. "Darryl told me about it a month or so ago. He was pretty high at the time. He usually was, which I suppose is why that stolen car ended up in the river. It's a wonder he didn't kill himself and some innocent parties on his way to Alpine. There's plenty of treacherous highway along the route, especially in winter."

"Would the dogs have been for Darryl's own use?" I asked. "He sounds pretty small-time."

"He mentioned he'd like one. But mainly, the dogs were to be raised for some big-time drug lords with big bucks to pay for them," Destiny explained. "Darryl was the go-between. Frankly, I didn't believe him at first, especially since Hans was so against drugs. But somehow he must have disassociated himself from the product involved and seen only how he could make some money. I did some research on Hans's background and discovered how his wife had died. I knew she'd come from a wealthy family. I'm certain that's why he killed her. Or, should I say, trained his dog to kill her. Of course the authorities couldn't prove it, so he got off, and inherited a small fortune besides."

"Why," I asked, "did he need to make more money?"

"Hans was a miser," Destiny replied. "He was a genuine Scrooge. I think it was sheer greed that made him train that dog to kill his wife."

"What a horrible thing to do to someone," I declared.

Destiny's expression was full of compassion. "What a horrible thing to do to a dog."

Before she went home, I told Destiny I honestly wasn't sure how much of her information I could use in the *Advocate*. It wasn't that I didn't believe her, but we had only the word of a small-time drug dealer. If Milo didn't like to speculate in his job, I didn't like to when it came to mine. At least not in print.

Destiny had grumbled a bit, but she seemed far less hostile. Maybe airing the tale aloud had helped her disposition.

The lights had flickered a couple of times before I headed out again a little after eight. I'd almost reconsidered my original intention, but if I put it off, I might never carry through. I was determined to confront the survivor who had been named in Julia Blair Berenger's obituary.

A few branches had blown across the road, but there was no rain or snow. As long as a ninety-year-old Western red cedar didn't fall on my Honda, I should be safe. At least while I was still driving.

The black wreath on the front door was swaying in the wind as I rang the bell. It took Justine Cardenas a couple of minutes to respond. She didn't look surprised to see me.

"Come in," she offered, bracing herself against the door to keep it from blowing shut. "Would you like a drink?"

"No, thanks." I followed her into the handsome, sterile living room.

"I finished the footstool cover just an hour ago," Justine said after we were seated. "It was very peaceful this evening with Nat attending the Board of Trustees meeting. Would you like to see the finished product?"

"Yes, I would," I said.

Justine got up and went over to a lowboy next to the French doors that led outside. "Here," she said, picking up the piece and coming to the uncomfortable muslin-covered armchair I'd sat in during my previous visit. "What do you think?"

I thought it was beautiful, and I said so. The intricate design was of two fair-haired women in eighteenth-century dress gathering flowers in a pastoral setting. In the lower right-hand corner I spotted the initials JBC. Underneath was another trio of letters—JBB.

I licked my lips, which had suddenly gone dry. "The figures represent you and your sister, Julia, don't they?"

"Yes." Justine moved the needlepoint so she could see it more closely. "Yes," she repeated. "We were twins. That's Julia on the right. I'm on the left. She's the one who looks as if she's laughing. I'm more solemn. But there was a time when we both laughed frequently. I haven't laughed since she died."

"Honestly," I said, "I don't know what to say."

Justine shrugged before returning her handiwork to the low-boy. "There's nothing to say." Slowly, and with great dignity, she returned to her chair. "I knew you'd figure it out. You're very intelligent. But there's nothing you can do about it, is there?"

I wasn't quite sure what she meant. I chose the safest response. "I can offer you my sympathy and understanding."

Justine gave a quick shake of her head. "That's not what I meant."

I didn't reply. I merely waited and listened to the wind. It seemed to be blowing all the way up the coast from San Diego.

"I didn't know Nat was hiring Hans Berenger until after the fact," Justine finally said. "Nat doesn't talk to me much about his work. And we never talked about Julia after she died. Nat had only met Julia twice after our wedding. He'd forgotten what her married name was—you know how men are—and he had no idea that Hans was Julia's husband. I never told him."

I was feeling bleak. And apprehensive. "Not even after Hans was killed?"

"No. What was the point?" Justine smiled sadly. "Nat has other things on his mind. He still hasn't decided whether or not to accept one of the positions he's been offered. You know about that. He did mention his lunch with you. He felt you could be trusted."

Which, I assumed, was why Justine was speaking so freely to me. Or maybe, as with Destiny, this was the night for Emma to sit behind the screen in the confessional.

"But you shared your grief with him over Julia's loss, didn't you?"

"I've tried very hard not to burden him with my sorrow. He has to concentrate on his career. It's been very difficult for me to bottle it all up inside. Yet I've done little but grieve for the past eight years. Eight years ago on the twentieth of February." She turned in the direction of the front door. "I almost went to

pieces when you saw the wreath on the front door and insinuated that it was for Hans. It was for Julia, of course. But I realized then that you would become suspicious. You would also
have the skills and the resources to investigate."

I didn't comment on her observations. Instead, I pointed out
that she and Nat had children. "You have a role not only as a
wife but as a mother. Surely you could involve yourself—" I
stopped. It was futile to suggest that Justine Blair Cardenas
should have put her life to better use. All of her energy had gone
into grief and keeping her emotions under iron-clad control.

"The children don't live nearby," Justine said. She opened
a cherrywood sewing box next to her chair and took out what
looked like a new needlepoint canvas. "Our son and our daughter have their own lives. They're better off not being close to me.
I would only make them unhappy. They never knew their Aunt
Julia, you see."

"Why did she marry Hans in the first place?" I asked.

"She was in love." Justine grimaced as she carefully threaded
a needle with pale blue yarn. "Julia was brilliant. She'd never
dated much, she was always too wrapped up in her studies. Then
Hans came along when they were in graduate school at Wisconsin. He was actually quite good-looking then, one of those lean,
dark-haired types who probably reminded her of a Brontë hero.
And of course he was very bright. Our parents favored the match."
She paused and pursed her lips. "Much more so than they did
my own. They called Nat 'that Mexican who's on the make.' It
was Hans who was on the make, not Nat. My parents were poor
judges of people. So was Julia."

"Did you ever confront Hans after he went to work for the
college?"

"I avoided him." Justine looked away as if she could see him
sitting in my place. "I couldn't bear the sight of him. When Nat
would mention his name I'd have to exert every ounce of self-
control not to react." Her gaze fixed on the empty canvas and

she began to stitch with automatonlike precision. "Then, this past year, we gave a Christmas party. Hans rarely attended faculty social gatherings, but that girlfriend he had, Rita, apparently insisted that they go. To be honest, I don't know if Hans knew who I was. I mean, as far as being Julia's sister was concerned. We weren't identical twins. But I took one look at him in our house and I couldn't stand it. I . . . I'd had a couple of cocktails, and I told him that if he ever came to our home again, I'd kill him." She hung her head. "Nat didn't know what had gotten into me. I told him Hans had damaged one of my needlepoint pieces."

I twisted around in my place. It wasn't just the chair's construction that was making me uncomfortable. "Was that when you decided . . . something had to be done?"

Resuming her stitchery, Justine nodded slowly. "That and the fact that Nat told me if he took another position, he might recommend Hans for the president's job. I had no idea what I should do. Then Destiny asked me to read her play. She wanted my opinion. It was dreadful, of course, but I didn't have the heart to tell her. But it gave me an idea. The only comment I made to Destiny was that I felt she should change the part of the café owner to a man. I spoke to Clea—she's become somewhat of a friend—and asked her to insist on casting Hans. Naturally, Clea wanted to please me, so she did. The only sad part—ironic, really—was that it was Nat who had to pull the trigger. There was no way around it, of course, and he did it in all innocence."

I tried not to fidget, though it was very difficult to keep my feet and hands still. "When did you switch the blanks for the bullets?"

Justine looked up from her work. "Cartridges, not bullets." She almost smiled. "My father collected guns. He taught Julia and me how to shoot." She bent her head to complete a vertical row at the top of the canvas. "I'd bought the bullets out of town in early February," she continued. "I went backstage before the last act on the pretext of using the rest room for the cast and crew. No one paid any attention to me. They were all so busy. By chance, Boots Overholt was helping Reverend Poole with his angel wings. It was really quite easy to make the exchange."

It probably was. Justine knew guns. She had gifted fingers—for exacting needlework and for sleight of hand with blanks and bullets. But I wondered what would have happened if Nat had missed Hans and hit one of the other actors. Or no one at all.

The silence between us had grown awkward. Justine obviously noticed it. "Are you certain you won't have that drink?" she asked, as well mannered and constrained as ever.

"Yes. I mean, no, I'm fine. I have to drive home in this wind. I need to stay alert." I was alert, but not fine, hoping my hostess wasn't a reincarnation of Lucrezia Borgia, wondering if I should jump up and race out the door, praying that I would be allowed to leave this unhappy house that seemed more like a cell.

Justine held up the canvas. "I'm going to make a small tapestry to hang in the upstairs hall. The pattern is an angel. I'm starting with the sky."

An avenging angel, maybe. "That sounds lovely," I said.

Justine put the canvas on the top of the sewing box and stood up. "I hope you won't think too ill of me," she said. "The newspaper has always treated the college most fairly."

I stood up, too, though I stumbled over the hooked rug by the chair. "The college has benefited the town most admirably," I replied, sounding as formal and stiff as Justine.

"Yes, it has," she replied. "It's saved Alpine in many ways, in great part because Nat has been so dedicated to its success. Nothing should be done to besmirch the school's reputation. Or his."

We were walking to the door. I felt faintly queasy, but I forced myself to speak. "Does Nat have any idea of . . . what happened?"

"I don't really know," Justine responded. "If he does, he'll keep it to himself. As you will, I'm sure."

I must have worn an uncertain look on my face. Justine offered me one of her cool smiles. "You have no proof, you see. If you were ever to mention any of what we've discussed, I'd simply deny it. All the sheriff would have is surmise. I understand Milo Dodge doesn't like that sort of thing."

Justine opened the door. I felt the wind blow into my face. It appeared that she was letting me go.

I stumbled again.

"Be careful," Justine urged, grabbing my arm to keep me from falling. She and I both looked down. The mourning wreath had blown off the door onto the porch. "Oh, no!" she cried, and bent down to gather up the wreath. I watched her as she hugged it to her breast and then examined it closely. "It's not really damaged. I'll wait until the storm's over before I put it back."

I was standing on the bottom stair. "Don't," I said.

She stared at me. "What?"

"Don't," I repeated. "It's over."

She kept staring and then, still clutching the wreath, went back inside her cold, cold house and closed the door.

I knew it wasn't over for Justine Cardenas. She would be haunted for the rest of her days. She'd already served eight years of a life sentence.

No. That wasn't quite right. She could still walk and talk and ply her needle, but she was dead inside.

That was the worst punishment of all.

The news that Nat Cardenas had resigned as college president reached me as I was going into church the next morning. Mary Jane Bourgette came rushing up to me before I could get through the double wooden doors.

"Nat's taking a job at a two-year college in upstate New York," she announced in a breathless voice. "That's what the emergency meeting was all about. You'll get the full story for the paper first thing Monday."

I was stunned, though upon reflection, I shouldn't have been. Mary Jane obviously took my expression for mere surprise. "Now the college will have to find a new president *and* a new dean of students. Nat leaves at the end of March. We tried to talk him into staying through the academic year, but he was adamant. Honestly, you'd think he wouldn't want to rush off. It sure puts us in a pickle."

In her no-nonsense manner, Mary Jane hurried inside. I waited a moment, absorbing the news. It was just as well. Leaving Alpine was the best thing for Nat and Justine Cardenas. I'd pray for them. And for me. My conscience was unsettled.

Father Den's homily for the first Sunday in Lent was about forgiveness and understanding. We mustn't condemn others for their actions, he said. We don't know what's in their hearts. Only God knows; only God can judge.

My conscience quieted.

After communion, I looked up at the altar where Father Den had placed a large, bare wooden cross. After the glories of Rome, St. Mildred's seemed so plain, so homely. But faith is simple. Lent reminds us that we all have to carry our cross. Milo carried loneliness and disappointment. Tom had borne the burden of his unstable wife, Sandra. I carried Tom's loss. Justine's cross had drained her of life.

Father Den's addition to the altar didn't look like a T. It looked like a cross.

Ben hadn't wasted his money after all.